Firefly

Also by Henry Porter

Remembrance Day
A Spy's Life
Empire State
Brandenburg Gate
The Bell Ringers
The Master of the Fallen Chairs

Firefly

HENRY PORTER

The Mysterious Press
New York

First published in Great Britain in 2018 by Quercus Editions,
an imprint of Hachette UK

Published simultaneously in Canada
Printed in the United States of America

First Grove Atlantic edition: October 2018

Library of Congress Cataloging-in-Publication data is available for this title.

ISBN 978-0-8021-2895-9
eISBN 978-0-8021-4675-5

The Mysterious Press
an imprint of Grove Atlantic
154 West 14th Street
New York, NY 10011

Distributed by Publishers Group West

groveatlantic.com

18 19 20 21   10 9 8 7 6 5 4 3 2 1

For my brother, Michael

PROLOGUE

His head went under. Seawater filled his nose and mouth; his eyes opened and he saw the black depths of the ocean below him. A moment later something knocked his legs — maybe part of the wreckage, he couldn't tell. All he knew was that he was going to die. Then it came again. This time there was a distinct shove on his buttocks and whatever it was that moved with such intent beneath him lifted him up so his head and shoulders came out of the water and he was able to grab a plastic toggle on the section of the rubber craft that was still inflated.

He clung to the toggle and retched and blinked and blinked again.

The sea was very strange to the boy, with its violence and the salty water that stung his eyes and the gash on his head that had been made with the handle of a gun by one of the men when they were being herded onto the raft. He rubbed his eyes with the knuckle of his free hand and cast around.

There was nothing to see in the dawn, not even the shadow of the coast they'd spotted a few minutes before the boat had begun to sink.

The waves were getting bigger in the wind that had got up at first light, bringing with it the smell of woodsmoke from the shore. They had taken this as a good sign: if they could smell the fires on the beach, they weren't far from their destination and safety. But that was before the front section suddenly deflated and water poured in, and the people panicked and grabbed the young children that were huddled in the centre, and the section that remained inflated began to rock uncontrollably. Then the boat flipped over and they were all thrown into the sea.

The screams died the instant the people hit the water, and now there was nothing except the sound of the waves.

He turned his head as a particularly large wave raised him and the wreckage, and he found himself looking down the slope of water at a bright blue life jacket that was spinning round in the trough of the wave. He knew he must get to that life jacket, because the orange one he'd bought on the street had split open at the collar, revealing nothing but the wads of paper it had been stuffed with. The blue life jacket became his only objective. He began paddling furiously with his free arm, but realised he couldn't drag the whole weight of the collapsed rubber boat through the water. He didn't know water – he had no idea about what you could and couldn't do in it. Until two days before he'd never seen the sea, nor anything like it, still less been plunged into its shocking cold immensity and had to swim for his life. On the few occasions he had swum, his foot had danced along the bottom of the pool as his arms thrashed atop the water; and he had fooled nobody, not even his doting father.

A few seconds later, an even bigger wave came along, and this one seemed to pause at a great height to contemplate him before crashing down and obliterating all his senses in a foaming rush that sucked at his body and tried to tear him from the wreckage. But he clung on with all his strength, and when he blinked the water from his eyes he saw that the blue life jacket was right in front of him. He took hold of it and dragged it towards himself, realising in that moment that it was much heavier than he had expected. He spun it round and found himself staring into an inflated hood and at the face of a very small child, no more than a year old, whose eyes and mouth were wide open in disbelief.

He was cross that the life jacket would be no use to him, but instinctively he wrapped his free arm around the blue bundle and wedged it between himself and the rubber dinghy so the sea could not drag the baby away. And there he remained, rising and falling in the waves, with the baby's face a few centimetres away, staring at him with intense concentration. Every time the boy felt his fingers grow numb on the toggle, he swapped hands; and sometimes, when he thought that he could not hang on any longer and he should give himself and the baby up to the sea that seemed so desperately to crave their lives, he felt a shove from below and was pushed up a little and held above the water for a few seconds, and the baby looked even more surprised. It was as though the ocean floor rose to take the strain from his arms.

How long they were out there he had no idea. Sometimes he tried to play with the baby, popping his eyes and rubbing his nose against the baby's face, and the baby even managed to gurgle a laugh. The baby became his purpose, for he knew their fates were locked together: if he could keep the baby alive, God would allow him to survive too, and they would live long and happy lives, and maybe one day they would become friends. But he was very tired, and so cold that he could not think, and he allowed himself once or twice to close his eyes – just for a few seconds – and to dream of his home and his three sisters. And when he did, all sorts of strange things started to happen in his mind and he began to believe that the sea was just part of a dream. And once, just before he heard the roar of the two jet skis come out of nowhere, he imagined a monster with an enormous beak rising out of the water beside him to search his face in wonderment, as if trying to fathom why there were so many bodies in the sea and what a boy was doing floating there with a tiny baby.

ONE

Paul Samson leaned back in the desk chair used by his mother in the upstairs office of her restaurant, Cedar, and waited. Below him, Cedar's kitchens were at full tilt, producing food for the most privileged Arab customers in London. He was always content in this room, the place where his mother and father used to sit opposite each other at desks pushed together, she running the restaurant and he his import and export business. His gaze moved across a wall of photographs – his mother Marina's shrine to the family's early life in Lebanon, and more especially to his father, Wally. His eyes came to rest on the black and white picture of them taken in Beirut in 1967. The photograph was famous in the diasporas of both their families – spread across the globe since the Lebanese civil war – for its natural glamour and the memories it evoked of old Beirut. Marina, in a bold floral swing skirt, was on one foot as she hugged her new husband, who in a light suit and open collar leaned against a Buick sedan and, with cigar in his hand, saluted who knows what – the city, his new young wife, his good fortune? The photograph might easily have appeared in one of the fashion magazines of the time, and yet it was just a snap taken by one of the city's street photographers. Wally had paid a very few Lebanese pounds for the framed photograph to be delivered almost immediately to the café where they were celebrating their marriage. This was the only photographic record of their wedding, and there wasn't a day when his mother did not look up at it, smile and mouth an endearment to the long dead love of her life.

There was knock on the door and Ivan, one of the two maître d's at Cedar, half opened it and showed his face. 'He's here,' he said.

'I can see,' said Samson, glancing at one of the CCTV monitors.

'You need a table? It's pretty tight tonight – full house.'

'No, show him up – and ask what he wants to drink. Thanks.'

Samson studied the screen. He saw a tall, dowdy individual, with a brush of fine grey hair, dark rings under his eyes and a stoop. A second, much younger man was waiting by the bar with his hands folded in front of him. Samson tracked the tall man on various screens as he climbed the staircase and proceeded along the corridor over Cedar's kitchens, where his mother, at the age of seventy-two, was supervising her staff like a general.

'Can we do something about your bodyguard, or whatever he is?' said Samson as Ivan showed his guest in. 'I don't want him spooking our customers. Most are from the embassies and you showing up here like this will already have been noticed.'

The man said to Ivan, 'You can tell my friend to wait in the car – I'll be quite all right here.'

He turned to Samson and put out his hand. 'Peter Nyman.'

'I know – Special Operations Directorate.'

'Something like that.' A dreary smile flickered across his face. 'Though we try to avoid that kind of acronym.'

Samson gestured him towards a chair, but remained standing.

'It's quite a place, Mr Samson,' said Nyman, looking along the line of monitors. 'I've long wanted to dine here.'

Samson smiled. 'You're welcome anytime, Mr Nyman. I occasionally see people from the Office. With our clientele, it's hardly surprising.'

'You serve alcohol?'

'Yes, the finest Lebanese wines. Do you like Château Musar? We have the prized '78 and '82 vintages.'

'Out of my range,' Nyman said, sniffing. 'I'm grateful to you for seeing me and I'll come straight to the point, if I may. We were wondering if you'd come back – just for one operation.'

Samson threw his head back and laughed. 'You slung me out. Cashiered like a bloody crook, I was.'

Nyman closed his eyes and pinched the top of his nose. 'I gathered it was the amount involved. These were big bets – very big bets indeed.'

'And my private business. I opened my books and we went

through it all. I showed a much greater return than any of you make on share portfolios. What's the difference?'

'These were horses,' said Nyman.

'You know how many bets I've had in the last year?' Samson said, now rather enjoying Nyman's discomfort.

'I've no idea.'

'Take a wild guess.'

'I really wouldn't know – maybe thirty? Fifty?'

'Seven. Five wins and two that didn't perform as well as I expected. Hardly compulsive behaviour, is it? You see, this kind of gambling is not so much about risk as patience and good judgement.' Without turning, he pointed to his right, to a photograph of Wally Samson taken in 1989. 'My father spent his whole life looking for reasons not to make business investments. I spend my time looking for reasons why I shouldn't make a bet. It's how I've made money.'

'You were betting in tens of thousands,' Nyman murmured.

Ivan returned with sparkling water and two glasses. Nyman fished the lemon out of his glass and looked around. Samson remembered the man's remote, disapproving presence at one or two meetings, though he had never heard him speak and did not know precisely what his job was. He was part of the scenery, and those in Samson's intake knew better than to enquire too closely about his role. Besides, Nyman wasn't seen in the Office much – a migratory figure who was said to be often in the United States and Canada.

Nyman sighed and put down his glass. 'Frankly I don't

give a fuck what you do with your money, Mr Samson. I was aware that you were an excellent intelligence officer and a loss to the service when you went.' Another insipid smile. 'So, can we talk on the basis of my distant admiration for you?'

'I always insist upon it,' said Samson.

'I want you to come back for a particular job – one you're especially suited for. I'm afraid I can't discuss the details here, but I would like you to hear me out later this evening and then give me a very quick answer. We're against the clock on this one and I need a decision almost immediately.'

'I'm not sure I want or need to come back,' said Samson, returning to the chair behind the desk. 'My view of the people at the top hasn't changed. The Chief was like some bloody mother superior.'

'You weren't alone in that view,' said Nyman. 'He's gone on to better things at an Oxford college and will enjoy the talk at high table, no doubt. As you know, we have a new chief – Hugh Fairbrother – and things have changed front of house and are much improved backstage. I'm not asking you to rejoin the cult, but I want you to consider this one very important assignment. I wouldn't be here, practically on my knees, if I didn't think it were important.'

Samson pulled his cuffs from his suit jacket. 'I don't know a lot about you, but I don't imagine you have ever been on your knees.'

Nyman looked him up and down, taking in the tailored suit and Samson's handmade shoes. 'Are you working here tonight?'

'Good Lord no – my mother has more sense than to employ me. She runs this on her own and, believe me, there's no one in London who does a better job.'

'But you are working, aren't you?'

'The odd assignment for Hendricks-Harp, right here in Curzon Street; a bit of travel; the occasional enquiry – nothing that keeps me away from London or the racecourse.'

'Really?' From his inside pocket, Nyman drew a photograph of a bearded man in sunglasses, an Arab *keffiyeh* and scarred leather bomber jacket and pushed it across the table to Samson. 'Recognise this individual? It's you, of course, on the Turkey–Syria border about seven or eight weeks ago.'

Samson didn't react, just ran his finger round the rim of his glass and gave Nyman a pleasant smile.

'I'm just making the point that this particular job has kept you from the racecourse for weeks on end, and that you are still very much in the game.' He paused 'What were you doing there?'

'It's a private matter – utterly legal of course, but very private.'

'That's not what we think – I mean about the legality,' said Nyman.

'What you think is your business. I'm afraid I just can't tell you about it.'

'In that part of the world, illicit shipments over those particular borders usually involves one of three commodities – drugs, armaments or fuel.'

'Check with Hendricks-Harp. I'm not at liberty to discuss

it. And, by the way, it's no business of the British government.' Samson's eyes met Nyman's with an unflinching gaze,
although the good humour in his face did not fade.

'I've been in touch with Macy Harp,' said Nyman,
retrieving the photograph. 'We overlapped for a few years
at the Office, you know. He told me a story about artefacts
being rescued from the iconoclastic barbarians of IS.'

'Right.'

'And you were responsible for seeing their safe conveyance
over the border to people who would look after them until
peace came. It's an operation financed by parties who are not
thieves but people with genuine interest in Syria's heritage.
And you were the main man in this operation, is that right?

'If Macy says so,' said Samson.

Nyman nodded as if to acknowledge he wasn't going to
get anywhere. 'Anyway, I told Macy that we were on to
something important, which meant he listened and agreed
that you were the right person to approach.'

'I don't work for Macy Harp. I'm a free agent.'

'I know that, but you are close and you listen to him. I
don't think I could get you to hear me out unless Macy asked
you.' He stopped and looked at his watch. A few seconds
later Samson's phone began to vibrate in his inside pocket.
He took it out and saw a familiar number.

'Fancy that – it's Macy,' he said to Nyman with a sarcastic
look before answering the call.

The next couple of minutes were spent discussing the
upset in the second race at Newmarket and the breeding of

the winner in the fourth. The turf was still the first interest of the Cold War warrior who'd set up Hendricks-Harp with a colleague from Germany's BND in '97, and created one of the biggest private intelligence companies in Europe.

'I believe you are playing host to a friend of mine,' said Harp eventually. 'He's your typical service ghoul, but it would be helpful if you'd give him an hour or two, old cock. Just listen to his story. That's all he's asking.'

Samson looked at Nyman, who had got up and was studying the wall of photographs. 'Fine,' he murmured, and hung up.

'I must say you do bear a striking resemblance to your father,' Nyman said without turning to him. 'It could so easily be you in these early photographs. But you're taller and his nose is straight, while yours looks like it was recently broken. But you both wear a suit well.' He straightened. 'I do enjoy a wall of photos like this – tells you so much. More people should do it, though I suppose it's only a family like yours, which has been through the mill – losing and gaining so much – that needs to keep the past in front of them in this way. It's rather moving.' He gave Samson what seemed a genuine smile, then dug in his inside pocket and withdrew a card. 'I'll see you at this address in . . . shall we say an hour? And thank you for agreeing to come.'

When Nyman had left, Samson rang Macy Harp back. 'He has no idea about the Hisami job, right?' he said.

'No.'

'Because it would be in keeping with their MO to use our search for Aysel Hisami for their own ends.'

'They don't know about her or her brother. When he asked me what you were doing I prattled on about artefacts, but watch him. He has a good nose and he doesn't miss anything. We don't need them finding out about Denis. He is very, very keen that nothing gets out, as you know.'

Samson recalled the slight, dapper figure of the billionaire Denis Hisami and remembered noting, as he spoke about his sister, the huge intelligence in the man's eyes.

'What about this thing Nyman wants me to do? Did he tell you about it?'

'Not much. It might be up your street, and it could be important. See what he's got to say. It's up to you, of course. The main thing is that we haven't got anything on at the moment. And won't have for a few weeks.'

The boy moved from the shadow of the huge port building to the dock where the ship would berth. He was anxious about showing himself, because just as he had been boarding the ship for Athens without a ticket two nights before, the police spotted him and took him back to the compound in the camp for unaccompanied minors.

The boy ignored the families that were gathered in little groups on the edge of the quay and moved quickly, with his head down, to the orderly line of young men waiting for the water bottles that were being handed out from the back of a truck about twenty metres away. He was looking for someone to help carry out the plan he'd formed two nights before. He had a particular image – a teenager, slight in build and from Iraq or Syria. In other words, someone who could pass as his older brother.

He walked along the line of young men, smiling as he went. It was amazing to him how alike they were. They all wore jeans and trainers and, because a sharp wind was blowing from the harbour's mouth – the very same wind that had capsized his raft two weeks ago – they'd put on hats and as many jackets as they could get. Some were wrapped in the blankets given out at the camps to every individual with a note: *Winter is coming. Keep this blanket with you at all times. It is a gift.* The boy had left his blanket at the camp. He knew he would be able to steal someone else's when he needed one.

He talked to several youths in the line, sounding them out gently about their plans. This was hard, because he felt so young and several of them made it clear they didn't want him around. One told him to get lost. Eventually he came across one kid of about sixteen, in a hat with earflaps, who brightened when he introduced himself. He was Syrian and alone in the world, his family having been wiped out by a government airstrike eighteen months before, a horror he'd witnessed and spoke about in the first minutes of their conversation. His name was Hakim and he had the strange habit of looking at the ground with his mouth hanging open when he listened. He definitely wasn't stupid though, he just seemed keen to oblige, and as they spoke he offered the boy half an apple and then a sweet. The boy gave his real name – Naji. He knew he had found his mark and began to describe his predicament, which was simply that he was deemed too young to travel by himself and was therefore unable to acquire a ticket for the Blue Star to Piraeus, even though he had the money for the fare. All he needed to do was get to the Greek mainland, and to pay anyone who would help him.

Hakim looked at him from beneath the peak of his hat. 'How much?'

Naji suggested thirty euros.

'I'll think about it for forty.'

'Thirty-five.'

Hakim nodded and they shook hands and bumped fists. 'Tell me your idea,' said Hakim.

'When we've got the water bottles we'll go over there and I'll show you.'

They practised for a long time. First Naji walked ahead of Hakim with Hakim's hand on his shoulder; then they swapped so Hakim was leading, but that didn't work much better. Naji asked Hakim to play the part so he could watch, but no matter how much direction Naji gave him, Hakim was a very poor actor and he kept dissolving into giggles. He said he hadn't laughed like that for a long time. Naji found himself getting very stern. At length he gave up on him and said he would play the main part himself. They went through what Hakim would say several times and he more or less had it right by the time the huge ship reversed into the dock and trucks began to unload containers from the stern.

Two gangways were lowered to the quay on the left of
the vehicle ramp and lines hurriedly formed, families on the
left and single travellers on the right. The queues snaked for
a hundred metres across the dark quayside. But there was a
hold-up and they couldn't start boarding. A container had
toppled over during the crossing and it had to be lifted by
a squat, mobile crane with four-wheel steering, something
that fascinated Naji, who was drawn to all machinery. If he
hadn't been so worried about getting on the boat he'd have
left the line to watch the operation on the vehicle deck.

The delay turned out to be really useful because another
big ship was due in the port and would need the dock.
Once the rogue container was out of the way the crew were
anxious to load the new cargo and the two thousand-odd
refugees waiting on the quay as quickly as possible. Police
and soldiers walked along the lines urging people to keep
moving forward and told them not to rest their possessions
on the ground every time the line stopped.

What had inspired him two nights before was a similar
urgency. He'd watched a couple of young men, one of
whom was blind and was being led by the other. Just before
the police seized Naji, he saw the pair reach the top of the
gangway and keep going without anyone inspecting their
tickets. Naji thought the blind man might have had something else wrong with him because he was very slow to
react when the other man spoke to him, and he guessed this
helped smooth their way onto the boat

It was now past 1 a.m. and the ship was an hour late

leaving the port. The soldiers were herding the last few dozen migrants up the gangway. Among them were Naji and Hakim. As they waited on the gangway, shivering in the cold, just a few paces from the ticket inspection, Naji poured most of the contents of his water bottle down the front of his jeans, creating an impressive dark stain. He let the bottle fall into the sea then, with one arm clamped on Hakim's shoulder, strained forward with his eyes roaming sightlessly in their sockets. He may have overdone things a bit by dribbling and twitching but it certainly had the desired effect on the man collecting the tickets, who looked away with embarrassment. Right on cue, Hakim went through the charade of looking for and finding his ticket, which he produced with a flourish. Then they set about looking for Naji's non-existent ticket, but this was delayed by the discovery of the young man's little accident. People behind them began to complain. A police officer called up from the dockside to ask what the problem was. For one moment it looked like both of them were going to be thrown off the ferry, but the inspector relented when Naji's twitches seemed to indicate that he was building up to some kind of seizure, and he waved them through.

Once they were up on the highest deck, watching the port retreat, it took them a good hour to stop congratulating themselves and reliving the moment when Naji was struck with the shakes. They were laughing so much that Naji quite forgot to hand over the thirty-five euros and Hakim was forced to remind him gently about the money.

★

It took Samson twenty minutes to walk to the address – a stuccoed town house tucked in the streets behind the run of clubs in Pall Mall. He remembered it well from his first interview with SIS twelve years before, an interview that he hadn't sought and certainly had not expected to pass. The place was used for discreet meetings and lunches with people who did not necessarily want to be seen going into the SIS headquarters on the Thames. Samson was surprised that it hadn't been sold off to save money.

Sitting with Nyman around the table were three other people, two of whom he recognised: Sonia Fell, a very sharp Balkans specialist of his generation, whom Samson liked but did not trust – far too ambitious – and Chris Okiri, an Anglo-Ghanaian from counter-intelligence, whom he rated very highly. Another man, compact and efficient-looking, got up and introduced himself as Jamie O'Neill.

Nyman was in a hurry. 'The Official Secrets Act which you signed all those years ago obviously still pertains, Mr Samson.'

Samson nodded. 'Of course. And you can call me Paul.'

Nyman took no notice. 'Would you take us through it, Sonia?'

Sonia Fell tapped once at her keyboard and a photograph of a large number of grey sacks appeared on a TV screen on the wall. 'These are body bags,' she said quietly. 'Unusual for Syria. They contain the 150-odd victims of a massacre in a town named Hajar Saqat, about fifty miles west of the Iraq–Syria border, in territory then held by IS. Most of the victims were Christian men, but we believe there were some women among them. Satellite imagery tells us that it took place on or just after the ninth of September last year.'

Another image appeared – four pickup trucks moving in a dust trail across the desert. 'We think these are the killers leaving the village. The vehicle with the black mark painted on the bonnet is associated with other incidents. The party dispersed in the late afternoon and it wasn't possible to follow these vehicles by satellite, but we were able to draw some inferences from cell phone usage at the site and match those phones with other atrocities and actions.

'Usually phones are changed or dumped, but two of these phones were kept long enough for us to really make a study of them. When the individuals using them changed phones we were able to continue to monitor those men and plot their travels – we had very accurate voice signatures. About three weeks ago we lost them. The voices went off air, so to speak. The last we heard from these individuals was within an hour of each other on the Turkey–Syria border. We concluded that the phones were thrown away or destroyed as the men left Syria – just about here.' She brought up a map with a circle marked on the border, south of a Turkish town named Harran. Refugee camps were also marked on the map, all of which Samson knew well.

'You're assuming they crossed over,' said Samson, 'but they might just as easily have dumped their phones and stayed on the Syrian side of the border. Anything could have happened. They could have been killed.'

'That's where Tim McLennan's information comes in,'

said Nyman. 'You probably remember McLennan. He's been in the Athens embassy for the last year. He has come across an interesting story. Chris, take over, would you?'

Okiri, who had been distractedly unscrewing and screwing up the top of a water bottle, moved forward in his chair, suddenly very engaged. 'The trio connected with the Hajar Saqat massacre were observed by a witness to those events in a refugee camp in Turkey two weeks ago – we don't know which one. That same witness claims to have seen at least two of these individuals more recently in one of the camps in Lesbos. That means they are already in Europe and may be planning an attack. Trouble is we don't have any idea of their identities and we don't have photographs – none of the usual boasts and posts on social media. In fact, there's nothing except the intelligence of this witness, which was brought to Tim McLennan's notice by a contact of his in the NIS, the Greek security service. The head of NIS doubted its value.'

He took a swig from his water bottle. 'But we do have something. We have a voice, and we have tied that voice to a phone used in the truck with the black square on the hood, as Sonia explained. The guy using this vehicle was the commander of the death squad. He speaks Arabic with a hint of Europe in his accent. The language experts say he has probably spent most of his life in Northern Europe – maybe Holland, Germany or Sweden – although he does speak good Arabic. This makes us think that the men under him are also of European origin, as that is the way these goons work. But there's something else about his voice – he has a very rare speech impediment, which occurs in only one in every hundred thousand people. Someone at GCHQ noticed that he makes a strangulated sound every few sentences, at which point his voice drops to a whisper and words get lost.'

'We had a speech therapist listen to the recordings,' continued Okiri, 'and she identified the condition as spasmodic dysphonia, which is caused by a spasm in the vocal cords and gives the voice that choked quality. This character – we call him Black Square because he used that vehicle a lot last year – has it bad. Sonia is going to play you a recording of one of the intercepts.'

They waited as she searched for the file on her desktop. 'Here you go,' she said brightly.

There was a man's voice shouting a tirade in Arabic, punctuated by clicks and sudden whispers. Then, right at the end, came a snatch of what seemed like song, in which the same threats were repeated, but in quite a good singing voice.

'Goodness, what's that?' asked Samson. 'I mean the song.'

Okiri smiled. 'As an Arabic speaker you will know that he is telling his associate that he is going to cut off his testicles and insert them in his rear end because of his failure to fill all the vehicles with gas. But you can only really hear that when he sings the line. The therapist says that singing is the only way he can make himself understood when the condition kicks in badly, and that it happens a lot when he is stressed and the vocal cords go into spasm.'

'This is how Black Square was recognised in a refugee camp in Turkey,' said Nyman, anxious to move proceedings along.

'The witness who escaped the massacre at Hajar Saqat was in the camp a year later and heard the voice of the man he had seen slaughter his neighbours. He was able to put a face to the killer, who had been masked that day. The witness was able to identify two others as probably being in Hajar Saqat.'

'So this witness knows what they look like,' said Samson. 'Presumably there's some photographic record of these men. They have to be registered, fingerprinted and photographed if they are to be accepted as Syrian refugees, right? So it's simply a matter of taking your witness through the photographs and circulating the faces.'

'We don't know which camp it is,' said O'Neill.

'The witness vanished before we could act on the report,' said Nyman. 'He's on the road to Northern Europe. I am afraid we don't even know the boy's name.'

'Boy? You said boy!'

'Yes, the source of this intelligence is a boy of about twelve or thirteen. But I should stress that he's exceptionally precocious – very bright and well able to look after himself, apparently. An exceptional individual, by all accounts.' He stopped and peered at a paper in front of him, then looked up at Samson. 'What we want you to do is find him.'

Before he'd finished, Samson was shaking his head. 'Let me just get this right. You're asking me to find a boy on any one of the four or five migrant routes into the EU, each of which is at least two thousand kilometres long and has many thousands of people on it? These routes change every day – you know that.'

'I believe you'll pick him up quite quickly,' Nyman said.

'We'll circulate information to the border guards, police and NGOs, telling them that this boy needs to be apprehended for his own safety. And then you can interview him.'

'I'm just wondering why McLennan's not doing this,' said Samson. 'It's his information and he's on the spot in Greece.'

'McLennan's wife is about to give birth,' Nyman said. 'Besides, have you seen McLennan recently? He's put on a lot of weight – he couldn't possibly do this. You're perfect for the job. You speak Arabic. You are utterly familiar with this territory and the situation with refugees because of your recent assignments for Macy Harp.'

Samson held up a hand. 'Can we just go back a bit? How do we even know the men have recognised this boy?'

Okiri gave Nyman a doubtful look, which he ignored. 'It's in the psychologist's report,' Nyman said. 'The whole story comes from a woman who works in one of the camps in Lesbos as a psychologist and counsellor to the refugees. She didn't believe the lad's story at first but then she emailed the essence of what he'd told her to the man who ran the camp. She wrote in English because he is Swedish. He gave it to the police who passed it on to the NIS. She said the boy had tried to make a run for it because he knew these men had seen him in the camp in Lesbos. She suggests that they had pursued him from the camp in Turkey to the Turkish coast, and somehow located him on Lesbos.'

'When did the boy go?'

'Not exactly sure, but within the last thirty-six hours.'

'Do we have the report?'

'McLennan has not been able to get hold of it yet. That's why you're going to have to talk to this psychologist before you start looking for the boy. We've got you a seat on a plane. The CIA is flying some of their people to Cyprus – the plane leaves from Northolt at 5.30 a.m. tomorrow. They've agreed to drop you off at Mytilene on Lesbos. Of course, all this depends on whether you'd consider helping us out.'

'There's something I don't understand,' said Samson. 'If these men were known to be IS killers, why weren't they taken out by a drone attack?'

'They were providing very useful information on various aspects of IS. We were anxious not to lose that.'

Samson sensed the usual fuck-up. If they'd taken these men out they would not now be on the road to Europe and that surely counted for more than any intelligence they were providing. It reminded him why, after his interview with the HR people, he hadn't minded leaving SIS. So much time in the Office was spent reacting to, or covering up, completely avoidable disasters. He smiled pleasantly, as he always did, but groaned inwardly. Hell, he wasn't part of it all any longer – he could say what he damned well liked now. 'So, you let them go, and now you want me to find the only person who can identify them by sight – a very young boy. You're asking me to clear up your mess.'

Nyman was unfazed. 'The product of the surveillance was good – we weren't the only agency to benefit from their incontinent use of phones – the Americans were in on it too. Many were involved.'

'I see,' said Samson, after a long silence. 'But someone screwed up and now they're in Europe?'

Nyman looked at the others round the table. 'Perhaps Mr Samson and I could have a moment.' They all got up and left the room. Nyman's gaze followed them then returned to Samson. 'There was, I agree, an element of our missing an opportunity. We're trying to locate these men with voice recognition techniques, but they don't appear to be using phones.'

'So all you have is the boy's word that they were in the camp in Lesbos?'

'Yes. That's why we need to discover more about him, and, if we find him, talk to him. You're well equipped for that.'

'Really? Why?'

'For one reason, your early life mirrors his. You've been where this lad is now. Lebanon in the eighties – almost as bad as Syria today. Your folk were made homeless and lost everything. The flight from the country of your birth and all that follows that – the disorientation and dispossession.'

'There's a very vague similarity, but that's all.'

'And you're familiar with what's going on in Syria. You've been inside the country several times. The story about the artefacts is all bullshit – right?'

'Talk to Macy Harp,' said Samson equably. 'He handles these inquiries.'

Nyman put his hands together in an attitude of prayer and rested his chin on his thumbs for a moment. 'Harp's not going to say anything, but we know what you were doing. You were looking for someone. I cannot hazard at the status of your operation. Let's just say that we'll keep our ears open for information that might interest you and let you know if we hear anything – is that a deal? There are connections to be made – links between apparently different strands of the Syrian nightmare.'

'Whatever you say,' said Samson

'Look, you know these bastards and you know how they operate. My view is that it will take a person of your calibre to find the boy and lead us to these individuals. I've talked to the Chief and he agrees with me; he wants you to do this for us. And of course we will pay you – very well, as it happens.'

Samson said nothing.

'Think about it – take a walk, go and have a drink. But give me a decision within the hour.' And with that, Nyman got up and left.

There was nothing in it for Samson. He turned to his reflection in the window and thought that on the whole he'd prefer to spend the next few weeks wearing some nice suits and visiting the racecourse. The last trip into Syria had taken it out of him physically, and in his reflection he could still see that odd, rather eclipsed expression in his face. You mislaid something of yourself in the hell of that country, and it remained there forever. He thought of Aysel Hisami, the young woman doctor whom he had failed to find but whose photograph remained in his wallet. Maybe he could help with this young boy, and it surely wouldn't be an arduous job. He'd like to help nail those bastards and if that meant pursuing a kid for a few days in Greece, he would be happy to oblige.

TWO

Ten hours after his first conversation with Nyman, Samson left his former colleagues in the Secret Intelligence Service, in possession of a new phone and satellite sleeve provided by O'Neill, who turned out to be the communications specialist, and parked the dusty Toyota Camry a hundred metres beyond the entrance to the refugee camp, on the western side of Lesbos. He walked back up the road, passing three fruit stalls, half a dozen hustling taxi drivers and a couple of booths from which girls in red mini skirts were selling phone cards. He hadn't wanted to draw attention to himself by nosing the car through the camp's open gate into the crowds beyond it, and besides, he needed to get a feel for the place before meeting the psychologist, Anastasia Christakos.

Sonia Fell had made an appointment with her, saying that Samson was just checking a few details of her story for the European intelligence agencies. In her experience it helped to elevate a national intelligence effort to a European level whenever you could.

He had fifteen minutes to spare, so he walked beyond the high razor wire of Compound B, where Christakos worked in the camp's medical centre, into an open area that resembled a bustling marketplace, except there were no stalls and nothing to trade. Maybe a thousand people had divided into lines for registration, food, water, clothes and blankets. Huddles of men urgently debated issues about the route north, each man listening as if his life depended on it, which it almost certainly did.

The sun was bright, and the wind whipped up eddies of dust and paper, tugged at the headscarves and dresses of the Arab women and turned the foliage of the ancient olive grove that surrounded the camp silver. On the hillside above, scores of white shelters were placed among the trees, and between these and the trees were hung brightly coloured cloths to give shade. Shafts of sunlight cut through the smoke from countless little fires.

It was all too familiar to Samson, reminding him of the refugee camp for displaced persons where his mother and sister had spent many months, while his father headed for London, looking for ways of getting them out and settling them in the damp, grey city, away from everything he knew and loved. He remembered the pall of anxiety, kids running wild, the garbage, the smell of food cooked in the open and the lassitude, particularly the hangdog expressions of the older men who'd lost everything and would never adapt to a new life.

He returned to Compound B, followed by three young men who wanted cigarettes. Samson smoked little, but he usually had a pack on him as a means to open conversations. He gave them each a couple and was cheered like a king.

At the gate, he was let in by a uniformed police officer and escorted to the medical centre, which occupied several large container cabins that formed a square. He entered one and a neat young woman, her fair hair tied back, rose from her desk and shook his hand lightly. As well as speaking fluent English – it turned out that she had trained at Bristol University in England – the psychologist took care of her appearance. She had a trim figure, clean white shirt, pressed chinos, good make-up, and a pair of large hoop earrings that framed her face.

They had coffee – rich Greek coffee – and Samson asked about her job, mentioning the stress and disorientation that he imagined were the chief problems she dealt with. This was a conversational gambit, nothing more, but the woman suddenly looked very serious. It had become part of her job as the camp's child psychologist, she explained, to look after the grieving parents and to accompany them to the island's morgue to identify the bodies of children who had been drowned on the crossing. Hundreds were washed up or picked out of the sea by fishermen, and it was her duty to help these people through this trauma, and, she added, to grieve with them and show her sorrow at their loss. This was how her day began two or three mornings a week.

'I'm sorry,' said Samson, 'I didn't mean to be insensitive.'

'That's okay – really. It's important visitors know the kind of pain these people have been through. Migrants are seen as a problem. We try to deal with them as individuals, not as problems.'

'I'm sure you make a great difference,' he said.

She lifted her shoulders and opened her hands. 'Who knows? I do my best.' She smiled. 'So, tell me who you are. Do you work for an intelligence agency? Are you a spy?'

'I'm not a spy,' he said, smiling.

'Then what do you do?'

Samson thought. 'I find people.'

'That's what you do all the time – find people?'

'Seems to be, though I didn't set out to do this.'

'And that's really all you do?'

'Sometimes these people are very hard to find.'

'Is it dangerous?'

'Not often.'

'But now you're working with an intelligence agency and you want to talk about our clever young man?'

'I hope my associate made it clear that I am here just for an off-the-record talk. You okay with that?'

She nodded.

'The report you sent to the camp commander found its way to our people and it intrigued my superiors. It seemed like there might be one or two things that fit with information that they have from other sources. This young man may have some really valuable things to tell us.'

She angled the desk fan away from her face. 'How much do you know about his story?'

'Very little.'

'When his raft turned over in a storm and was destroyed on some rocks, he somehow grabbed hold of a baby girl and held on to her until some Spanish guys on their jet skis rescued them. He saved that baby's life, but what was really fascinating is that rescuers say they saw a dolphin very close by and they believe it was keeping them both alive by holding them up in the water. The boy confirmed this. There are many dolphins around Lesbos and they often show interest in the rafts and follow them across, so maybe it's not too incredible.'

'That's quite a story.'

'Thank God the media hasn't got hold of it. But you know there is a resonance here in Lesbos. Maybe you know the story from Greek mythology about Arion, the poet who was saved by a dolphin after being captured by pirates and shipwrecked near Lesbos.' She stopped. 'As with so many of these kids, we know very little about him.'

'So, he isn't registered – no photograph, no fingerprints. Did he have Syrian papers?'

'No, but he told us he was Syrian, and the other boys who were held here with him accepted that he came from Syria because of his knowledge of their country.'

'In your report, you stated that he had been in a Turkish camp. Do you know which one? He would have had to register there.'

She shook her head. 'No, I don't think so – the situation is pretty chaotic and procedures are not always in place.'

'So, when did he escape from here?'

'Two nights ago, but this was the second time. We don't yet know how he did it. The fence around the Protection Unit for Unaccompanied Minors is very high. You'll see it on the way out.' She pursed her lips and frowned. 'You should know that this young man is very smart. He looks like an ordinary kid, but I did a test with him, just to establish his mental state and capabilities. His IQ was 145 to 150, the top 0.5 per cent of humanity. He could be the smartest person I've ever met. He has incredible language and technical skills. Let me show you something.'

She went to retrieve a folder from a filing cabinet and spread a few drawings on her desk. 'I asked the boys to draw the place they would most like to be right at that moment. So they made pictures of their homes and their families – things like that. Actually, these tell you a lot about what these kids have lost.' She handed him a drawing. 'This is what the boy drew.'

Samson found himself looking at five tiers of red rectilinear shapes. Each plane had a distinct character with repeated features. The structure resembled an architectural elevation but was, if anything, more intricate. It was executed in a perfect perspective scheme and with different tones of red shading that were so even they might have been printed. There was an extraordinary precision and care to the work.

'Isn't it remarkable?' she said. 'And he has musical ability as well. He plays the Arabian flute quite beautifully. You are not dealing with an average kid.'

'Well, it's really impressive. Can I take a picture?

She nodded and he took pictures of the whole drawing and the signature.

'Let me get this right,' he said putting away his phone and handing her the drawing. 'He told you he'd seen two, maybe three terrorists in the camp here – is that right?'

'Yes, that's why I wrote the report to the camp overseer. I can send it to you.'

Samson pushed his card with his email address across the table. 'Where did he see them? Did he say what they looked like?'

'He gave me no kind of description. He saw two near the entrance to this compound, and they saw him. He was sure of that and he said they would kill him if he remained here, because he knew where they were going and what they planned to do. That's why he escaped the first time.'

'He said that?

'Definitely.'

'Did you ask him details?'

Anastasia looked agonised. 'No, I regret it, but I hear a lot of stories from these boys.'

'What made you believe him?'

'I'd had a bad day the day he told me – many difficult cases and a lot of stress. It was hard, you know? And the next morning I remembered one characteristic of this kid. He didn't tell anyone about the dolphin and he didn't brag about saving the baby, either. We only heard that part of the story after one of the rescuers from the beach brought the mother and father to see the boy so that they could thank him. Their gratitude was something to see. It was their only child, their firstborn, and yet he made nothing of it – he was just embarrassed. That got me thinking that this is a kid who doesn't like to boast and he doesn't make up stories. He steals a lot but he doesn't lie. So that's when I sat down and wrote the email. But he had already gone when I got to the camp.'

'Could he still be on the island?'

'Maybe, but I'm sure he headed for the port, which is where the police picked him up last time. A Blue Star boat for refugees left for Piraeus that night. He may have boarded that.'

'Let me just get the timings right. If he sailed that night he would have reached Piraeus the next morning – two and a half days ago.'

'Yes, then he would make for the border with Macedonia.'

'How far's that?'

'More than five hundred kilometres. He'd have to take the train, but there are many wanting to travel so there's a long wait. And the police might pick him up because he's on his own and has no papers.'

'So he could conceivably be in Athens still?'

'Possibly.'

'Can you give me an idea of his appearance?'

'He's about twelve or thirteen but he hasn't reached puberty yet. He's slight in build though I guess he's about average height for his age; dark hair, quite a light skin, and light eyes – a brownish, pale green colour. They're very striking. He told me they were like his mother's.' She stopped to think. 'I only had two sessions with him one to one, and that was how I learned about his really amazing language skills. His father taught him English, now he's learning German using the web. But there was . . .' Puzzlement and anxiety flickered in her expression in quick succession. 'I felt something was there – some big tragedy or shame in his life.'

'He talked about a family – did he give you any clue which refugee camp they're in?'

'I don't even know if they were in the camp with him. That was the thing with him – he kept everything so tight. He never gave up anything voluntarily.'

'Do you have any idea why he's on the road by himself?'

'I had the feeling that he'd been entrusted by his father with this mission. It's quite a common story. If the family don't have money, they send a boy to get asylum in Europe. It's a huge responsibility for these children and you can imagine the psychological impact when they fail. They're unrealistically optimistic about their chances and they have no idea of the dangers on the road. But this boy, he was the most determined I have ever seen. Maybe surviving the wreck when so many people were drowned has given him a feeling of invincibility.'

She straightened slightly. Through the window, her gaze followed two large men in Arab robes and loose red NGO vests who were making their way through the lines of people waiting for medical attention. A few seconds later they were ushered into the office by a Canadian aid worker, who pulled

up chairs around a desk at the far end of the room and gestured for them to sit down. They were from the north of
England, though Samson couldn't quite place the accent.

He cursed their arrival. The psychologist seemed to have
warmed to him and he had a lot more questions for her,
but her manner had suddenly become formal again. She
scribbled a note and handed it to him. *Bar Liberty, Mytilene 9
p.m. – OK???* She walked over to his side of his desk, put her
hand out and began addressing him in Greek. He nodded,
though he hadn't the slightest idea what she was saying.

'See you later,' she mouthed at the door.

THREE

After sending Anastasia's email to London, together with his notes on their conversation, Samson drove back to Mytilene and found a room in a hotel overlooking the port. Even though the boy might still be in Athens, he was sure Anastasia could tell him a lot more.

He took a can of beer from the mini bar and went out onto the balcony. He drew a cigarette from the pack and examined it before lighting up.

The Turkish coast lay no more than ten miles away, clouded by haze, which Samson realised was caused by the wind scooping spray from the waves. As he smoked and thought about the camp and Anastasia's work, his gaze came to rest on a few tiny strips of orange out to sea. He fetched a small pair of binoculars from the side pocket of his rucksack. Three long rubber dinghies loaded with people in orange life jackets were moving at an agonisingly slow speed through the waves. Each disappeared in turn as it entered the trough of a wave.

He became aware that one of his two phones – the encrypted set – was vibrating in the back pocket of his jeans. He pulled it out, entered the code with his thumb and answered.

'We're just looking at the stuff you sent over,' said Chris Okiri. 'The man says he wants much more on what the boy saw and heard in the camp. Take her through what he told her and get her to flesh it out. The man points out that she seems to have written the word Stut before the word Germany. There are one or two mistakes in the email and he wonders whether she meant to write Stuttgart. If the boy is trying to reach a relation in Stuttgart, the German authorities may be able to work out who that is and get a family name then we may be able to track him back to the Turkish camp.'

'I'm seeing her later,' he said. He watched as two large motorboats approached the dinghies.

'You there?' asked Okiri.

'Yes . . . As it happens, I'm watching a rescue of refugees from my balcony.'

'Right,' said Okiri, plainly uninterested.

'The point, dear Chris, is that more migrants are coming every day and they'll all soon be on that road. Where's McLennan?' He put the binoculars down, reached for the cigarette that had gone out in the ashtray and relit it.

'McLennan's wife is in the hospital, so it's just you at the moment. We've told the French, Germans and several Balkan governments about the boy. The trouble is that we have so little information it's hard to really interest them right now. We need everything you can get from that woman. Hey, by the way, I love that story about his rescue.'

'Yes,' Samson said, and hung up. He raised the binoculars and stood for a few minutes watching the rescue operation. Eventually one of the craft was taken in tow and the people from the other two scrambled, or were lifted, onto the larger of the two motorboats.

He napped for half an hour then walked along the harbour in the late afternoon light. Recently arrived migrants were occupying every available bench and patch of grass, while the town's population continued as if the strangers weren't there. The atmosphere seemed harmonious enough, though Samson had learned from the hotel reception that it had been anything but in the summer, when the migrants were sleeping and cooking and washing – as best they could – in all the public spaces in the centre of town. Things had settled down since then. Restaurants and cafés were now doing a brisk trade serving the better-off refugees – those that had come on clapped-out launches and motor yachts, rather than the big rubber inflatables.

Young men were everywhere. Samson learned to recognise those who had freshly waded ashore by the dried saltwater tidemark on their jeans. At a food station, beneath the shade of large umbrella pines, just beyond the port, he chatted to those waiting and counted a dozen different nationalities – men from as far away as Bangladesh, Eritrea, Mali and Morocco. He offered them cigarettes and found out which way they planned to enter the European Union Schengen area. On the side of a caravan he read advice – provided in English, Arabic and Urdu – about the countries the young men would be travelling through. There was one particular warning: 'Bulgaria is very difficult, with a lot of walking through mountains and forests. Independent reports of police beating, robbers and many bad dogs.'

He took pictures of the notices with his phone to capture the websites that were listed. New routes would first appear on these sites, together with emerging hazards and other news. He wondered if it might even be possible to use one of them to communicate an offer of safe passage to the boy.

As dusk fell, he walked back into the centre by a different route, and came across a store that had once sold sun cream, towels and beach mats, but was now mostly stocked with waterproof gear, rucksacks, tents and warm clothing. He bought himself a torch, hat, gloves and anorak to wear over his battered leather jacket. It amused him that the female assistant took him for a migrant. 'If you're going north you'll need these,' she said, handing him three Freytag & Berndt maps covering Macedonia, Bulgaria, Serbia, Croatia and Slovenia. 'They cost much but they're good.'

He paid her and took the maps, then asked if she could remember a young boy with light eyes and good English visiting the store in the last few days. She called into the back room and a man with glasses propped on his forehead appeared with an open newspaper in his hands. He spoke English, too. Yes, he remembered the boy because of his polite and intelligent manner. It was two days ago – around seven in the evening – and he had bought everything he needed and had shown particular care in choosing the items.

'You are certain it was two days ago?' asked Samson.

'Yes,' said the storekeeper. 'I remember that he went to the boat – the boat was leaving that evening.'

Anastasia Christakos must have got the sailing dates confused – she was, after all, some way from the port. 'So, the Blue Star went two nights ago, not three?'

'Yes, there's one every other night. Another one for refugees sails this evening.'

'The boy had money?'

'Yes, euros, and he bargained with me.' The man searched his mind for a phrase. 'He has something this kid.' He looked at his assistant and said something in Greek.

'Self-possession,' said the assistant.

The storeowner examined him. 'What do you want with this boy?'

'I believe he's in danger. We're trying to find him,' said Samson, gesturing to the bags of equipment at his feet.

'It's possible that I may be able to help you. The boy could not afford the maps, so I allowed him to take photographs.'

'With a phone?'

'Yes, they all have phones.' He then showed Samson on the maps he'd just purchased what sections the boy had photographed. 'He's smart, this kid. It means he has the map even when there is no Internet.'

Samson made some notes on his set of maps and ringed

the areas that the boy had photographed. He thanked the man and his assistant and set off to the ferry terminal, where a Blue Star ship had backed into the dock and was now disgorging trucks from its stern. Night had fallen. There were hundreds of people standing or sitting in family groups on the quayside, with all their possessions piled together. Except for the tractors removing containers from the bowels of the ship, there was very little noise in the terminal. There was a kind of hushed reverence for the great vessel that would set these people on the European mainland the next morning.

He wandered over to a group of older men who were watching a Greek fisherman hand-lining for small oval fish, sat down on the sea wall and wrote an encrypted email to Fell and O'Neill, the communications specialist. *The boy has a phone. May have been bought on Lesbos in the last few days because it seems unlikely that phone would have survived his raft going down. The provider could be Junophon. If you can get details of numbers sold in the last few days, we may be able to run checks on calls made to Turkey. I think he has papers that he hasn't showed anyone – maybe a Syrian passport. Also see if you can get access to registration records of the Lesbos camp. Maybe the bad guys show up in them.*

An email returned from Fell. *We're on it!*

He watched the scene for a while then sauntered over to a camper van run by Médecins Sans Frontières and started speaking in Arabic to the young man he'd seen marshalling the line of people waiting for attention. The row of white plastic chairs was now empty and the man was at a loose end.

He told the man that he was doing some research for Al Jazeera. After a short time he discovered that it was possible to buy a ticket for the ferry on the black market without the documents that confirmed refugee status, and it wasn't unknown for people to board without a ticket. The authorities weren't overly diligent because they were eager to get people off the island as quickly as possible.

He emailed SIS with the news that the boy had almost certainly landed in Piraeus just thirty-six hours before. Given the delays on the bus service and trains to the north, he might still be in Athens.

Later, he found Anastasia in a boisterous group of aid workers in the Bar Liberty. She detached herself from the party when she spotted him and they went to a table in the smoking section outside, where she demurely lit a cigarette, as if it were her very first time. They ordered food and Samson asked about the two men who had come into the office.

'Oh, yeah – those guys. They're always trying to get access to the boys for religious instruction. And you know what? The kids really don't want it. They are stressed as it is – we protect them from more pressure.'

'Where are those men from?'

'I don't know – somewhere in the UK, maybe Leeds. They're a bit creepy. And they hang around a lot. I found them in the office the other day on their own, which I didn't like, and I asked them to leave. I just didn't want to talk in front of them.'

'If these men come asking about him, could you let me know? And their names would be helpful.'

She nodded. 'OK.'

He brought the copy of her email up on his phone and looked around to make sure they were out of earshot of the other customers. 'Would you mind if I read this to you and asked a few questions? It's obviously important that I get this right in my mind – I mean exactly what the boy told you.'

She picked up her drink. 'Of course, be my guest. Remember I wrote this in a rush.'

'Maybe we could talk a bit about the detail?'

'Sure,' she said, then blew a stream of smoke from a pout.

'Okay, so, the relevant part is this: "After he was returned to our charge, I talked to the boy about why he escaped and he told me that he had to save his own life. He said that he saw two men here on Lesbos who were with him in a refugee camp in Turkey (which he refuses to identify) and that he was sure they were going to kill him. I asked him why they would do that and he replied that he recognised them from the mass killing in his village in northern Syria and that he was sure they were the same men. He told me he overheard conversations between the men while they were speaking of an attack in Europe."' Samson stopped as a waiter placed several small meze dishes on the table and then asked, 'Shall we just talk about this bit?'

She nodded and took some pitta bread.

'Firstly, did he tell you how he recognised these men? We have reports of massacres and mostly these men wear masks.'

'He recognised the voice of one of the men — it is a strange voice and then he recognised the others from their mannerisms and also their voices. I am sure he said that. He seemed so sure.'

'Anything else?'

'When they were alone they called each other by names he recognised. He didn't tell me the names.'

'How did he and his family escape the killings? How were they allowed to witness this crime with impunity?'

'Maybe it was because they were Muslim. He mentioned that his father had been tortured by the regime, but he did not use that word, he used the word mistreated. He said that these men killed only Christians. He was rather vague about all this — I got the feeling he wasn't telling me everything he knew, or was making up details as they came to him.'

'But the vital part of all this is that he recognised these men in the camp. Is that right?

'This is what he said, yes.'

'So how come this boy then learns of their plans to carry out an attack? It seems improbable.'

Anastasia frowned. 'I know, and this is why I did not believe him at first. I believe he said he was spying on them and maybe they had tried to groom him into their ways. Maybe they were recruiting him and he had gone along with that and spied on them. The story was complicated and I didn't follow all the details because at that moment I was sceptical.'

'Do you think that in fact he may have imagined it all?

That is surely a possibility. If he had spied on them while being groomed, it would require a lot of courage and a cool temperament. Does he have those qualities?'

'Yes. He saved that baby and he escaped twice from detention. I think he's a very brave kid and I also think he could be quite ruthless and dishonest. He may have stolen one or two items when he was in the camp – a knife that had been taken by one of the guards from a kid. I think he stole that from my desk.'

'A knife?'

'Yes, I saw him playing with it. I told him to put it down. I never saw it again.'

Samson asked her about the word Stut in the email. It had turned out that she had in fact written Stuttgart, but then wasn't sure whether the boy had definitely told her that he was heading for the German city and she had failed to delete all of the word before sending the email.

'So when did he tell you this?'

'It was in our second one-to-one session, when I was trying to get him to talk about the trauma of the people from his boat being drowned. He wouldn't open up. He said that he was protected and that the same mysterious force would get him all the way to Germany. That is when I thought he mentioned Stuttgart once, but I can't be sure, which is maybe why I half-deleted it.'

'Did he tell you anything about the route he planned?

'He said nothing about that.'

'Did he own a phone?'

'Not sure – we don't search the kids. Their private possessions are exactly that. His stuff was all drenched, but most people take precautions with a phone because it's the most important thing in their life and they need them on the way over so they can call help – the smugglers give them numbers. They wrap phones in several plastic bags.'

'Did he have money?'

'I don't know.'

'Did he form a relationship with anyone – people he could make the journey with?'

'He was like a celebrity in the camp – the story about the dolphin and the baby. Maybe he made some friends, made contacts. Yes, a lot of people came to see him when they heard his story, because everyone is bored in the camp and they like to be distracted. I don't know if he had a particular friend.'

'What was the nature of your treatment, your therapy?'

'These boys have a lot of responsibility on their shoulders, because each one is hoping to get asylum and bring their families to Europe. He left his family behind in a camp in Turkey. Imagine that! The only way these kids can handle that pressure is by a kind of reality distortion. You have to prick that optimism. I told this boy, there are evil people out there – paedophiles, people traffickers, murderers, corrupt police, criminal gangs and robbers. Winter's coming and people will die of cold on that road. I told him, you go out there alone and you could wind up frozen to death or murdered. You have to say these hard truths to them.'

Samson got up. 'I need to tell my people what you have told me. Can I get you another drink while you wait?'

After he had brought Sonia Fell up to date, he went back and they ate. He had had almost nothing to eat for twenty-four hours and began to feel a lot better and ordered more beer. He liked Anastasia and admired her lack of sentimentality and self-importance. He could see why people opened up to her, and he admitted to himself that he was a little sorry to be leaving the island so soon. They talked about what Europe could do about the migrant crisis and the psychologist concluded rather bitterly that whatever happened, it would always fall to the Greek islands to deal with the influx.

'They are drowning in our seas, crawling up our beaches, and that isn't going to stop soon,' she said. 'Just because Europe has suddenly decided that these people are not wanted doesn't mean they aren't going to give up getting on those little rafts. They have nothing to lose – there's nothing where they come from. They look at the Internet and they see kids their age with money and girls and freedom and they think why I can't I have that? It's not just about war – it's about inequality. You try having absolutely nothing . . .'

'I have once,' he said. 'My family were refugees. I was in that boy's position.' This visibly surprised her and she was about to respond but he moved quickly on. 'From your talks with the boy did you get any sense of his background? Is there anything I can use?'

'Yes, I drew some vague conclusions. I felt he was maybe the eldest child because of his sense of responsibility, and maybe he was brought up with sisters rather than with other boys. He interacted better with women and girls than with males. He could be a little awkward with boys of his own age, perhaps because he's so intelligent and finds them dull, but maybe it's because he wasn't used to boys. He's solitary and self-sufficient – most of the time he was in the facility he sat in a chair by the gate looking intently around him, or reading. A person gave us a load of books in English and he found a science book – I think it was about physics – and he liked that a lot.'

'Sounds like he'll be an interesting adult,' said Samson absently.

'That's exactly what the director of the documentary said.'

'What documentary was that?' he fired back.

'There was a French documentary crew here. They were making a series for Canal Plus. We gave them full cooperation. It's about child migrants – kids travelling on their own.'

'They filmed your work?'

'Yes, and many other things, as well. They were at the camp for five days.'

'Did they film this boy?'

'Maybe, I don't know . . . Yes, they probably did.'

'Where's the crew now? Are they still on the island?'

'No, they're in Athens filming. I know they'll be there for four days. Why are you so interested?'

'You just said they may have filmed the boy – we need a picture of him.'

She put her hand to her mouth. 'How stupid of me – I didn't think of that.'

She fished in her bag for her wallet, from which she plucked the card of Jean-Jacques Pinto, the bright new star in French documentary-making. Samson had seen a full-length feature by Pinto about the *banlieues* of Paris earlier in the year.

'Do you know him well enough to call and ask him to see me tomorrow in Athens?'

'Of course.' She smiled and took out her phone.

'Don't say anything about the boy. Just ask Pinto if he can spare the time to see me. Say it's important and I will explain when I see him. Tell him I work in a Europe-wide security operation,' he replied. 'You know the sort of thing.'

She dialled the number, still smiling.

Anastasia deployed all her charm on Pinto and he agreed to meet Samson the next day, though he was wary. All that was left for Samson was to catch the early flight to Athens, and Anastasia said she could arrange it, even though the flight was usually full. She made another call and told him he had a ninety per cent chance of a seat if she was with him at the airport by six, for which reason she suggested he check out of his hotel that night and stay with her in the house she shared with two aid workers on the coast road.

Half an hour later they arrived at the villa. The place had once been a desirable holiday home but now it looked onto one of the main landing beaches for migrant dinghies. As they swung into the drive their headlights picked out a pile of discarded life jackets.

'Okay,' she said, as he let his things down softly in the hallway. 'The others are asleep. I think we should go to my room.' When the door was closed behind them, she turned to him with a perfectly charming smile 'You can sleep on the bed, but that is all.'

'That's fine with me,' he replied. 'Feels like I haven't slept for a week.'

But instead of sleeping they talked for another hour, staring up at the fan in the half-light and talking about their lives. 'How do you speak Arabic so well?' she asked. 'Did you learn it for your job?'

'It's my first language,' replied Samson. 'I was born in Lebanon – but we had to leave and I was brought up with my sister in London after '85.'

'But Samson is an English name, no?'

'It's anglicised from the Arabic name Shamshun. That was my father's first name. Actually my family name is Malouf. We dropped it when we went to England.'

'You had to leave Lebanon?'

'Yes, it was during the war. I was eight or nine, I forget. We lost everything and went to England, where my mother set up a famously good restaurant in the West End of London.'

'And what about your father?'

'He died early. He was the archetypal Levantine trader. He needed the Mediterranean. He could have lived at any time in the last two thousand years and he'd have made a living doing exactly the same thing – buying and selling.

But he got us out, and somehow found the money to set up a home in London.'

'But you're not a trader – you find people,' she said, turning to him so that he could feel the breath of her words on his cheek. 'What does that actually mean?'

'It's not my profession; it's just something that's developed over the last couple of years. I work for a company that sometimes helps clients find people.'

'Who have you found recently?'

'We lost track of the person I spent most of the year trying to find. She vanished.'

'Was it someone you knew?

'No, I didn't know her. She was doctor – a brilliant one, by all accounts. I was working for her brother.'

She waited a couple of beats. 'Do you have a partner – someone special in your life?'

'No,' he said at length, 'no one special, but that's not for want of trying.' He laughed.

'You find people but no one for yourself – is that it?'

'Look, I should sleep,' he murmured.

They fell silent, but it was a while before Samson stopped thinking about Aysel Hisami. Just before he dropped off he hurried through that old reel from his childhood in the camp, where his family had been for over a year before his fast-talking, handsome father got them out.

Next morning, the words that had passed between them seemed every bit as intimate as sex and they were somehow much closer. When they had dropped off his car keys at the airport she turned to him with a candid interest. 'I hope we meet again,' she said. 'Maybe you'll come back some day.'

'Oh, I'm sure I will, Anastasia,' he said, and he took her hand and held it. 'I've really enjoyed talking to you, and I know we will speak about the boy again. You have my number and my email, right?

She nodded and kissed him on the cheek. 'Good luck. I hope you find him. He's going to be something really important, I am sure.'

'Maybe he already is,' said Samson, smiling, and he turned to the departure gate.

FOUR

He waited at the hotel in Athens for Jean-Jacques Pinto for over four hours. It seemed the filmmaker had forgotten about their appointment and was not prepared to come back to the hotel until after he'd completed shooting scenes at the city's main bus station, where boys travelling alone were identified and detained, and then at the orphanages where they were kept.

Samson was frustrated and angry. With every hour that went by the boy was getting further away from him, and soon he would be lost in the wilderness of the Balkans.

When Pinto eventually materialised in the lobby with his crew, Samson's mood did not improve. Pinto, a short, volatile young man with cropped hair, a scarf loosely tied around his neck and a great sense of his own importance, flatly refused to show Samson the footage from Lesbos. The more Samson reasoned with him, the more he protested. 'Who is this fucking Englishman to tell me what I should do with my film?' he asked his crew. What right did Samson have to interfere with the journalistic process? Did the English not appreciate that in France the activities of journalists and filmmakers were still sacred?

Samson waited until Pinto ran out of steam, then took him by the arm and steered him firmly to a less public part of the lobby. He released him, looked at him hard and inhaled.

'In your footage from the island there's likely to be vital evidence that will save lives. I need to look through it. And I am not going away until I do.'

Pinto averted his eyes. It was all Samson could do not to hit the jerk. 'You don't know me,' he began quietly, 'so I do understand your reservations, Monsieur. But let me just say that if you refuse to show me this material, the permissions you hold to film in Greece will be withdrawn immediately. Just one call from my government to Greece's National Intelligence Service will ensure that happens. Do you need that kind of delay?'

Pinto glanced around the lobby but said nothing. He scratched his stubble, fiddled with his scarf and rattled a pillbox he'd taken from his pocket.

'I really don't understand this reluctance,' continued Samson. 'Anastasia told me there would be no problem. We talked about your work and she said you were the sort of guy who would readily help. This boy we are looking for is in real danger.'

The man looked at him doubtfully and popped a pill from the box. Samson knew he was about to fold. He shook his head regretfully. 'I really don't like to insist, but take my behaviour as a measure of my urgency.'

Pinto blinked several times then turned to an assistant and said, '*Laissez cet homme voir ce qu'il veut*' – Let him see what he wants. And with that he disappeared into the elevator.

His assistant, a young woman named Suzanne, came over with a laptop. She evidently thought the exchange highly amusing. 'Jean-Jacques, he is a truly great director,' she said with a smile, 'but also he can be a little bit of an arsehole.'

'We all can,' said Samson, grinning. 'I just was. Is there somewhere we can go where I can watch this undisturbed?'

She offered her own room on the second floor and ordered coffee to be brought up.

When they were settled, she explained that the footage was arranged thematically in five sections: general footage from the island; film of rescues and rescuers; film that dealt with the processing of refugees; film of the camps; film of the children. Since child refugees were Pinto's subject matter, this section was where he should direct his attention.

But first she'd play him some material that she was working on at the moment and was to hand. It was of a rescue in the northern tip of Lesbos, the place on the island closest to Turkey. 'This is amazing footage,' she said. 'It captures so much of what the refugees endure. It's just a few minutes.'

Dawn had just broken on a stormy day. The film crew had obviously arrived in some haste, and the camerawork was shaky as the four of them leapt from the car. There was pandemonium everywhere, with people clad in wetsuits sprinting up a track beside the beach; others were yelling into radios and aiming high-powered torches out to the murky sea. A wind tore at the fire in a large brazier, sending streamers of smoke and sparks across the waves. More people came running with gold and silver survival blankets. Everyone was shouting.

It took a few moments for the cameraman to find his bearings and work out what he should be shooting. At the same time, the film crew managed to get their lights working and the sound became more consistent. Pinto could be heard taking charge. The camera panned from two trees beside the track to the sea, where three large rigid inflatable rescue boats were going back and forth about one hundred metres from the shoreline, the beams of their searchlights slashing across the waves. The camera picked up two bodies, motionless in the water, then a couple more. Samson counted five in all. The camera zoomed in on the rescuers jumping into the water and dragging the bodies towards the boats, where they were hauled aboard. On the largest of the rescue boats, two crew members worked furiously, trying to bring people back to life, pumping at their chests and bending down to give them mouth-to-mouth.

This went on for a minute or two, though it seemed much longer. Then Pinto appeared on camera, stumbling across the wet stones on the beach, scarf flying around his head. He had seen something. The camera followed him, then moved beyond him to focus on a body in a life jacket bobbing in the sea. Pinto waded into the water to seize hold of the person and drag them the last few metres to the beach. The person's arms began to flail as he did – they were still alive. With one arm, Pinto was also gesturing ahead, towards the trees. The camera jerked up and focused on a powerful jet ski that had arrived at a rickety jetty built below the trees. Attached to its rear was a platform and clinging to this were five exhausted people. Men ran into the water to help them make the short distance to dry land, which allowed the jet ski almost immediately to turn and head back out to sea. Once ashore, the sounds of people's distress could be heard in snatches above the roar of the sea and the wind in the trees. They were pointing out to sea where their loved ones were drowning, and one or two had to be restrained from going back into the water.

Now medical workers arrived and began to deal with the survivors, wrapping them in foil blankets, holding them, comforting them, guiding them towards the glowing braziers and checking them for injuries as best they could in the poor light. The camera seemed wary of intruding and, as one of medics stepped forward and gestured angrily at the crew, the picture wobbled before Pinto appeared and told the cameraman to stop filming. But in those few moments Samson saw a boy among those being led towards the fire. He had been one of the last to be plucked from the sea by the jet skis. He was clutching a backpack and was wrapped in a blanket, so his face was hidden. This could be any young boy but maybe – just maybe – Samson had witnessed the rescue of the boy he was looking for.

The screen froze on the final image. 'Jean-Jacques is thinking of opening the film with this.'

'He should – it is very powerful,' said Samson, 'and very shocking, too. How many people were lost?'

'Twenty-five I think,' she said, still gazing at the blank screen. 'Maybe you should tell me *exactly* what you are looking for?'

'You saw the boy on the beach just now? Somewhere out there is a boy of his age who is in danger because he has information about some terrorists. We desperately need to find him. But we don't have a photograph of him. We don't even know his name. We heard a dolphin might have saved him. Does that ring any bells?' She shook her head. 'He was in the care of a woman called Anastasia at the camp. She's a psychologist. Did you meet her?'

Her eyes lit up. 'Yes, a truly great person. I liked her a lot. We filmed her.' She went to work on the laptop and quickly found the film shot at the medical centre. Samson was suddenly looking at Anastasia as she conducted a group therapy session through an interpreter. All the boys' heads were turned away, so the camera focused on her as she laughed and joked with them. There were several other scenes featuring Anastasia – an art therapy class, one-to-one therapy and some sort of role-play session – but always the boys' faces were hidden or indistinct.

'Damn,' he muttered as the sequence came to an end. Partly this was because he liked watching Anastasia with the kids. She was so good at engaging them and making them participate.

'Don't give up so easily,' said Suzanne. 'When we left that day, after being with Anastasia, Jean-Jacques had this idea that we walk out of the camp with a following tracking shot.'

'What's that?'

'It is when the camera moves with the subject. It's like the famous scene in *Goodfellas* when Henry Hill is going through a restaurant – such a great piece of cinematography, because you really get the wise guy thing. Do you know what I'm talking about?'

'Afraid not.'

'Scorsese is a master. Jean-Jacques admires him a lot. Anyway, we did this shot and Pierre – that's our camera-man – followed Jean-Jacques from the medical centre out of camp to give the idea of the scale.'

She searched the laptop and clicked play.

The camera began to move down a long, winding pathway bordered on both sides by a high fence that was topped with razor wire. Wherever Pinto looked the camera followed him; whenever he paused the camera paused. First he peered right, through the wire, at a line of women waiting for the camp's maternity and paediatric services. Then he looked left, at some police dogs that were being fed and watered. He glanced at the light in the trees and at his feet walking through the dust.

The pathway reached the gate, and he looked left, at three boys in the yard of a small compound.

'Can you stop it now?' Samson said. He pulled out his

cell phone, selected the camera option and held the phone to the screen. He took three separate close-ups of each boy, checked it and attached it to an email which he sent to Anastasia. A few seconds later, he called her and asked her to look at her inbox.

He waited, listening to her breath and the tapping of her fingers on her keyboard.

'Okay, I got the emails,' she said. 'The first one – no, that's not him; the second – no, that's not him, either; and the third – no, sorry! But you have the right group of boys.'

'I'll call you back,' said Samson.

Suzanne had already moved the film on to a couple of smiling girls who were calling through the perimeter fence. The camera came to rest on them and then returned to the object of their attention, a boy of about the right age, sitting in a white plastic chair very near the gate. His hands gripped the arms of the chair; his feet kicked at the dust. Instinctively Samson knew this had to be him. He took a picture and emailed it to Anastasia. He rang immediately and she confirmed his instinct.

'Fantastic,' said Samson. 'That is wonderful news. Speak soon.'

'I really look forward to that,' she replied. 'Good luck, Paul – I know you'll find him now.'

'I hope so,' he said. He wanted to say how good she was with the children and what a terrific impression she made on the film, but for some reason he didn't. He thanked her, said he hoped they would meet again and hung up.

'Can you give me the best still you've got of this kid?' he asked Suzanne. 'And send it to me at this address?' He gave her his card. Then he had another idea. 'Is it possible you could turn up the volume? I want to hear what those girls are saying to him.'

They went through the whole sequence several times. It was clear that the girls were calling to the boy. Samson and Suzanne both strained to hear what they were shouting.

'Sounds like *na gee*,' said Suzanne.

'You're right — it's Naji. It's a name. You know what it means in Arabic? Survivor!'

He called Anastasia again. 'Me again! Do you think his name could be Naji?'

'Could be — I heard someone call that out in the compound a few times.' She thought for a second. 'Yes, I think that may be it.'

'That's what I'm going with,' he said. 'Hey, you were terrific in the film — the kids obviously love you.'

'Thanks — see you.'

The wire mesh that cut across part of Naji's face in the still provided by the film company was digitally removed and the image enhanced so that SIS had an almost faultless portrait of the boy.

Looking at the face in the photograph, which came by encrypted email later that afternoon, Samson thought he could perceive much of what Anastasia had been saying about the boy. There was indeed an intelligent light in those

pale brown eyes, which looked out from beneath a mop of
dark hair. Naji had fine features and a mouth that spread into
the habitual smile of those rare people who find things come
easily to them and are usually ahead of the game. Naji was
good-looking and also had a kind of grace. Samson understood why those young girls had been shouting his name
through the fence.

What to do with the image was the subject of long deliberation in SIS headquarters. The first idea was to circulate
the picture of Naji as widely as possible – to all police and
border forces in the Balkans and Northern Europe, as well
as to the NGOs and government organisations operating
along the migrant route. But how sensible was that? From
the Middle East to Northern Europe, people-smuggling
organisations had penetrated the police and border agencies,
corrupting them with the money from a trade worth well
over a billion dollars annually in Europe alone. If it was
known that the intelligence services considered Naji vitally
important in the fight against terrorism, circulating the photograph might be tantamount to putting a price on his head.
It didn't take too much to imagine how a people smuggler
might turn kidnapper and seek a ransom for Naji's release.

Then there was the enemy to consider. It was not known
exactly how well IS operated in the Balkans, but it was
assumed that there was some kind of crude network, at
the very minimum a list of numbers and maybe addresses
to provide support to terrorists using the migrant trail. A
photograph released to all and sundry might easily come

into the possession of the very people that wanted to make
Naji and everything he knew disappear. It would show just
how valuable he was to the European intelligence services.
In short, it would provide confirmation, if it were needed,
that his death was a priority.

The result of the discussion was that Nyman and the Chief
decided that the photograph should only be shared with key
partners – the French, German, Austrian and Italian intelligence services – and, informally, with one or two trusted
contacts among the NGOs. It went without saying that
Naji's name would not be released either. Already Okiri
and Fell had begun searching databases held on refugees in
Turkey, in the hope that they could make a match with a
family who had sent their young son, Naji, to find a new
life in Europe. This was crucial, for it would then locate the
terrorists to a particular camp and, if their luck held out, lead
them to the false identities and registration photographs of
the men who now sought to re-enter Europe as legitimate
refugees. The boy's destination was important, too, and the
German Federal Intelligence Service – the BND – were
making a considerable effort to identify exactly which individual or family in the Stuttgart area the boy was aiming to
visit, though clues were woefully thin on the ground.

Nyman called, but he didn't have to explain to Samson
the implications of keeping the boy's name and photo secret.
Samson knew it meant that he alone would be on the trail
of the boy for the next few days, at least. Nyman told him
there would be help, once he got past the Greek border with

Macedonia, although he was confident the boy would be found before that.

'Thanks for the vote of confidence,' said Samson, 'but I have little idea where to start.'

'Why not Athens, where you are now? As you said, you're not very far behind him. and I can't believe he will travel too long on his own.'

'He's escaped twice from detention – over a fence that might have surrounded a maximum security prison – and he certainly got on that ferry without showing any papers. He knows what he's doing, this kid.'

Nyman ignored this. 'Stay in touch at every moment of the way,' he said and hung up.

A boy could get where he wanted in a crowd, and also *what* he wanted, if he was light-fingered and swift enough, which is exactly how he had acquired several of the items in his pack. Naji learned that you could use a crowd almost like a medium and swim through it, though nowadays he did not much like the idea of swimming. He had slipped from the side of the crush at the station into the centre and worked his way forward, saying that he had lost his father who was at the front and was about to board the train without him. He showed some tears and people let him through. It was all an act, of course, just like his triumph boarding the Blue Star ship at Mytilene.

He was now very near the front of the crowd for the train that would take them near to the border with Macedonia, and was waiting patiently to be summoned forward. He looked around and took in his surroundings. The train station was not nearly as large as he had imagined it would be when he bought the ticket from a man in Victoria Square, and he was a bit disappointed.

It was then that he heard the voice.

He didn't turn to look, because he was certain this was Al-munajil's voice – the croak of the devil. And worse, he could tell from the murmured conversation happening just a few paces behind him that Al-munajil was with Usaim, one of his sidekicks. He treated Usaim appallingly, but the man was like a slave to him, and one of the cruellest of all the fighters.

Naji froze, astonished that they had not already seen him. If he got on the train he might be placed in the same carriage as Al-munajil and Usaim and they would be sure to spot him on the long journey and then they'd hunt him down at the other end and kill him. He waited, listening to them talking, and remembered the long days and nights that he'd spent with them, riding in the back of the pickup – those months that he could never tell anyone about, not even the nice woman in the camp who'd shown so much interest in him.

He pulled his cap down over his eyes and moved sideways very slowly, for he realised that he must be in the direct line of sight of the two men. He waited until armed policemen came forward and told the people in the first few ranks of the crowd to have their tickets ready. The crowd surged forward and people began to shout. Naji spun to his left and was soon weaving through the ragged margins of the crush.

He glanced back and scanned the crowd for a few seconds to make sure they weren't following him. It was then that he caught sight of Ibrahim, Al-munajil's terrifying deputy. All three had left the island and were travelling together. This was really bad. Somebody had to stop them. For one moment he thought of telling the police officers at the station, but then they would ask him why he was travelling alone and they'd throw him in one of the orphanages he had heard about. Besides, he wasn't sure they would believe him.

He hung around outside the station and managed to get a little money for his ticket, though nothing like the price he had paid to the man in the square, and then he took himself to a park a hundred metres away and found a shaded spot where migrant families were resting. He ate the cheese and bread he'd saved from the boat and finished the bottle of water he'd bought for the train ride, yet the terror he felt wouldn't go away. He was shaking.

He took out his flute and played, more for himself than anyone in the little park, although he did place his cap on the ground in front of him. For some reason the music conjured the image of his mother baking bread and calling for his sisters to help her with her work. He rarely allowed himself to think of his family, but he did so now because it reminded him why he was making the journey – so one day they could be together again and he could play while his mother baked bread for the family.

A few people gathered around him to listen and he began to grin and play up to the crowd with some jaunty tunes that were harder than the wistful piece he had started with. A tourist came along and stopped in front of him, and her husband filmed him with his phone. They dropped a note into the hat – not coins, but a ten-euro note! He could barely believe his luck, and not for the first time thanked the force that seemed to be watching over him. He played for another half-hour and earned a few coins and some kindly glances from passers-by. Things were looking up. He'd made back most of the money he'd lost on the train ticket. Then, to his astonishment, he heard someone call his name. He turned and saw the two girls from the camp in Lesbos, Hayat and Sana.

He gave them a big smile and a wave. Without Hayat and Sana he would probably still be languishing in the detention centre for boys. Hayat had given him the smock and hijab that had allowed him to escape the second time. The clothes meant he didn't have to climb up the back of one of the huts and scale the fence in the middle of the night like he had done before.

The second escape had been a lot less frightening. He noticed that when the aid worker came to check on the boys in the early morning, he never locked the padlock and just left the gate closed behind him because the boys were always asleep. He popped his head into each hut, starting with the first on the left, which was Naji's. The moment the man had looked in, Naji, who was already wearing the girls' clothes, scrambled off the bed, leaving the blanket covering some black bags filled with rubbish, crept out of the hut and slipped through the gate. The man didn't notice and no one bothered to question Naji at the main gate. Dressed as a girl, he walked all the way to the port.

'Have you still got my clothes?' Hayat called out. Naji prayed no one had heard that.

'I left them on the island. I didn't think I'd see you again.'

'What a shame!' said Sana, who was two years younger than her cousin Hayat. 'I bet you looked really good as a girl. You should have gone all the way to Germany like that, Naji – as a pretty young girl.'

He felt himself flush and he began to put away his flute. 'I'm sorry,' he muttered.

'It doesn't matter,' said Hayat. 'As you can see, we dress as Western girls now.' She came round and sat on the bench next to Naji's bag. Sana joined her. 'When are you going north?'

'Soon,' he replied.

'We're taking the bus to Thessaloniki tonight with our families,' said Hayat. 'Why don't you come with us?' She said it as though it was some kind of holiday outing. He didn't think these girls had any idea what lay ahead of them.

'I have to find a cheap way of travelling, I have little money.'

'The bus is going to be great,' said Sana. 'Did you hear what happened to the trains?'

'No.'

'They are being delayed because there's trouble in the north. All the people have to get off the train at a station and wait. They say there's a demonstration by Greek people. Nobody knows what's going on. It will be better on the bus.'

'How do you know this?' Naji said.

'It's on the refugee website, but the links are all in English.'

'Can I read them?' he asked, taking the phone from Sana.

There were several stories in the English media and one or two in German newspapers. Naji sat down and very quickly worked out what was going on. He reminded himself that he must find a way of charging his own phone.

The girls waited impatiently. 'Yes, you're right, ' he said eventually. 'There are two problems: the Macedonian border is closed, and there's a demonstration by Greek farmers who have blocked the track with their vehicles. They expect it to be cleared soon.'

'You read English *and* German!' said Hayat.

'I'm learning German,' said Naji. 'I will bring my family to Germany, and I'll need to speak the language. I can read it quite well now.'

The girls exchanged looks, as if they now had confirmation that Naji was some kind of freak.

'If you can read German, can you help my father?' Hayat asked suddenly. 'He has documents that he must translate.'

Naji knew Hayat's father was a big shot from Homs and that he had once owned a shopping mall as well as two hotels, but he'd lost everything in the war. Hayat had boasted about her family's former wealth when they were in the camp.

'I can try to help,' said Naji. 'German can be hard.'

'I'm sure it's worth the price of a bus ticket to my father,' Hayat said.

There were two families sitting on mats under a tree: Sana's mother and uncle; and Hayat's father, mother, sister and brother. Hayat's father was fat with a double chin and his face was set in a permanent scowl. When the girls introduced Naji, he said he didn't much like the look of the street musician they were associating with. Just because they had been brought down in the world didn't mean they should mix with scum, he said, as he shook roasted pumpkin seeds from a paper bag. Hayat's mother told Naji not to take any notice – her husband was always in a bad mood these days.

But eventually he handed the documents to Naji, who took himself off to read through them. There were just three pages, with not much text, and they were very hard to understand. After an hour, during which he used Hayat's phone to translate some phrases into Arabic, he realised her father was in danger of missing a deadline. He had to sign at the bottom of each page to show he had read and understood all the terms of the agreement for a partnership he was setting up with a Syrian businessman in Hamburg, and return it to him within the next five days. It seems he had had the document for two months.

When he heard this, Hayat's father cupped hands in a gesture of helplessness. What was he to do?

Naji replied that he simply needed to buy an envelope, find a post office and mail the documents to Germany. His daughter nodded when Naji suggested that maybe she could address the envelope in the Western alphabet for him.

He took the documents from Naji and let them drop on to the mat beside him and went back to his pumpkin seeds.

'Can I have the money for the bus ticket, as we agreed, sir?'

The man looked straight through him, as though he was no longer there.

Naji repeated his request a little louder.

'Go play your music, boy,' he said nastily, 'and stop bothering me.'

Not so long ago, Naji might have accepted that someone like Hayat's father could do what he wanted, but this man was an ignorant fool and Naji had likely saved him a lot of money. Everyone was equal on the road.

'We had a deal, sir,' he said. 'You agreed to give me the bus fare if I helped you translate this document.'

'Get out of my sight.'

'You owe that money to me, sir. Everyone here knows that.'

The adults in the party looked away, but Hayat caught his eye and began tipping her head in the direction of the document, which still lay beside her father. Naji knew exactly what she meant: he bent down, grabbed the document and ran for the park exit. There was uproar behind him but he was too fast and no one attempted to pursue him.

He left it for fifteen minutes before returning to the edge of the park. Hayat spotted him and ran over. She was giggling by the time she reached him. 'I got you forty euros,' she said as he handed the document to her. 'It was great that you did that. My father isn't used to people standing up to him – he's such a bully.'

Naji pocketed the money and looked at her ruefully. 'Thanks. I know I owe you twice over now.'

'I'm glad,' she said, the coquettish look returning to her face. 'You can find me on Facebook, then you can work out how you are going to pay me back.'

'When I reach Germany I will pay you back.'

'Stay safe, clever Naji,' she said, glancing behind her to make sure she was out of sight of her family. 'Be very careful out there: you're young to make this journey alone.'

'Not much younger that you.'

'Yes, but you are still quite slight,' she said.

There was no point in denying that. 'Maybe we will be on the same bus,' he said.

'I hope not – my father would kill you.' She examined him as if memorising his face, and started tugging at something on her wrist. She handed him a bracelet of red silk that had a charm dangling from it. 'This is all I have. Maybe it'll bring you luck on your journey.' Then she gave him a smile that he was sure would stay with him for the whole of his life, turned and walked back to her family.

'That's him,' said Andre Procopio, the Greek intelligence officer who had passed the story of Naji to McLennan a few days before.

'Which?' Samson asked, peering forward.

'The man with the red shirt, lighting a cigarette – that's Iliev, the Bulgarian. He's the man we need to talk to.' They watched for a while. Procopio, a rather laid-back former policeman with a ready smile, wanted to see whom Iliev was talking to.

'It's okay,' he said. They left his car and walked quickly to the centre of the square, where there was a flowerbed full of garbage.

Procopio called out to the man in Greek. Iliev turned, seemed to consider running but thought better of it and grinned, showing them a mouthful of gold. A rapid exchange ensued in which it was clear that Procopio was threatening the Bulgarian, though never at any stage did he lose his smile. Eventually he turned to Samson. 'All is good. My friend here is going to introduce us to his associates. One of them is bound to have encountered the young man we are looking for. He will call his associates and we will meet them in the bar over there.'

Samson wasn't surprised that Greek intelligence had such good access to the networks sending thousands through the Balkans every week. It was, after all, in the Greek national interest that people landing from the Middle East spent as little time in the country as possible. The smugglers who operated in Turkey – tempting migrants of every sort with websites that promised blonde women, free accommodation and benefits in Northern Europe – were detested, but members of the same trade in Greece were grudgingly tolerated, at least for the moment.

The first two of Iliev's associates had no memory of seeing the boy in the photograph, but the third, a parody of sleaziness, wearing a medallion and with a scar across his chin, said he'd sold the boy a train ticket two days before. He was certain of it – the boy was young but he had bargained hard and knew what he wanted.

Samson knew which train the boy had likely taken and when it arrived in the north, and it was now clear that he stood a good chance of catching up with his quarry at the border, if, as was reported, it was only intermittently open. His main concern was to work out the fastest way to get there, but then a fourth and a fifth smuggler arrived in the bar and Samson decided to show them the photograph anyway. Both had seen Naji in the square and one even knew his name because he had overheard a conversation with some girls. The other was quite certain that he'd sold Naji a bus ticket and that he'd seen him busking to raise money before he bought it. He admired the little fellow and said he had balls.

It was odd, for both men swore that they'd seen the boy in central Athens long after his train had departed. There was no reason for them to lie, so maybe the man who said he had sold Naji a train ticket was simply mistaken. But someone who worked the street for Iliev, fleecing desperate migrants eighteen hours a day, wasn't likely to make that kind of error.

When the two men had departed, Samson said, 'The boy has little money. We know that because he was playing his flute to earn a few coins. So why did he waste the train ticket?'

'Maybe he heard about the demonstration blocking the line,' offered Procopio.

'Yes, but a few hours added to the journey isn't going to make any difference to him. A kid like that can't afford to waste thirty euros.'

'Is it important?' asked Procopio.

'No, but it is interesting. I'm learning that this boy is very hard to predict.'

Samson called London and told them he might be no more than twelve hours behind the boy. The good news was that the border was closed and that would delay him further. He would make for the border immediately.

FIVE

The bus travelled through the night and arrived early in the morning in the city of Thessaloniki, where Naji achieved two things: he earned more money from busking in the street and he charged his phone. The man in the kiosk selling newspapers and cigarettes waived his usual three-euro fee for phone charging when he saw Naji's playing bring him trade. People who stopped to listen remembered they needed cigarettes, or decided to buy a magazine or a lottery ticket. The kiosk owner, who wore a skullcap and a long black jacket, sat stroking his grey beard and telling Naji that he should come every day and they'd make money together. Naji declined, but offered to buy the phone charger from him, whereupon the old guy shook his head and in a kindly enough way told him to get lost.

Buoyed by the thought that he could make money and wouldn't have to spend all of his family's savings, which his mother had sewn in neat little plastic packets into his backpack, jeans and jacket, he boarded the bus for the two-hour trip to Idomeni on the border. He was hopeful about his journey after coming so far so quickly, and now he had the idea of love to spur him on. What else could Hayat's smile and her gift of the red bracelet mean? He admitted to himself he knew nothing about this aspect of life and wished he had Munira, the eldest of his three sisters, to tell him whether he was now in love, or if this was just a pleasant preliminary.

The Idomeni transit camp brought him back to reality. As he trudged with the others from the bus towards the camp, he knew that his problem hadn't changed. Without registration papers he couldn't cross to the town of Gevgelija in Macedonia; yet even if he had them, he would not be allowed to pass because he was too young. There was another reason that he didn't want to go through the process of being photographed and fingerprinted. He suspected the terrorists had influence everywhere, and might get access to the database that tracked refugees through Europe and find out where he was. So, he would wait and watch and make his own luck. But it was going to be hard. For one thing, the border was closed and he'd heard people say that Greece would start sending refugees back to Turkey. All Europe seemed now to hate and fear the migrants.

There were four huge tents set up by Médecins Sans Frontières and the UNHCR and these were already packed with families. More arrivals were expected from the trains that night. Things hadn't been made any easier by the first big rainstorm of the autumn, which had turned the tracks and the ground near the tents into a quagmire. People put up their own tents and had improvised shelters by tying plastic sheets between trees, but nothing kept the rain and mud out. Those that didn't have shelter hung around in groups, cold and wet, some cloaked in foil survival blankets they'd kept from the beaches of Lesbos and Kos. They smoked cigarettes, made fires that fizzed and steamed in the rain, and gazed at the vast, dark clouds that had rolled down from the mountains to the north and were now spreading menacingly across the lowlands of Macedonia.

Naji joined a food line and after an hour of queuing received bread and soup. Then he found a place in one of the big tents between two family groups, where he could just about lie down. It proved hard to get any sleep. The air was foetid – the men pissed in water bottles so as not to lose their places; babies cried all night long and old people groaned and complained to God about their discomfort and misery. After a few hours he'd had enough of the smell and the man snoring next to him. He got up and picked his way through the prone bodies. Outside, he went to join a circle of young men who had built a blazing fire at a safe distance from the tents, and were standing as still as statues, watching the sparks fly into the sky. One of them offered him a drag on his cigarette, which made him feel sick.

At six, just as dawn was breaking, a youth ran over to the group and said the Macedonians were preparing to let five hundred refugees through to allow them to catch a train from Gevgelija to the border with Serbia. The young men all immediately gathered their belongings and rushed to the border crossing. News had spread quickly: families were emerging from the tents, shouldering backpacks and dragging bags across the sodden ground; fathers were hoisting babies and mothers screaming at their kids. They were wild with a mixture of hope and desperation.

Naji waited a moment before detaching himself from the young men and joining the families on the left-hand side of the track, for he was sure that the people with children would be allowed to go first and he had an idea of tagging along with one of the bigger families. But he needed to judge it well. If he made his move too early, or too late, he might be stopped by one of the soldiers and asked for his papers.

The crowd was silent. The sound of cockerels crowing and dogs barking came from across the border and then, to everyone's amusement, a small, honey-coloured dog sauntered up to the gate, cocked its leg and went through the border as though no border existed. The soldiers beckoned the crowd forward, making it plain with their guns that this was not going to be a stampede. Everyone's papers were to be inspected thoroughly and they started checking photographs by shining torches into people's faces, even though by now it was quite light. Naji fell in behind a family of six, which consisted of two young children being carried by the parents and a couple of boys, aged about six and eight. He started talking to the boys about the magnificent train they would soon board.

The father wearily handed all the family's documents to a soldier. He flipped through them nodding and then gestured the family forward. With his heart thumping, Naji went with them, wrapping his arm round the smallest boy's shoulder.

They went five paces, and a further ten. He'd got through!

Then he heard the soldier shout, 'Stop!'

Naji kept walking but the soldier ran after him and grabbed hold of his backpack. 'Stop!' he shouted again, and cursed at him in his own language.

Naji turned and gestured to the family.

The soldier called out to the man, 'This boy is your family?' The man shook his head and continued up the newly laid road towards the Konska River bridge, which led to the town.

He was practically carried back into Greece by the huge soldier and was told to stand by a fence post until he was handed over to the Greek authorities. An officer came over to underline the message that if he valued his life he wouldn't try any more tricks to enter Macedonia illegally; besides, he was plainly underage and needed to be confined somewhere. Naji was appalled: to be stopped from entering Macedonia was one thing; to be detained because he was a child was another.

A harassed-looking young Swiss woman from the UNCHR was eventually summoned by radio. She interviewed him beside the road as refugees streamed past. To her he told the story of becoming separated from an adult brother who had gone ahead with both their papers. He pleaded with her: at that very moment his brother was preparing to board the train to Serbia. How was it possible that the authorities would prevent the reunion with his beloved brother, who was the only person he had in the world? What had he done to deserve this cruelty? His eyes began to water at the thought of this terrible injustice, and he saw that the woman was beginning to believe him and might even persuade the soldiers to let him through.

'You stay there,' she said, and walked over to the officer. Naji saw him shaking his head and smiling. She returned. 'I don't believe anything you say. It's one story after another with you – first you pretend to be a member of a family with young children, now your brother has left you. You are going to have to come with me, and we will decide what is to be done with you.' She put her hand on his collar and began to march him back towards the transit camp.

As they passed near some trees, where a group of African migrants stood, Naji broke free of her grip and ran for his life towards the Africans, whom he rightly guessed would do nothing to help her. In fact, they cheered as he headed towards them and crashed through their midst to the bushes beyond. He knew she wasn't following – she was too heavy for that – but he kept going, weaving through an area of scrub and bushes until he came to a stony pasture, where a few sheep were grazing. He sat down on a large boulder, out of breath and dejected, but soon he began to feel better. The sun came out. He ate half the energy bar given to him by the old man in the kiosk, propped his backpack against the boulder and dozed a little. Then he watched a mad spiral of little yellow butterflies and a bird of a species he had never seen before darting about in the grass catching insects.

There was now warmth in the air and he began to think that with a little luck he might be able to complete his journey before winter set in. Naji's optimism, so often sunk, had revived once again.

He laid out all his possessions in the sun so that his pack could dry. Apart from what he wore and the money secreted around his clothes and in the pack, he had few belongings. He looked down on his smartphone; the sleeping bag he'd found on the road in Lesbos, which must have fallen from someone's pack; a map of the Balkans which he'd shop-lifted from the store in Mytilene; the little silver frame backed with goatskin that contained the photograph of his mother and his three sisters, Munira, Jada and little Yasmin; an English paperback book entitled *The Cosmic Detective: Exploring the Mysteries of our Universe*, which the nice woman in Lesbos had given him; a metal cup; a plate; chocolate and assorted energy bars; two apples; a packet of bread; gloves and a woolly hat; spare trainers and spare jeans; his favourite striped shirt; his flute; a compass he had bought at the store; and the knife he'd taken from the office of the therapist, Anastasia.

He packed everything away very neatly, just as his mother had shown him, though now he had much more to fit into the pack. He looked at the knife. There was something beautiful about it. With a cutting edge on both sides, the blade was slightly wider at the point than where it was fixed into the plain wooden handle. He hadn't been able to examine it properly before now and, balancing it in his hand, he realised that there was a good reason it was weighted at the sharp end – it was a throwing knife. He tried it out on a nearby pine tree and every time he threw it, it sailed through the air and stuck straight into the trunk with a satisfying thud. This pleased him, for he felt that if he practised, he might become really good at knife throwing and always be able to find his target. He spent an hour trying different techniques, first holding the knife by the handle like a hammer then gripping the blade between his thumb and forefinger, which he found less accurate over twenty throws. The best results were achieved by using the hammer grip. He found that the trick was to start with a straight arm above his head and let the knife fly from his palm as he brought his arm parallel with the ground.

He was wiping the pine resin from the blade with some leaves when he heard voices from the bushes. He moved over to his pack and slipped the knife in his back pocket. Two young men appeared from the scrub, smiling – an African and a European in a camouflage T-shirt.

'Hi,' the African called out.

Naji nodded.

'You speak English?'

Naji nodded again.

'This guy, he is from Bulgaria and he wants to know if you go to Macedonia,' said the African.

'Yes, I go to Macedonia,' replied Naji.

'You go to Macedonia with me,' said the local, gesturing in the direction of the border. 'I bring you in Macedonia.'

'He says he can take you there for money,' said the African.

'How much money?'

The African looked at the man. 'He says seventy euros. He has to pay the police.'

Naji thought about this. If he had to spend that amount at every border he would quickly run out of money. 'Forty euros – maybe. Seventy euros too much,' he said.

The smuggler looked hurt. The African explained that he'd seen what happened at the border that morning and he'd brought the smuggler to find Naji because he thought he needed help. The guy had put himself out to come and make this offer, he said. Naji knew he was probably getting a cut for introducing clients – just a few weeks in refugee camps had educated him in that particular way of the world. 'I will pay forty-five euros – twenty-five now and twenty on the other side.'

'Sixty euros,' said the smuggler. 'Forty now; twenty later.'

They both looked at him without saying anything. He returned their stare. The black guy seemed okay – as straight as you were likely to find in the camps and on the road, he thought. The other man he didn't trust. But he'd be much more frightened if he hadn't got the knife in his back pocket. For once people couldn't treat him as just a kid and he didn't have to be scared rigid, so he stared back at him, good and hard. Then he asked the African where they planned to cross.

'They are making a hole in the fence tonight a few kilometres that way.' He pointed to the west. 'We go in the dark. We meet in four hours.'

'Where?'

'The Fire of the Africans.'

'Where's that?'

'The place where we have our fire under the tree – you were there.'

Naji nodded.

'He wants the money now,' said the African. 'Forty euros now.'

'I'll give it when I see the hole in the fence.'

'But it is necessary to pay police,' said the African.

Naji asked them to turn away, took the money out of the slit in the strap of his pack and reluctantly handed it to the smuggler. Then he hoisted his pack.

'Ciao,' said the African.

'Ciao,' said Naji, using the word for the first time and feeling good about it.

Naji told himself that he'd just learned a valuable lesson. He must never again put himself in a position where he might be attacked. Throwing a knife at a tree a few metres away would never save his life. If he was to survive, he needed to find people to travel with. He needed friends.

★

Samson picked up the call, from Macy Harp's Curzon Street number, on his personal phone, twenty miles from the Macedonian border. He asked the driver – supplied by the Greek intelligence service – to pull over on the mountain road so he could keep the signal. He got out of the car and walked to the edge of a drop to face the stupendous view.

'That thing we've been working on – it's over,' said Macy.

'You're sure?'

'Yes, we are.'

'Have you told the client?'

'No, he told me. He had a lot of people working on it and they have established it beyond doubt.'

Denis Hisami, a Silicon Valley investor in his late forties and billionaire several times over, had come to the Curzon Street offices of Hendricks-Harp and told Macy Harp, Samson and two other ex-SIS people about his sister, Dr Aysel Hisami. A distinguished medical scientist in her prime, the thirty-two-year-old had returned to Kurdistan from California as IS rampaged through Iraq in 2014 to serve as a frontline doctor for the Kurdish forces. She was captured by IS. Her family feared the worst, but two Yazidi teenagers who had escaped from sex slavery brought news that she was alive and being held with forty other women deep in IS territory. Hisami had set about trying to buy her freedom and Samson had gone three times into northern Syria and Kurdish-controlled territory in Iraq to meet with possible intermediaries who seemed to stand a chance of purchasing Aysel Hisami in the horrendous slave markets that operated in northern Iraq. Locating her, keeping track of her as she was moved from place to place, finding out exactly which IS commander controlled her fate and trying to cross-check the information was a very delicate operation. It required enormous patience, which Hisami did not have because he knew that his sister, brave as she was, could take only so much of the sexual violence and torture that the young Yazidi women had reported. She was owned by a particularly sadistic IS commander, they said.

Hisami, a quiet, thoughtful man whom Samson liked a lot, had become increasingly impatient and opted for another approach. Eight weeks ago he had flown into London to tell Hendricks-Harp that he was standing the firm down while he developed new lines into IS. It was typical of the man that he had done this personally. Macy suggested that their client had spent so much money on the contract that they should keep the job ticking over, just in case things didn't work out. Samson went to Syria once more to talk to his contacts about Dr Hisami. What he learned about the treatment of the slaves in the process would, he was sure, stay with him for the rest of his life.

'Do we know what happened?' Samson asked.

'She committed suicide about ten weeks ago,' said Macy. 'There are two independent reports from escapees. She saw no other way out of her situation. I am sorry, Paul. I know you were deeply committed to her release.'

Samson was silent for a couple of seconds. He was appalled, because he had for some reason believed that as long as they were looking for her, and as long as they kept the brave young woman in their minds, she would live. It was a kind of superstition with him when searching for someone. He had to think of them all the time, and even though he didn't know the young doctor, this compulsive imagining of her had brought her close to him, and now he felt a very powerful sense of loss. 'I feel for her brother,' he said. 'He's a good man.'

'I've just had him on the phone. He's not giving up. He's putting all the money that he set aside to bring his sister home towards the identification of her captor – the man who tormented her and caused her death. Knowing Denis, I don't fancy that individual's chances. How're things going your end?'

Samson was silent.

'You there?'

'Yeah, I was just thinking about her – sorry, I err . . .'

'I know – it's very disappointing for you. You did everything you could, Paul. No one tried harder to get her out.' He paused. 'How's it going with the boy?'

'Some small successes – we'll see.'

'Let me know if you need anything. I'll keep in touch with the authorities this end.'

Samson hung up and got back into the car. The driver read the anger in his face. 'You okay, Mr Samson?'

'Yeah, I'm fine,' he said. But he wasn't. Over the last year, he had learned a lot about Aysel Hisami's research into a particular type of brain tumour suffered by young children.

He still had her picture in his wallet and on his phone. He'd showed it to hundreds of people in Turkey and Iraq and the reaction was always the same – what a nice-looking woman! She radiated integrity and dedication. It appalled him that those monsters pushed such a person to kill herself, while, of course, claiming that rape, torture and enslavement were part of their holy mission and the will of God.

Twenty minutes later they reached Idomeni. It was hot and the camp was heaving with people waiting for the border to open again. The Macedonians had closed it, saying that there weren't the facilities to cope with the vast movement of people. The transit camp at Vinojug, just over the border, was overwhelmed and the platforms at Gevgelija station, close by, were crowded with migrants waiting for the next train to the Serbian border, which was not expected until the following morning. A government spokesman said the town could not cope and added that the Macedonian people would not continue to tolerate lawless bands of young men roaming their country.

He got out and this time the other phone – the encrypted handset, with the satellite sleeve – rang.

It was Sonia Fell with an update.

Ten individuals in Stuttgart had been identified as possible candidates for Naji's uncle. They were being interviewed by the BND – the German Federal Intelligence Service – with the view to gaining information about the boy's family and where they were in Turkey. Calls from Lesbos to Turkey had been monitored for the period of Naji's stay on the island, as they were now from Idomeni. This seemed a hopeless task, except that they were looking for a comparatively rare caller – a boy whose voice had not yet broken. London had also reached out to contacts in the Balkans to get a clear understanding of the important figures in the smuggling networks that operated in the area, to see which might help trace the boy.

Sonia Fell was overseeing this inquiry. She also told him she was contacting the children's services of the main NGOs working along the route to see if there were any patterns of behaviour of children travelling by themselves; anything that could help predict what Naji might do. She was becoming aware of the level of abuse and violence visited upon young women and children on the migrant trail. If these crimes were committed against locals they would provoke outcry, but because they were happening in the flow of the vast transient population they were rarely recorded, let alone investigated.

'There are a lot of predatory men out there, Paul,' she said, 'and talking to aid agencies, I have no doubt that that this is going to be the greatest threat Naji faces on the road. We just have to hope you find him first, and that he understands what's out there.'

Chris Okiri, meanwhile, was examining the possibility of placing coded messages on various websites. This had originally been Samson's idea. Okiri was thinking in terms of a puzzle that referenced the dolphin and the rescue of the baby. It had to appeal to the boy's intelligence and it must mean something only to him. A member of GCHQ's staff, who was active in setting and solving challenges on various obscure puzzle websites, was helping to design the puzzle that might intrigue the boy.

Samson looked across the biblical multitude in the late afternoon sunlight. 'We're going to need more people on this,' he said. There was a silence the other end. 'Hello?'

'I've put you on speaker,' said Fell.

He repeated that he would need more people.

'We're not in a position to send anyone quite yet,' said Nyman. 'I'm hoping that Sonia will join you in a week or so. She was once stationed in Belgrade. And a man named David Cousins, whom you can call upon *in extremis,* is currently in that embassy – though I have to say that he may not be in the first rank of talent the service has to offer!'

'I don't think you quite understand the challenge,' said Samson firmly. 'We know this boy has very little money and no papers, so he's likely to be travelling on foot. That means it's going to be hard to pursue him by car, because they are using tracks and rail lines, as well as roads. But equally it would be crazy to attempt to follow him on foot because we might commit to the wrong route and lose a lot of time. We need at least two people – one on foot and one in a vehicle. In fact, I believe we may need three or four – the third and fourth would cover all the rail and bus stations and keep in touch with the aid agencies et cetera. The problems of communication in that territory are going to be huge, even with a satellite phone.'

'As I say, you will soon be joined by Sonia,' said Nyman, cutting him off. 'And we have also arranged for a top man to act as your driver and fixer while you're there, a man named . . . What's his name, for God's sake?'

'Vuk,' said Sonia Fell. 'Vuk Divjak.'

'Who's Vuk?' asked Samson.

'Vuk is an old contact of ours,' she said. 'A legend in the Belgrade embassy during the break-up of the former Yugoslavia.' She stopped. 'He's unusual, but absolutely reliable, and you'll need an interpreter. He's going to meet you in Macedonia if you don't catch up with the boy before then. And he will stay with you as long as you need.'

'Vuk!' said Samson doubtfully.

'Yes, the name means Wolf,' said Fell.

'Right,' said Samson. He hung up and went to tell his driver that he would no longer be needed. Then he shouldered his pack and headed to some trailers on the far side of the camp. On the way, he passed close to a group of women sitting in a circle. Suddenly, a squat female in a brightly coloured headscarf rose from their midst and launched herself at a much younger woman on the other side of group, shrieking abuse and tearing at her face and clothes. Samson sidestepped them and kept moving. Three men rushed to drag the assailant off. One of them remonstrated with Samson for not intervening. Samson shook his head good-naturedly and wished them luck over his shoulder. The woman was their problem, not his.

★

Naji, who was just a little distance from the same distur-
bance, waiting for an opportune moment to join the huge
food line, also ignored it. For a boy as camp-smart as he, the
spat between the women represented an excellent opportunity and he plunged into the line while everyone was
distracted. He did not notice the man with the pack walk
past the fight, for he was on the lookout only for signs of
his pursuers. The number of people in the camp had almost
doubled during the day and the aid workers were frantically
trying to cope with the demands for food, water and shelter.
He surged forward and grabbed a couple of extra bread rolls,
shouting that they were for his family, and then joined a
crowd around a pickup that had just arrived with thousands
of water bottles. He took three, drained one and placed two
in the side pockets of his pack.

There was still over an hour before he needed to go to the
Fire of the Africans. He wandered around, his practised eye
alert to any opportunity. He noticed a stick leaning against
a car and took it, then an elastic tie on the ground by one of
the tents that would help to compress his sleeping bag a little
more. He thought a sheet of plastic that had been spread out
to dry after the storm might come in handy, too. He folded
it neatly into a manageable square and strapped it to his pack
over the sleeping bag

The scavenging over, he wandered over to a trailer embla-
zoned with the UNHCR logo, inside of which were several
people working at computers. He found a woman smoking
a cigarette outside the trailer door and smiled at her. She

exhaled a huge plume of smoke and smiled back. 'How're you doing?' she asked.

'Thank you, I am well,' he replied. 'Please, missus. Do you have Wi-Fi? I want communicate to my sister.'

'You know there's free Wi-Fi over there,' she said, pointing in the direction of the tents.

'Not good,' said Naji. 'Too many people using.'

She stubbed the cigarette out and picked up his hand and wrote the password on the inside of his arm with a Sharpie. 'Keep it to yourself – okay, sport?'

'Thank you, missus,' he said, with what he imagined was his most charming smile.

She found this amusing. 'Where did you learn your English?'

'From my father – he is teacher,' he said.

'Well, he did a good job.'

'You are from where, missus?'

'Saint Paul, Minnesota in the US of A – and you?'

'Hajar Saqat in Syria.'

'Well, you go easy now. I hope you speak with your sister,' she said.

Naji liked talking to the American woman: it made him feel that he wasn't just some kid from a village in the middle of nowhere in a country that didn't exist. Naji looked down at the phone in his hand and turned it on. He wondered if there was something wrong with it – although he had charged the battery in Thessaloniki for an hour, it was only a quarter full.

He patted down his hair in the reflection of the trailer window, put on his broadest smile and took a photograph of himself against the UNCHR logo, which he texted to his eldest sister, Munira. He waited for a reply. None came, so he sent a message saying he was safe, happy and well and would call her soon. There was no reply to that, either. He guessed her phone wasn't charged or that she had no money on it.

Munira was the only member of his family who owned a phone. He was wary about calling, because on the only occasion he'd spoken to his family since setting out – to say he was safe and in Europe – he had found himself overwhelmed. He had stood there with tears in his eyes, unable to speak and at the same time desperate that his mother, who had seized the phone from Munira, should not guess he was upset. He kept it together – just – but afterwards told himself that if he was going to complete his journey and bring his family to safety in Europe, he had to behave like a man, and that meant that he should call Munira very rarely. He thought of her for a few moments. If he hadn't packed all his possessions so efficiently, he would have taken out the little goatskin-and-silver picture frame and gazed at the photograph of his family, especially the face of his eldest sister, the person he was closest to in the world.

SIX

In the glorious light of the late afternoon, Samson's luck continued. After an hour of searching, he found the man running the transit camp, a personable Englishman named Stephen Ingersoll who worked full-time with the UNHCR. More importantly, he had been at the University of Oxford at the same time as Samson and they knew each other vaguely. He suggested that Samson wait in his camper van until the 6.30 p.m. update, when most of the transit camp staff would be reporting on various aspects of the day. A huge influx was anticipated the following day and, with the frequent border closures, the camp would be at breaking point. There was no hope of providing more shelter, and food and water were in short supply.

'Things look serious for you,' said Samson.

'They are – very,' said Ingersoll, looking up from his checklist. 'Every time a border is closed, or there's a problem in one of the five countries these people have to pass through to get to the Schengen area, a chain reaction occurs down the Balkans. A border closes in Slovenia and a thousand kilometres away the Macedonians close theirs, too. And guess who's left with the problem – us.'

'But none of this applies to the illegal migrants,' said Samson, 'the people who get through the borders without papers, like the boy I am trying to find. Most of the migrants you're dealing with have to pass through Macedonia within seventy-two hours of entering, is that right?'

He nodded. 'Yup.'

'But an illegal can stay as long as he wants,' said Samson.

'True, but the borders are much harder to cross illegally. I mean, look at the Hungarians' fence. And the Balkan police forces are tough.' He paused and looked out of the window. 'What we're seeing is nothing new. Mass migration across the Mediterranean is thousands of years old. It is the way of things. The fascinating part is that migration actually works. Economies grow because of migration, the jobs that no one wants to do are filled and money is sent back to less well-off countries, making them richer and less dependent on the West. This is how it should be – that's the point, Paul.'

Samson nodded. 'I know. My family relied on the kindness of people like you, Steve. We were refugees in the eighties.'

'Really? I didn't know that about you.' Ingersoll looked genuinely surprised.

Samson told him briefly about his own experiences in a camp, which were so present in his mind since Lesbos. He told him that nothing much had changed, except that the people probably had more in the way of possessions and they all had phones. 'In Lebanon, we had nothing,' he said. 'But you can see why this number of people might frighten Europeans.'

Ingersoll looked irritated. 'I don't want to get on my high horse, Paul, but it's a bloody good thing for Europe to be reminded there's an outside world where people suffer and have nothing. We have a duty – it's as simple as that. These are people we're dealing with, not rubbish to be disposed of and forgotten about.'

Samson nodded. It was people like Steve and Anastasia Christakos who stood between humanity and chaos.

They walked a short distance to a tent where twenty key workers of the camp waited. They all looked tired and apprehensive.

At the end of the meeting, Ingersoll introduced Samson.

'This is a delicate matter,' Samson started. 'My job is to find a thirteen-year-old boy who is travelling alone. We believe he's been here within the last twenty-four hours – he may still be here, for all we know. He's a Syrian, recently come from Turkey via Lesbos, where he was very nearly drowned. He's in great danger from some extremely bad people who are actively searching for him. They may be here, too. The point is that he will certainly not survive these next few weeks unless we find him. I can't go into further detail, but let me just say that finding this boy is regarded as a priority by several European governments. In a moment I am going to show you a picture of him, which, for reasons of security, I cannot distribute electronically. I hope you'll take a long, hard look to see if the photo rings any bells.' He stopped and swept the exhausted faces in front of him. 'And can I ask you one more favour? We are working against the clock, and it is of vital importance that neither the boy nor any other party learns of our interest. So, I'd be very grateful if you didn't mention what I've said outside this meeting. Rest assured that my primary concern is to save this boy's life. That's why I'm here.'

He walked to the front row and handed his tablet to a woman. She glanced down then looked up at him with astonishment. 'I saw this boy this morning – he was stopped by the border police. I tried to bring him back here but he ran away from me.'

'So he didn't cross,' said Samson, equally surprised that she recognised him.

'No, he pretended to be a member of large family and they caught him and sent him back. Then he escaped because he can run a lot faster than me,' said the woman, who told him her name was Patricia and she was from Switzerland. '*Il est un délinquant?*'

'A tearaway,' said Samson, giving a kinder translation.

'Yes,' she said nodding vigorously.

The other aid workers gathered round the tablet. One recognised him from the food line because he'd pilfered two bread rolls and the other, an American named Anne-Marie Millet, had actually spoken with him. They were all certain it was Naji, and moreover, two could say definitely that he seemed to have hooked up with a group of illegal immigrants from North and sub-Saharan Africa, who had gathered beside the camp and were generally making a nuisance of themselves. Patricia saw him head in their direction and Anne-Marie Millet watched him join the Africans there just half an hour after they spoke. Samson thanked everyone and asked Anne-Marie if she could give him five minutes.

They talked as he walked with her back to her trailer. Naji had told her the name of his village in Syria – that was helpful confirmation, if any were needed, of his identity. He had mentioned a sister and that his father was a teacher – almost certainly of English – both useful details that would help trace Naji's family. Anne-Marie had noticed that he held a phone that was contained in a ziplock bag.

They reached the trailer. 'So it was right here that he used his phone?' Samson asked.

'Pretty much,' she said.

'Would you mind holding on for a few moments?'

'Of course not! By the way, he took a selfie by the trailer and I guess he sent it.'

He moved a little distance away and called Sonia Fell. 'Can you ask our people to get a fix on the exact spot I'm calling you from now and then see if we can pick up any communications to Turkey from this point between five and five thirty today?' he said. 'He may have sent a text message as well as used the broadband. I don't know about these things but it might be worth investigating whether this particular broadband router records any information from the devices using it. Maybe our Greek friends could look into that.'

'Sure – will do,' she said. 'How are things?'

'I'm really close, but the boy is going the whole way as an illegal which means we're not going to pick him up at the border crossings, and we're unlikely to find him at any of the transit camps through the Balkans.'

'But if he's a Syrian he doesn't need to do that – he's a legitimate refugee.'

'He's underage. If he's caught he'll be sent to some God-awful facility. I suspect that's his biggest fear right now.'

He returned to Anne-Marie and she led him to the spot where the Africans were standing around a fire.

At first they were suspicious, but Samson, speaking Arabic and some French, dispensed charm and cigarettes, together with the information that he was looking for his nephew, a boy called Naji whom he knew had been at this spot within the last two hours. He showed the photograph around the circle of men and they agreed that he had been there, but were reluctant to say much more.

'It's important I find him,' said Samson. 'He's just a kid.'

A Moroccan with a slightly menacing air said, 'That's what the others said. How do we know who you are? You could be police.'

'I am not the police,' Samson said quietly. 'How many others?'

'He has a lot of uncles, this Naji,' said the man. 'Many relations from Syria are looking for him.'

'How many?' Samson shot back.

The man didn't answer.

'It's important,' said Samson.

'Two,' said a good-looking African.

'Are you sure?'

They all nodded.

'Can you tell me where the boy is now? Did you tell these men that you saw him?'

The group fell silent.

'I need to know – he could lose his life.'

They said nothing more and Samson walked away in the dark. He wasn't done with them. He'd call Procopio and ask him to have all the men questioned by the local police. After all, he now had evidence that an IS cell was looking for the boy. He phoned London. Okiri and Fell were both busy. He left a message saying he'd had a breakthrough.

As he hung up, the African who had confirmed that two men were looking for Naji came up to him and said he might be able to help some more. Samson realised he wanted money and gave him twenty euros. The man started gesturing and speaking very quickly: the boy had gone with the group to a point in the fence where an opening would be made while the guards looked the other way. He didn't know what time this would occur, but it would be some time that night. He said that Naji was with a man named Joseph from Ghana. Joseph was a good guy. Naji would be okay with him. Most of the group were from North Africa, though there were also a couple of Pakistanis who had been twice thrown back by the Macedonian police, and two from Afghanistan. He personally suspected this was a scam by the Macedonians to take money from the migrants before returning them to Greece: that's why he hadn't gone.

'The men who asked about the boy, do they know where he is?'

'Yes, one of the people here told them. I think they went to the place.'

Samson swore under his breath. 'If you show me the quickest way to the place where they are going to cross, there's another twenty euros in it for you.'

The man nodded and went to collect his things from his friends. Samson phoned London to inform his colleagues that he might have to enter Macedonia illegally in pursuit of the boy.

Naji lay alongside Joseph the Ghanaian under a bush, watching the fence thirty metres away. There was no moon and the lights of the towns of Gevgelija and Idomeni were now far off to the east, yet the night was quite light and they could make out the fence. The whir of insects was unlike anything Naji had heard, and moths rose from the dry grass and flew into their faces, causing Joseph to splutter and manically fan the air in front of him. Around them in the bushes were hidden about thirty men and a couple of families with small children, all of whom had paid money to the smuggler.

He looked up at the stars and remembered when he and his father had lain on the warm concrete of their yard at home and his father had pointed out the constellations to him and talked about Darb Al-Tabbāna, the Hay Merchants' Way, which Europeans call the Milky Way. It seemed such a very long time ago – a lifetime away. His father took hold of his hand and dragged it across the night sky and told him that from end to end the Hay Merchants' Way was 100,000 light years. And Naji had protested that a hay merchant would die before he reached the end of his journey, so he couldn't have travelled all that distance, and his father, who was so playful and was never ever severe with his children, lay beside him shaking with laughter. 'You have many gifts, my son,' he had eventually said, 'but poetry has escaped you.'

Naji took no notice, because the truth was that he didn't have any idea what his father meant. He was just fascinated by the idea of light taking all that time to travel across the Darb Al-Tabbāna, and he asked his father if it were truly possible that some of the light that reached them as they lay in the yard had emanated from distant suns before human civilisation even existed. And his father said yes, he supposed that might be true, and for the first time Naji grasped the vastness of space and he knew that this was his subject – the subject that he would explore one day, just like the great Muslim astronomers of the past. Thinking of this now helped calm his nerves.

Half an hour later they became aware of some activity in front of them. Naji strained his eyes to see what was going on. He could just make out the shadows of two men working at the fence against an area of light rock. Then a low whistle came from the other side and suddenly there was activity all around him. Shadows he thought were bushes began to rise and were running towards the fence. Naji and Joseph were among the first to arrive at a hole of about half a metre wide: a section had been cut and neatly rolled back. They went through after a group of Afghans but then realised there was another obstacle to cross: a taller fence with coils of razor wire in front of it. The Afghans were now going up and down in the space between the two fences, searching for a second gap, and were beginning to sound quite desperate. Naji stood still, scanning the line of the second fence, and it was he who spotted the flame from a cigarette lighter being held against the other side of the fence, about seventy metres away. He touched Joseph on the arm and they jogged to the spot. At first, it wasn't obvious how they were going to pass through the razor wire, but, having dropped to his hands and knees, Joseph found an area where the wire had been raised and it was possible to crawl under it. Naji went first because he was the smallest. He soon realised he could only avoid being caught on the razor barbs of the wire by shoving his backpack along the ground ahead of him. Once he'd cleared the wire, he had to wriggle to a standing position and move a couple of metres to the right, where a hole had been cut in the mesh of the fence. But this was impossible without being snagged by the wire, so he placed the stick he'd taken from the transit camp against a rock and used the purchase to push the coils back. Joseph hooked the wire onto itself and they were able to move through the hole.

Naji suddenly found himself in the night of another country and realised he had no idea what he was going to do. He'd been so focused on getting across the border that he hadn't thought about the next part of the plan. Joseph didn't seem to have any idea either, so Naji decided to hang back and wait for Joseph's friends to come through the second fence. They'd know what to do and he would ask them if he could tag along with them.

But progress was slow. A man with a young child was snagged in the razor wire and was holding everyone up. People between the two fences were becoming extremely agitated and matters weren't helped by someone spotting a flash of light along the line of fence, which they thought might be the border patrol. Eventually it took several men with knives and a small torch to cut him free. The man with the child eventually came through the second fence, followed by his wife, and started fussing over the kid, who until that moment had been quiet. The child started crying and the father had to silence it by wrapping a hand over its mouth, and that caused the woman to scold him. Then she noticed that he was bleeding from his head and she started crying and he barked at her to stop her nonsense. Joseph swore under his breath – these people would get them all arrested if they didn't shut up, he muttered.

Naji was annoyed too, but he was also a little sorry for them. He remembered the time that his own family passed into Turkey, under the noses of Turkish guards, and how they had all been so terrified that they spent the night snapping at each other. His mother slapped his youngest sister, which she'd never done before, and his dear father, who was desperately frail after the hellish things that had been done to him, was so bewildered and fearful that he went to pieces and had to rely on Naji to get them across. But that was all right, because it had been Naji's plan in the first place.

They listened intently to what was happening on the other side of the fence, and they could tell from the direction of the voices that a few had turned back to climb through the first fence, so as not to risk being caught by the border patrol. Earlier, when they were making their way to the rendezvous with the Bulgarian, Naji had heard the men saying that it would be better to stay in Greece than encounter the Macedonians in the middle of the night, because they could rob you, kill you and bury you in the forest, and nobody would be any the wiser.

Naji was asking Joseph whether it was best to hide out in the woods or head in the direction of Gevgelija, but before he finished his question he heard a sound that chilled his blood.

From a few metres behind him came the unmistakable voice of Al-munajil cursing as he negotiated the razor wire. And then he heard the voices of Usaim and Ibrahim. It seemed one was caught up on the wire. Naji couldn't tell which and he wasn't going to wait to find out. He started backing away.

'Where're you going, kid?' asked Joseph.

'I can't be here,' he hissed. 'Those men talking now, they'll kill me if they find me here.'

'Which men?'

The conversation had already gone on too long for Naji. 'The man with the voice. I have to go now. I hope to see you again some day, Joseph. Thank you.'

He lifted his pack and, although he had never been in anything like a forest before and the thought of it scared him, he started walking quickly uphill towards the great black trees he could see silhouetted against the starry sky.

Samson received a text on the encrypted phone: *Advise do not cross into Macedonia. Enter legally and meet Vuk, who will be at Macedonian registration centre, Gevgelija, with car.*

He texted back: *Too late, am already in. Will find Vuk later.*

Chief says return now, came the reply. *Call us.*

Return NOT possible – way back closed, wrote Samson. *Can't speak now. Will call when I can.*

Nothing came in response to that and he returned the phone to his pocket. He had of course lied about being in Macedonia, because he knew how close he was to the two, or maybe three, men who were posing as Naji's relations and were almost certainly IS killers. To return to the transit camp on foot, which would take an hour and a half, cross legally into Macedonia and then try to pick up the trail on the other side of the border would waste too much time.

As he approached the breach in the border, the African who had showed him the way, and was now himself intending to go over the border, recognised the voices of a pair of Moroccans he knew from the camp. They were stumbling through the dark with a huge tube that turned out to be an irrigation pipe, which one of them had noticed in a field on the way to the rendezvous with the smuggler. They explained they needed something to lift the razor wire between the two fences because there was a bottleneck and a lot of migrants were waiting to get through.

Samson and the African followed them to the opening in the first fence and helped pass the pipe through to the Moroccans. A little way down the slope, they came to the second opening and the tangle of razor wire that was now holding everyone up. One of the Moroccans scrambled under the wire and the pipe was fed through to him. He placed the end on top of the far fence. It was then a simple matter to lift the other end of the pipe so that the coils of wire rose and people could pass beneath them, barely having to stoop. They all got through, even the last man, who had to bear the whole weight of the pipe as he moved under the wire. He let it go and it fell to the rocky ground with a clank that rang through the night.

Samson went around asking the huddles of figures if they had seen the boy, but he got nowhere and so returned to his companion, who was in animated conversation with another African named Joseph. It didn't take long for him to discover that Naji had fled, having recognised the strange voice of someone he said would kill him, and that Joseph had subsequently encountered three men who wanted to know if he had seen a young Syrian named Naji. With one of them holding a knife to his throat, they had demanded to know which way the boy had gone. Joseph pointed them in the wrong direction, but he wasn't sure they believed him and in the dark it was difficult to know which way they had ended up going. After a certain amount of persuasion, he told Samson that Naji had headed straight up the hill.

Samson set off, but after a few hundred metres he stopped, got out the phone with the satellite sleeve, and pulled up the map of the area. Naji was headed north and into an area that, apart from a few tiny settlements, consisted almost entirely of mountains and wilderness. He didn't think the boy would last long in that kind of country, even if he managed to avoid the killers.

He sat down on a rock, took out a cigarette and considered whether to smoke it. He soon lost any reservations, lit up and began to imagine what he would do in the circumstances. There was only one answer for a boy who had been brought up in a sparse desert landscape and who'd never seen a forest, still less spent any time in one at night. He would go a little way, then hunker down until morning. When he thought the danger had passed, he'd return to the spot where he started out. Samson was quite sure he would eventually come back to the border fence and use it as a way of finding his way to Gevgelija and the station.

He checked his text messages. There was one from Sonia, telling him that Vuk Divjak had arrived in town. He replied, giving his rough coordinates and suggesting Vuk meet him on a track about three kilometres from his current position at 6 a.m. It wouldn't be hard to find because it was at the point where the track grazed the border with Greece. He stowed the phone, looked up at the stars and let his senses attune to the forest around him. It wouldn't be long until dawn.

Naji's terror took him far. He climbed straight up the hill – not easy in the dark, the ground still slippery in places from the storms of a couple of days before. As he went higher, he realised he had to keep going rather than turn back, for descending would be more dangerous in the dark than climbing. He reached the summit, felt his way through a kind of miniature gorge and came to a gentle slope where the trees were taller and there was much more undergrowth. This he did not like because he imagined all sorts of animals lurking at his feet. He feared snakes particularly. In his reading about the Balkan Mountains on the web he had discovered that there were a number of different types of snake in Macedonia. He took out his throwing knife and his torch, which was safe to use now he was far away from the fence, and found a path of bare earth through the undergrowth. After a few minutes he came to an outcrop of rock that rose through the trees. It was an easy climb. He got halfway up and decided to make camp on a flat area that was sheltered by a wall of rock and an overhang.

He busied himself with the plastic sheet, which he spread to keep the sleeping bag dry, and inspected his store of food, deciding what he would eat and what he would save for the morning. This kept his mind from Al-munajil and the memory of the terrible things he'd forced Naji to witness, which had been stirred up by hearing that voice twice in the last couple of days. He concentrated on eating his bread, a chunk of hard cheese and the chocolate he'd filched from the kiosk in Thessaloniki, just before the old man had made him a gift of an energy bar.

His gaze drifted from the shapes of trees against the night sky to the forest floor and he became aware of something astonishing. Below him were thousands of tiny yellow pulsing lights: some were stationary; others wandered in the night like crazy, slow tracer bullets. His first insane thought was that the stars of the Hay Merchants' Way had fallen from the sky and were dancing in the forest, for that was exactly what it looked like – a minute swirling galaxy among the trees. And then the word firefly came into his mind, not that he'd ever seen a firefly or read anything about the insect. But he knew such a thing existed and this must be what he was seeing – thousands upon thousands, blinking in the night. He had perhaps never been so desolate as when he climbed up onto that rock, but now optimism surged through him and he gave a yelp of joy to the forest, which seemed to have welcomed him and contained no threat whatsoever. He wished he were with Munira so they could see this wonder together, especially now the breeze was pushing the fireflies up the hill towards him, some of them rising to the branches that spread over the outcrop to make a canopy of lights. This was not just magical, he thought: it was a sign – like the big fish that had saved him – that his journey was blessed and that he would succeed in reaching his destination.

He took some photographs with his phone, most of which weren't very good because the insects came out as yellow squiggles, but one was clear and he decided he would send it to Munira as soon as he could because it was just the sort of thing she loved. He remained watching for a long time as the fireflies pulsed in the night, eventually going to sleep covered by his sleeping bag and leaning against the wall beneath the overhang. He slept for three or four hours, dreaming many fantastical stories, but then someone intruded by repeatedly calling his name. He woke up with a start and looked around. Dawn had broken; birds were calling and mist hung in the treetops.

'Naaaajiiii,' cried the voice, extending the syllables of his name for a few seconds.

'Naji, we are your brothers. We want to help you,' came another voice.

'Tell us where you are,' came the first voice, 'we've brought you food and Coca-Colaaaa.'

'Naaaajiiii . . .'

'Naaaajiiii . . .'

He reached for the knife he'd left out on the rock and dragged the corner of the sleeping bag towards him so it couldn't be seen from the ground. The voices circled him slowly and seemed to be getting nearer. He prayed they didn't come across his footprints or any signs of his movement in the undergrowth the night before. The men kept on checking each other's position between shouting his name, and once or twice he heard Al-munajil's instructions – the cracked call of a crow sometimes rising in response to the executioner's terrifying sing-song voice.

This went on for twenty minutes, until Naji heard one of them moving right beneath him. He had approached the rock and was now urinating – he let out a groan of pleasure and a fart as he relieved himself. It was Usaim and he was with Ibrahim. After Usaim had zipped himself up, he started bellyaching about being kept up all night without any food to look for a treacherous piece of infidel shit.

'Our brother is obsessed, but what is the boy once we've completed our mission?' said Usaim. 'The boy is nothing! We should concentrate on our mission.'

'You tell him that,' said Ibrahim. 'He won't like it.'

'But it's the truth,' said Usaim.

'Tell him and see what happens,' said Ibrahim. 'There's plenty we don't know about our mission. Understand that, my short, fat friend.'

For one moment, Naji considered pushing the boulder that was balanced on the edge of the outcrop over the side, but thought better of it. He'd make too much noise shifting it, and besides, he probably wouldn't hit them. Instead, he shrank into the shadow beneath the overhang to wait them out. If they scaled his rock, he would fly at the first man to show himself and try to stab him in the heart with the knife.

The two men eventually ambled off to meet up with

Al-munajil, who was shouting from the other side of the valley. They called Naji's name as they went, but they didn't bother to hide the frustration in their voices now. He peeked through the crack under the boulder and watched them make for a stream at the bottom of the slope, about seventy metres away. He could tell by the way they were moving that they were tired and had had enough of looking for him. He found himself loathing them, as he never had before, hating the swagger and terror they'd brought into the forest, which only a few hours before had been a paradise for him.

For a few seconds he gazed up at the boulder, trying to work out its weight and whether he could shift it. Yes, he murmured to himself, he would do it. He silently folded the plastic sheet and rolled up his sleeping bag, secured both to his backpack with the elastic tie and looked through the crack again. Usaim and Ibrahim were still at the bottom of the slope, waiting for Al-munajil, One of them was chucking stones into the stream; the other scratched his balls and looked up at the sky.

Naji slipped his arms through the straps of the backpack, placed both hands against the boulder and started rocking it. It was several times his weight and at first it barely moved, but after five or six good shoves above its centre of gravity it began to roll a few millimetres back and forth, in the process making a crunching noise on the rock beneath it. He timed his pushes to give the mass momentum as it moved away from him. Suddenly the shelf on which it was balanced gave way and it fell, hitting the ground with a soft thump. Very slowly – almost without a sound – it began its journey to the bottom of the valley.

He'd have given anything to watch, but he grabbed his stick and scrambled down the other side of the outcrop. In no time at all, he was moving quickly towards the path he'd found the evening before. He dodged the thickest undergrowth beneath the trees so as to make as little noise as possible, and very soon he'd reached the point where he knew they wouldn't catch him if they set off up the hill after him: he was fast and they were tired. He stopped to listen, but heard nothing except the feathering of the wind in the pine trees. He thought that maybe the boulder had become stuck on the way down, or perhaps it had veered off course.

He dropped to his haunches, hoping to catch any sound.

And then came a cry and several shouts and a further cry of pain. All three men were now shouting and cursing. He wished he could see what was happening below him. He listened for a few seconds, slapping his thigh, then turned and made for the crest of the hill that was now lit by the rising sun. He clapped his hands, laughed to the sky and took off through the forest.

SEVEN

Early next morning, Chris Okiri, who had worked through much of the night, and Sonia Fell were summoned, with a number of other intelligences officers, to Nyman's office to review the boy's story. Things weren't adding up.

'The BND in Stuttgart have drawn a blank so far,' Nyman said to the room. 'They've been to all the obvious people in the Muslim community and can't find anyone who's expecting a boy to turn up. No one can think of a distant relation even remotely like Naji. The description of his family rings no bells. No one knew anyone at Hajar Saqat and what's odd is that we have found no matches in the Turkish camps for a family of the correct configuration – teacher father, mother who worked in Syria's northern governorates, three daughters and a son. Maybe the registration process is far from perfect in Turkey. There are millions of refugees and of course people lie about where they've come from and what they were doing, but we would have expected to find that family by now. The Turks have gone the extra mile, because they're as keen to locate these operatives as we are, so it isn't for want of trying.'

'Let's look at this a bit more,' said Peter Nyman, levering the lid off a tin and spraying coffee granules onto the conference table. 'Obviously he's telling the truth about the men who are pursuing him, because Samson has come across three men looking for the boy in Greece. We also have the match of the boy's description of the individual with the speech impediment and our own information about one of the killers at Hajar Saqat. That's right, isn't it?'

'Absolutely,' said Okiri. 'But we aren't seeking to undermine the importance of the boy. Rather, our conclusion is that he may be even more important than we previously thought.' Sonia Fell nodded as Okiri continued. 'We believe that he has lied about his family because he's protecting them and is anxious that no one finds out where they are.'

'To protect them from IS,' concluded Nyman.

'The question is why, when the family is apparently in Turkey, are they still at risk from IS?' asked a Middle East expert named Lehan. 'The answer could be that Naji and his family were more entangled with IS than we thought, or maybe that his family is still in Syria.'

'Evidence?' asked Nyman.

'Nothing hard,' said Sonia Fell. 'I had a conversation with Anastasia Christakos in Lesbos yesterday. I wanted to follow up on some things Paul spoke about. Her thinking about the boy has developed somewhat. She believes there are areas where he's lying and areas where he's underselling the truth. She thinks he may be lying about his family – its composition, the professions of his parents, their place of origin and so forth, but that he's telling the truth about the men. She spoke about the burden the boy is carrying with him. She thinks that he witnessed something or was party to something terrible. So, quite apart from the responsibility of bringing his family to Europe, which is part of the story there is no reason to doubt, there is something else – some knowledge or experience which may be relevant.'

Nyman looked unimpressed.

'I wonder,' she went on, 'if it is perhaps better to deal with what we know is true, rather than speculate about his family?'

'Go on,' said Nyman.

'What we know is true,' Sonia said, 'is that these men were in the camp in Lesbos during the boy's confinement there. We know they must have registered as Syrian refugees, and that they would have to do so at the camp in order to get off the island legitimately and travel through Greece to Macedonia. That's the start point for us. Somewhere in the registration files for the period are the fingerprints and photographs of the men we're looking for. We'll have access to photographs later today. Obviously there'll be thousands of faces in these records, but we can develop some processes of elimination.'

'And this is where Turkey comes in,' said Okiri.

'How so?' Nyman asked.

'We can check registrations in Turkey against the ones from Lesbos for the relevant period and begin to refine the list of likely candidates,' said Okiri. 'For example, those who've been in Turkey for a considerable length of time are not the ones we're looking for. We're searching for men who registered in Turkey soon after those phones were dumped – then moved quickly to register in Lesbos.'

'That works,' said Nyman. 'You're aware that the Security Service has a very useful resource in the shape of half a dozen or so people who were in Syria and Iraq and have returned to this country disillusioned with IS. These individuals have not been prosecuted because we make use of them on occasions like this. You can get MI5 to sit them down with the photographic record for the relevant period from Lesbos and see if they recognise anyone.' He looked around. 'Good! This all sounds like it's coming on well – is there anything else?'

'His phone,' said Okiri. 'We know the boy has got himself a phone and we have been trying to trace his calls, texts, Internet usage et cetera. We need the number so we can track him when he's got the phone on.'

Nyman swivelled away from them to look at a large seagull that had landed on the ledge outside with something in its beak. 'I've been rereading some material – a report from an organisation that campaigns against the use of child soldiers. It's gruesome reading but I think it offers some clues as to the psychological impact on children exposed to, or compelled to participate in, extreme violence. I'll have it distributed to you all and, Sonia, you might run it past Ms Christakos and ask her opinion. Reading her email, it seems to me that young Naji may have seen a lot in his life. Why does this matter? It may explain Naji's relationship with the men. My hunch is that he's more involved with these people than he let on to Christakos, and that this is the reason he's protecting his family. Like you, I have reached the conclusion that the family is, for the moment, irrelevant in tracking down these men, even though he is propelled to risk so much to bring them to Europe.' He stopped and turned to face the conference table. 'I agree with your thinking about the start point being Lesbos; and we know something else about these men – we know they passed through Athens.'

'Yes,' said Okiri, 'so they must be on CCTV somewhere.'

'Exactly. Obviously you had all thought of that,' said Nyman, slightly mischievously. 'If you read Samson's report from Athens, you'll see that the boy bought a ticket for the train but went by bus to Thessaloniki. Why would he do that if he has little money?'

'Samson said there were delays on the train that day,' said Fell.

'Then why did everyone else get on the train?'

'Presumably they weren't especially bothered about the delay.'

'Exactly, and why would Naji be bothered about a delay, if no one else was? I know the boy was in a hurry, but no more so than anyone else. Maybe he saw someone at the railway station and decided at the last moment to change his plans. We should have our friends in Athens do a search for any relevant CCTV from its station and its environs and see if we can find the boy and then look for other faces in the footage. Maybe we'll find matches with faces from Lesbos.'

'I'll get onto it,' said Okiri.

'Good,' said Nyman. 'Now, what else is there? Oh yes, I have a name for you. Actually, it is a nickname used by his IS comrades – Al-munajil. It means machete. Our source – actually a very important asset developed recently in collaboration with the Americans – suggests that this is the name of the man who was driving the vehicle with that black mark. Our source has never seen him, but worked it out from reports within IS of this man's actions. Like all truly evil regimes, IS keeps scrupulous records on its barbarities, so that has helped us identify him. The asset is ninety per cent sure that we're searching for Al-munajil. So, we have a voice and a name. Surely it won't be long before we get the image.' He stopped and looked out of the window again. 'The boy is important, but these men are the priority. We'll put our major European partners in the picture this afternoon. Sonia, you will prepare a brief. We're going to need people along the route – eyes and ears at the border crossings, registration points and main transport centres looking for a man with a pronounced speech impediment. We'll need help from local intelligence services in the Balkans as well, and that must be handled delicately. The Chief is of the opinion that an interception is undesirable, unless Al-munajil presents an immediate danger.'

'What about Paul?' Fell asked.

'He should stay looking for the boy. By the way, have we heard from him today?'

'I had a text very early on to say he was going to meet Vuk Divjak.'

'And?'

A flicker of doubt passed across her face. 'We've heard nothing from him.'

'He didn't meet Divjak? Does that suggest to you he's in some trouble?'

'No. Paul is always okay. It's probably a communications problem. We're working on finding him.'

'Well, get hold of him.'

Thousands upon thousands of feet had beaten the path smooth and even the recent rain had made no impression on its surface. On either side, the bushes and ditches were strewn with litter – the broken shoes, plastic bags, food containers and discarded water bottles that marked the migrant route from the Greek islands to the Alps and the Schengen area.

Naji was in an elated mood, and even when he looked up and took in the size of the mountains ahead – many of them already capped by snow – he experienced the same thrill that had run through him when he witnessed the fireflies in the forest. The mountains were indeed intimidating. From west to east, through 180 degrees, they dominated the landscape and appeared to Naji like a massive wall, erected to keep people like him out of Europe. Had he not been walking with his new band of friends, he'd have felt too frightened to undertake the journey. But now he knew anything was possible. Despite the terror he'd felt when Al-munajil and his killers had come so close to finding him in the forest, he was not afraid.

He had crept into town that morning feeling that everyone was looking at him, but he soon realised nobody was giving him a second glance. The town was overwhelmed with a new influx of legitimate migrants who had been allowed to enter Macedonia to ease the strains in the transit camp in Greece. This would make it much harder for anyone to find him and also gave Naji the cover he needed for buying provisions for his journey.

He hovered for a while at a fruit store, where there were bananas for sale, which he hadn't seen for as long as he could remember. He bought three and laid them out on his special clean cloth, which was much less clean than it used to be, and took a photo with his phone and sent it to Munira. Then he remembered the photographs he had taken of the fireflies in the forest and scrolled through them to choose the best one, which he sent with the caption '*Alyiraeat*' − fireflies − and a message: *Sweet sisters. I am in a country called Macedonia and these are the insects that light up the way for your loving and respectful brother. I am well and happy and safe. I send my love to you and our revered parents. Naji.*

The other reason for Naji's good mood was that he'd grabbed as much food as he could eat and carry in his pack from the feeding station at the Macedonian registration centre, which was jammed with families and wailing children. As well as eating to the point that his stomach was hard and protruded slightly beneath his T-shirt, he'd managed to wash himself and scrub the worst of the dirt of the forest from his clothes. With his mother's voice in his ear, he'd even washed his hair with the cheap apricot-scented shampoo provided by a charity. He had emerged into mid-morning sunlight feeling a new person. It was then that he ran slap into Joseph and his friends.

Joseph asked anxiously what had happened to him. He said he'd been worried and thought he might never seen him alive again, for at the fence he had been questioned by three men who'd threatened to beat him up and, later, another guy, who was much more polite and seemed to be concerned for Naji's safety. Naji would have brushed the whole thing off with his usual bravado, but the news of a fourth man, who spoke good English, had two phones and somehow did not seem like a migrant, concerned him and he asked Joseph to tell him everything he had noticed about the man. Joseph hadn't been able to see much in the dark, but the one thing he was sure about was that the fourth individual had nothing to do with the first three – he was polite and educated and, Joseph added, he didn't smell like a donkey. Naji smiled, but the news of the fourth man worried him.

He began to cross-examine Joseph about going north, and asked him outright whether he could go with him and his friends. Joseph saw the question coming and looked down at him earnestly. 'You are brave, little man, but are you strong enough for this?' It was going to be the toughest thing he had ever done in his life, he continued. While everyone was going to look after each other on the trip – for they were a band of brothers now – they would not be able carry him if he became exhausted. They were all illegals and that fact would be obvious to the police when they left the crowds of legitimate migrants who were waiting for the trains to the Serbian border. They would be harried and chased across the country. They would risk beatings and deportation, and they would certainly experience hunger, thirst and great hardship. Some might not survive the journey.

As he spoke, half a dozen North Africans gathered round, together with a trio of Afghans they'd teamed up with. They nodded solemnly and stroked their chins in agreement with Joseph. Naji knew they thought he would hinder them.

He moved to the centre of the circle to address them all. 'It is true that I am but a boy,' he said slowly, 'but I have seen more in my life than all of you put together. If you have suffered as I have, or have seen the things that I have, then you have my pity.' Aware of the tremor in his voice, he stopped to get control of his emotions. 'I have seen men tortured, burned, crucified. I have seen the bodies of the people Daesh beheaded. I have seen war and bombs. I have seen people lashed for smoking a cigarette, women stoned to death because someone accused them of going with another man. I have watched my neighbours – people I knew since I was a very small child – plead for their lives before they were killed for no reason, or because they were of another faith. My father's best friend and his uncle were killed. But none of this has stopped me.'

Joseph told him that he needn't go on. But he continued.

'It was I, Naji, who led my family to safety, dodging Daesh fighters and under the noses of the Turkish border guards. I travelled alone across strange countries. I was nearly drowned in the ocean, but a dolphin saved me. Yes, a dolphin – a huge fish – kept me floating until the rescuers came. But for the good fortune that Allah has shown me, I would not be here now. Yes, I am but a boy, but I have experienced the worst things life has to offer, more than any man here. There is nothing that will stop me from reaching Germany and I pray that I will bring my luck and share it with you all. Let me come with you.'

Naji had never spoken like this before. In fact, he had never assembled all the horrors he'd witnessed in his mind at one time, and this made him feel self-conscious, as well as ashamed. He looked down at the ground. His face was hot and his hands were shaking.

'If you are Syrian,' asked one of the Afghans in Arabic, 'why do you not get papers and travel with the people from your country?'

'Because they're like you. They think I'm just a boy, who should be locked up in a place for children,' he replied fiercely.

'You will come with us,' said Joseph, placing a hand on his shoulder, 'and we hope for some of Naji's luck.' And to underline to the others that Naji could be useful, Joseph told them all about how he had found the spot where it was possible to crawl under the razor wire.

The band of brothers numbered fourteen, but as they left town they split up so as not to cause suspicion. Two groups walked separately up the rail track and a third took the road. About an hour later they met up again on the bank of the river, just where it veered away from the road and railway into flat farmland. And this was when Naji experienced a sudden burst of hope, which he realised was as much to do with the lushness of the land as the fact that he was for the first time travelling with a group of people who treated him as an equal. As they went, they told their stories and sometimes Naji was able to translate from the English spoken by the Africans into the Arabic used by the men from Algiers and Tunisia and, haltingly, by the Afghans.

They walked for five hours, until one of the Afghans was stung by a bee and it seemed like a good moment to find somewhere to sleep. They made a small fire beneath some fruit trees and cooked what they had and shared it out, and Naji received much praise for the plastic sheet, which kept most of their belongings dry during a short rain shower in the early evening.

To mark this moment in his journey he took several shots of the group in the orchard with his phone, then asked one of his new companions to take a photograph of him sitting in the middle of the group, which he planned to send to Munira. The man was slow and wanted to look through the shots taken so far. Joseph seized the phone, told both of them to join the others and took a shot.

Only one incident spoiled that first hopeful twenty-four hours. Deep in sleep – the best sleep he'd had for a long time – he became aware of fingers moving lightly over his body and gently probing his bag, the strap of which was hooked around his left arm. He thought it was part of his dream, but something made him withdraw the hand that held the knife in his sleeping bag and wave it in front of him. At the same moment the man beside him murmured in his sleep. The fingers stopped moving at once and a few seconds later the presence withdrew, leaving only the smell of spicy breath in the still air above Naji's face. Very soon after that he went back to sleep.

'Where are you?' Fell asked.

'In Vuk Divjak's car,' replied Samson, surveying the clutter on the dash of Vuk's Land Cruiser. 'Which is more like a bloody folk museum.'

'Is he with you?'

'No, he's in a café,' Samson said. 'Where the hell did you find him?'

'You'll get to like him,' said Fell. 'I'm going to put you on speaker now. You can guess for yourself who's here. We also have other colleagues whom I won't identify. You're encrypted, but . . .'

'Fine,' said Samson.

'And just for the record, tell us what happened,' Fell asked.

'I was picked up by the Macedonian border police because they said they suspected that I'd entered their country illegally. I was held for a few hours, but they couldn't prove anything because they don't stamp EU passports at the border. The absence of a stamp in my passport told them nothing.'

The arrest had been unnecessary and he felt a little foolish, which is why he didn't go into it with Fell. Having decided that the boy was not going to make his way back to the fence, Samson sent a text to Vuk and began walking to their rendezvous. On the way he came across an old Arab man hobbling with a sprained ankle and scratches on his arms and face. He was bewildered and frightened. Samson felt he couldn't leave him wandering in the scrub alone and led him back to the track and told him that it wasn't far to the town, where he could rest and maybe find something to eat. At this point the border patrol came along and he and the old man were loaded onto a truck. It was something of a relief for the old man, who was probably suffering from dementia, but not to Samson, who was within a few minutes of meeting up with Vuk. He was held for five hours, roughed up and told that he was not welcome in areas sensitive to national security.

'They told me I had forty-eight hours and then I had to leave, but that's not going to be a problem,' he said.

'As long as you're okay,' said Fell.

Nyman came on the line. 'Is it your view that the men pursuing the boy are still in the area?'

'Hard to tell,' he said. 'If I hadn't been delayed we might have seen who came out of that forest this morning. My guess is that they've joined the migrants going north. There are very large numbers in town today. The border was opened to those with registration papers, but there were also coordinated breakouts with as many as five or six separate breaches in the fence.'

'You've seen our email outlining the main points of this morning's meeting. What do you think about the reasoning that the boy was more involved with these men than we originally thought?'

'I agree, and you're right to concentrate on evidence that we know we can lay our hands on in Greece. I can't say what his involvement might have been.'

'I want you to stay on the boy anyway,' said Nyman. 'I appreciate it's going to be hard but Vuk will have spotters along the way – good men he works with on a regular basis.'

'Great,' said Samson.

'I'll leave you with this thought: I'm certain we haven't got the whole picture. We're missing something, I'm sure.' He paused. 'Oh yes, there's one other thing. We've come up with the coded message to the boy and are arranging for it to appear on various migrant websites and the Facebook pages they're using. It will also be printed and posted in places along the route – registration centres, feeding stations, medical centres etc. It will mean nothing to anyone else.'

'It could be an idea to mention the psychologist from the island,' said Samson. 'She's about the only person he trusts in Europe – he opened up to her. Why don't you make her part of the message?'

'You think she might help us bring him in?'

'Yes, but you'd better check with her.'

He clambered out of the car at the end of the call, lit a cigarette and watched Vuk Divjak coming towards him, trailed by a young thug in a leather jacket whose hair was shaven at the sides. Vuk's walk fascinated Samson. The Serb moved with a kind of a regretful determination, like a farmer on his way to slaughter his favourite pig – fists clenched, eyes averted and lost in a strange, angry sadness.

'What's up?' said Samson.

'Nothing up – everything down. Life is bitch.'

'I'm sorry to hear that.'

'This Aco – he is working with me. I tell him we look for spy boy come from hell.'

'The spy boy come from hell – indeed,' said Samson. 'It's important that we find him.'

'Spy boy, he gone on Vardar River.' He turned to the thug in the leather jacket. 'Maybe Aco see boy playing pipe today.'

Samson showed him the still from the documentary on his phone. Aco tugged the ear with the diamond stud and nodded.

'Where?'

'By market, then near the station,' he replied.

'Then boy go up fucking Vardar River,' said Vuk, gesturing to the north.

'Aco follows the boy – he goes with others.'

'Did he try to get on train?'

'No. He took shower at registration centre. He ate food then he goes with others up Vardar,' said Vuk.

'Take me to the place where you saw him,' said Samson.

'No point. We wait for Simeon and Lupcho. They come now.'

Samson went to buy food and water to put in his pack. He returned as Vuk's helpers arrived in a black BMW with low-profile tyres, several dents and an air of criminality. Simeon, the rougher looking of the two, wore trainers, tracksuit pants and an open khaki military shirt over a T-shirt that featured an AK-47. Lupcho, who was taller, was dressed in black and wearing sunglasses and red trainers with a silver trim.

'These magnificent cunts,' said Vuk, wrapping an arm around each of them.

'You know that's not an especially flattering term in English,' said Samson, shaking their hands in turn.

'I say cunts are *magnificent*! What is matter with this?'

'Nothing,' said Samson, shaking his head. He entered their three mobile numbers in his phone contacts and sent them each the photo of the boy, saying that they had to keep it to themselves. Vuk said he'd castrate all three if any of them leaked the photo, and added that he would be doing a service to the women of Macedonia, Serbia and probably Albania, too.

He brushed the dust from the bonnet of his car and spread out a map.

Samson traced his finger along the Vardar River, from its source in the western mountains near Kosovo through the capital, Skopje, to the point where it plunged south through the central highlands to Greece. He noted that for all that stretch the river was tracked by the Alexander the Great Highway as well as the north–south rail line. This was very rugged terrain and proximity on a map was no guarantee of access from either the rail line or road to the river.

It was decided that Simeon and Lupcho would watch a gap forty kilometres north of Gevgelija, where the land begins to rise sharply. Any migrant planning to walk to the Serbian border would have to go through that pass, whether by rail track, road or by following the river course. Aco, meanwhile, would go on his trail bike to patrol a place where the rail track and unmade road ran along the eastern bank of the river. If they didn't find the boy in the next twenty-four hours, Vuk would redeploy them. He told them to keep their cell phones on and find a place where they always had reception.

'It's important that they don't scare the shit out of the boy,' Samson said to Vuk. 'Can you tell them not to approach him if they see him? But if they see anyone attacking this boy, they're to do their best to save him.' When Vuk had finished translating, he added, 'They should know that the men trying to harm the boy are extremely dangerous. They won't hesitate to kill anyone who gets in their way.'

Vuk nodded and turned to the men, who produced various expressions of contempt and patted what Samson assumed were concealed weapons. Vuk looked at Samson with a piratical leer and told him that these were his best men and that they had spent many hours in the mountains dealing with Albanians and Kosovars and there was no better way to test a man. 'These men not disco pussies,' he said as they departed in a cloud of dust. 'They fucking lions.'

On the second day the band of brothers started in a misty grey light that stole across the plain. They walked through the morning until the October sun was above them and burning their necks, but the wall of mountains seemed as distant as when they'd set out the day before. About midday, Naji became aware of soreness in his right heel. He stopped and took off the trainer – hard material was protruding from the inside of the shoe and had caused a blister to form at the back of his heel. He cut the material off, but the damage was done and the little dome of the blister had to be burst, which he did with the point of the throwing knife. He changed into the trainers he'd stolen on the boat, but before putting them on he cut a piece of his special clean cloth to tie round his heel. This became dislodged as he hurried to catch up with the group, but the soreness was much less.

He found them sitting in the shade of a lone carob tree. Some dozed; others stared silently across the shimmering yellow fields. The land was tinged with autumn colours but the temperature was more like summer and each of the men was showing signs of exhaustion. He sat down and ate a banana, a piece of bread and a chocolate bar that had melted in his pack, noting that chocolate – hard or melted – was the best thing in the world.

There were no jokes and no stories – the banter had gone. The group wanted only to talk about the route. The Africans, including Joseph, were for staying by the river, because they said they were less likely to attract attention there, but others, including an Iraqi, three guys from Afghanistan and an Algerian who had come through the hole in the fence just behind Joseph and Naji, wanted to cross the river at a road bridge, head to the rail track and walk up the line to Serbia. They said this would be the shortest route north, whereas the path they were currently following meandered with the river and would add days to the journey. The debate went on in at least three different languages for about half an hour. Although Naji wanted to remain with the Arabic speakers and the Afghans, he felt loyalty to Joseph, so he said nothing. Eventually, the talk petered out and soon they were all getting to their feet and hoisting their packs.

The afternoon cooled and a little of the spirit of the first day returned. Naji went off to forage for bunches of hard, yellowish grapes from a vineyard that stretched for kilometres to the east. It was when he approached Joseph and gave him a handful of grapes that he smelled his breath, the same breath he'd smelled when he was half asleep the night before. It had been Joseph's hands that had prodded and felt him and his possessions, trying to find his money. The man he liked most in the group had tried to rob him! He looked at Joseph's smiling face and knew he would try again and that sooner or later he'd be successful. Now he understood why Joseph had persuaded the others to let him join them: all along he had planned to rob him and leave him in the middle of nowhere without money.

He dropped back from the main group, burning with anger. Not knowing anything was wrong, one of the Afghans started to talk to him, and gradually Naji calmed down, although he knew he had to get away from Joseph and find other allies in the group. The two of them stopped by a bend in the river where the water washed into a little bay and the Afghan, whose name was Lashkar, showed him how to skim stones, but only on the condition that Naji taught him how to throw a knife, which he'd seen him do the previous evening.

They'd fallen behind quite a bit, so they quickened their pace to catch the others. A few minutes later, when they were still a hundred metres or so behind the others, they became aware of a mechanical thump in the air. Curling round a low hill of pine trees ahead of them was a large, camouflaged helicopter. Naji knew the model of the aircraft instantly – a Mil Mi-17 two-engine turbine transport helicopter – and he could recite by heart the details of the design, range and lift of the Russian-made helicopter. But that was not what entered his mind. What made him yell at the others and start running back down the track towards a bed of reeds was remembering seeing his first barrel bombs.

There had been two, and they were dropped from a much larger Russian helicopter as it went into a climb over the town. He'd watched the bombs tumble chaotically through the air, stubby fins glinting in the sun as they spun round. He knew instantly what they were but it seemed impossible to him that they would cause so much damage, so he just looked on, wondering at the crudeness of the weapons. They landed either side of a school. The shock wave blew him over. He struggled up to see several buildings gone and huge white plumes of smoke that looked like two ears. Later, he heard of the children – all of them girls – killed by the explosions. They never found anything but the smallest traces of them. He thanked Allah that his own sisters went to another school and had not been targeted.

Now he rolled into a ball and stuck his fingers in his ears, expecting to be buffeted by explosions. He waited, scarcely breathing, but nothing happened. Then he began to think that the helicopter was too low to drop bombs without blowing itself up. He waited some more and parted the reeds to look out. The helicopter was hovering about five hundred metres above the path. Instead of running with him to take cover in the reed bed, his companions had stayed rooted to the spot, gawping at the machine with good-natured smiles. One or two of them actually waved. They began to move up the hill. The helicopter drifted to the right, dipped its nose and roared off to the north.

He scrambled out of the reeds, wondering where Lashkar had gone, looked around for the stick he'd thrown away in his confusion and, glancing up the track, brushed himself down. Worried that he would not catch the others by nightfall, he set off at a lick, but as he reached the hill his legs began to give out and his arms just flopped by his side. He stopped and took some water. The idea of walking through these mountains seemed truly crazy, but he slapped his cheek and told himself that if he were to be defeated by this little hill, he would never bring his family to safety. He braced himself and summoned the image of his dear sisters and the new girl in his life, Hayat, who had looked at him with so much concern in her eyes. He'd show her! Gritting his teeth and forcing one foot in front of the other, Naji trudged on and reached the crest of the hill.

He looked down on the river, about a hundred metres below him on his left. Then he saw two men sprinting up the hill towards him. The first was Lashkar, the other was a Moroccan whose name he didn't know. Their fear and the effort of running uphill distorted their faces. Further down the slope, about three hundred metres away, he saw army trucks pulling up on the track in a cloud of dust. Sitting in the dirt beside a truck were at least thirty young men, while another group, which include one or two of his companions, were being prodded at gunpoint towards them. He took all this in before Lashkar grabbed his arm, whirled him round and dragged him down the hill. Several followed, including Aziz, the Libyan who'd made the fuss over the photograph, two other Afghans, two more Moroccans, a Gambian and an Algerian. At the bottom of the hill they ran to the reed beds, where they hid for the next hour. Only when it was dark did they venture out to find a piece of dry ground, away from the roar of the river, where they could make a fire and share out what they had to eat.

Naji's self-confidence was restored by Lashkar's praise for his astuteness over the helicopter. He said it was obvious the chopper was part of the operation to herd the illegal migrants coming up the river path into the trap; only Naji took notice of the military markings on the aircraft and thought to ask himself why the crew was showing such interest in them. Naji smiled modestly and told them the truth about his fear of helicopters, but they still insisted on hailing him the hero, and that made him feel pretty good about himself. And something else cheered him. As the evening wore on and they prepared to bed down, they spotted a few fireflies blinking in a field of maize, which he took to be a good omen. He reminded himself, as he dozed off, that Joseph had been among those rounded up with the others. 'I am with good people now,' he told himself, 'I can make this journey, God willing.'

Samson spent a frustrating day following up sightings of young boys in the mass of migrants walking the 180 kilometres to the Serbian border. Twice Vuk's spotters were sure that they had identified him through binoculars trekking through the countryside, but on both occasions they were wrong.

He'd slogged up the rail track in the pursuit of a boy about Naji's age, who had been seen by Aco from his trail bike, but caught up with the group to find the boy was travelling with his father and uncle. However, he learned a lot during those few kilometres, chiefly that the stone in which the track was set, known as the ballast, was exceptionally hard on the feet and ankles, so the only way to walk was to use the concrete sleepers between the two rails. But that meant you stood in the path of an oncoming train and, as Samson discovered, trains came out of nowhere and made very little sound as they approached. Many had been killed on bridges and in narrow cuttings where there was no escape. His other insight was that no person could carry all the water they needed for the punishing heat on the rail track. Every walker would have to leave the rail line at least once a day to find water.

He retraced his steps to a gate where he was due to meet Vuk. It was a beautiful afternoon. He smoked a cigarette and briefly watched a helicopter circling over a hill to the south-east of him, on the other side of the river. His personal phone went – it was Macy Harp.

'I wanted to remind you that Kazinsky Red is running in Dubai at the weekend,' he said. 'And I'd have thought you'd want to be on that.'

'Think I'm going to pass this time – he could easily be beaten by that gelding Beauty Tip.'

'You're not going to take a small interest?' Macy asked.

'Nope,' said Samson. 'I'm looking at Ascot next week.'

'But you won't tell me the name of the horse?'

'Not on it yet,' said Samson, smiling into the phone.

'Look, the reason I called is I wanted to know how things are going. They're not telling me much.'

'No joy yet – it's going to be tough.'

'Well, keep in touch and good luck.'

Samson checked the Office phone and saw an email with an attachment. The subject line read, *Taken last evening. Sent this morning*. He opened the attachment. It was a photograph of a group of migrants with bags slung over their shoulders. They looked like a soccer team on an away fixture, and right in the middle of the group was their mascot, a boy wearing an enormous grin on his face – Naji.

Seconds later the communications man at SIS, Jamie O'Neill, was on the phone. 'Thought you'd like that.'

'You've traced the phone. Who'd he send the picture to?'

'His sister Munira in Turkey.'

'Great news! So you've got his location?'

'We knew where he was when he took the photograph, from the data embedded in the image – twenty kilometres north of the town you were in, the name of which I cannot pronounce, and half a kilometre east of the Vardar River.'

'Right, so he's on the other side of the river to me – that's helpful. Have you got a position for him now?'

'No. He keeps the phone switched off. He hasn't had it on since we picked this up. We intercepted a couple of other messages and three photos: a selfie taken exactly where you predicted – by the UNCHR trailer; a weird study of some bananas; and a photo of lights in the forest, which are apparently fireflies. Actually, it is a rather good photo, so we've given him the codename Firefly.'

All the photos were sent to the same messaging account, belonging to Muzpaho2, his sister Munira.'

'So you have the number and you've got what's on the phone?'

'Yeah, we have the number – obviously – but we need him to switch it on in order to get to grips with the data. I guess you now have the option of calling him and offering help. That's what his lordship wants.'

'I don't want to risk spooking him. I'll think about it.'

As well as giving a current location, Samson knew that a smartphone could supply a wealth of information about a person's habits, who they were communicating with online and who they were texting and speaking to. It could be commandeered to transmit the owner's conversations and tasked to take pictures of them and their surroundings. With very little effort the smartphone could be converted to a perfect surveillance and tracking device.

Yet all these things could only happen if the phone was switched on long enough for the hack to take place. And the problem with Naji, O'Neill said, was that he hardly ever seemed to use his phone. Since GCHQ had intercepted the messages with their attachments, the phone had remained off. They discovered that he'd made almost no calls, although the phone had been credited with nearly €100 in Izmir, where Naji had been three weeks before. Most kids of his age with that kind of credit on their phone would burn through it quickly. Not Naji. He turned on the phone to take a picture or send a message, then immediately turned it off. He'd made just one phone call – lasting under three minutes – in the past four weeks, and that was from Lesbos. Samson said that the boy had an inbuilt respect for money, but O'Neill suggested there was maybe another explanation for the lack of activity. The phone was an old model – maybe the battery was faulty and wouldn't work unless it was on more or less permanent charge, and anyway, charging a phone on the road couldn't be easy.

But they had his location from just twelve hours ago and that was vital information. If the group he was with had stayed on the eastern bank of the Vardar, their current position could be estimated to be between about fifteen and twenty kilometres north of where the group had been on the previous evening.

Samson ended the call, looked across the fields for signs of Vuk's Land Cruiser, and, seeing nothing, called him.

'I need you here right now. I have got a position for the kid.'

'I am coming in ten minutes tops,' Vuk replied.

'Where are you now?' demanded Samson testily.

'I am beyond you, but very near,' said Vuk emphatically. 'Just hurry.'

Then the Office phone vibrated with another message from O'Neill: *Call me when you've read this: The man in the top row of the photograph, three from the end on the right, is a bad guy. CT recognised him as Mohammed al Kufra. He is a Libyan who studied two years of law in Italy. CT checked with Five's group of identifiers who have just got back to us. He is definitely IS and was recently in Syria. We know he was an important figure in the administration of the caliphate. He raised money with oil deals, drugs and selling slaves. He was sending hundreds of thousands of dollars worth of Captagon – the amphetamine IS manufactures – to the Gulf States and Saudi Arabia. After oil, it's their main source of revenue. A large shipment of the drug was recently intercepted in Beirut. We knew that was his.*

Samson examined the photo again. The individual spotted by counterterrorism and confirmed by MI5 seemed to have been caught unawares. Whilst the rest of the group plainly knew that the photo was being taken and were smiling or pulling faces, Mohammed Al Kufra looked surprised. He wore a bandana and a Roma supporters' shirt. He was certainly the oldest in the group. There was something about Al Kufra's profile that was ringing bells.

He spotted Vuk bumping across the field and waved frantically. Then he called O'Neill.

'This doesn't look good,' he said.

'On the other hand, Al Kufra may not know who Firefly is,' said O'Neill. 'He could be travelling independently from the three men you were following last night.'

'Doesn't sound right to me. He's a big wheel. What's he doing on the road with these no-hopers?

'Friends over the water think he may be on the run, having pissed off his masters by dealing drugs on his account. But that's beside the point. If Al Kufra knows who Naji is, he won't last long.'

'I'll do my best to find him today, though we haven't got a

lot of time before nightfall. What's happening about Turkey – the boy's family?'

'Sonia Fell's already on her way,' replied O'Neill. 'We know where they are, but haven't yet made an approach. We should have a lot more information by close of play tomorrow, or the next morning at the very latest.'

'Keep on Naji's phone – let me know if you get a new position,' he said, before hanging up and running to meet Vuk's car.

They went north to a tunnel under the rail line, which led to a bleak little hamlet sandwiched between the tracks and the river. They passed through the hamlet and followed the road south towards a bridge over the river that was missing part of its parapet. As they drove, Vuk spoke to Aco and told him to meet them at the bridge. He was already there when they arrived. He had his arm through his helmet and was speaking on his phone. The moment he saw them, he put on his helmet, kicked the bike off its stand, waved for them to follow him across the bridge and roared off. 'What the fuck he doing?' said Vuk more than once.

They went due south on narrow gravel track. They were now about twenty-five kilometres north of where the boy had sent his photograph that morning, which Samson reckoned was the maximum distance the group could have travelled that day. The track rose for a few hundred metres, and at the top of the incline Aco skidded to a halt with a spray of gravel and pushed his bike back on its stand. Vuk pulled up and they got out and walked over to him. Aco gestured down into a small valley, where they saw army trucks being loaded with migrants. Samson understood immediately what had happened. As the stream of migrants moving north had descended the slope on the other side of the valley, they'd walked slap into a squad of soldiers hidden in the trees near the river. There was no escape, unless they ran back up the hill. Aco told them that Simeon and Lupcho had seen a helicopter in the area, then out of curiosity had followed one of the army trucks and come across the operation. They'd phoned to tell him what was happening when he was on the bridge.

Samson swept the valley with his binoculars. There was no sign of Naji on the ground and, as far as he could tell, he wasn't among the men on the trucks. It was a pitiful scene. The migrants, most of whom looked to be from West Africa, sat cowed and with shoulders sagging.

Samson called down to Vuk, who had walked ahead. 'Can you ask your two guys if they know what's going to happen to these people?'

Vuk called Simeon, who said he was talking to the soldiers. He had learned that the trucks were to be driven to the border that evening and those people without registration papers – mostly likely all of them – were going to be escorted back into Greece, whatever the Greeks had to say about it. He'd discovered that the operation had been going all day and that the Macedonians were detaining a lot of Africans, some of them walking with children. But no one of Naji's age had been reported – they were quite sure of that. Apparently, a few migrants had escaped the net, but the officer in charge wasn't concerned because they would be rounded up sooner or later. It was enough that they had apprehended sixty illegals over the course of the day, and these people would no longer be a threat to their country. That was how he'd put it.

Samson texted O'Neill: *I need a good file photo of the Libyan right away.*

O'Neill replied immediately: *Coming up.*

It arrived a minute later. Samson sent it to Vuk's phone. 'Can you find someone in the intelligence services here to share this with?' he said. 'Tell them that this man is a dangerous jihadi and he may be on one of those trucks down there.' Vuk goggled at him, astonished by Samson's information. 'If he isn't on the trucks, he's got to be somewhere in this area.'

'How you know that, boss?' he asked.

'London told me,' he said, lifting his binoculars again.

His attention went to a very tall young African, who rose from a squatting position. With his bag slung over his shoulder, he started walking away from the trucks towards the river. Nobody seemed to notice until he had gone some distance, then a soldier shouted for him to come back. The man kept going. The soldier raised his gun and yelled again but did not shoot. The African passed the trees where Samson assumed the soldiers had concealed themselves to catch the migrants coming down the hill. It was now obvious that he was heading for the river. The soldier dropped his weapon and began running; two others joined him. They knew what the man intended, and so did Samson. His walk told you that something in him had snapped. His hope, his resilience, his stamina – whatever it was that kept these young men going – had finally given out. The man sat down on the riverbank with his feet in the water, looked up at the sky and then lowered himself into the milky brown torrent. In no time at all he was dragged out into the main current, and all that was visible of him was his perfectly round head and his bag bobbing in the middle of the river.

Samson watched, horrified, until the man's head disappeared around a bend in the river. There was no way of telling whether he might be washed ashore, or be swallowed by the waters of the Vardar. He caught Vuk's eye. Vuk shook his head gravely, as if to say no one could possibly survive the river in spate. Samson moved the binoculars back to the valley and to the soldiers walking to the trucks. They looked genuinely appalled. The migrants who had been waiting on the ground in a stupor had all jumped to their feet, and those on the trucks were craning to see what had happened. Samson found himself hoping that someone down there knew the man's story – who he was and where he'd come from and why he had taken his own life.

EIGHT

When he was awoken in the early hours by a prod and a tug at his backpack, Naji assumed that they were about to set off, for the remaining nine had agreed the evening before that from now on they would try to travel as much as they could at night. But soon he realised that someone was trying to undo the fastener on the pocket of his backpack. He shot up in his sleeping bag, ready to pull his knife, but the man was too quick for him: a hand closed around his throat and he was pinned to the ground by the man's body. It was then that he smelled the spicy breath. The man continued to work at the fastener and eventually got it undone and took out what he was looking for. He twisted as he placed it in his pocket, then Naji felt the full force of the hand around his neck and the air being pressed out of his lungs by the man's weight. He would be dead in seconds. He writhed in the sleeping bag and kicked out and miraculously landed a blow on Lashkar's head. Lashkar woke, immediately realised what was going on and seized the only thing to hand – Naji's stick, which was being used to hold the plastic sheet in place. With a scything motion he caught the man on his back. Then he beat downwards, repeatedly connecting with the man's head and shoulders, causing him to cry out. The others woke and began shouting. The hand released Naji's throat and the weight rolled away. Naji was aware of people jumping up and someone waving a torch but his whole being was focused on getting air back into his lungs and on the terrible pain in his windpipe and neck. But even while he was being strangled under the waves of the man's noxious breath, Naji had known the man had taken his phone.

When he stopped retching and his breathing finally returned to normal, he told the others about the precious phone that had survived the sinking of the raft and was his only link to his family in Turkey; he mentioned other important things on that phone, which he said he could not talk about. He was very near to breaking down, but controlled himself by squeezing his tear ducts with his thumb and forefinger. Someone poured tea into his battered aluminium cup and tipped sachets of sugar into it to give him energy, and Lashkar put an arm round him and told him that things would be okay.

It had been Aziz the Libyan who had tried to kill Naji, stolen his phone and escaped into the night. When he believed Joseph's hands were crawling over him like a huge spider the night before, it had been Aziz. And now Naji thought about it, Aziz was always chewing that chilli and ginger jerky. He felt terrible that he had cursed Joseph and had bad thoughts about him when he had done everything to help Naji.

The others began to talk about Aziz, and it emerged that none of them liked him. No one knew how he had joined the group, because he had no friends – he had just fallen in with them outside Gevgelija and started walking. When Lashkar had asked him why he had not taken a boat from Libya to Italy, Aziz came up with a crazy story that his vessel had been swept away in a storm and he had ended up in the Aegean. He took more food than he should and one of them pointed out that he always stuck close to Naji – they thought he maybe wanted to have sex with him – and he looked over Naji's shoulder whenever Naji took out his phone. 'Maybe he got your password,' said Lashkar.

Each in their own way tried to make him feel better and let him know that they cared for him. Slowly they began to get their things together and stagger off into the night, for they were determined to press on up the river until they reached a bridge a few kilometres beyond the valley where their companions had been arrested. This would lead them to the hamlet and to the rail track and the highway. They were all of them done with the river and had decided to remain as close as possible to the columns of legitimate migrants, those that had papers but who could not afford transport to the north. On the way, Naji ate all his food, including his last banana, for he now believed that the exhaustion he felt on the hill had been due to lack of food and water, and the food did make him feel better, though his throat was sore and it hurt to swallow.

By dawn, they reached a bridge where some kind of accident had taken place. This improved their mood, although Naji was inconsolable about his phone and showed no interest in the wreckage of a small truck that had taken the parapet with it into the river. It was not just the severing of his only link to his family that he regretted; it was the loss of the old messages and the photos that Munira had sent, which he sometimes scrolled through to make himself feel better. The phone was like having them with him, and now that it was gone he felt more alone than he had done at any moment in his journey. This weighed heavily on him, but at the back of his mind he also knew that he'd lost the means to access all that information he had collected on Al-munajil and his crew. One day he might be able to recreate the codes he'd devised in his head, hunched in the back of Al-munajil's pickup, but it would take time and there was a lot he would have to recall without making a single error. If he could manage that, he'd be able find the material on any device in the world. But for now that was the least of his concerns.

The group of nine kept walking until they came to the hamlet. There was no sign of life; the windows were shuttered and the only store was closed. One or two dogs showed interest in them, but they saw not a single human being and, having filled their water bottles from a tap on a water butt, they moved on. At length, they found the road leading to the tunnel under the rail line and it was here the party split, with the two Moroccans, the Algerian and the Gambian opting to walk the rail line. There was suddenly no sense of them being a group any longer and the four Africans barely said goodbye before climbing the embankment and vanishing in the vegetation that bordered the track. Naji and Lashkar and the two other Afghans headed towards the Alexander the Great Highway, which was surprisingly free of traffic.

Over the next couple of hours, they saw no more than a few hundred vehicles, and the only moment of interest during the whole morning was when they came across a snake sunning itself in the litter on the side of the road. The Afghans threw stones at it and it flashed away through the dry grass.

Just after midday, by which time they had been walking for eight hours, they spotted a service station ahead of them, on their side of the highway. They were mightily relieved, for they had run out of food; their water bottles were again low and they were all exhausted, particularly Naji, who again began to wonder whether he had the strength for the journey. There were only a few cars and one truck in the car park, and the man running the café and mini market seemed pleased to have their custom. Lashkar bought Naji a strip of four painkillers for his throat. He swallowed two with some Coca-Cola and went outside with a chicken roll and a chocolate bar. He had noticed the toilets on the side of the building and wanted to use them before the others. He went down some steps to find a pristine washroom that was decorated with photographic wallpaper to give the impression that you were in a forest. There was music playing over a recording of birdsong, plentiful soft paper, mirrors and hot water – all that he needed. He used the lavatory, washed himself all over and rinsed his underpants, socks and a T-shirt, which he hung on some railings at the back of the building to dry in the midday sun. For a while he sat in the shade with his arms wrapped around his knees, looking out across the mountains, feeling a sense of his own smallness. Then he dozed off.

A cold wind, a sign of the coming winter, woke Naji at five that evening. He snatched his now dry clothes down from the railings, packed them quickly into his backpack and rushed round to the front of the service station. Lashkar and the two other Afghans were nowhere to be seen. He searched everywhere with mounting panic. Maybe they had found somewhere to sleep, or they were playing a trick on him. He looked under the trucks in the car park and behind every car.

Eventually the man at the counter got his attention by calling him on the PA system, used to speak to drivers filling their vehicles, and beckoned him inside. The nametag – in Cyrillic and English alphabets – told Naji that the man's name was Zoran. Speaking in English, he said the Afghans had left in a truck. Naji must have looked devastated because the guy came out from behind the counter and sat him down in the little café area. He said that Lashkar and his friends had been sitting in the café, at that very same table, when they were approached by a people smuggler, a person known to his colleagues at the station for his regular trips to the north. It was this man's habit to stop there to pick up stray migrants and buy water, which they assumed he resold to his passengers at a greatly inflated price. It was anyone's guess what he was making out of each trip. He charged Naji's friends three hundred euros each to go all the way to Austria. There were perhaps thirty other men, women and children in the truck, so Naji could do the maths for himself. Naji's friends had searched high and low for him, including in the toilets, but the driver was in a hurry and after a few minutes said he would leave without them if they didn't climb into the back with the other passengers.

Aside from being extremely apprehensive about being on his own again, Naji was angry with himself. A trip all the way to the Schengen area! Lashkar and the others would be there within a couple of days. A chance like that wouldn't come along again. He slumped back in his seat and desperately tried to stop the tears welling up in his eyes. He took deep breaths, as his father had taught him. He knew that if you gave way to your feelings, you would be overwhelmed by your situation. To survive the horrors of the homeland you had to stay strong and never give vent to despair, for the expression of it would always make it worse.

He knew also that if he had had his phone with him he would have been all right. Just to speak to his family or text his sister would give him the boost he needed to continue with his journey. But that connection was lost. He must face the truth that his luck had run out – the guardian angel that had saved him in the sea and allowed him to find solutions to the problems that he met on the road had deserted him.

He bought a Coke and made a conscious effort to order his thoughts. No one else was going to help him, so he had to come up with a plan himself, and that thought alone gave him some encouragement. He had screwed up and now he would find a way to retrieve the situation and stay true to his plan of bringing his family to safety in Europe. Somehow he would work it out – somehow.

The few drivers in the café began to leave. Naji smiled at them hopefully as they passed his table but no one offered him a ride to the Serbian border, or anywhere else. The place was soon empty. The two other people working there departed and Zoran prepared to close. He came over to Naji, carrying a secure black case that contained the takings of the day. The owners of the service station would be along soon to collect the money, he said, and Naji couldn't be there when they arrived.

'I'm sorry,' said Zoran, 'you have to go.' Then he had an idea. He was about to close the toilets, but if Naji were to run ahead of him and make sure he wasn't visible when he came to check everything and lock up, he could spend the night there. He would be safe and warm. Naji headed for the door, but before he reached it the man called after him and lobbed him two sandwiches and a roll filled with cheese. They were out of date and would be taken off the shelves in the morning – Naji might as well have them.

And so it was that Naji spent his most comfortable night since he'd slept in a bed on Lesbos, and because the hot water had not been turned off he was able to wash his jeans and trainers and dry them on the hot pipe beneath the sink. He took out *The Cosmic Detective*, the book given to him by Anastasia, and read by the blue light from the electronic insect killer that was high on the wall. Things were okay – in fact, they were pretty good – and even the recorded birdsong, which seemed to be on some kind of timer, stopped after a while. Tomorrow he would ask the man behind the counter if he could use his phone to send a message to his sister.

Vuk found rooms in a farmhouse owned by a friend of a friend. It was a pretty place with a mountain view, a large vegetable plot and farm animals wandering about a ramshackle yard. Samson was woken a little before six by a cock crowing. He went in search of coffee in the kitchen, where the cheerfully ample lady of the house was at work. Through the open window he saw that Vuk was outside and talking to the farmer, who held the halter of a large white bull with backward-facing horns. Vuk rested his arm on the bull as though it were a vehicle and gestured with his cigarette hand. It was evidently a setting he felt comfortable in.

'The guys, they check the lorries at border,' he called over, when he saw Samson. 'No boy and no fucking terrorist.' He withdrew a flask of quince brandy from an inside pocket, poured some into the flask cap and knocked it back. 'What we do now, mister? Fuck the goats?'

'Not sure yet,' replied Samson. 'There's no point chasing round these hills unless we have something to go on.'

'We catch boy today, Mister Samson – I know we do catch him and we do kill all those fucking terrorists.'

'Well, here's to our success,' Samson said, toasting Vuk with his coffee. He grinned at him and wondered what Vuk's thoughts were like in his own language.

In London it was even earlier in the day, but the Office was calling him. Samson answered. 'Hello, Chris.'

'How'd you know it was me?'

'Because you are a sadistic arse and you hoped I was still asleep.'

'The boy's phone is on and we have a position for him,' said Okiri.

'Great! What else did you get?' Samson asked.

'We found good pictures of his sisters and mother which we've sent to Sonia in Turkey. His texts and phone calls have given us a patchy log of his movements in the last few months, including in Syria, but mostly of his journey from the camp in Turkey to Izmir and onwards to Greece. The battery isn't great, but as long as he doesn't use the phone, it shouldn't drain too fast and we can keep track of him.'

'Where is he?'

'He must have got a lift because he is about thirty kilometres north of where we thought he was yesterday. But he's on foot again, walking up the rail line.'

Samson cursed under his breath. He wasn't keen to repeat the previous day's toil.

'I've sent you the coordinates by text – tap on the link and it will find his place on the map. Later we'll work out a system so that you can have a live feed that shows you exactly where he is from minute to minute.'

'That would be helpful,' said Samson, moving towards the Land Cruiser and twirling his hand in the air to suggest that Vuk wind up his conversation about bulls.

'Have you thought what you're going to do when you get to him?' Okiri asked. 'He's going to be pretty wary after all he's been through.'

'Yes, I need Sonia to find out as much about him and his family as she can and then we can maybe put them together on the phone and hope they'll tell him to trust me. Then I guess we'll find him a hotel in Skopje and start debriefing him, as far as that will be possible, and develop things from then on . . .'

'Right,' said Okiri sceptically.

'Let's just find the boy,' said Samson. 'Is there anything else on that phone?'

'It's being looked at. I think we'd like to get inside the actual phone, so when you find the boy, don't forget that.'

Samson hung up and Vuk reluctantly moved from the side of the bull and went to his car with that strange, regretful walk. Samson tapped the link in the message from Okiri – a light pulsed on the rail line about twenty kilometres from the farmhouse. He showed it to Vuk, who grunted and phoned his three spotters to tell them where to meet. Only Aco answered. He told Vuk he could be there inside the hour. He added that he knew the spot and that it was exceptionally difficult terrain. The train track was wedged between a sheer cliff and the Vardar River, and it was a stretch of line where there had been several deaths that year.

They avoided the highway and took the old road that followed the course of the Vardar even more closely than the highway until they reached the town of Veles. There they found a road to take them to the place indicated by Naji's phone. On the way, Samson wondered why the boy had chosen to join the train line at the most hazardous place. Perhaps someone had given him a lift, it had come to an end and he had had no option but to get out of the vehicle and walk the line. It was also odd that the boy, so scrupulous about saving his battery, had turned on his phone.

London called again on the satellite phone; this time it was the communications officer, Jamie O'Neill. 'The reception is poor in the area where Firefly is now,' he said, and Samson noticed the trace of Northern Irish accent when he said Firefly. 'But we have a position for him seven minutes ago, so he can't have gone far. He's north of a train station named Rajko Zinzifov. Sending that position to you now. We'll fix you up with the feed ASAP. We don't have live satellite coverage but we've got some excellent imagery that shows that it's a very tight fit along that stretch. You wouldn't want to be on the track when the Thessaloniki–Belgrade express passes in forty minutes.'

'Have you got all the train times?'

'Yes, but we can only estimate when they pass along

that stretch by adding or subtracting from the arrival and departure times at Veles station, which is about eight to nine minutes away. Maybe you should try to find a spot to intercept him after that stretch, but I'm looking at it now and I don't see any obvious place.' He heard O'Neill breathe heavily. 'Once he's walking on that track there's no choice but to follow it. It's a bloody long haul for a young lad. A few miles up the track and he'll have to pass through a tunnel. There's no way round.'

When the call was over, Vuk scratched his stubble ferociously and offered his flask to Samson.

'Maybe when I've got the boy safely off the track,' Samson said.

'Then I drink for you.' Vuk put the flask to his mouth.

It was then that Aco came on the scene, but not on their side of the river. He called Vuk and explained that the only way they would know who was on the rail line was if he remained on the eastern bank. He would act as Samson's spotter and he'd also have a better view of approaching trains, particularly those coming around the bend.

Samson and Vuk moved off and drove up a hill of stunted trees and bushes. They bumped along a track that was no more than a depression in the grass. Vuk insisted that it was an ancient way – the road that people had used to pass through these valleys for thousands of years. It was little more than a shepherd's path now, of course, but Slav warriors of the past had once marched along it to do battle with the Greeks. Samson ignored the history lesson and kept his eye on Aco's bike flashing through the trees that lined the banks of the Vardar. About fifteen minutes into the journey, he saw him pull up in a meadow of hay stooks. Moments later Aco was on Vuk's speaker saying he had seen half a dozen migrants spread out over fifty metres, just a little ahead of Vuk's car. There was no sign of the boy.

Samson called O'Neill. 'Can you give me a new position for him?' he asked. 'We've found a group and I want to know if he's with them.'

'Give me a moment,' said O'Neill. Then a few seconds later he added, 'I've got your position and his, and I'd guess you're pretty much on top of him. You have to be damned careful – a train is going to pass from the north.'

Samson got out of the car and moved to where the hillside dropped onto a wooded cliff. The track was almost totally hidden by trees, and he could hear nothing above the noise of the river. There was no way to tell that trains passed at great speed beneath the trees. He crawled over a protruding shelf of turf and began his descent, keeping his body pressed to the cliff and clinging to saplings and branches to stop himself plummeting in a hail of earth and stones onto the line.

He had dropped down about ten metres when he paused to wipe his face with his shirtsleeve. He heard voices, looked down and glimpsed people walking along in the shade immediately below him. He counted eight men. Aco was right – the boy wasn't among them. And yet the phone signal was giving this place as his exact location. He waited a few minutes and then completed the rest of the descent by sliding noiselessly down a gully of moss and earth to land on the track ballast.

He waited in the shadows with his back pressed to the rock. He called Aco, who told him in halting English that he was sure there were just eight men on this section of the track. Then he called London. The satellite phone didn't work so he used his own cell phone. O'Neill and Okiri were watching the boy's signal together. It was still moving along the track, approaching the bend where the river and the train line veered westwards. The signal was no more than seventy metres ahead of Samson.

The penny was beginning to drop. He stepped out on the line and raised his binoculars. The man walking second last in the group wore a dark red and yellow shirt. He had seen that A. S. Roma supporters' shirt before – in Naji's photograph from the orchard.

'It's the Libyan,' he whispered to London. 'The bastard's got Naji's phone. God knows what's happened to the boy.'

Okiri and O'Neill absorbed this.

'Mr Nyman's here,' said Okiri. 'I think we need to involve him in this. Hold on a moment.'

Samson waited a minute, watching the men walk. Nyman's voice came on the line. 'We need that phone, Paul. We think there could be important evidence on it that we can't access remotely. Can you intercept Al Kufra?'

Samson was silent.

'You there?' demanded Nyman.

'Yes, I'm here – I'm thinking.'

He looked up the line. The eight men had gone past a recess in the sheer embankment, where an electrical transformer was housed, and were moving slowly in the shadows on the left-hand side of the track. That gave them limited options if a train passed any time soon. The embankment was too steep to climb in a hurry and on the other side of the track there was very little space between the rail line and the river. The only way they could escape would be either to run back to the recess, climb into a tree by the river or fling themselves down in a cable trough and hope for the best. All this assumed they would have enough warning to take action. Samson suspected that if the train came from the south, they might not see it until too late, because they were facing the other way. If it came from the north, the bend would mean they wouldn't know until the train was upon them. The only clue to the approach of a train on an electrified line was the twanging sound in the electric cables above.

'You said there was a train due – how long before it passes?' asked Samson.

'The Thessaloniki service from the north is about eight minutes away, give or take. But then you've got another one coming from the south a few minutes later. They pass just a mile below you, where the line opens up and there are two tracks.'

'What do we know about Al Kufra?'

'He's a nasty piece of work, so be careful. We think he's headed to Italy.'

Samson dialled Vuk. 'Have you got a gun?'

'Of course – I tell you this many times. Now you want gun?'

'Does Aco have a gun?'

'Of course Aco has gun!'

'I need you to go thirty metres up the track. You'll see a gap in the trees. There's a green box on the line. I want you to throw a gun down to me. Then tell Aco to start shooting ahead of the group – I need him to make a lot of noise so he frightens them. But I don't want him to shoot any of them, you understand?'

'Of course, mister.'

Samson started running. He reached the recess without the migrants noticing, looked up and saw Vuk. The gun landed a little distance above him and he retrieved it easily. It was a common Czech-made pistol. He checked the safety catch and stuffed it into his back pocket. At that moment he heard the snap of gunfire from Aco's side of the river. The men froze on the line and looked around, bewildered. Then Samson stepped out into the open and started shouting in Arabic. 'Brothers, come back. The soldiers are firing at you. Over here!' He waved furiously. 'You'll be safe here.'

They looked uncertain. The five in front simply crossed the line and crouched down, close to the river. The other three, including the Libyan, began to run towards Samson with their heads down.

The Libyan arrived first at Samson's side. He cursed and looked up the line, trying to determine the source of the gunfire. The other two – who, from their looks, he guessed were both from the Horn of Africa – were too terrified to say anything. They slumped to the ground with their bags. But the Libyan remained standing. He turned to search Samson's face. He had rather liquid eyes, which oscillated with suspicion, a deep frown mark in the middle of his forehead, tight curly hair and pockmarked cheeks and neck. This was certainly Al Kufra. He began speaking in a harsh Maghrebi Arabic that Samson found hard to understand. 'Who the fuck are you?' was more or less what he said.

'*As-salaamu alaykum*,' Samson said. 'I have come to help you and these men.'

Al Kufra didn't hear him.

'You will be killed by the soldiers or by the train on this line,' said Samson. 'We have a vehicle. If you climb this bank we can give you a ride to safety.'

Al Kufra looked Samson up and down and took in that he was carrying nothing and had none of the grime and fatigue that marked the faces of those on the road.

'Who the fuck are you?' he repeated. 'Why are you here?' This time he used the Middle Eastern dialect, which had none of the Punic and Berber influences that Samson had learned about on the refresher course MI6 had sent him on in Lebanon a few years previously.

'I'm here to help you,' said Samson. As Al Kufra looked up the line and across the river, trying to determine where the gunfire was coming from, Samson studied him closely. He assumed that Al Kufra had killed the boy and that was why he had the phone. But when the Libyan wiped the sweat from his forehead with his right hand, something else sparked in his mind. During his sorties to the rebel- and Kurdish-held territory of Iraq and Syria, Samson had heard more than once of the commander in whose hands rested the fate of every young woman kidnapped and enslaved by Isis. It was after this commander's disposal of Dr Aysel Hisami, in a revolting public sale, that she became unreachable. Samson just could not make the connections to buy her freedom from the man or men who owned her. He heard more than once that the commander, who was in charge of monetizing any asset IS could lay its hands on – ancient artefacts, drugs and, of course, thousands upon thousands of mostly Yazidi women – was tattooed on the right hand, between his thumb and forefinger, with three small circles. Tattoos are regarded as sinful in Islam; they are uncommon and tend to be remembered, even if the actual crime of being tattooed has been washed away by sincere repentance. That is was why the man was sometimes called '*Thlath Dawayir*' – Three Circles. Al Kufra's hands were filthy, but a crude tattoo of three circles was clearly visible.

Samson dragged his focus back to the boy and that phone. He became aware of the jangling and singing in the overhead cables. The Thessaloniki express was approaching. He spotted the locomotive and it was no more than a few seconds before the train roared past, carriage after carriage of passengers looking dully out onto the landscape. Samson stepped back and took out the gun and levelled it at the back of Al Kufra's head. The two men on the ground looked up, astonished, and began to scramble to their feet, ignoring Samson's attempt at a reassuring gesture. As soon as the train had gone they were legging it up the line. It was only then that the Libyan turned and saw the gun.

His eyes widened. A vein at his temple pulsed. 'Who are you?' he stammered. 'What do you want?'

'What did you do with the boy?'

'What boy?'

'The boy you stole the phone from. Did you kill him, Mohammed?'

Al Kufra reeled at the use of his first name. 'What boy? I am not this man. I am Aziz Abdul Hussain.'

'You are Mohammed Al Kufra, a Libyan national, student of law in Rome, a former inmate of Poggioreale prison, Naples. Deported to Libya 2008. Imprisoned Abu Salim prison, Libya from 2009 to 2010. Since 2013 you have been a commander in Islamic State. We've been tracking you ever since you stole the phone from a boy called Naji. Did you kill him to get the phone?'

'What you're saying is . . . you're crazy!'

Samson pulled his cell phone from his back pocket and pressed the home button a couple of times. Then he held the phone in front of Al Kufra's face. 'You know this kid? That's the boy called Naji. Did you kill him?'

He shook his head. 'I did not kill this boy.'

'Why did you take his phone?'

'He made a photograph with his camera.'

'Right, because you are Mohammed Al Kufra and you

thought the photograph would be used to identify you as a senior Daesh commander – which you are, of course. So you killed him and deleted the photograph.'

Al Kufra shook his head. 'I did not kill the boy Naji. I could easily have killed him but I did not. I liked him. He has balls.' He didn't even bother to deny that he was Al Kufra. Samson could see he was struggling to compute the situation he found himself in. How had he been pinpointed to this wild part of the Macedonian rail network? How was this stranger so sure of his name? Why the hell was anyone bothering with a kid like Naji? Samson thought he was probably high on something, and that wasn't helping his reasoning powers.

He told the Libyan to put his the hands on his head and turn round, and he began patting him down. He found a battered phone which was almost certainly Naji's – the screen was cracked and taped at the corner. Then he took another phone from Al Kufra's trouser pocket. This was on. He touched the screen to make sure it stayed unlocked. He told the Libyan to empty the contents of his backpack then lie face down. Spread on the ground was a phone charger, a knife – with no visible signs of blood on it – some clothes, a plastic cup, a Syrian passport using the Hussain identity, a Koran and various religious paraphernalia, a few packets of jerky, bread, tea and maps of the Balkans, a wallet with five hundred-euro notes and a few fifties, a toothbrush and shaving equipment.

'Maybe we can help each other,' said Samson. 'All I want is the boy. I didn't come after you – I don't give a damn about you. What did you do with Naji?'

'I didn't kill him. That's the truth – Allah knows my heart.'

'How did you get here so quickly?'

'I walked.'

'You walked pretty fast. Why didn't you take the train for Gevgelija? You have money.'

He didn't answer.

'Because you're hunting the boy and knew he was on foot? Is that why you started out walking?'

The Libyan raised his head from the ground and strained round to look at Samson. 'I do not hunt the boy. Why would I hunt the boy? He is nothing to me.'

Because you're part of Al-munajil's group – Al-munajil's killer squad.'

'Al-munajil?'

'Yes, he is a famous IS commander. Everyone knows Al-munajil. He has a speech impediment and he likes to hack people to death with a machete. You're with him, right?'

'Al-munajil?'

'You do business with him? Is that how you know him? You are part of his team.'

'I do business with many brothers. Maybe I do business with him. I do not remember this man.'

The shooting had stopped. He heard a noise behind him. It was Vuk, who had found a cable attached to metal posts used by engineers to climb down to inaccessible parts of the track. It allowed an easier descent than Samson's. Samson gave him the gun and told him to turn Al Kufra over so he could photograph him. He also took a close-up of the passport. He rolled him over again and picked up the back-pack and weighed it in his hand. He felt the perforated back panel from inside and out, and realised that something had been hidden in the layers of material. Eventually he found the opening at the bottom and took out a bag of pills: he guessed there were around a thousand green triangles, each embossed with an eagle's head. He took a picture of these, too, sent the three photos to London, then walked down the track so he could phone the Office out of earshot.

Okiri answered. 'Yeah, that's him – that's Mohammed Al Kufra. Well done: you've got quite a catch there. What's he say about Firefly?'

'I think we must assume he's dead, although he says he just wanted to delete the photograph on the phone and did not kill him. He denies he's part of the team hunting Naji – says he doesn't know Al-munajil. He has another phone with him. It's unlocked. He must have used it recently. I'll call you with it in a few moments.'

'Great. What do you make of him?'

'A nasty piece of work: a killer, without doubt. He's high on something – not sure on what – probably Captagon. He has a load of pills hidden in his backpack. Ask the boss what he wants me to do. Should I hand him over to the Macedonians?'

'We'll get back to you on that. But I guess you need to get him off the rail line. We'll probably want to talk to him with European friends.'

Samson returned to Vuk, who was flipping the top of his old Zippo cigarette lighter open and shut as he stood over

Al Kufra with the gun. 'You want me kill him, mister? Put bastard in river?'

Samson gave him a weary look. 'Of course not. I want to get him up to your vehicle. He needs water. He looks dehydrated to me. We'll need Aco's help.'

Half an hour later they had got their captive up the embankment and, having bound his hands and feet with rope, they pushed him down in the shade of the Land Cruiser. Aco stood over him with a gun

'What you waiting for?' asked Vuk.

Samson didn't respond. His phone started to vibrate in his pocket. He answered to Okiri.

'Just to bring you up to speed,' he said. 'Sonia is with Naji's family. Looks like things are going well.'

'But, Chris, I can't guarantee he's alive. I don't see the point interviewing them if he's dead.'

'We're going ahead on the assumption that the boy is alive. There's a lot of good material to be had, the boss is sure of that. On the question of what to do with Al Kufra, we have arrangements in place. You're going to be joined by Macedonian intelligence and a French intelligence officer and our guy in Skopje – Sonny Small. We're sensitive to the rendition issue, so they're going by the book. Mr Nyman's view is that Al Kufra is not part of the team, but that he himself may be on the run from Daesh. There's information that he was skimming from the shipments going out of IS-held territory to Saudi Arabia. Your friend Mohammed had to leave in a hurry, or face certain execution. That's another reason why we think he's going to talk. Everyone here is really pleased about this, Paul.'

'You want me to wait here?'

'Yes, they're sending a chopper. We've looked at the satellite imagery. There's a good place to land not far from where you are. They have your position. Shouldn't be more than an hour or two. By the way, can you call me with his phone and we'll start working on it.'

Samson did as he was asked then returned to Al Kufra. He stood looking down at him for a few seconds, knowing that it was precisely this kind of low life that had caused the death of Aysel Hisami. Then he got out the map of Macedonia, spread it in front of him and told him to trace his journey from Gevgelija and mark the position where he last saw the boy.

Al Kufra did it without hesitation, showing the exact spot where the group had been intercepted by the Macedonian security forces and giving a convincing account of what happened afterwards and how they had eventually found each other after hiding from the troops. He told Samson that he had tried to steal the phone the evening before but Naji had woken and pulled the knife. The second time he had been careful to pin him down so that Naji couldn't move and he, Al Kufra, wouldn't be stabbed. He stared up at Samson. 'It would not have troubled me to kill him, but it was unnecessary. I let him live because I found the phone.' He stopped. 'I liked the boy's spirit.'

'You're saying he's alive?'

He nodded, then a wild look entered his eyes. He began

to cough violently and eventually spat out a hoop of bloody phlegm. Aco jumped backwards and cursed him 'He's with the Afghans,' said the Libyan eventually. 'They're walking – maybe on the rail track. That's what they said they planned to do.' His chest went into spasm again.

'You have quite a problem there,' said Samson.

'*Marad alsili*,' he replied, giving the Arabic for tuberculosis.

'You'll need treatment for that. Is that why you've come to Europe?'

The Libyan didn't respond.

'Or did you have to leave because you were ripping off the caliphate with your drug deals? That's what we heard, Mohammed.' Al Kufra shrugged. Samson guessed he was not only suffering from TB, but was also in the first stages of withdrawal and desperately needed one of his pills. He wasn't going to get that any time soon. 'So they are behind you on the rail line?' Samson said.

'Maybe.'

'How many in the group?'

'Seven with the boy.'

Samson turned to Vuk and told him to direct Simeon and Lupcho to check the rail line below them. Just then he got a text from O'Neill on his own phone: *Boss says check out DealistXB app on the bastard's Samsung. It will interest you.*

He went to a rock in the shade, noticing that while the sun was still hot there was a cold breeze blowing down from the mountains. He found the DealistXB hidden in another app and opened it.

NINE

Early that morning, the door to the washrooms had been unlocked and an old woman carrying a bucket and mop had shooed him out. He went round to the front of the service station, where there were already several trucks parked. Men with big stomachs were gathered around a coffee machine in the café. Naji waited for them and then used the coins he'd earned in Gevgelija to buy coffee, which he thought would make him look grown up. He didn't like it much, but it was better when he added a lot of sugar. No one took any notice of him, least of all Zoran, who looked exhausted and was in a poor mood. Naji thought it wasn't the right moment to ask him if he could pay money to send a text to his family. He wondered about asking one of the drivers for a ride to Serbia but he had no idea how to approach them and guessed that they wouldn't understand his English anyway.

He went outside and propped himself on a post to eat the roll Zoran had given him the night before. The sky was clear except for wisps of cloud trailing from the peaks of the high mountains in the west. He felt good, but had no idea what his next move should be. Maybe he should start busking with his flute, but the truck drivers didn't look as if they would like flute music, so he decided to wait. He was staring at the view when Zoran barked at him on the PA system and told him to come inside quickly.

Everyone was gathered around the TV screen mounted on the wall, looking up at pictures of a truck that had crashed into a stream in Serbia. The cabin had been wrenched forward and almost torn off, so that you could see the entire engine. There were gashes along the side of the cargo hold and the doors at the back were open. Emergency workers crawled over the wreckage, attaching chains from a crane to the chassis and widening the holes in the side. There were a few bodies, roughly covered up, on the bank of the stream; also sitting there, with their heads in their hands, were one or two passengers who had got out alive. The camera focused on the shocked faces of the survivors then panned up to the broken crash barrier where the truck had left the highway and careered down into the stream.

Zoran put his hand on Naji's shoulder and pointed to the logo on one of the doors and on the side of the truck – a cockerel wearing a crown. He explained to his customers in the Macedonian language what this meant, then to Naji in English, although by that time it was unnecessary. From their expressions, Naji knew the truck was the one that had left the service station with his friends late in the afternoon the previous day. Falling asleep behind the building had probably saved him – the spirit that watched over him had not deserted him after all.

Zoran translated the report in short bursts. The crash happened at night . . . Serbian police said that so far ten people were known to have died . . . truck was carrying migrants . . . driver and his mate dead . . . conditions good . . . truck left highway for no apparent reason . . . no other vehicles were involved . . . driver may have been using mobile phone . . . many hours before the truck was spotted . . . not known how many people were trapped . . . cries are coming from within the vehicle . . . rescuers can hear children inside.

Naji searched the screen for any faces he recognised and prayed with all his heart that Lashkar, who had taught him to skim stones and told him all about his love for a girl on Kos, had somehow managed to escape injury and death. If Naji hadn't fallen asleep while his clothes dried he would have been in that truck and might very well have been killed. It turned out that his guardian angel had protected him, but this somehow seemed to him at the expense of the three Afghans who had been so good to him. He was too shaken to make any sense of it. He heard his father's voice in his head: if those men had died, their deaths, as well as your survival, were God's will, and that was all there was to say about it.

Zoran seemed to understand what was going on in his head. He told him that he could stay in the café as long as he wanted that day, but he had to find a way of continuing his journey – otherwise the police would find him and arrest him. Naji asked if he could use his phone to send a text to say that he was all right. His family might see the news and worry that he was in the truck, which was stretching things a bit because this news was very unlikely to reach Turkey. Zoran wouldn't accept Naji's offer of money and handed him the phone. But then he had to show Naji how to change from Cyrillic language to Arabic before Naji sent his usual, slightly formal text: *Honoured father and mother, beloved sisters. I hope you are well. I am safe and happy and well. I am making progress with my journey and send you my greeting and love. Naji.* He changed the language back to Macedonian Cyrillic and handed it back.

Naji sat down and the truck drivers returned to their coffee and sandwiches. Zoran busied himself with the till, studying a receipt with his big, black-framed glasses on the end of his nose. Without looking up, he said. 'That musical instrument in your pack – what is it, my friend?'

'It is the Arabian flute – the *ney*,' Naji replied. 'For five thousand years it is played by my people.' He lifted it from the pack, unwrapped it and demonstrated how different effects could be achieved by obliquely blowing across the mouthpiece. He told him that the *ney* played in the country-side, often by shepherds, was usually higher pitched than the instruments used in religious music. This flute had belonged to his great-grandfather, who was a farmer. 'My father, he gave me this flute because he is without the gift for music,' he told Zoran.

'Maybe you should play for us,' said Zoran, adding hastily, 'but not in here. Perhaps people would like it out there.'

He went outside, wiped down the instrument with his clean cloth, worked his lips and began to blow softly into the mouthpiece. He began with a very slow tune that had many long notes and pauses, which he'd learned from a Sufi recording, long before the war, when IS had come to his village and told people what they could and couldn't play. He felt that the tune fit somehow with the morning light and the cold mountain air, and as he played he thought of Lashkar and his lost love. And that made him think of Hayat and the red ribbon she had given him so solemnly in the park.

As the truck drivers came out, they stopped and watched and nodded with appreciation, and one or two handed him some small change. Zoran asked him to move away from the door so as not to be in the way. He took up a position at the edge of the shade near the car park and played for forty-five minutes without pause, collecting in the process much loose change and many more smiles and compliments than he had either in Athens or Gevgelija. Naji knew he was playing well, improvising in ways that he never had before.

There was one man who watched him for a long time, standing close to him and smiling and flipping the fob on his key ring. He was large and wore a suit, an open collar, sunglasses and his hair slicked back. He looked rich to Naji: he was driving a new Opel Zafira. Eventually he raised his sunglasses and spoke to Naji, but not in a language Naji understood. There was something greedy in his eyes that reminded Naji of the man who tried to do things to him in the alley when he was buying a life jacket. Naji had elbowed him in the stomach and smashed his glasses before running off with the life jacket, which turned out to be a dud.

The man kept talking, trying a combination of English and German. '*Möchtest du gehen* in Serbia? You go in Serbia? *Zwei Stunden* – two hours in *mein auto.*'

When he got no response, he smiled and went inside the service station. He reappeared a few minutes later with two cans of Coke, one of which he placed beside Naji, then he went to his car and leaned against the driver's door, smoking and drinking from the can.

All the pumps were occupied with vehicles, so Naji didn't see the pickup roll into the far side of the service area until too late. Two men lounged in the back. With a start, he immediately recognised Ibrahim and Usaim. At the same moment they recognised him and jumped up and hammered on the roof, but Al-munajil was already looking in Naji's direction. The pickup stopped. Ibrahim turned round to speak to Al-munajil through the passenger window. They were deciding what to do. Then Ibrahim leapt down from the back and started walking to Naji with his arms open, as though he was overwhelmed with joy.

Naji's mind froze. He lowered the flute and just stood staring at the killer as he walked towards him.

'And look who we've got here – Naji, my long-lost little cousin!'

Naji glanced left and right and back into the café, where Zoran was busy with customers.

'My good friend Naji – your troubles are over. You may ride with us.' Ibrahim was at his side and had slung an arm around Naji. 'Now pick up your bag and come with your friends – your brothers.' He was now steering Naji towards the pickup and Naji was walking and doing what he said simply from habits of past terror. That was how he had survived before – when they told him to do something, he obeyed. Ibrahim's hand gripped his neck and Naji felt the pressure of his thumb and forefinger just under his ears.

'And your brother Usaim wants to talk to you about his injuries. The big boulder in the forest – that was you, wasn't, it, Naji?'

'My stick – I need my stick,' Naji said, suddenly twisting round. 'It's over there.'

'You don't need your stick now, Naji,' said Ibrahim through clenched teeth. 'You come with your brothers. You don't have to walk any more.'

Naji wriggled free and ran back to his stick, which was leaning against a stack of gas cylinders. Ibrahim whipped round and went a few paces after him, but then stopped. He knew that he couldn't very well drag Naji across the forecourt in front of the people filling their cars, so he just stood beckoning to him with a phony smile on his face. And that was what broke the spell. Naji understood that if he moved one step towards Ibrahim he would be dead by the end of the day. Ibrahim glanced at Al-munajil, who made an impatient gesture to tell him he should go back and get

Naji, whatever the fuss. At that moment the pickup moved forward and started turning towards Naji.

It was obvious they were going to bundle him into the vehicle. There was only one way out for him. His hand folded round the handle of his knife in his pocket and he raised the stick with his other hand so that people could see he was in trouble and Al-munajil's men meant him harm, and then he shot a desperate look in the direction of the man who had bought him a Coke and had been watching the proceedings with detached interest. He seemed to get the picture straight away. He straightened and jumped into the Opel, started the engine and moved forward to block the path of the pickup, which was easily done because he was much closer to Naji. As he arrived by Naji, he shouted and opened the passenger door from the inside. Naji hopped in.

The Opel sped out of the service station and onto the highway. The pickup made a wide arc around the petrol pumps and followed the Opel, unnoticed by the few people around, least of all Zoran, who was busy with the routines of running the service station.

The app on Al Kufra's phone opened on a list of works of art, with thumbnail photos of Assyrian statues, amulets, decorated antique pottery and cuneiform tablets – in other words, a huge catalogue of the looted artworks that IS now sold through networks of dealers and brokers to the art markets in the West and the Gulf States. Samson had made it his business to understand the trade, because some of the individuals disposing of the artefacts for IS were also responsible for maximising the income from sex slaves. They were divisions of the same vast criminal enterprise and he suspected there would be an overlap somewhere. So he reverse-engineered the networks he found, passing messages back up the line to IS that an interested party would pay a lot for the release of a certain female doctor held in IS captivity. He didn't have much success tracing Aysel Hisami with this, but other approaches had proved more hopeful and at times he thought he might just get her out.

He scrolled through the price list of artefacts, remembering how much art IS had wantonly destroyed before the US air attacks on its oil refineries and tankers forced it to think of replacing the revenue by selling ancient works from the Sumerian, Akkadian, Babylonian and Assyrian cultures, all of which had sprung up at one time or other in 'the land between the rivers' – Mesopotamia.

He wondered why London had directed him to the app and began looking at the items for sale, clicking on the brief, almost comic descriptions of the works for sale. A 3000-year-old sculpture from the ancient city of Nimrud was labelled 'Old head with no nose and big beard'. He clicked on the photograph of this piece and suddenly a photograph of a naked girl filled the screen – a very young girl, who was looking away from the camera and trying to cover her breasts and pubic area with her hands. She was no more than fifteen. Beneath the photo was a price – $120.

Behind each picture of a work of art there was a woman

for sale. There were hundreds, maybe thousands of them, all photographed in more or less the same humiliating pose and almost all bearing the signs of mistreatment and even torture. One young woman had two black eyes and bandages on her wrists, evidence of an attempted suicide. Her price tag was just $70. Sometimes the price received by an auction or private sale was recorded. In this case it was just $64.

He'd come across a lot of this kind of material in his search for Aysel Hisami, and had watched videos of slave markets, released for propaganda purposes by IS. On one occasion he had viewed the appalling films of fighters raping the captives, just in case he glimpsed her. He had acquired a profound loathing for the evil young men in these films. But never before had he encountered one of the individuals responsible for the entire apparatus. He looked across to Al Kufra and, suppressing a brief desire to beat the life out of him, got up and went over to him.

The Libyan was looking a lot worse and had acquired a tremor in his right hand.

'How many of those pills are you taking every day – five or six?'

The Libyan shook his head. 'Maybe four.'

'And you need one right now?'

He nodded.

Samson examined him again. 'You've got a really bad case of withdrawal there. It's not just from these pills, is it?'

The Libyan shook his head vigorously then fell back against the tyre of the Land Cruiser. He was sweating profusely.

Samson picked up the backpack and started feeling the lining, never letting his eyes leave Al Kufra. He reached the wide waist belt that stabilised the pack when it was being worn and thought he felt something rustle beneath the material – silver foil – and further along there were some small packages. He retrieved some scorched foil, a plastic biro tube and five packages of the Golden Crescent's finest heroin.

'I get it,' said Samson, glancing at Vuk, who looked down with contempt on Al Kufra. 'You're bringing the pills into Europe to trade for heroin. You're addicted to speed – Captagon – but this is the major drug in your life.' He stopped and sat down by the Libyan, so close that he could smell the man's odour.

'I need your help on two matters. If I think you are lying to me, I will destroy all these drugs immediately. If you tell me the truth, I will maybe let you smoke some of this. Do you understand me?'

The Libyan nodded.

'If there's the slightest doubt in my mind, this stuff goes into the river.'

He nodded again.

'Firstly, I want the truth about the boy. Did you kill him?' He took hold of the Libyan's chin. 'Did you kill the boy?'

'No.' There was no flicker in the man's eyes.

'Okay,' said Samson, moving away. 'On your phone there are pictures of many naked women with price tags. You were offering them for sale, is that right, Mohammed?'

He exhaled deeply. He was shocked that Samson had found the pictures of the women so quickly. 'They are the caliphate's property. This is not me.'

'Remember our deal,' said Samson. 'I need the truth, so don't pretend this was nothing to do with you. You were the dealer, the broker – whatever you like to call it – and you arranged for these women to be sold into sex slavery. That's right, isn't it? When this phone is investigated further and we start to track down the history of your communications, there'll be much to learn about you and your trade. You won't be able to escape responsibility for your actions.'

The Libyan lifted his shoulders hopelessly. 'I was doing what they told me.'

'I think you'll find that excuse has had its day in Europe,' said Samson. 'Now I'm going to show a picture of a woman. She was older than these young Yazidi and Christian women that you sold: she is in her mid-thirties. Her name was Dr Aysel Hisami. She was captured about a year ago, not far from Mosul. She was serving as a doctor in the front line of the Peshmerga forces. We know she was sold into slavery and we know she subsequently killed herself.' He let that hang in the air.

'Many women committed suicide,' said Al Kufra. 'It was a problem for us.'

Samson was known for his exceptionally calm disposition, inherited from a father who could sit without blanching at a card table knowing that he might lose everything on his hand, but it was all Samson could do not to take Vuk's pistol and put a bullet in the Libyan's head there and then. 'Yes, a problem indeed,' he said very quietly. 'I have two pictures of Dr Hisami here and I want you to look at them very closely.' He showed him the picture on his own phone, which was from the website of the UCLA medical school where the doctor had carried out her research. The Libyan nodded. 'Don't say anything yet. Just look at this one.' He held out the phone again. It was the last known photograph of her. Dr Hisami was in battle fatigues and wore the red beret of the Peshmerga forces.

The Libyan asked him to shift the phone because of the reflection, then he seemed to nod. 'Maybe I remember her,' he said.

'Maybe?' said Samson, his anger showing for the first time. 'Maybe? I need more than that.'

'There were many women.'

'This one was different. She was very educated, a brilliant doctor and she spoke English fluently like an American, though perhaps she never allowed that to be known. She had dignity, the bearing of an accomplished person – a person who has already done much in her life.'

'I say maybe.' The Libyan shifted his buttocks on the ground. 'I'm not sure.'

Samson stared down at him hard. The man's eyes avoided his. 'I think you know her, and I think you know what happened to her, too,' he said. He waved the heroin in front of the man. 'Tell me and you can have as much of this stuff as you want.'

The man took a couple of deep breaths and the hacking cough began again. Samson asked Vuk to give him some water, which he did reluctantly. Vuk knew exactly what kind of man their captive was.

The Libyan wiped his mouth and started again. 'Maybe she was the woman the caliphate sold to Abu Wassim. Maybe the caliphate even gave her because Abu Wassim is one of the greatest servants of the caliphate. I do not remember.'

'Abu Wassim – you're certain that was his name?'

The Libyan nodded. 'That is his name – the woman was this man's property.'

'And who is this man? Where is he now?'

'I never met him.'

'But all these women passed through your hands. You have hundreds of them on your phone. You must know the man who bought her.'

The Libyan started shaking his head. 'No, you misunderstand the situation – I was in charge of the records of the disposals and allowing brothers to see what women were available before the disposals, while they were in the field.'

'By *disposal* you mean the slave market – the auctions,' said Samson firmly. He desperately wanted to punch Al Kufra's face in and so looked away to the waters of the river below them. 'But you saw what happened to the doctor,' he said eventually 'Where was she held?'

'Mosul – in a house with twenty others.'

This tallied exactly with Samson's information. It was from this house that two young Yazidi girls had escaped

and brought news of Dr Hisami's suicide. They reported
that they saw her rarely because they were held in different
parts of the complex, which was formerly some kind of
clinic. Two weeks before she hanged herself they found her
collapsed in a shower. They told of seeing rope marks on her
hands and ankles, bruises and cigarette burns across her mid-
riff and neck. Samson had spared Denis Hisami these details.

'Is she on your phone? Do you have a photograph of her?'

Al Kufra looked up at him slyly. 'I need what you've got
in your hand. Then I will help you.'

Samson stepped forward and seized the man's collar with
his left hand and jerked it up. In doing so the thumb of his
right hand slid across the screen. He saw the screen fill with
a dozen or so images of young women. He had accidentally
opened Al Kufra's entire catalogue of women for sale. 'You
are way past the point when you will ever make a bargain
with anyone again. Now show me the photograph.' He let
go and held the phone up so Al Kufra could see and began to
scroll through the faces of hundreds of women. 'Up? Down?
Which way? Where is she?' he demanded.

Al Kufra asked him to slow down, then said he should go
to the part of the record where there were two sisters. He
remembered the sale of the sisters, and that was close to the
time when she came up for disposal. The sisters were 'featured' together in the same photograph – that was unusual.
It was in the spring, he added.

'It was in the spring,' Samson repeated dully. The cliché
about the banality of evil was never truer. The key figure

in a programme of mass rape and enslavement was this loser with broken trainers, a filthy football supporter's shirt and an addict's restless eyes. The organised barbarity of what he had participated in was up there with the Khmer Rouge in Cambodia, the genocide of the Tutsi people in Rwanda and the slaughter of 7,500 Muslim men and boys by Bosnian Serbs at Srebrenica. In scale and cruelty, it complied with every definition of a war crime. Yet at the heart of the machine that destroyed Dr Aysel Hisami was this scabrous, raddled junkie. After months of patient search and a lot of money paid out in bribes and inducements, Samson had found him by chance because of a stolen phone.

He began to go through the vast album of victims but couldn't find a photograph of two sisters.

'Maybe in special section,' said Al Kufra.

'How do you get into that?'

'I have to show you. I need my hands.' He worked his way from the tyre and leaned forward so that Aco could untie his hands. The instant they were free, he struck with the speed of the cobra and in one movement seized the gun from Vuk and levelled it at Samson. But he hadn't taken into account that behind him stood a young man who was in all probability one of the most violent individuals in the Balkans. Samson was briefly aware of a slightly manic smile spreading across Aco's face before he punched Al Kufra hard on the side of the neck and sent him reeling sideways. The gun dropped from his hand and before Al Kufra knew what was happening Aco had him in a headlock and was preparing to snap his neck. Vuk retrieved the gun and used the opportunity to kick the Libyan in the ribs.

They lifted him up and placed him against the tyre. A few minutes later, with the gun pressed to his temple, Al Kufra opened up the 'special section' and led Samson to the heartrending photograph of Aysel Hisami, who was pictured naked, with a look of utter despair in her eyes. It was extremely hard for Samson to see, but he had to make sure that it was the doctor. Beneath was entered the name Abu Wassim and the price paid by him – $160.

Samson examined the picture briefly and walked away holding the sachets and bag of pills.

'We had a deal,' Al Kufra said, as Aco tied his hands again.

Samson tore opened the sachets and shook the powder into the breeze. He opened the bag of pills, placed a stone inside it and tied a knot in the plastic. Then he hurled it high over the scrub on the embankment and the river's edge and watched it plummet towards the waters of the Vardar. He did not even turn to see the devastation on the Libyan's face, but kept walking to get away from the man. 'Kill him if he so much as moves a muscle,' he said over his shoulder.

He took a screenshot of the page with Hisami's photograph and Abu Wassim's name and the price and sent it to his own email address, and then attached it in a message to Macy Harp's cell phone.

Macy called a few minutes later, just as Samson had lit a cigarette. Samson explained how they had apprehended Al Kufra that morning by tracing Naji's phone, and how he had found the catalogue of sex slaves quite by chance. 'That photograph is just one of hundreds on his phone.'

'I'm sorry you had to see it, Paul,' said Macy. 'I know how much she came to mean to you.'

'Yes, well . . .' For a moment he couldn't speak.

'What's Al Kufra like?'

'This is a man who flipped from playing Candy Crush to selling women for rape by text. But at least we got Abu Wassim's name.'

'Yes, Denis Hisami will be pleased about that. Did he say anything else about Abu Wassim?'

'Says he didn't know him.'

'You believe him?'

'No – I think there'll be more information about the man on the phone. Our friends have looked at it remotely already. I'll give them the phone when they collect this bastard, which should be any second now. The information about the missing women will be crucial to the families and I guess it could form the basis of some kind of prosecution.'

'That's good.'

'And you should make sure Nyman understands that I'm giving it to them on condition that you're allowed access to all relevant information about Aysel Hisami. Remind him I was hired to find the boy and that this is a bonus.'

'I don't have to – he's onside. You still believe the boy is alive?'

He took a last puff from the cigarette and stubbed it out carefully on a rock. 'On balance, I do. The kid's a survivor.'

They began to wind up the conversation. Before he said goodbye, Macy said, 'It's the last day at Ascot next week – the last meeting of the flat season. Any thoughts?'

'Plenty,' said Samson. 'But I'm keeping them to myself for the time being.'

'You're a cagey bugger,' said Harp, and hung up. It was odd, possibly inappropriate, that they talked about racing just then, but thinking about Ascot improved Samson's mood. It made him feel calm again. He kept his distance from Al Kufra from then on, although he was satisfied to see increasing signs of withdrawal. Even in his line of work, he had encountered very few people who had done as much harm as he.

About an hour later they moved him to high ground to be collected by a civilian helicopter, which had on board the SIS man from the Skopje embassy, Sonny Small, and two Macedonian intelligence officers. The Frenchman appeared to have been left behind. The Libyan struggled, protesting that he was an innocent refugee and that they had no evidence against him, but Samson showed the Macedonians what was on the phone. They took one look and Al Kufra was hoisted unceremoniously into the helicopter and forced to the floor with a gun in his face.

'London mentioned some drugs,' said Small, out of earshot.

'I disposed of them all. You don't want the Macedonians charging him with drugs offences? He'll be here for the next decade.'

'Quite right,' said Small.

'He's going to be crazy for a while – he's coming off speed and a high-grade heroin.'

'Maybe that's no bad thing.'

'Indeed,' said Samson, 'a little suffering would not go amiss. He says he has TB, so don't let him cough all over you.'

Small lifted his chin towards the two Macedonians. 'They want to know who you are and what you are doing here.'

'Tell them the truth – that I'm a private contractor looking for someone among the migrants. I'll be gone in the next twenty-four hours. I'm very happy for them to call Macy – he has a lot of contacts from the days of the break-up of Yugoslavia. Probably knows these guys' boss.' He gave Small the number.

'Right, I think that's everything,' said Small, moving to the aircraft. He had forgotten to ask for Naji's phone, and Samson wasn't going to remind him. He wanted to look at it more thoroughly himself – and besides, SIS had access to it, as long as it was on.

They watched the chopper take off. When the noise had died down, he turned to Vuk. 'I think we should find some-where to have a drink and some food.'

Vuk said he knew just the place in the local town where they could wait while Simon and Lupcho checked the stretch of rail line to the south of them on the slim chance that Naji was on it.

'What we do about boy?' he said.

'Wait,' said Samson.

TEN

From the moment they hit the highway, Naji's rescuer made clear the favour was not without its price. As he accelerated to 120 mph, he put his hand on Naji's leg and groped the inside of his thigh. There was nothing Naji could do. They were travelling faster than he had ever been in his life, and he couldn't risk distracting the man, even though the highway was clear. Naji screamed 'Nein!' and 'No!' several times, but it just seemed to make him more excited. He was enjoying Naji's panic. And then he showed him a card, which featured a blue shield in which there was a Cyrillic heading, the word Police and the initials PM between laurels.

He flashed the card at the first tollbooth and went through the barrier without paying. He pulled up in a truck inspection area on the right of the highway and waited there, revving his engine and glancing in his mirror. It wasn't long before the pickup arrived at the barrier to pay.

'They will kill us. *Sie . . . sind . . . Terroristen*,' said Naji. 'They are terrorists.'

The man raised his sunglasses and gave Naji a sadistic smile. The pickup passed through the barrier and drifted towards them. Usaim and Ibrahim were peering over the roof from the back. Al-munajil had one arm out of the window.

Naji begged the man to move. 'They will kill us.'

He put his foot on the accelerator and they moved about thirty metres.

The man touched him again, this time on his stomach, and searched Naji's face for a sign of compliance. Naji was shaking. He could have cried, but he was just too frightened. If the man left him on the side of the highway, Al-munajil would grab him and kill him. He tried to smile, and he gave the man a nod, as though he would accept his attentions. But this did not seem to be enough. The man allowed Al-munajil's pickup to approach them again. It was a game of cat and mouse. Every time they nearly caught them, the policeman's car shot forward. He didn't understand why Al-munajil had not drawn level and opened fire. If this were Syria, they'd be dead by now. Something was holding them back. Maybe they didn't have any guns – a person posing as a migrant couldn't risk being found with a weapon.

They played this game for about five minutes. Naji ended up with his eyes fixed on his backpack, which was wedged between his legs in the footwell, praying that something would save him from the situation. Quite suddenly the pickup roared ahead of them and started up the highway.

Naji soon saw why. Two police cars with flashing lights were passing through the tollbooth – they were the first of a motorcade that included a big black saloon, and a Mercedes SUV with darkened windows and another car with flashing lights behind its radiator grill.

Naji thought of opening the door and making a run for it right then, but the man read his mind and grabbed his arm at the same time as moving the car forward. The motorcade disappeared up the highway and passed the pickup, which began to slow down again. The Opel caught up with it, but as soon as it tried to pass, the pickup swerved into their path. This went on for a long time, despite other vehicles occasionally going by, and for most of it the man felt able to fondle and touch him wherever he wanted. Naji's face grew hot with rage and shame. The man called a friend on his phone and although Naji had no idea what he was saying, he knew from the lascivious looks and gestures that this wasn't good news for him. In Greece, he had been warned about predators on the road. He'd taken no notice, despite his experience when buying a life jacket. He realised that the man he was with now was many degrees more dangerous than the old bastard with the big belly who had tried to grope him in the alley.

And still one car blocked the other. The man got so bored that he used the camera to take a picture of Naji and sent it to his friend, and then rang him back to discuss him more. Naji felt like a little goat in the market. He resolved to try to escape, even if that meant jumping out of the car when it was moving.

After about twenty minutes, they reached an exit on the highway. The pickup's driver slowed down, presumably trying to work out whether the car Naji was travelling in would take the exit or keep heading north towards the border with Serbia. The Opel moved to the fast lane and accelerated, as if planning to continue on the highway. The pickup moved to block its way. The Opel swerved to the right and headed to the exit at great speed, clipping a bank of gravel. The driver let out a whoop of triumph, but before they took the roundabout to follow the road east towards the Bulgarian border, Naji saw the pickup go into the slow lane and begin to reverse, so it too could take the exit. They wouldn't be far behind.

The man's demeanour suddenly became much more aggressive. He kept cuffing him and grabbing him by the neck. For the second time that day, Naji's hand closed around the handle of the knife in his pocket, but they were going too fast for him to do anything.

The fields and vineyards gave way to unfarmed land and scrub. Suddenly the man turned left, up a minor road that meandered in parallel with one of the many tributaries of the Vardar. It was a beautiful area, though Naji was in no state to appreciate the wild European countryside. Without warning, they turned off the road and went down a leafy track towards the river, at the end of which was a deserted building with a tin roof and walls that were made from huge boulders. The man seemed to know the spot well. He reversed the car to the side of the building so it could not be seen from the road. He turned the engine off and grabbed Naji, trying to fondle him again. Naji fended him off. The man got out and went round to the passenger door, opened it and hauled Naji out. He was strong and Naji knew he didn't stand a chance against him. But he broke free and summoned all the German he knew to plead with the man to leave him alone. All he got in return was a shake of the head and a brutal smile. The man removed his jacket, laid it carefully on the car's roof, unbuckled his belt and came after him.

Naji took the knife from his pocket, feinted to the left then, ducking down, he moved to the right and plunged the blade into the man's thigh. He aimed low intentionally, but he could just as easily have stabbed him in the stomach. He pulled the knife out, stepped back and readied himself to lunge again. His assailant looked down at the spreading patch of blood on his left trouser leg and yelled. He lunged at Naji with his fist, missed, then took hold of his leg with both hands and let out another cry of pain. Naji stepped back, certain that the man was not yet finished with him. He knew that a thrust to the man's chest with the fat, long blade of the throwing knife might kill him, but he desperately didn't want to have to do this, even though the man was a rapist. Their eyes locked. Naji raised the knife again and silently shook his head to tell the man that he really meant business. He said something in Arabic, which came out without him even thinking about it. 'I come from a country where people kill each other every day of every week, and I will kill you if you don't leave me alone, sir.' Of course, the man didn't understand the sentence, least of all the honorific that Naji rather oddly tacked onto the end, but maybe he got some of its meaning.

Naji was breathing quickly and his heart was pounding. If he had been able to stop and think he'd have been aware of feeling something like surprise that adults could behave in this way. He would get that feeling when he saw something terrible in his homeland – the barrel bombs tumbling from the helicopter had seemed like something only a cruel child would do, not grown-ups. But it was the other way round – adults were the cruel ones. This man meant to hurt him, and he would take pleasure from it – he knew that. It was a pleasure he did not comprehend.

He wanted to get away – to grab his bag and stick from the car and run – but the man was still a danger and he obviously wasn't going to allow Naji to escape. So Naji threatened him, slashing the air in front of the man's face yet taking care not to allow him to grab hold of his arm. He stumbled, toppled backwards, clutched his leg and landed on his bottom. He yelled out again and writhed in agony and Naji thought he had hit his tailbone. The fury that had succeeded lust was now replaced by fear. He tried to get up but Naji told him in halting German, '*Ich . . . werde . . . töten . . . dich*,' which meant, more or less, 'I will kill you.' His voice made a weird squeak and then went deep.

He put it down to his poor grasp of spoken German and went to grab his possessions through the open door of the car. As he grabbed hold of his bag, his eyes came to rest on the phone. Then he saw the fob, which was still in the ignition. He could either throw it away, or he could start the car and just drive off. He wouldn't go far – just put some distance between him and his attacker. Of course, he had never been behind a wheel before, but he confidently supposed there was probably not much to it. At home, he'd seen countless idiots driving without any difficulty at all.

He brushed the man's jacket from the roof, jumped behind the wheel and started the engine. He knew about pressing the clutch, which he did, and then he rammed the gearstick into first and let the clutch out. This caused the car to shoot forward and stall. The man was now on his feet, hobbling after him and screaming. Naji repeated the actions and managed to move off. He was going, but not in the direction he wanted. There seemed to be a lot to think about, what with turning and changing gear at the same time. He managed the gear, albeit changing from first straight into third, and found himself accelerating down the track towards a flat, stony floodplain. He ploughed across a ditch and a low earth bank and drove onto the hardened mud. Just for good measure, he changed up to fourth, but found that he had to drive faster than he wanted, so changed down, hardly touching the clutch. He congratulated himself on the smooth gear change. He was now having the best fun he'd had in months. He went round and round, whipping up a huge dust cloud and sounding the horn every time he missed one of the boulders in his path. The man was far away and couldn't touch him, so Naji tried one or two manoeuvres he had seen on TV – going fast in a straight line and turning as sharply as possible. The first time he nearly rolled the car and ended up facing the direction he had come from; the car rocked gently from side to side and the engine roared because he'd neglected to take his foot off the accelerator. He also tried going as fast as he dared across the flats and braking suddenly, which made the car slide across the hardened mud. It was all too much, and he could have stayed there for the rest of the day, perfecting what he believed to be his natural skills as a driver.

He looked towards the stone building. There was no sign of the man. He turned the radio on to full volume, fiddled with the tuner and found a heavy metal number, and then writhed to the music in his seat for a bit. Naji wasn't a kid who thought he was cool – in fact, he knew he definitely wasn't cool – but right then he thought there was a chance that, if Hayat could see him, she might think he was.

He wondered what he should do. Going back to the highway was out of the question – he would be spotted and sooner or later arrested, and then they would want to know where he had got the car. He consulted the map and decided to take the minor road north and leave the car somewhere near two villages that lay close together on the river, about twelve kilometres away. He started off towards the building, negotiated the ditch and earth bank better than he had before and aimed up the bumpy track towards the road, revving the engine more than was perhaps necessary. He was so intent on steering that he didn't see the man stagger from the shade of the bushes with a boulder in his hands, which he heaved into the path of his own car. It landed squarely in the middle of the windscreen, creating a bulge to the right of Naji's head. Shattered windscreens were nothing new to a boy who had grown up in a civil war – he knew that all you had to do was punch through the glass and keep going, because the glass would never cut your hand. This he did, but he realised with horror that the passenger door was now open and the man was halfway into the car and desperately trying to lift his damaged leg. A snapshot of his crazed face and bloody hands imprinted itself on Naji's brain before he accelerated away, causing the man to let go and fall onto the track with a single agonised bellow.

He assumed driving would be easier on the road, but quickly discovered there was much less margin for error. When he met another car coming from the opposite direction he panicked and grazed the Opel along its right-hand side, giving it one or two minor dents as well. Because of the shattered windscreen, the people in the oncoming car did not see him until they were level with him, and then he was aware of two female faces staring aghast in his direction. He was new to Europe but it didn't take much to imagine what would happen next: they would find the man in the road; he'd tell them that he had been stabbed and his car had been stolen; and then the police would soon be looking for a migrant boy with a knife. He sped up but got caught behind a large orange earth-moving truck that was labouring up a short hill. He didn't trust himself to overtake without either hitting the truck or going over the side. After half an hour he reached the first village on the map and decided that he would leave the car a little way after it and walk along the river to the next village, which was larger and might have somewhere to buy food and water. In the end, the spot for disposal was decided by an ancient tractor that came round the bend on Naji's side of the road, the old man behind the wheel distracted by something in the back of his vehicle. Naji had no option but to cross the path of the tractor and careen towards a stand of dazzling yellow poplar trees that occupied a bend in the river. He braked, but this had no effect on the Opel's momentum and he crashed through a stook of hay, clipped a pile of fencing posts and eventually came to a halt when the car rolled into the trunk of one of the poplars. He was unharmed but furious, as if it were his own car. He jumped out of the driver's seat to yell in Arabic at the tractor driver, who continued on his way, apparently oblivious of the incident. He may not even have been aware of the Opel.

All this was watched by a young man with a large white dog, who rose from his place in the shade of the poplars. He had heard the burst of Arabic and, after checking there was no one with Naji, called out to him in the same language. He was tall and had a large open face that had something Asian or Mongolian about it. He was smoking and held an open can of Skopsko beer, which he offered Naji.

'My name is Ifkar, and I am Yazidi,' he said, surveying the wreck of the Opel with a grin. 'You are a fucking Arab, right?'

'Right,' said Naji, grinning in return. He pulled his ruck-sack and stick from the car, snatched the man's phone from its holder and straightened to introduce himself. 'What's the dog's name?' he asked, taking the can of beer.

'Moon, that's my name for her. She joined me a few weeks back in Bulgaria.'

'She has a beautiful coat,' said Naji.

'That's because I brush her every day and give her my best food. I took her from her owner, who was a very cruel man.'

Naji put his hand down tentatively and let the dog smell him.

'She likes you,' said Ifkar and, after a long pause in which he scrutinised Naji's face with almost rude proximity, con-tinued, 'You know where we are? I've been lost for weeks and I cannot ask anyone because no one understands me.'

Naji told him he knew exactly where they were, but he had to leave because the police would be looking for him and there were three other men on his tail and they were terrorists.

Ifkar was impressed. 'Damn fuckermother,' he said in English.

'No,' said Naji, 'it's motherfucker!'

Ifkar looked in awe at Naji. 'Damn motherfucker!'

They covered the car with fallen boughs, a few fencing posts and armfuls of hay, and very soon they had left the picturesque spot and were following the river north, with Moon leading the way.

★

'Firefly's alive,' said O'Neill. 'His sister got a text from him this morning. Sonia is with the family. She saw the text and got the number of the phone he's using. I'm sending you a location. Looks like a petrol station on the north roadway of the Alexander the Great Highway. Not far from you now. The phone's still there.'

Samson pulled the map towards him across the restaurant table and beckoned Vuk, who was in the doorway talking to the owner.

'Hold on,' he said to O'Neill, and turned to Vuk. 'Where are Lupcho and Simeon?' Vuk put his glasses on and stabbed a finger at the map. They would take a while to get off the rail line – he and Vuk would reach the service area much sooner. They would send Aco on ahead.

'Keep an eye on that phone,' he said to O'Neill.

Aco reached the garage ten minutes before them, having found a gap in the barrier on the highway and crossed the median to the northbound roadway. He looked everywhere and reported that Naji was nowhere to be found. Samson checked with London – the phone was still at the same location.

When they arrived, Samson went in with Vuk, sat down with a coffee from the machine and dialled the number supplied by Sonia Fell in Turkey. He heard a phone vibrating behind the till, but no one answered it. He called again and eventually an attendant with a woeful expression snatched up the phone and answered with irritation. Samson rang off immediately, got up and walked over to the counter, whereupon he held up the image of Naji on his own phone. 'This boy was here earlier – did you talk to him?'

The attendant was wary and said he wasn't sure that he had seen the boy. There were a lot of migrants who thought they could walk the length of the highway. There were many such boys and they were all trouble, he said.

'Zoran,' said Samson, reading the nametag, 'we know you allowed him to use your phone – the number I just rang – to send a text message at 7.45 a.m. this morning. It's extremely important that we find him, for his own safety and the security of many others.' He pushed a fifty-euro note towards him.

The man still looked doubtful, and wanted to know who they were.

'We are trying to save this boy's life,' said Samson. 'That's all you need to know. We mean no harm to you.' He paused and his eyes drifted to the people who could be seen on the CCTV monitors filling their cars. 'We know that you were kind to him. You let him use your phone because his own phone was stolen yesterday. The kindness of strangers means a lot today. Was he on his own? How did he get here?'

Then the story came out of how Naji had fallen asleep and his friends had taken a ride with a smuggler, only to be involved in a deadly accident overnight. Some of his friends were in all probability dead. Vuk said he had heard something about it on the news. It was a terrible business.

'Well, they all left here yesterday afternoon, pleased that they were going all the way to Austria in the truck,' said

Zoran. 'The police are coming tomorrow to interview me because they know the smuggler stopped here regularly. But what can I do? How could I know that the bastard would drive over the edge of the highway and kill sixteen people? What do you say to the migrants? How do you warn them that the smugglers are ruthless, bad people?'

'You mustn't blame yourself,' said Samson. 'They're desperate – they'll do anything.'

Zoran nodded.

'You have CCTV film of the smuggler?' Samson asked casually.

'Sure, the police will see it tomorrow.'

'So what happened to the boy?' Samson asked.

'He was playing his pipe out there and then he just vanished.' He clapped his hands. 'One moment he was there; next he was gone. I don't know what happened to him.'

'Did he take a ride with someone?'

'I didn't see. It was our busy time and there were a lot of vehicles filling up and there were people in here watching the crash footage on TV. They wanted to know what happened. After all, they were travelling on the same highway.' He paused to take a payment from a customer. 'The boy created a little interest with his music. It was nice. He has some talent.'

Samson nodded. 'Yes, the kid's quite special.'

'But maybe he stole some things from me – chocolate bars. I noticed some missing.'

'I'm sorry about that. Maybe we can compensate you.' He put another twenty-euro note on the counter. 'So you allowed him to use your phone to send a text at seven forty-five. When did you notice that he was gone?'

He frowned and sat back to think. 'I watched the seven thirty bulletin, which was when we saw the crash. He was playing his music for about an hour after that, so he had gone by nine at the latest.'

'That's very helpful – thank you. There may be something from the CCTV cameras outside that would be useful to us. I'd very much like to look for the relevant period.'

He started shaking his head before Samson had finished speaking. 'I can't do that – the company has a policy. Even the police have to get permission.'

'Yes, but whereas the police are investigating a road accident that's already happened, I and my friend here are trying to prevent many more deaths in the future, and the boy that you were so kind to is the key to the investigation.'

'Who are you?'

'I'm sorry – I should have told you. I'm Paul Samson and this is my associate Vuk Divjak, who is well connected in your country. And out there on the trail bike is our colleague Aco, but I don't think you want to meet him because he a psychopath.'

'Yes, but what is your job? Who are you with?'

'I find missing people. In this case I'm helping organisations that are trying to prevent terrorist attacks.'

Zoran dragged his hands through his hair and peered over his round glasses. 'And this boy who spent the night in the toilets is important?'

'We think so, yes. He's also likely to be killed if we don't get to him soon.'

The man absorbed this information while he dealt with another customer. Samson looked around and saw that Zoran had a biography of John Lennon beside him. He wondered what it must be like for an educated, decent person like Zoran to spend his life selling fuel and filling the coffee machine. He had warmed to him.

'Look, I know we're taking up your time,' he continued, 'but I wouldn't ask unless I thought this was vital. I really do need to look at the footage.'

'If this is so important, why is Macedonia's intelligence service not involved?' Zoran asked.

'Just three hours ago I was dealing with the Macedonian authorities about another individual. We are cooperating with your people but this just cannot wait, I'm afraid. I wonder if this would make any difference.' He took five fifty-euro notes from his wallet and put them on the counter, bringing the total offered to Zoran to €320.

Zoran considered the fold of notes for a few seconds then swept them up, placed them in his shirt pocket and led Samson and Vuk into the back office. 'I go off in an hour. You need to work fast,' he said, closing the door behind him.

It was a digital system with an eight-channel recorder and a split-screen monitor. Most of the cameras faced the pumps to record the car registration numbers of the customers. But one was angled along the front of the building, another covered the entrance to the washrooms and toilets at the side and a third watched the parking area.

They guessed rightly that Naji would be found on the camera that was trained on the front of the building, and quickly located him at eight twenty-two that morning, moving from the entrance to the northerly end of the building, where he could be seen playing the flute. Samson smiled, partly because he had found him so quickly, but also because there was something about the boy's irrepressible spirit that he admired. By then, Naji would have known that his companions might very well be dead, but he'd picked himself up and started busking in the unpromising circumstances of the motorway service area in the early morning. It was undoubtedly him, but he was thinner and tanned from the sun, although his forehead was paler where it had been protected by the peak of his cap.

At first he attracted no attention whatsoever from the few customers at the station, but presently one or two began to stop and nod their heads and occasionally drop money into his cap. They fast-forwarded and saw a man in sunglasses paying close attention. It was clear that Naji didn't like him, because he was refusing to acknowledge him, even though for some minutes he was the only person listening to his playing. The man went into the café, returned with a couple of cans then passed out of view. Samson made a note of the time – 08.35 – and flipped to a recording of the car park for the same period.

'Look, he's watching him,' said Samson, pointing to the man standing by a dark blue Opel Zafira.

'This guy, he likes fuck the boys,' said Vuk.

'Maybe,' said Samson.

They watched the man for a while, then Vuk pointed to the small section of the screen that still showed Naji. Samson clicked to enlarge. Naji had stopped playing and was staring in front of him. The time was 09.12.

'What's he seen?' murmured Samson.

They searched the feeds from the other cameras. Beyond the petrol pumps, the bottom half of a metallic grey pickup was visible. It has just pulled up and the exhaust pipe was smoking badly. An arm hung out of the passenger window and a hand patted the door. A man in navy sweatpants jumped down from the back – a tall, lean individual who was wearing a cap beneath a hoodie. He strode under the cameras that were covering the pumps, then was seen coming from the left in the shot of the front of the building which featured Naji.

He approached Naji and took hold of him. Samson and Vuk watched him marching Naji towards the pickup, then Naji breaking free and running back, not to the building entrance as they expected, but to some gas canisters, where he picked up a stick. The man stopped and whipped round. He seemed to want to go after Naji, but hesitated and decided to return to the pickup.

Over the next five minutes, flipping from camera to camera, they pieced together the order of events around 09.14 that morning: the attempt by the pickup – a Nissan – to snatch Naji; the interception by the dark blue Opel; and the beginning of the pursuit up the highway. The footage supplied much vital information. Samson froze the shot of Naji's would-be kidnapper as he lifted his cap, and got a very clear image of his face, which he photographed with his phone and immediately sent to London. He also sent a more blurred picture of this individual and another man in the back of the pickup, captured as it circled the pumps before driving away. One of the men was wearing a bandage, so identification might be difficult. He grabbed a good image of the man in the Opel and photographed the registration plates of the two cars. The Opel Zafira hatchback had a two-letter area code – DE. Vuk told him that meant it came from Delčevo, a small town in the eastern part of Macedonia, close to Bulgaria. Vuk thought he could get the details of the Opel's owner quickly, but the Nissan had a Bosnian plate and that would take a day or two.

The significance of the vehicle from Bosnia, whence increasing number of jihadist recruits were coming, did not escape Samson. He sent the registration number to London, to be forwarded to the British embassy in Sarajevo, which could establish whether the plates were fake or genuine – and track down the owner if they were the latter. Normally he would have made arrangements to copy sections of the film, but he didn't want to alert the manager of the service area to what precisely was on his system, particularly as the police were due the next day. Besides, he had all that he needed.

They left the back office with plenty of time to spare.

The manager of the service station looked up from the cash register: 'Got what you wanted?' he asked.

'Yes, you've been a great help,' said Samson, holding out his hand. 'We're grateful to you. And can I just say it was good of you to let him rest in the toilets last night? I have an interest in the boy's survival – I meant what I said about your kindness.'

Zoran blushed and said it was nothing

When he got outside, Vuk was already talking to his contacts in the police about the owner of the Opel. Samson moved away from the pumps and rang London to bring the Office up to date.

Chris Okiri answered. 'This is really good – marvellous stuff. You bagged three of the bastards in one day.'

'It's just a photograph, Chris.'

'Yeah, but a photograph that matches some images from Athens – this guy was a few feet behind Naji in the railway station. The quality of the pictures from Athens is not good, but it's definitely the same man. And now we're examining the other men around him, trying for matches in imagery from camps in Lesbos and Turkey. Really, this is fantastic.'

'No one has any clue about his ID?'

'No, but we're searching all the databases. In a couple of hours we'll be showing the photograph to the people who have been in that particular part of the world. We should get something out of them.'

'He's not the machete man,' said Samson. 'He wouldn't have risked showing his face like that. But I get the feeling he was in the car. So we need to find that pickup damned fast.'

'Believe me – we're working on it. By the way, how the hell did they know the boy was going to be there?'

'They didn't – it was pure chance.'

'And he left with this other man – the bloke in the Opel?'

'Yes, that may be a problem,' said Samson, looking over to Vuk, who was gesticulating angrily into the phone. 'We're looking into that now. We'll be going east later.'

'You may have to delay that. The boss is flying in. He's expecting you in the capital. And our friend in Turkey will be there, too. She's got a hell of a story to tell.'

'I'll be in the east, as I said.'

'This stuff has to be face to face – you know that. You can delay for a few hours, surely?'

Samson was silent. He was familiar with the discreet signals his former colleagues gave out, the gentle steers and nudges towards a particular course of action. It was like the dance performed by honeybees to communicate a message. They wouldn't say it, of course, but the boy was no longer important to them.

'What's going on, Chris?'

'Nothing. Everyone's absolutely thrilled with your brilliant work today. The man you brought in this morning is really valuable – we're sure of that. He knows a lot about what's happening in Libya, too. And this photograph you just sent is a breakthrough. We're going to be building on that through the night. Believe me – you've done a wonderful job. Look, go and hear what they have to say. I'll send the details.'

'But you're giving up on the boy?'

'No, of course not! We're committed to Firefly. That's why you're on the job.'

Samson shook his head as he listened, surprised that Okiri thought he'd fall for such obvious bullshit. 'Thanks,' he said. 'When is our friend going to arrive from Turkey?'

'Last flight from Sofia tonight. So, you'll be in the capital. What shall I tell the boss?'

'I'm not sure what *you* should say to *your* boss. But I'll be there if I can make it back from the east.'

'I'll tell him you'll be there.'

'He's got my number, if he wants to check in,' said Samson, and hung up. He went over to Vuk, who apparently had no anxiety about smoking in the petrol station. 'Any luck?' he asked him.

Vuk shook his head. 'Maybe police bastard.'

'You're saying they're not giving out registration details for police officers, is that right?

'Yes, this is what I am saying. New vehicle so he maybe police bastard.'

'So the boy was picked up by an off-duty cop – that's really not good news for several reasons.'

'Why?'

'For a start, a policeman who has a taste for little boys is going to think he can get away with more. He'll take bigger risks.'

'He maybe in the government also,' said Vuk.

'The same applies.' Samson looked around. 'Where's Aco?'

'Hunting jihadis.'

Samson immediately understood he'd been redeployed at London's behest. 'And Lupcho and Simeon, too?'

Vuk confirmed this with a regretful nod.

'So, we no longer give a shit about the boy. Just one of the many kids that disappear on the road, is that it?' He almost said it to himself.

'I give shit for Naji.' Vuk put his elbows close together and let his hands fall open like an aggrieved Italian. 'I give many shits, mister.'

Samson had some time on his hands without the address to visit in Delčevo. He drove with Vuk to Skopje airport – also, to the fury of the Greeks, named after Alexander the Great. There, they rented a car from a pathetically grateful young man who represented one of the smaller car hire companies – in Samson's view, the bigger ones had all given up trying long ago – and loitered in the almost deserted airport, waiting for Sonia Fell's delayed flight. He received a couple of oblique texts from Nyman, who was already at the British embassy, but ignored them. He knew exactly the game Nyman was playing. This all reminded him of the enormous amount of communication that occurred in the Office, designed to give out various discreet signals but saying absolutely nothing. He didn't miss that institution-alised waste of time, or the furious search for meaning in emails between colleagues. In fact, he didn't miss much about SIS – certainly not characters like Nyman, nor, now he came to think of it, Sonia Fell, who for a brief moment he had been attracted to. They'd had a mild flirtation that lasted a few dinners and an outing to the theatre, but went no further because Fell insisted on examining him on past love affairs, of which there were quite a few, and talking about work and her ambition. And, it went without saying that she disapproved of his passion for horseracing, which was more or less a deal breaker for Samson.

He tried to persuade her that making a large bet could be a thoroughly rational business – indeed, like investing in a promising stock – and that there was no element of addiction to his behaviour because he did not get a kick out of the risk, or possess some deep-seated need to lose. He explained that since he was a student at Oxford, he had successfully made money by being careful and very, very disciplined. He even showed the little book where he kept the record of all the bets he'd made since he was nineteen, and pointed out that in some years he had not gambled, but she was unimpressed and also rather shocked by the amounts risked in the most recent punts. In her mind, the gambling was not only a weakness in itself, but indicative of, or at least allied to, what she thought was his sexual incontinence – her expression, not his.

His mind moved to the prospects of Dark Narcissus, a four-year-old mare with one good win to her name, in the last big flat race of the season at Ascot. Lightly raced, she was a sharp little racehorse and he particularly liked the way she'd rounded a bend with such purpose in a race of one mile and one furlong at Sandown. But it hadn't been the jockey's

finest hour: he took the wrong line in the final three furlongs and got boxed in, with the result that Dark Narcissus
was sixth. What attracted Samson to the bet was that she
wasn't given credit for the way she ran the race until that
moment, and no one seemed to notice that the jockey eased
back once he knew he'd screwed up. At 16–1 she was a good
price. The favourite, a horse called Snow Hat, was at 4–1.

While a morose man worked a floor polisher around him,
he did some calculations, which involved betting on both
horses at different times. The first bet would be on Snow Hat
and he'd make it with Jay Judah, a bookie from whom he had
taken a lot of money in the previous year. The moment he
placed the bet the price would come in: £5,000 on the nose
should do the trick. Judah would gab away about Samson's
interest in Snow Hat and start a minor fashion for the horse.
That would probably mean the prices on the less fancied
horses would go out, particularly as it was a big field. He
could see Dark Narcissus drift to 20–1 or even 25–1.

He made the bet online through his account and wasn't
surprised five minutes later to receive a call from Judah,
whom he knew kept a wary eye on the market at all hours
of the day. 'This is unusual for you,' said Judah after some
stiff pleasantries. 'What do you know about the animal?'

'Not a lot, but it seems to have improved over the season.
I just like the way it competes.'

There was silence from Judah for a few seconds. 'Bollocks,' he said. 'Bloody bollocks. You know something.
What do you know?'

'Really, I know nothing about Snow Hat. Just a feeling – that's all.'

'You don't do feelings, Samson. You're a fucking shark. I'm laying most of this off.'

Samson now had a good banker bet on Snow Hat that would produce a large profit if it won and cover much of his stake on Dark Narcissus. Now he'd wait and watch the price move out on Dark Narcissus.

Sonia Fell arrived at just before ten and was surprised to see him. 'They didn't say you were picking me up,' she said.

'They didn't know. I wanted to talk to you about Naji before . . .'

'I talk to Nyman?'

'I have a feeling they've lost interest in Firefly.'

Fell was too good a politician to comment on that. 'What do you want to know?'

'Everything you can tell me about him.'

She thought about this and he realised that she was working out what she could and couldn't share.

'I'll give you an outline. Have you eaten?'

'A sort of mutant sandwich-wrap, which I got over there,' he said pointing to the last remaining outlet open. 'From your time in the Balkans, you must know a good restaurant where we can talk?'

They slid into a corner table at a self-consciously folksy restaurant called The Eagle, where the waiting staff wore traditional Macedonian costume and shouted over the music of an accordion and a guitar. Fell ordered a martini and he a beer. She caught him eyeing the waitress and grinned at him. 'You haven't changed, have you?'

'Just wondering if she heard me right,' he said good-naturedly. 'But, yes, she is pretty.' He paused and engaged Fell's smile, but said nothing. She still had something for him, a kind of prim sexiness that had become more pronounced as her ambition increased.

She seemed to know what was in his mind. 'You had your chance,' she said.

'Did I? I was unaware of that.'

She looked away. 'But we were unsuited, Paul – that's the truth, isn't it?'

He followed her gaze across the restaurant. He had never seriously considered making a play for her, but evidently she had expected it, which was maybe why she could be so damned chilly on occasions. 'You probably right – but you know you're one hell of an attractive woman, Sonia.'

She studied his face for signs of insincerity. The drinks came and he raised his glass to her. 'I mean it – you're looking terrific these days.'

She accepted this with a nod.

'So, Naji . . .' he started.

'Before I talk about him, just tell me what went on today.'

Samson gave her ten minutes on the events on the railway line and at the service station and ended with his attempt to track the driver of the Opel through Vuk's contacts.

'You think he's going to be one of these children who just vanish?' she asked.

'I pray not. Nyman has redeployed Vuk's boys, so it's going to be doubly hard to track him down, but if we can get the details of that police officer we stand a chance. So, Naji . . .'

'Full name Naji Touma. Father – Faris Touma, a teacher; mother – Nada, sometime civil servant. His father's family came from the countryside, near Hajar Saqat. Her people are city dwellers – storekeepers of one sort or another, and quite well off. She had some money of her own from her father, who owned a dozen minimarts in the north of the country. Faris had very little money. They met and fell in love at university. They have three daughters and Naji, whose fourteenth birthday is in a few weeks' time. He's the second child. Faris was also a writer . . .'

'Was?'

'Yes, he died. The boy never accepted it, but he was present at the death.'

'He didn't tell that to the psychologist in Lesbos. He was quite specific that his family all came out to Turkey together.'

'They did, but his father died from a stroke in the camp.' She stopped to order for them both. 'Faris was a teacher of literature and English studies in quite a big town near Raqqa,' she continued, when the waitress had scooped up the menus and left. 'When the uprising against Bashar al-Assad began in 2011, he took no part. He was a peaceful man, according to his wife

– basically apolitical and not particularly religious either. Early in the revolution he went in search of two sixteen-year-old students who had gone missing from his class. The relatives of the boys had appealed to him as a man of standing in the local community and asked if he would make inquires with the authorities about the boys on their behalf. He went several times to the local police headquarters. I'm not sure which town this was, but she implied that he made a considerable journey each time. He wouldn't give up and eventually the government security people took him into custody and tortured him very badly. At some stage he received a blow to the back of his head and lost some of his sight. Once she knew where he was, his wife expected never to see him again, but after four months he was dumped by the roadside in a shocking state – fractured limbs, missing teeth, lacerations and that sort of thing – and he was brought home to his family. He recovered much of his sight, but he was a broken man. He couldn't work and was in a state of nervous collapse, from which he never properly recovered. Nada had lost her job, so they went back to his village where they could receive help from their extended family and tribal connections. Naji, who had been in the same school as the two missing boys and was taught by his father, took it upon himself, on his father's arrest, to become the man of the family, and did a lot to keep food on the table. He made a fruit stall, fixed people's computers and phones, ran errands – that kind of thing.'

Samson shook his head. 'So they were in the village when IS appeared?'

'Yes, and at first the fighters were welcomed in this village and were given billets and as much food as they could eat. They were all Sunni people in the village, and Naji's family had been victimised by the Alawites, so they believed that IS would be their protectors. They had no idea that IS would turn out to be as brutal as the government torturers. Nada's time was taken up with looking after her husband and her daughters. She didn't see what was going on around her, or, in the first weeks, notice anything different about Naji, who was spending a lot of time out of the home. She's now certain he witnessed terrible things; maybe he even participated in them, though she's not sure. She began to notice changes in him, but he provided food and money and they were just so grateful that she ignored it. That's something she regrets.

'As we know, he's an exceptionally smart kid. She told me he breezed through every class at school and it became almost impossible to teach him because he already knew it all. IS spotted this potential. She thinks now that they were training him up to be a suicide bomber, but they recognised his gifts and decided that one day he would be an asset to the caliphate. These people think they're going to be around for a thousand years, so they'll need brains like Naji's. The upshot was that Naji achieved the position of a privileged young disciple, which benefitted his family in all sorts of material ways.'

'So his sponsor was Al-munajil?'

'Looks like it. He seems to have swallowed all their bullshit and was apparently dedicated to the cause. This wasn't an act – he really was buying into it. This went on for almost fifteen months, but then Naji heard that his eldest sister was being lined up as a bride for Al-munajil and he started plotting their escape to Turkey. This was all entirely Naji's doing apparently, but his father went along with it. Naji handed over the money to the smugglers and arranged for the family to be transported separately to the border and led them across at night. This was in the summer. The father died a few months later from a stroke that was probably caused by the same blow that damaged his sight.'

'When did Al-munajil appear in the camp?'

'She doesn't know exactly because she never saw him. But she thinks it could have been about the time Faris died, because Naji was very tense and secretive. This was when Naji and the father were planning Naji's journey into Europe. Faris blessed the trip and sanctioned spending a lot of the family's resources because Naji had managed the escape from Syria so well. He persuaded his father that he could get to Germany in a matter of weeks. The psychologist talked a lot about his reality distortion – making up his own version of reality for his needs. She mentioned Steve Jobs, who was half Syrian, in this context. She says Naji has equal powers of self-delusion, although she called it self-indoctrination.'

'What about the relative in Germany?' Samson asked. 'Where's Naji going?'

'He made it all up. He told a lot of lies to the psychologist – there was never anyone. He has no particular destination, which is even braver, when you think about it.' She stopped as the waiters set down several wooden bowls and two skillets loaded with cabbage rolls, beans, sliced sausage, pastry filled with cheese and an earthenware dish containing *turli tava*, made out of peppers, potatoes, rice, onions and minced meat. Samson investigated the dishes, thinking of his mother's love of food.

'We need to concentrate on this,' Sonia said, and they were silent while they helped themselves.

'How soon after Faris died did Naji leave?' he asked eventually.

'The poor woman can't remember – she's still devastated. It's just a few weeks since he died. We have to remember Faris was only thirty-eight. She expected a long life with him.'

'I thought of him as being well into middle age,' said Samson.

'They married young after university.'

Samson looked across the restaurant and reminded himself to talk to Anastasia as soon as possible and get her unfiltered opinion. He briefly wished he was sitting with her rather than Fell, but pushed the thought away. 'Does Anastasia think Naji understands that his father is dead?'

'In a way, he has because he has taken on responsibility for looking after his family – that can't be doubted. But she believes he hasn't absorbed it emotionally – that he's still doing this for his father. He may in some strange way think that if he gets to Germany his father will still be alive.'

'So he fled the reality of his father's death?'

'Possibly.'

'I'm trying to work out whether that triggered his departure, or if it was seeing Al-munajil and his associates in the
camp.'

'Does it matter?'

'It may do,' he said,

She gave him a sideways look. 'What are you thinking?'

'If he left Turkey to escape the reality of his father's death,
he may not know as much or have brought out as much
intelligence as we originally thought. It's a different matter
if he went because he was fleeing Al-munajil – if seeing
those men he knew in Syria was the trigger.' He looked
at her hard and took up his glass, wearily resigned to the
realisation that his former colleagues were acting in what
they regarded as a hard-headed way, but which in fact was
rather stupid. The boy was everything in this investigation
– the IS team was clearly interested only in finding him –
and yet MI6 was now shifting the focus from the quarry to
the pursuers. 'I assume he's now focused on the three men,'
he said.

'You'll have to ask him that yourself.'

'Oh, come on, Sonia. It's plain that's what's going on.'

She raised her eyebrows. 'If you say so.'

'What about the rest of Naji's family?'

'The three girls are lovely – the older one, Munira, is a
true beauty. She's nearly sixteen. I can understand why he
wanted to protect her from IS. She and Naji are very close.
She looks like him and is extremely bright, with near perfect

English. Their father taught them all from an early age. He read them Robert Louis Stevenson and H. G. Wells, would you believe?'

'Did you talk to Munira properly?'

'No – the mother did all the talking for the family, though Munira translated. Then Nyman called to bring me to this meeting, so I couldn't stay and get Munira on her own. We could surely use her to get to Naji.'

'If Naji had a phone she could call him. Does she know anything?'

'Yes, there were moments when I could see that she knew a lot more than her mother.'

'Like what Naji saw in Syria and maybe what he saw and heard in the camp?'

'Perhaps. It's clear that his mother is finding it very hard without Naji as well as her husband. She kept on bursting into tears. I felt for her. Munira was on the point of saying something but I don't think she wanted to upset her.'

'When are you going back?'

'After the meeting tomorrow – there's a lot more to do.'

'What the hell is Nyman doing pulling you out so quickly?' he said suddenly.

'Paul, you know I can't tell you. You're the hired gun and outside the loop.'

'Thanks.'

'This is Office stuff. See what he says. We're meeting at 7 a.m. at the embassy. Everyone will be there.'

'Who's everyone?'

'You'll see.'

He dropped her at the embassy – a functional but not unattractive building beside a park – and found a hotel for himself near the Vardar River. It was late but still warm. He went out to the promenade along the riverbank and ordered another beer at a bar with tables of smokers outside. In front of him were two huge galleon ships that housed restaurants and bars, and which were fixed into the riverbed with all too visible metal struts. Skopje tried hard to look like a capital, but the state buildings were too white and neoclassical and there were too many supersized statues of heroes, including the disputed Alexander. The galleons made it look like a stretch of Las Vegas.

He messaged Anastasia: *Need your advice on your client if I find him.*

Am at dinner with my boss, came the instant reply. *Can't talk. Tomorrow any good? How are YOU? A.*

Great. Can we make it early – like 6.30 a.m.? he replied.

Sleep well. Xx, she wrote.

Samson considered looking at Naji's phone. He'd bought a charger for it at the airport and it now had full battery. The password had been remotely disabled by London after he had found the phone in Al Kufra's pocket. He assumed they'd been looking through it all day, but it was odd that O'Neill had not been in touch to find out when he was going to hand it over. Samson was not technically capable of dealing with any encryption that might be on it, but he scrolled through the photographs, stopping at the few shots of Naji's family, all of them caught unawares in the last few months. He wondered if he had taken them knowing that he was about to go on the road. But much of it meant nothing to him, for Naji appeared to have different ideas to most about what made an interesting photograph. There were shots of machines, many diagrams and some geometric schemes like the one he had drawn for Anastasia in the camp, which all attested to his scientific bent.

At midnight, Samson received a call from Vuk. It took a little time to understand what he was saying because Vuk's English was more haphazard late at night, but the substance was that he had seen an item on the local news bulletin about an off-duty police officer who had been found by two women on a country road, suffering from blood loss after being stabbed by a migrant. One of the women happened to be a nurse at the hospital fifteen kilometres away and she was able to stem the blood coming from the single wound. He later told his colleagues that he had given a ride to a youth, not a boy, who had demanded money, attacked him and stolen his car – a blue Opel. At the end of the report there was a picture of the victim in his uniform. Vuk was certain that this was the same man they'd seen on the service station CCTV footage. They had all the information they needed, so it was now just a question of finding him.

Samson paid and got up, noticing the twitch of interest in a man a few tables away. He had felt there might be watchers at the restaurant. With British spies flying into the capital, it wasn't surprising that the locals were showing interest. He would be careful what he said on the phone in the room.

The next day, he woke at dawn and drew the curtains to see the vast Russian-owned power station belching a vertical plume of steam into a murky sky. He eventually managed to make a mug of instant coffee, having sprayed the contents of one sachet across the room and squashed two of the little milk pots while trying to open them. He took his mug to the stairwell and phoned Anastasia.

Before she said anything, he told her, 'Perhaps better not to use names.'

'Okay,' she said brightly. 'So, how are you? Is it all going well?'

'Yes, but I'm concerned about your *nephew*. Maybe he did not accept the death of his father. I believe he thinks that he is still alive, even though he was there when he died.'

'That's going to be a problem. Have you found him?'

'No, but I'm not far behind him. I'm trying to work out how to handle him when I do and whether there's a way to predict his behaviour. The one thing I have learned is that this boy is a born survivor, and tough with it. He has escaped death and capture and he just keeps going. What he's going through is very rough for an undersized kid of not even fourteen. Is his stamina likely to hold out? Will he crack? Will he press on until he meets an obstacle that he just can't get round?'

'No way to tell, I'm afraid. But you saw his persistence in

escaping the camp. And to survive the sinking of the raft, to hold on with that baby in his arms, took a lot of courage.'

'I don't believe he told you anything like the full story of what he's witnessed in the last couple of years, or how closely he's been involved with some very bad people. He has had to make some serious calculations and compromises to get his family out, which most adults would find too hard. Does this surprise you?'

'No, a lot of these children get used to taking life-and-death decisions. Young people are resilient and more adaptable, yet he has a bigger load than any I've met. And the failure to accept his father's death, well . . .' She fell silent.

'When I find him, I wonder if you could take a couple of days off and help me? He trusts you. We need him to tell us everything he knows as soon as possible, but I don't want to push him.'

'I've worked here for a straight ten months without a day off so I have a ton of holiday owed to me. Say the word and I'll come.'

'That means a lot. Thanks. I'll cover the costs.'

'Not an issue,' she replied.

He looked out on the power station and was reminded of the city in Germany they once thought Naji might have been aiming for. 'You remember I questioned you about something in your email, when we thought that you had started to spell out a German city but failed to?'

'Yes.'

'Don't say the name now. I just wonder where you got

that name. Do you think it might have come up in a talk with your nephew?'

'Yes, but I can't remember in what context – that's why I probably did not complete the sentence. I maybe thought he was going there because of the relative he spoke about.'

'That was all made up. There's no one in Germany.'

'Really! He was so convincing.'

'But the name of the city definitely came from him.'

'I am pretty sure, yes.'

'So, I wonder why he had it in his mind. I mean it's not the first place you'd think of in Germany, if you were spinning a story.'

'Who knows – is it important?'

'Probably not. But I'll tell you when we meet.'

'If you find him.'

'I will.'

'Ah, here cometh the hero of the hour,' exclaimed Nyman with unusual bonhomie. 'Welcome, welcome, Mr Samson.'

Nyman had less natural cheer than a pebble. As well as embarrassing Samson a little, this effusiveness put him on the alert. He nodded, sat down and looked around the seven faces. Apart from Nyman, he only recognised Fell. 'Apologies for my lateness,' he said. 'I had an important call to make and then it took longer than I expected to get out here.'

'Don't worry,' said Nyman. He made the introductions – to Hans Spannagel from Germany's BND, Louis Fremon and Anna Houlette, respectively of the French foreign and domestic intelligence services, the DGSE and DGSI; Giles Rogerson from MI5 and Nik Verhoeven of Belgian State Security Service, the VSSE. They nodded in turn and at the end of the roll call Fell gave him a conspiratorial wink that Samson didn't trust.

'Owing to Mr Samson's efforts, ladies and gentlemen,' said Nyman, 'we are now in a position to know that a three-man active service unit is travelling through the Balkans at this moment. We believe that these men are headed for Bosnia but that they have yet to cross the border with Serbia. Bosnia is the staging post on their way to central Europe. We anticipate that they will rest and recuperate there before making the onward journey. We know their identities and we have images of two of them. We expect to have a photo of their leader – Al-munajil – very soon. This is all entirely due to Mr Samson's efforts in tracking the boy Naji Touma, whom we sometimes refer to as Firefly. We owe him our thanks.'

There were nods of appreciation around the table, but Samson knew this was the big brush-off. 'I haven't traced Firefly yet,' he protested.

'Quite so,' said Nyman, anxious to move on. He raised a hand to cue Fell, who went to work on her keyboard. Two images of the same man were projected onto the wall, one of which was the still made by Samson from the highway service area CCTV. The second showed him in a turban, standing over a cowering figure in an orange jumpsuit. His long, gaunt face was much clearer. Samson thought that if the face in this photograph were isolated, ninety per cent of people would certainly recognise the gaze of a killer.

'This is Ibrahim al Almania – a name that admits his German association. He is variously known as Rafi Abu Saif al Almania and Abu Alamia, which we guess is a kind of joke that broadly means Father of Pain. We believe his original name to be Ibrahim Anzawi. He was born in Iraq and fled Saddam's persecutions with his family in the 1990s and went to Sweden. He has lived and worked in Germany, and is a fluent German speaker. He's thought to be Al-munajil's right-hand man and to have taken part in mass executions in Iraq and Syria. He's thirty-five years old, has been a part of IS since the early days and is a thoroughly evil individual.

'We were able to identify him after collecting imagery from Athens railway station, Turkey and Lesbos. He registered under the name of Zaman, having provided a passport in that name, and his photograph was taken for the registration papers.' He nodded to Fell, who brought up the picture taken in a Turkish refugee camp, together with that of another man standing against the same background. 'He registered at the same time as this man – Usaim al-Mazri. They didn't bother to disguise the fact that they were travelling together.'

Two photographs of Usaim al-Mazri appeared – one from the railway station CCTV, the other a head and shoulders shot taken in Turkey for his registration papers. Usaim was stockier and looked quite a bit younger than Ibrahim. Another photograph showed him wearing a beard and turban and carrying a rocket launcher. 'In the background you can see a severed head on the fender of the Isuzu truck. That is thought to have been Usaim's work.'

'Usaim has lived in Cologne and Amsterdam. Last night, Britain's Security Service ran his photograph past some "reformed" IS fighters and he was recognised by several. He has been in Iraq for the last two to three years and took part in the early IS offensives with Ibrahim. As yet, we do not know much about his associations and network in Europe. We believe he studied as an engineer in Hamburg and that he is active on social media as "DogkillerX", but he has posted nothing in the last seven weeks.'

Samson cleared his throat. 'I'm sure this was the other man in the back of the pickup. He had a bandage.'

Nyman nodded without interest and turned from the wall to face the table. 'It's obviously only a matter of time before we have a photograph of Al-munajil. The question is whether we make an interception now, or do we wait and watch? Our people in Bosnia believe that if we delay we will learn much about the network there and its connections to Northern Europe.'

Spannagel from the German BND spoke first. 'Since these two men have connections with my country, we may assume that they are returning to Germany with a view to mounting an attack. We are strongly in favour of the earliest possible interception, but we recognise that this is your operation, so my government is prepared to consider a time limit of between three and seven days.' Verhoeven from the Belgian

State Security Service was content with that and the French wanted an assurance that there would be arrests within a week. 'Intelligence is important but we have to balance this against the risk to our citizens,' Anna Houlette said. 'No intelligence is worth the mass slaughter of innocent people.'

Nyman nodded. 'Then it's decided. We will track these men with the help of local security forces, drawing on any assistance the Americans can give us for the next seven days. But if at any stage one of our governments calls for an interdiction, then it's incumbent on us to respond as soon as it's feasible. Is that agreed? We will have complete information sharing so that each government has the ability to raise a red flag at a moment's notice.'

Samson shifted in his chair, prompting a less than friendly look from Nyman. 'Do you know where they are now?' he asked, allowing his frustration to show.

'Not at this minute, no, but we expect them to cross the border into Serbia soon, and make their way to Bosnia. We believe we know the identity of the man who's driving them.'

'What about the boy? I understood this was all about him, about the things he'd learned and witnessed in Syria while with these men. It's clear from Sonia's interview with his mother that he spent a lot of time with them. What did he learn during that period? What does he know that's so important to them? I'm just wondering if we are reading this wrong.'

'How so?' asked the BND man.

'We're making the assumption that the boy is not important to these men,' replied Samson, 'yet they have clearly followed him through Turkey, Greece and now Macedonia. Is this coincidence, or are they, as we originally suspected, a team sent to kill him?'

'Which do you think it is?' asked Louis Fremon from the DGSE.

'I believe they are pursuing Firefly and need to eliminate him before they leave the Balkans,' said Samson. 'Whether they plan attacks in Europe after that I cannot say.'

'Of course, there's no evidence for the primary motive you suggest,' said Nyman.

'It wasn't my suggestion,' said Samson. 'It's what you told me when you hired me to find him. I believe that holds true today and it's worth putting some effort into finding the boy.'

'But we have no idea where Firefly is,' said Nyman. 'You lost him yesterday and admitted he could be anywhere.'

'I'm hoping to have something to work on by the end of the morning,' he said.

'But he's not the danger,' said Fremon. 'These men are known to be killers and they are on European soil and travelling to the heart of Europe. We can't divert valuable resources to finding a boy who represents no threat whatsoever.'

'Unless you believe he is the reason they are here,' countered Samson. 'That's my bet.'

'That's exactly what it is,' said Nyman curtly, 'one of

your bets – a punt, a gamble. We have to be sensible about this. Our focus now must be these men.' He looked round the table for agreement, which came with a series of nods. 'Obviously you will all report back to your heads of service and ministers. Unless I hear to the contrary, we will assume that we have a week to observe these individuals and then we'll decide what action to recommend to our governments.'

Samson's personal phone began to vibrate. He looked down and saw a familiar number. It would be a good excuse to leave. 'Sorry, I must take this,' he said, getting up.

In the corridor, he answered. 'Mother, how are you?'

'Where are you?' asked his mother accusingly. 'You're abroad – there was a strange type of ringing. Why didn't you tell me you were going away?'

'I did – you didn't listen,' he said, smiling into the phone. 'What's up with you? How's business?'

'I haven't called to talk to you about the restaurant. Where are you? What are you doing?'

'I'm having a very pleasant time. I've been to a Greek island and now I'm doing some walking, looking at marvellous scenery and eating very good rustic cuisine in the mountains. But Mother, I'm a little busy right now. Can we speak later?'

'You be sure to call me.'

'Of course, Mother.'

She sighed again. 'You come back soon.'

'I have to go now. It was lovely that you called. I'll see you very soon.'

'Be safe,' she said before hanging up. His mother was no fool; she had some idea of what Samson did for work, though she never went so far as to ask him directly because she didn't want to know the details.

Fell came up to him with her keen, happy-to-be-at-work smile. 'He wants to talk to you. He's just having a word with our French colleagues, but he hasn't got long. He's going to see the head of Macedonian intelligence with the ambassador. They expect it to be a difficult meeting. Then we're going to Belgrade.'

'You and Nyman?'

She hooked her hair behind her ear. 'Sure.'

'You aren't going back to Turkey?'

She shook her head.

'And you knew last night you weren't returning.'

She shrugged. 'I wasn't absolutely certain what he wanted me to do. But I was in Belgrade and I know some of the people there.'

'I get it. Nyman sent you on your little day trip to Turkey to find out about Naji. You know that the kid is exceptional – you told me yourself that the caliphate valued him for all his gifts, but then you reported back that there was no evidence that Naji knew anything that was worth our continued effort to find him. Doesn't that seem contradictory? But I guess the point is that with the picture of Ibrahim from the service station CCTV, plus the imagery from Athens, Nyman has all the evidence he needs to mount a full-scale search for the Al-munajil unit.'

'That's our job, Paul – to find the terrorists.'

'Meanwhile O'Neill had a look at Naji's phone and found nothing, and Nyman concluded that the boy could be forgotten. Is that about right?'

'I'm not saying any of this,' she said quietly. 'You just worked it out for yourself, okay?'

'Of course.' He looked down.

'You did such great job, Paul. Without you, we wouldn't know these men were in Europe.' She stopped and laid a hand on his arm. 'I'm sorry.'

He shook his head at her insincerity. 'Don't be. This is the business we're in. I'm not going to talk to Nyman. He's just going to formally cancel the contract to find Naji.'

'He wants to thank you as well.'

'No need for it. Tell him he can settle up with Macy and I'll put my expenses in the post.'

'Paul, have a word with him, please. He's fantastically grateful about Al Kufra, which they didn't mention just now. He's already singing. Everyone in there will benefit from the intelligence he provides. He wants to thank you for that too, not least because the Macedonians feel they were involved and that will help him in his meeting later.'

He stared at her. 'This is the usual bullshit, Sonia, and you know it.' He stopped and took a breath. 'The boy is still important to this investigation, whatever anyone says, but he is also a human being who needs our help, and whether we like that or not, we are stuck with that responsibility.' He turned, went a few paces, then stopped. 'If you're not going back to Turkey, you won't mind giving me the family's coordinates – numbers and details of the camp et cetera?'

Samson noted the look that entered her eye. Bureaucratic possessiveness, he supposed.

'Well, I'm not sure that I can . . .' she began.

'You wouldn't have found them without me. You owe me – Nyman owes me. You just said that.'

'Okay, I'll email you later.'

'Text me now, so I know I've got everything,' he said firmly.

With her mouth a tight line, she worked at her phone. The text arrived. Samson read it before turning to the door again. 'Thanks, Sonia, and good luck. You're going to need it,' he said bleakly.

Outside, he walked a little way before lighting a cigarette. He was angry, but also pleased that they had not the slightest control over him and that he could do what he wanted. It was colder now, and through the veil of the city's pollution he noticed the peaks to the north and west were showing much more snow. An icy breeze tugged at the dirty yellow leaves of a nearby cherry tree. Winter was coming. He would get a parka at the store next to the hotel. He took a couple of puffs and dropped the cigarette. He dialled a number. 'What've you got for me?' he asked when Vuk picked up.

He was on his second cup of coffee waiting for Vuk in the hotel lobby when he became aware of movement to his right. He looked up to see not Vuk, but the impeccably dapper figure of Denis Hisami, brother of Aysel Hisami.

'I'm sorry to spring this surprise on you, Mr Samson,' he said, peeling off his gloves.

Samson smiled and began to clamber out of the awkward, low chair.

'Please don't,' said Hisami, slipping into the chair next to him. 'The moment I heard from Mr Harp, I knew I should come. My plane landed three quarters of an hour ago. Not bad – about twelve hours door to door.'

Hisami had one of the most intelligent and calm faces Samson had ever encountered. He looked eagerly at you through small, rimless oval glasses, the sort that you might see in photographs of musicians and artists from the early twentieth century. His hands rarely moved, and he always wore the same expression of polite anticipation, as though his interlocutor was about to say something incredibly fascinating. He was dressed in a white polo shirt, a light sports jacket, tan trousers and sneakers with olive green and pale orange flashes that picked up the colours in his jacket. If you ignored the men who had arrived in the lobby with him, the only sign of the wealth that had brought him to Skopje so fast was a large gold watch on his wrist.

'That is fast,' said Samson. 'Coffee?'

'That would be very pleasant. A large espresso, if they run to that.'

Samson signalled to the receptionist, whose antennae had already picked up on Hisami, and he rushed over.

'Just so you know what's going on,' said Hisami, 'through contacts he has had here since the break-up of the former Yugoslavia, Mr Harp arranged for me to hear first-hand from the people interviewing Al Kufra and to gain from them as much knowledge of the fate of my sister as I am able.'

Samson nodded but said nothing.

'I know what you're thinking, Paul. You believe this will be a painful experience for me. That's true – it will be. Mr Harp has warned me that the pictures of my sister are extremely distressing. But I have prepared myself. I owe it to Aysel to know her in her final despair.' He stopped and looked across the wide, dreary lobby of polished marble and pot plants. 'As a family member of one of Al Kufra's victims, I am to be allowed access to this man.'

Samson was surprised that Hisami had pulled strings so quickly, but as an early investor in social media and in Apple's revival by Steve Jobs, Hisami was one of the richest men in the world. He also had Macy Harp on his side, which helped to open doors across the West.

'You may think that you have steeled yourself,' said Samson, 'but I strongly recommend that you do not see those photographs.'

'You must say that. I would say the same to you. But you should understand that I am honouring my sister in this way. I loved her very deeply, Paul. We had been through a lot together – moving to America when most of our family members were wiped out under Saddam Hussein. We were each other's witness – do you understand what I mean by that? That's why I've come. This is an act of witness to my sister's final days.' The equanimity of his manner had not changed, but his eyes betrayed profound grief, and he looked straight at Samson to show that he didn't mind him seeing it. 'You've done a remarkable thing in finding this man. I cannot thank you enough.'

'It was luck. If Al Kufra hadn't stolen the phone from the young boy I'm looking for, we'd never have caught him, and then it was only by chance that I looked on his phone and investigated the photographs.'

'Are there many?'

'Yes, several hundred. Our people have downloaded them and are in touch with Yazidi, Kurdish and Christian organisations that are working with the families of the missing.' He paused. 'I am very sorry I didn't get her out. I hope you know that.'

'I knew you were putting everything you had into it, even when we tried other avenues apart from yourself. You will, I hope, forgive me for using other people. I understood that she couldn't withstand that treatment for very long.' He looked away. 'My sister operated only in the sphere of good. I know that sounds pretentious, but it is true. There was no time for love or emotional self-indulgence, either. She devoted herself to the care of others, to the memory of our family and to our cultural heritage. No one was more Kurdish.' He smiled. 'And you know what? She was also very funny – a really fantastic mimic.'

'Yes, you told me when we first met.'

'I am sorry – I'm inclined to go on about her. She would be embarrassed and annoyed with me. You know that I'm building a medical facility at the hospital where she carried out her research? We're going to be treating an awful lot of kids there. It will be named after her.' The espresso arrived and he sipped it, studying Samson. 'I don't know much about what you're doing here, except that you're looking for this boy. Is there any help that I can give? Anything you need?'

'Nothing I can think of. We just have to find him as soon as possible.'

'You have all the resources you need, I take it? This is a government operation, right?'

Samson said nothing.

'It is fully resourced?'

'The emphasis has moved from the boy. He's not the priority he was.'

'I'm not sure that I understand what you're saying, but I surmise that you're continuing to look for the boy, if your conduct in my sister's case is anything to go by.'

'Yes,' said Samson. 'I may need to buy some help at a later stage, but there's no point until I have an idea where he is. We lost him yesterday.'

'You only have to say the word. I'd like to reward you for this breakthrough, and for all the work that I heard you did without being paid. Mr Harp told me you went into Northern Syria after we started exploring other possibilities, and that you were very nearly killed.'

'He's exaggerating quite a bit.'

'I doubt it,' he said, and gave Samson a card. 'These are all my numbers. You can always find me.'

'How long are you going to be here?'

'As long as it takes to identify the man who caused my sister's death. To that degree I'm an unreconstructed Middle Easterner, Mr Samson. I cannot turn the other cheek. I think she'd disapprove, but then I'm not as good a person as she was. She had no idea of the nature of this enemy. They were different to anything she had experienced, even in wartime, but she went because she knew her people needed her.'

'Yes,' said Samson. 'She was very brave.'

'Do you know what I feel like? A cognac. What about you?' Samson shook his head. Hisami nodded to one of his people, who went off to find the drink. 'Is there anything I can do for you – really, I'd like to help you. I won't feel happy unless you let me repay you – that's my way.'

Samson thought. 'You'll think this frivolous in the circumstances.'

'Try me.'

'I'd like you to place a bet today on a horse race next week.'

Hisami smiled. 'Really? That is an interesting request.'

'The horse stands a good chance of winning, so it's not a bad bet.'

Hisami's eyes narrowed a little.

'I'm thinking of a small amount, for you at least,' continued Samson. 'A few thousand pounds to win.'

'That's certainly possible.'

'Maybe five.'

'Five thousand pounds! Let me see – this must be a bet you don't expect me to win.'

'You could win, but I'm hoping that you don't.'

'So you favour another horse and are seeking to influence its price.'

'Yes, but I've bet on this particular horse, too. If the horse I really favour wins, I'll pay you the amount you put on your horse, which is currently favourite to win, as well as make a donation to the facility that you're building – but only if mine wins.'

Hisami smiled. 'So, there three possible outcomes for me – win, break even or lose. I'll be betting against your choice, but I stand to gain if you win – or at least Aysel's centre does. And I assume that you're not going to tell me the name of the horse in whose favour you're seeking to influence the market?'

'Correct.'

'This'll certainly be a novel experience, and I think Aysel would have approved of the idea. Yes, I think she would have liked this rather dubious scheme of yours, Paul, and I believe she would have liked you, too. So, yes, I'm in.'

'Great. There's one other thing: I want you to open an account at a particular bookmaker in London under your name and make the bet on that account.'

'Is this some sort of sting?'

'No, it's exploiting a market. The bookmaker I have in

mind has probably already laid off the bet I made, and he will do the same for yours, so he won't be exposed.'

'Very well. You'll give me the details by email?'

'Of course. It's important you do it today.'

'Fine.' He swirled the brandy glass that had just been handed to him then raised it to Samson. 'Here's to our bet. Here's to Aysel's bet.'

'Thank you.' Samson liked Denis Hisami and admired his cool and his good manners.

'It is I who owe you, Paul. I'll enjoy watching how this works.' He paused, and his expression grew serious again. 'I want to keep in touch with you about Al Kufra. You may be able to help me with one or two things. Mr Harp gave me your numbers.' He rose and winced as he downed the cognac.

'Call whenever you need,' said Samson, getting up and taking Hisami's hand. 'And good luck!'

'The same to you – it's been a pleasure.' He gave Samson a slight bow and left the lobby, his men following him.

Vuk Divjak appeared half an hour later, clutching a map marked with the exact spot where the women had found the off-duty police officer on the road, about thirty kilometres east of the highway. He'd learned that the police had been actively searching for their colleague's car over the last twenty-four hours. Although they had kept watch on the highway and all roads north to the Serbian border, there was no sign of it.

An attack on a policeman provided a considerable incentive for his fellow officers to seek out the perpetrator, but in this case Vuk sensed a strange lack of enthusiasm for the investigation. Although the officer had claimed a migrant thug had stabbed him and taken his car, it turned out that the women who went to his aid reported they'd seen a young boy driving an Opel with a smashed windscreen. There was something in the man's past that suggested to his colleagues that maybe he'd got what was coming to him, but of course they could not ignore the incident because of the publicity surrounding it. Migrants were hardly flavour of the month.

Samson left the hotel in his new parka, noticing that the surveillance detail appeared to have gone, and drove south then east. He found the place, parked the car and walked until he came across a few blood droplets on the road. He followed the trail until he reached a farm track on his right, where he found more blood and pieces of windscreen glass. He continued walking until he came to an abandoned stone farm building and saw tyre tracks on the damp soil in the shade of the building. The impressions were very clear and there was no doubt in his mind that the same car had reversed alongside the building at least three times. Whether this was on separate occasions or all on the previous day, he could not tell. He also noticed the car had been driven erratically around the sun-baked mud of the floodplain.

But this all interested him less than the building. He went inside and saw a dirt floor, a table, chair, coiled rope and some wire, an oil lamp, plastic tablecloth and various farm implements. While the place was uninhabited, it was clear that it had been organised and that someone visited regularly, for there was a tin can on the table containing butts of the same brand of cigarette, some empty wine and beer bottles and a tumbler with the dried residue of red wine. He walked round to the back of the building and noticed that a little way up the wooded bank there was freshly turned earth. Someone had tried to conceal the diggings with turf and clumps of weeds that had been moved from elsewhere. Branches had been laid across the earth and he wouldn't have noticed anything but for the angle of light slanting through the trees and illuminating the patch of ground. He looked back to the building. On the roof tiles, which could be easily reached from the bank, lay a spade and a roll of plastic sheeting. He shook his head grimly. He was beginning to get a very bad feeling about this place and, now he came to think about it, there was definitely a rotten presence in the air on the bank that was familiar to him from his trips to Syria – the smell of decomposition.

If Naji had been here, he had clearly managed to escape, but had there been others? He took a few photographs with his phone, returned to the road and sent them to Vuk. A few minutes later, he called and found him drinking in a bar, waiting for further instructions from Britain's Secret Intelligence Service.

'You know that place on the map?' said Samson. 'Close to where the policeman was picked up? I went to it and found an abandoned building that I think you should tell your friends in the police to investigate. There may be a body buried there. I've sent you photographs.'

'Body that is dead!' Vuk exclaimed.

'I'm not certain, but someone should take a look. Maybe that man who tried to abduct Naji used it regularly. Feels like there's something bad there.'

Vuk's speed of comprehension was not at its best. 'A body that is dead?'

'Yes, that's what I'm saying,' said Samson, beginning to lose patience. 'Make an anonymous tip-off, if you're worried about it. I think the man who picked up Naji maybe has a lot to hide, but I haven't got time to look into it any further.'

'Okay, boss,' he said, and abruptly hung up.

Samson drove north, investigating every turning and track and as much of the scrub as was accessible to a car. He moved very slowly through the empty countryside, with one thought in his mind. The women who had seen Naji on the road said he was driving very poorly – that's what had made them look to see who was behind the wheel. They thought it was possible that the kid had never driven before, which led Samson to think that he might not want to go very far, especially as the Opel's windscreen was smashed. Also, Naji would appreciate he stood a very good chance of being picked up if he kept the car. He had, after all, stabbed a man.

It took two hours before he came to the village on the bank of a river that meandered through heartrendingly beautiful countryside. He only noticed the heap of hay and fencing posts after he had spotted tyre marks leading from the road down to the stand of poplars. The tracks were fresh so he got out of his car and investigated. He found the Opel and looked back to the road, wondering how it had come off the bend, ploughed through the mown hayfield and come to rest at the base of one of the trees. Naji had obviously got out unhurt and covered the car with hay – quite effectively, as it happened – and continued on foot. But someone else had been there before Samson – someone in a vehicle with large, wide tyres – and that person had uncovered some of the front of the Opel so that the metallic blue paint of the bonnet and the smashed windscreen were just visible. They had also opened the driver's door, because the hay was brushed aside. Traces of the larger vehicle's three-point turn were visible in the flattened grass.

Samson opened the door and looked inside. There were no signs of blood, not even on the windscreen glass, which was everywhere. He noted that there was no phone in the holder, but a charger lead was still plugged into the cigarette lighter and there were some papers in a bulldog clip on the back seat. From these he deduced the name of the owner was Captain Ylyo Nikolaivic. He closed the door, noticing one or two scrapes in the paintwork, then circled the Opel, looking again, with a certain amount of awe, at the path it had taken once it had left the road. Naji had again escaped with his life. Not long before he crashed the stolen car, he had probably been in even greater danger and he had managed to defend himself by stabbing the predatory policeman with the knife he'd stolen from Anastasia's room. Samson had no exact theory about what had happened at the deserted stone dwelling, but the place had stayed in his thoughts for the last couple of hours. Sooner or later, this kid's luck was going to run out.

He also pondered the tracks of the vehicle that had drawn up alongside the Opel. It seemed odd to him that its occupant had taken the trouble to investigate the suspicious mound of hay and fencing posts, yet hadn't done more to uncover the car: that would be the natural reaction of the inquisitive passer-by, surely. Instead this person, or persons, had left the Opel and gone on their way.

He returned to his car and looked at the map. He reckoned that Naji was about sixteen hours' walking time ahead of him, which might be twenty kilometres or more. It was impossible to know whether he had followed the course of the river, on which lay one or two settlements, or had taken a road that veered away into the wild country, which, at some stage, he would need to cross to reach Serbia. If he had followed the road, Samson thought he might well find him by the end of the day.

ELEVEN

Ifkar was the most singular – and handsome – person of their age that Naji had ever met. He didn't seem to worry about anything: whether he had food or a place to sleep, where he was going or which country he hoped eventually to settle in. None of it seemed to matter to him. He told Naji that he had been wandering in Bulgaria and Macedonia for several months without the faintest notion where he was. He was just happy to be free and travelling with the dog he called Moon, which he told Naji he'd taken from a cruel shepherd three months before. The dog had been tied to a tree on a short rope and the shepherd was laying into her with a stick. Ifkar watched for a while, expecting the man to stop at any moment, but he kept on beating the dog, and Ifkar knew that if he didn't intervene he would kill her. He approached the shepherd and spoke to him, hoping that the man would understand that it was wrong to go on punishing the dog. The shepherd did not even lift his head, so Ifkar tapped him on the shoulder and, when the man looked up, delivered one big punch to his chin, which knocked him out cold. He untied the dog and bathed her wounds with water and gave her some food. Eventually, the shepherd began to come round. Because Ifkar didn't feel he could strike the shepherd again without killing him, he got up from the dog's side and began to walk away. And Moon limped after him.

Ifkar said he knew what was in the dog's mind because he had been in a very similar situation when he lived with an uncle who beat him for reasons that were still mysterious to him. One day he decided he would rather starve than accept these beatings and he upped and left and went in search of a new life, which turned out to be a good decision. Within a few months, his homeland had been overrun by ISIS and many thousands of his people were killed or taken as sex slaves by the men who wore black turbans and headscarves. This appalled him but, as he pointed out to Naji, if he had not suffered the terrors of those early years at his uncle's hands, he might very well have stayed in his village and ended up being slaughtered with the rest of the men. Furthermore, he had taken all his uncle's money and valuables on the night that he made his escape, and these would have ended up in the enemy's pockets. So, that, too, was evidence of the exceptional inner wisdom that occasionally spoke to him.

At the end of this speech, Naji looked Ifkar up and down and asked why someone who was as strong as he would put up with years of beating. Ifkar said he had sometimes wondered that himself, though he had to confess that he had become much stronger as he'd travelled through Turkey and Bulgaria during the last year. He'd made a point of doing exercises every day, no matter how tired and hungry he was, just to make sure that no one would ever take advantage of his peaceful nature again. He showed Naji his flexed biceps, which Naji agreed were enormous, and said that he was now working on his chest and on his thighs, which he felt were undersized.

These exchanges all took place in their first hours together as they walked along the river, chatting like old friends and stopping to peer at interesting things on the way. Ifkar had a very quick eye. The slightest movement of a tiny speckled fish in the river, or the iridescent glint of a beetle in the grass, was enough for him to drop to his knees to peer at or closely inspect whatever had caught his attention. He had time to investigate the wonders around him and follow his curiosity wherever it led because he had no particular place to go. He told Naji he was working on a plan, but that it had not advanced very far, so he was just waiting for his inner wisdom to speak to him again. Meanwhile Moon, so called because of her pale yellow coat, which was almost white now that Ikfar washed her regularly, seemed very much to share his relaxed attitude. When he stopped, she immediately sat down, glanced at his face, then followed his eyes to the thing that interested him.

About two hours after they'd met, they came to a place where the river widened and there were two shallow pools

beside the main current. Ifkar claimed he spotted the movement of a fish that was quite a bit larger than any he had seen
before. However hard he tried, Naji simply couldn't see it.
They sat down on the bank and waited. Presently the fish
showed itself by nibbling at the dozens of black flies that
struggled on the surface. Ifkar left the bank and went and
found a tree and cut some sticks, which he bunched together
at one end and tied tightly with a twisted plastic bag. When
he'd finished it looked a bit like a big fan. He told Naji to
go to the top of the pool, enter the water and wade downstream. Ifkar would approach with Moon from the side and
they'd hope to push the fish back to the gravelly shallows
where there were just a few centimetres of water. Then he
would use his scoop to flip the fish onto the bank.

Naji felt this was all extremely optimistic and he complained bitterly about the sharp stones hurting his feet and
the chilly water making his legs ache. Ifkar told him that he
was a whining Arab and he needed to shut up so that he could
put all his concentration into stalking the fish. Very slowly,
they persuaded the fish to drop back rather than make a dash
for the fast-moving current in the middle of the river. Ifkar
cornered it and eased the scoop forward in the water. The fish
had nowhere to go and started darting back and forth in panic.
Naji couldn't see what was happening, so Ifkar gave a blow-by-
blow commentary on the fish's huge size and stupidity. Finally
he got the fish exactly where he wanted and lifted the scoop,
but it immediately disintegrated with the weight of water.
The fish, however, was thrashing about in the tangle of sticks.

Moon pounced and Ifkar flung himself onto the fish. Grabbing hold of it, he struggled to his feet, shouting with the shock of the cold water. They hit the fish on the head and stared down at it in the grass, marvelling at its size. Ifkar said that it was least two kilograms, which, from Naji's experience in the fish market at home, seemed generous, but he knew it would be enough food for all three of them. They took a photograph of the fish and themselves with the fish and Moon.

Then they took their catch to higher ground because Ifkar said that the coldest air rolled down from the mountains at night and lay in the valleys. They made a shelter about a hundred and fifty metres up the wooded hillside, placed boulders in a circle and built a fire at its centre. Moments of joy on Naji's long journey were very few, but sitting there while his new friend delicately cooked the fish on a stick, was a happy time. He reflected that the day, which had started out at the service station and included three episodes of sheer terror, as well as the new experiences of driving a car and catching a fish – or at least being part of the team that landed it – had been one of the most scary, exhausting and interesting of his life.

Ifkar pronounced the fish cooked, divided it up with Naji's throwing knife – which, despite being washed in the river, may still have had a little of the policeman's blood on it – and gave the head and a lot of the back end of the fish to Moon. He opened a can of beer and they took turns with it as they ate chunks of white meat in their fingers. It felt like they had been travelling together for months.

At length, Ifkar rolled a couple of the boulders on the outside away from the fire so he could warm their sleeping bags before they got into them.

'Who gave you the red bracelet?' he asked when they were settled with two of the chocolate bars that Naji had lifted from the service station.

Naji told him about Hayat and her cousin and how they had helped him escape from the compound in Greece by giving him their clothes, then how he'd bumped into them in Athens. He said that he might have fallen in love with her but that he hadn't thought of her recently so now he wasn't sure.

Ifkar asked him about his family and where he came from and Naji began to tell his story in fits and starts. He was aware of Ifkar and Moon, who lay between them making contented whimpers, but it was as if they weren't there and he was just talking to himself.

'My mother, she didn't tell us much when my father was arrested by the government, but Munira – that's my older sister – found out from a girl in her class in her school. We didn't understand why they would take our father, because everyone knew he was a peaceful man and a good teacher. Many people were taken – the boys who protested, their parents, too – and we never saw them again. My mother told me not to go to school any more because she thought I would be arrested as well. I was young and I didn't know anything. I was just a boy then.

'I wasn't at school and we had no money and there was

little for us to eat, so I went with a friend and we took a handcart to the edge of town, where we bought fruit and vegetables, then brought them back into town and sold them for more because there were no stores open. One day my friend who helped with this business vanished. I don't know what happened to him. Maybe a bomb killed him; maybe the police . . . They tortured people, you know that? Even kids.' He stopped to put the last piece of the chocolate bar in his mouth. 'Then I got into shoes.'

'How was that?' asked Ifkar.

'I found this guy who was dead who was wearing these perfect new Nike trainers – size 44. I took them and I sold them from the handcart, and then a man asked me to sell the shoes of his dead brother because he needed money, and that is how I got into buying and selling shoes. Even in the bad times, people pay money for shoes. And women wanted fancy shoes, and they paid for them because they still had money. I sold maybe ten to fifteen pairs a week. One week I sold eighteen pairs, including a new pair of Vans SK8-Hi sneakers – you know, the canvas ones. I made a hundred and fifty Syrian pounds on that deal.'

'How much is that?'

'It was like four or five euros – that was the profit on one pair of shoes! So I gave my family money, and my mother was pleased, but she said that my father would be angry if I wasted my life selling shoes and she told me to keep studying. One day I went to the school. It was strange, because no one was there. I found my father's friend, the science teacher, and I told him that I could not come to classes because my mother was worried about me being arrested by the security forces because of my father. He had heard the same story many times, so he wasn't surprised. He gave me loads of books, but made me swear to keep them secret because he didn't want the police to know he'd helped the son of Faris Touma. This is how I continued my studies.'

'Are you clever, Naji?' asked Ifkar.

'Maybe – I don't know. I made money for my family so I guess that was pretty smart, and I felt proud about that. I didn't always make money, though. Sometimes I lost money, like when I bought a pair of sunglasses and they never sold, so I wore them myself, but they were too big and they had stars on the frames and Munira said I looked like an idiot.

'That was the day when she told me that my father was found on the road. They made it look like he'd been hit by a truck. It was four months after he was taken. My mother didn't let us see him for a long time. His arms were broken and he was bruised all over; his front teeth were knocked out and he couldn't see because they hit his head so hard at the back, and that is where your visual cortex is.' Naji stopped to control his voice. 'And they starved him. Those men from the government, they are devils. They starved my father. That's why I . . .' He stopped and fell silent.

'Why you what?'

Naji didn't answer a few seconds. 'It doesn't matter. I wanted to take revenge on those people, that's all.'

'I understand that,' said Ifkar.

'Anyway, my mother waited until night and then she took my father to the hospital, and she told them that he'd been in a traffic accident – she couldn't say he'd been in a military prison, because the doctors wouldn't have treated him. But they knew from the injuries what had happened to him because they'd seen the same wounds before. My grandfather gave her the money to pay the bribes to get my father out of prison, and then he paid for him to be treated. We were broke. When he came out of the hospital we went to live with my father's family, in a village called Hajar Saqat. There's a big Roman stone in the desert there, like part of an arch or something, but it fell down a long time ago. The village is called after the fallen stone. It's the only interesting thing that's happened there for centuries. Everyone is poor. They talk to their donkeys and sheep – that's what they do for amusement. They don't buy shoes and they have all the fruit and vegetables they need. Even though we were away from the war and didn't hear any bombs, I didn't like it. My father was very weak and we never talked like we did before, because he was sick in the head and all the time he shivered as though he was cold. It was the shock of what they did to him and what he saw them do to ordinary people who had done nothing wrong, like his two students he went looking for. They said to him, if you want to see your students, you must come with us, and he went with them and the next thing he knows he's locked up with the two boys and is being beaten and starved like them!'

'What happened to the two boys?' Ifkar asked, moving

to prod the fire with a long stick. Sparks flew into the night above them. Naji asked him to do it again and again. Eventually Ifkar prompted, 'The boys, did they live?'

'They were strangled in front of my father.' He said it very quietly, as if it were his own shame. 'My sister overheard my father tell my mother. It made them weep.'

'I am sorry for you, Naji. Sorry for your father.'

'I have to be positive,' said Naji. 'That is the only way. This was when I began to play the flute properly and I played for my father often. Then I got a new profession – I became a phone engineer. A man asked me to look at his phone to see if I could mend it. I found a site in English that tells you how to repair phones, and I made his work. Soon, I was mending maybe four phones a week, and that was because I could read the American site, and ask people all over the world for their solutions. It's pretty cool asking people on the other side of the world for help. One of the village kids wanted me to erase all the anti-government songs on his phone. A song like that was enough to get you killed, if they found it on your phone at a checkpoint. So I cleaned up his phone and hid some other stuff so no one would ever find it.' Ifkar had gone quiet and Naji sensed his interest in phones might not be great, since he didn't even own one. 'So, gradually my father became stronger and his sight began to return. I read to him in English and he liked this because he corrected my pronunciation and it made him realise that he would teach again some day. Things were getting a little better.

I bought and sold phones and it was more profitable than buying and selling shoes or tomatoes.'

'And your sisters. What did they do in the village?'

'They helped my mother. They looked after my father. Munira learned to weave with two women in the village and she became their apprentice. But she is going to university to be a lawyer. She is smart, as well as very, very beautiful.'

'Can I marry her?'

'She says she will never marry anyone: she doesn't want a man telling her what to do.'

Ifkar muttered something under his breath.

'She says all men are stupid because we invented war,' said Naji.

Ifkar poked the fire again and it flared up and the crackle reverberated around the trees. They saw an owl glide past about ten metres away. There was something about watching the flames that made Naji open up.

'Then IS came to the village,' continued Naji, 'and we hoped they would protect us from the government. They were welcomed and we gave them food and the villagers opened their homes to the fighters because they needed to rest. And some of them were injured and the village made a little hospital, which was like two rooms, where they could be treated. But then we learned what they were really like. There were many foreign fighters and they were arrogant and they treated us like we were dirt. They had their own laws. Women had to go covered; no music; no smoking; and no phones were allowed. A young woman was given sixty lashes for using her phone! They came to our house and demanded to know why my father didn't go to prayers, and my mother told them that he had been tortured by the government and he was too weak to leave his home, and they told her he must go to prayers or he would be beaten. And they executed people outside the village and everyone was forced to watch – even young people.'

Ifkar was silent. Naji thought he might be asleep, but he let out a long sigh then said, 'I'm sorry for the memories you carry in your head.'

'I don't think about them much,' said Naji.

'What happened then? How did your family get out?'

Then Naji told him about the man who came to their home because he'd heard in the village that Naji was good at mending phones. Naji didn't know then that this was Al-munajil, the one that executed people with a wide sword that resembled a machete, but he could see that the man was important, and he had a terrifying aura. Naji corrected a simple fault with the phone, though he made more of it because he wanted to impress the man, who was very stern and showed little respect to his family. Al-munajil spoke Arabic perfectly, because, as Naji later found out, he came from a city named Tikrit in Iraq, though he had spent many years in Germany. His name was Abu Wassim, but everyone called him Commander, or Al-munajil. No one knew his real name: Naji did because he later found it on one of the man's devices.

Naji's mother brought Al-munajil tea, though he never let

go of his gun and he kept speaking on the newly mended phone in a harsh voice that kept breaking, as though someone was throttling him. He showed an interest in Naji's technical ability and when he asked him what he thought of the government, Naji replied that he loathed the people who'd imprisoned his father. At this, his father, who had said nothing since the man had entered his home, muttered from where he was sitting in the breeze from the window, and Naji realised he'd said too much and immediately stopped talking. On the way out, Al-munajil put a hand on his shoulder said he might be able offer him a way of getting back at the government. 'He said a boy like me with technical knowledge could do some real damage. Then he said he wanted to get to know me better.'

'What did that mean?' asked Ifkar.

'I didn't know then, but my father spoke to me and said he could smell the man's evil. He had seen such men in the military prison where he was tortured. They were different to other men. He told me never to see Al-munajil again. But it was too late. Next day, Al-munajil's men came early and they told me to get into the back of his pickup. I was with them many days. My father and mother thought I was dead.'

'Where did you go?'

'Everywhere. Al-munajil was the commander. They drove hundreds of kilometres. He was checking on things. When Al-munajil and his men went to a house to sleep, I was left in the back of the pickup with a sheet. I didn't know why he wanted me. Then Ibrahim, who was his right-hand man, said Al-munajil was considering me for a very holy mission against the enemy. Everyone did what Al-munajil wanted – he decided things.'

'A suicide mission?'

'They didn't say that. They just told me I would avenge the crimes that were done to my father.'

'With a vest?'

'They had another idea – a vegetable cart, like the one I used in the town.'

'He knew about that?'

'Al-munajil knew everything about me. I'd told him how we made money when my father was in prison – that's how he knew about the vegetable cart. They were going to put the bomb under the vegetables in the cart and then I would detonate it with a trigger in my hand.'

'And you would kill yourself.'

'They didn't tell me that, though of course I knew. But they never said I would be killing myself, too. During those first days, he never spoke to me. The other men – Usaim and Ibrahim were the main ones – said he was testing me. Maybe I failed that test because when they showed me stuff . . . I didn't react well. Maybe they thought I wasn't strong enough, or I was too young – something like that.'

'What did they show you?'

'I can't say,' said Naji. 'People were killed . . . women, girls . . . they put them in cages. Yazidi women.'

'You were just a kid! How could they show you these things?'

There was anger in his voice, which worried Naji. 'I don't remember a lot – it made me sad. Sometimes I cried.' He had never told anyone that before.

'Anyone would,' said Ifkar. 'All the women in my uncle's village were taken. When I was in Turkey, I heard that many of them killed themselves rather than go with these men.'

'They are all evil, but Al-munajil is worse because he makes people around him become evil.'

Ifkar propped himself on one arm. 'You too?'

Naji didn't reply.

'You said they followed you,' said Ifkar. 'Why would they come all this way to kill you?'

'I took something from them. I had it all on my phone. Then a Libyan arsehole stole the phone, but he will never find anything because it's hidden too well.'

'What kind of thing is on it?'

'I copied stuff from one of Al-munajil's phones, not the one I mended, but another one he used to keep records on. He asked me to encrypt it, so I copied that material and put it somewhere.'

'On the phone?'

'Yes . . . and no. I worked on his phone and the other devices for a long time. There were a lot of alterations he wanted on the actual phone. I took the microphones out, disabled the cameras and the geolocation. He never used it for communication – never ever. He knew he could be hacked. He had lots of phones, but he never spoke on this one.'

'A kid like you can do all that?' asked Iflkar, not bothering to hide his scepticism.

'Yes, I learned a lot in the last year, because I was working for them all that time and travelling with them and I was allowed to use a laptop. I fixed a lot of phones. Al-munajil knew I would build something no one could get into. I put all the data I stole in a place they could never find.'

'He'd have killed you if he found out.'

'He did find out and that's why he's here.'

Ifkar began stroking Moon, who stretched luxuriously in the glow of the fire. 'Why did you take the risk?' he asked.

'As I told you, my sister Munira is very beautiful, and one time when they came to get me, Usaim saw her unveiled at the back of the house. A few days later Al-munajil started asking questions about her, like how old she was and whether she was obedient and a good cook. And the next week he asked more questions and said he would come to my home to see how my father was. Like he cared! I spoke of this to Munira, and she said she would rather kill herself than become Al-munajil's wife. I knew what those men did, especially Al-munajil, who was very cruel to the women. I heard what they said to each other. They thought I didn't understand, but I knew what they were talking about . . .'

'There was a place they used to go in Iraq. I didn't know exactly where it was because they never told me, but I knew we were in Iraq. It was an old building – a hospital or something – and that's where they kept their women. I was left outside, but I saw women at the windows and at night

I heard crying and sobbing and screaming and all that – and I knew this was where he would bring my sister. They hurt women when they refused to do what that they wanted. Once Al-munajil told Ibrahim how he was going to punish a woman who would not have sex with him and he would make it so that she would never refuse him again.'

'They are beasts,' said Ifkar.

'I was frightened for Munira,' continued Naji, 'so I went to my father. At first he was very angry with me. He said everything was my fault because I had brought Al-munajil into our house and it was all due to my obsession with phones. I told him I was trying to make money for the family, but he replied that the money was less important than studying and reading. This was the only time he raised his voice to me in my life – the only time, I promise you that. He was very angry and even when he calmed down I could still feel it. He told me that he no longer recognised me – that I had lost all my values. The coarseness of the company I kept showed in my behaviour. He said I was arrogant and thought too much of myself.'

'Did you explain to him that you had to go with Al-munajil?'

'I didn't say anything, because he was right. He accused me of talking about our family outside our home and revealing things that I knew were private, things that were only for him to speak of.' Naji stopped for a few moments, again feeling the pain of that day. 'He told me to go outside in the yard and to remain there until I recognised the trouble I had brought upon our family. I was there all night for I was too ashamed to face my mother and my sisters. But Munira came out to me and gave me bread and a can of pineapple juice, which she had saved because it is her favourite, and she looked at me and told me it wasn't my fault – she asked me how I could be blamed for her beauty. Even then she could make a joke of it, which tells you something about her.

'The next day, my father called me into the house and told me he was no longer angry with me. He and my mother had decided that we were going to Turkey, no matter how much it cost, and then we would find a new life in Europe. He wanted to go to England because he spoke good English. He told me to find the smugglers that would take us over the border because he knew I was in a better position than he was to make such contacts. He held my hand and gave me his forgiveness and said that the fortune of the family – all our lives – depended on me. It was the proudest moment of my life when he placed that faith in me.'

'But you were just a boy – how could you find a people smuggler?'

'I knew people. When my father was in prison I met a man who offered to take my family out. Everyone knew who he was. He went to Turkey and ran operations from Gaziantep, but he has agents in the city and they were looking for clients all the time. I had money of my own because I stole from Al-munajil. There were sacks of money, which they picked up from different places and took to a place in the city at night, and I knew they didn't count it all until it got to the city. I stole a little each time and put it in my shoes. I stole a lot in that way.'

'Why did they trust you?'

Naji was slow to answer. 'I never spoke out of turn. I spoke only if they asked me something. I did not complain. I asked for nothing, not even food. I hated Al-munajil, but I learned how to play him and I tried to please him and make him like me. I began to learn German because of him – he spoke fluently. He said I would soon be part of his family, meaning he was going to marry Munira, and I smiled to make him think that I was flattered that he was thinking about my sister. It was during those days that I copied everything from his phone and hacked computers in their buildings. Their security is shit! And I stole the most money from him then. I knew we were going soon.'

'How did he know you did that? Who told him?'

'I did.'

'You did! Why?'

'I'm really tired,' said Naji. 'I will tell you tomorrow. I must sleep now.'

'Me too,' said Ifkar.

'Thank you for the fish,' said Naji. 'And everything else, Ifkar. You are now my friend.'

'There will be more fish,' said Ifkar several seconds later. 'And I will marry your sister instead of that bastard.'

But Naji was already asleep.

TWELVE

For the remainder of that day, Samson travelled north, stopping frequently to scan the valleys with his binoculars. There was no sign of Naji. The landscape was almost totally empty and he began to question himself about the wisdom of pursuing the boy. He could not seriously argue that Naji was still out there, and he certainly couldn't be sure the boy was the terrorists' priority, as he had stated in the meeting, but the dogged side of his nature pushed him to keep going.

As it grew dark, he found a village with a supermarket in what looked like an old agricultural depot. It was a hangover from Yugoslavia's communist days, when stores offered basic supplies and did not bother to appeal to passing trade. He bought salami, bread, cheese, water, a bottle of red wine and a few chocolate bars and returned to his car. Outside, he came across four young German hikers, all of them looking like they were in training for the military. They were stocking up before moving on somewhere to pitch their tents. Samson fell into conversation with them in English, and after some chat about the route they were taking, he asked whether they had seen any migrants, particularly an Arab boy on his own. They shook their heads and said they had seen a few migrants but they were all in groups. They moved off and Samson started packing the food away in his rucksack. Then one jogged back to him.

'We should mention that we did see two young Middle Eastern guys walking up the river with a dog. They were a hundred metres below the place where we crossed about five hours ago. They were taking a picture of a fish with a phone. They had a big white dog with them.'

'Did you see what they looked like?'

The young German shook his head apologetically. 'They were too far away. We could only just see the fish, which the smaller of the two guys was holding.'

'Can you point out this place for me on the map? It's really important I find this kid before anyone else does.'

The other hikers trickled back to join their companion.

'Why do you want this boy? What are you doing?' asked one.

'This minor was abducted earlier today and escaped a serious sexual assault. You ask what I am doing: right now, it's called child protection. This boy is in serious danger, and not just from the local population of paedophiles. There are people out here who are trying to kill him for what he knows.'

They shook their heads in turn.

'What can I do to persuade you?' Samson asked. 'Maybe I could call a member of your government who knows exactly what my work is and he can vouch for me.' He pulled out his personal phone, found the number for Arnold Jager and tapped to call him. Jager was a counterterrorism expert for the BND; they'd been good colleagues on a couple of operations and had kept in touch since Samson left SIS. 'Hi, Arnie. I am in the Balkans with four of your countrymen. I am looking for someone and I need their help. Can you tell them that I'm legit?'

Arnie laughed. 'Sure, put me on speaker.'

The German boys gathered round the phone to hear Arnie at his most crisp and menacing. '*Guten Abend*, I am an officer with the Bundesnachrichtendienst. I can assure you that if my friend is asking you for your help, it concerns a security matter of the utmost importance. Please provide him with everything he needs and do anything he says. Do I make myself clear?'

One of the hikers began to mutter his doubts.

'Give me your name and address. I will phone you on your personal phone with your passport number in five minutes.'

'But you don't have my mobile number,' said the hiker.

'Exactly,' said Arnie. 'Name and address, please.'

To Samson's mild astonishment, the young man gave his name as Helmut Muller and said he lived in Munich.

'Fine,' said Jager, 'I'll speak to you in a moment.'

Samson spread the map and lit a cigarette. It took Jager exactly three minutes to make his call to Muller's phone,

at which point the others, highly amused by his embarrassment, returned to the map and lit it with two phones. They
had seen the two young migrants at a spot where the river
widened and it was possible to wade across, which is why the
Germans had made for that place. They could not tell which
way the migrants were travelling, but they suspected they
were going north, because that side of the river was an easier
route. A few kilometres above that point they would have
to make a choice between two valleys, one that went north-
east and one that went due west but then veered north. In
both valleys were roaring torrents because of a recent storm.

Samson wished them well and finished packing away his
provisions, then stood checking his messages for a few seconds. He looked up, thought for a moment, then slapped his
forehead and cursed his stupidity. He immediately dialled
Vuk's phone.

'Where are you?'

'With new girlfriend,' Vuk replied.

'Did you talk to the police about that place I mentioned –
the place where the policeman took Naji before he stabbed
him?'

'No, I do this tomorrow. I am doing new girlfriend now.'

Samson grimaced. 'Vuk, I need you to leave your new
girlfriend now and track down that policeman.' He ignored
the protests at the other end and continued, 'We need to find
out if his phone was in the car when the boy stole it.'

'Boy maybe have phone?'

'Exactly – if he stole that phone, I have a way of maybe

communicating with him and locating him. I hear he was using a phone this afternoon to take a picture. It may have belonged to someone with him, but let's try. You have to get that number and make sure that policeman doesn't call his service provider to have the phone blocked. That's why you need to find him as soon as possible. You understand what I'm saying?' He heard Vuk grunt with effort, as though he was getting up.

'Yes, I understand this. But the policeman, he does not give number for love of Vuk Divjak.'

'Then you offer him money – a lot of money.'

'How much?'

'One thousand dollars to start with – go up to five. The money will be available from tomorrow morning in Skopje – okay?'

'And maybe he does not cooperate with Vuk like this.'

'That's when you tell him you have concerns about that place where the stone building is. You tell him you are worried about what might be out there. That's all you say – nothing more. I'm pretty sure he'll cooperate.'

'Okay,' Vuk said with little enthusiasm. 'I go now.'

'I'll make sure you are well compensated,' said Samson. 'And Vuk – thank you.'

He hung up and stared into the night for a few moments before messaging Denis Hisami to ask whether he could provide upwards of $1,000 in cash at short notice. *I think this could be a breakthrough*, he added.

Hisami replied immediately: *By all means – let me know*

when and where. We learned a lot in the first session today. Am staying for duration. Keep in touch.

Samson thanked him then texted Anastasia. *I need your help ASAP. Can you make it? Understand if you can't. Eternal thanks.*

He waited for a reply. Nothing came, so he got into the car and examined the map. The German group had seen the two migrants with a dog at around five o'clock. At most, the pair had a couple of hours of light before they would need to make camp for the night, but not all that time would be spent walking. He reckoned they would make it between one or two kilometres north of the crossing place before finding somewhere to sleep. The trouble was that he would have to leave the car by the road and, not having any clear idea where they were, commit himself to entering some pretty rough terrain. The chances of finding them would be slim and again he would lose time. He drove north, passed the place where they had been spotted and parked on a patch of rough ground at the point where the road swung right away from the river and up a hill. From there he could see about one kilometre to the south and much further to the countryside in the north, which was dotted with the lights of occasional farmsteads.

He got out and scanned the landscape with his binoculars. There was some cloud cover, but the night was quite light, and when the moon came out the river became a strip of silvery ribbon meandering through the shadows of the woods. He saw nothing, and after a few minutes of looking opened the wine and drank a little from the bottle. He tore some bread from the loaf and cut slices of sausage, which he consumed slowly and without much enthusiasm while staring dully at the insects that had been drawn to the interior light of the car.

His reverie was disturbed by his personal phone, which was lying on the passenger seat. He reached for it through the window and, as he answered his mother's call, noticed that he had also received a text from Anastasia.

'Hi, how are you, Mother?' he said, moving to perch on the warm bonnet of the car.

'Worried,' she replied.

'Oh, I'm sorry to hear that. What about?'

'Where are you?'

'Just taking the air, having finished a meal.'

'I know when you're lying to me, Paul. Please don't tell me stories full of untruths and fantasy.'

'It's completely true, Mother. Anyway, it's great to hear from you. Is there a special reason you called?'

A sigh of exasperation came from the other end. 'I wanted to talk to my only son – is there any harm in that? Is that a crime? I was thinking of you this morning.'

'How nice,' said Samson, knowing, almost to the word, what was about to follow.

'I woke this morning with thoughts of your father, as I do so often.'

'Yes, Mother.'

'Such a lovely man: such perfect manners, and so handsome. I miss him very much, you know.'

'Yes, I know,' said Samson.

'And he was such a very good father, too.'

'Yes, he certainly had his moments – a great father.' While his father had been more glamorous and funny than anyone Samson had ever met, he could never have been described as a great family man. This wasn't the slightest source of resentment for Samson. His father was a trader, a dealer – a man who lived in the marketplace, for that was where his charm worked best.

'More than moments! He was very good with you, Paul. He loved you and he understood you. I woke this morning thinking that you, too, would be a very good father. You remind me of him in so many ways.' She muttered something he couldn't hear, and probably wasn't meant to hear. 'I was talking to your sister last night and she agrees with me that it's time you took a proper job and had a family.'

'Right, my sister! Please give her my love. You think Leila should be giving me advice on marriage when her second has just failed?'

'She has your interests at heart, as you know. You spend your life thinking about horses and doing these mysterious consultations. That is not a man's life, Paul. You should take on responsibilities and become someone.'

'I will put some thought into it, I promise. But I need to find someone who will put up with me, Mother. That's not going to be easy.'

'Nonsense. There are plenty of nice young women who would be happy to marry you. Your problem is that you do not stay with any of them long enough to know if they would be suitable.'

'You're probably right,' he said absently, his gaze coming to rest on the lights of the vehicle that had stopped at the place where the road rejoined the line of the river, about one and a half kilometres to the north. The lights swept to and fro as the vehicle turned. He watched the car begin to move in his direction, stopping every so often for a few seconds. He could not see enough to have any idea what it was doing, but decided that he would leave the side of the road and find somewhere less obvious to park before it reached him.

His mother now moved on to the subject of his sister's children – his two nephews and a young niece – and the problems with the eldest boy, whose father took no interest. She asked Samson if he would talk to the boy when he returned to London.

'I have absolutely no idea what to say to him.'

'Of course you do – don't be silly,' said his mother with a tone of finality.

'I don't remember me and my father having many heart to hearts.'

'What are you saying, Paul? You talked all the time! You were the best of friends.'

That part was true. There had been plenty of laughter and many conspiratorial winks as his father roughly patted him or grabbed his knee, but they never talked properly, which was why Samson missed him still. If anything, that void was now larger than in the months immediately after he had suffered a heart attack while parking the cherished Alvis coupé outside their home. He'd enjoy his father's raffish company now, and he'd like to hear what he thought of the world and of his son's life, though he would almost certainly disapprove of his current occupation. And the gambling – he'd like to ask his father where that came from. His father was cautious when it came to business, which is how he had made his money, and yet he could win or lose £100,000 without moving a muscle, and confessed to feeling sick after either eventuality. That was pretty much Samson's experience, too. A big win was relief, but it was never the pleasure that people imagined.

'You come back to us soon, son.'

'I will,' he said.

'And start thinking about having children. He would be saying the same to you if he were alive today. You owe that to him.'

'I will,' he said automatically, before gently ending the conversation and raising the binoculars to the car that had pulled up in the distance. He couldn't make out much, although he thought he glimpsed a figure passing in front of the lights. He got back into his car and read the message from Anastasia: *I'll come when you need me. Have you found him?*

Not yet. But great that you can come! Thanks. Will have a man named Vuk meet you. Will advise on status of your client tomorrow.

He turned the car and headed for what he took to be a forestry track a little distance down the road. He drove slowly up the incline to a spot where he found he could see much more of the valley, reclined the seat a little and hunkered down for the night. Eventually the car he had been watching disappeared, but later, when he was dozing, he heard a vehicle pass below him. He jumped out to train the binoculars down the road, but saw nothing except a pair of red lights vanishing into the distance at some speed.

At about 11.30 p.m., Vuk called and opened the conversation with, 'Bastard policeman, he want five grand.'

'He can have it because we're in a hurry, but you be sure to tell his colleagues in Skopje about that place when we don't need him to keep the phone open any longer. I believe Naji was fighting for his life at that ruin. The money will be available first thing. Where are you going to meet the cop?'

'Skopje.'

'And that's where the money will be delivered to you. After that I want you to pick up a friend of mine at the airport – a young woman doctor who is going to help me. I will send her your details and you can make the arrangements directly with her.'

'Okay, I go now and fuck my new girl.' He stopped and grunted. 'Oh, I forgetting. They tracking terrorists in Serbia. They follow car to Bosnia-Herzegovina.'

'Are you sure?'

'This is true. They see these three men.'

'Good – that makes things a lot easier.'

Naji and Ifkar woke with the cold just before dawn. Ifkar sat up in his sleeping bag and prodded the fire with a stick;

when it failed to catch light he got up and hunted around to find tinder. He boiled water in an old can and made them tea. Naji fished out the sachets of sugar he had taken from the motorway service area. They drank in silence, watching the sky between the trees grow lighter. Ifkar did some exercises, pulling himself up on a branch then performing countless press-ups and sit-ups. He found a log and placed it across his shoulders and proceeded to do squats. Moon and Naji watched, and then Naji, feeling warmer and still tired, dozed for another hour until the sun rose above the mountains in the east and sunlight dappled their campsite. Ifkar had packed his own things and was ready to leave long before then, but he waited for Naji to wake, stroking Moon and gazing up to the treetops where some butterflies spun round in a double helix.

They stamped on the fire and threw a little water on it, which sent a billowing cloud of smoke through the trees and made the logs fizz. It was Ifkar's idea to keep to the ridge above them rather than return to the river, because they would cover more ground. The cold night air reminded them that the seasons were changing, but the sun was still strong during the day and they kept to the shade of the trees for as long as they could. They made good progress. Naji drew the flute from his backpack and played as they walked, which greatly pleased Ifkar, who occasionally danced a step or two, clicking his fingers in the air. They were thick as thieves, and Naji wished he had his phone to tell Munira in person how well things were going, for he was now sure

that with Ifkar at his side he would soon find his way to
Germany. When he had time, he would sit down and write
an email telling her all about Ifkar and Moon, using the
phone he had taken from the man's car. The phone was fully
charged, and not protected by any meaningful password – it
was 1234 – so he was able to see where they were on the map
in the rare moments when there was good reception.

They continued for two hours until the woods opened
up to a bare, round mountain, its gentle slopes rolling into
pinewood valleys on either side of them. They lost sight of
the river, but they had filled their water bottles the evening
before and would have enough water for the day. Ifkar said
he loved being on top of the world with the views all around
– it made him feel freer than any other time in his life. He
had never been in a more beautiful landscape, not even in his
homeland, and he sang strange, mournful songs in his own
language to honour it.

They decided to circle the mountain on its shaded side
and drop down into the woods a few kilometres on, but first
they had to cross a stretch of hard ground that was strewn
with broken rock; their feet crushed the plants and filled the
air with the aroma of herbs as they went. Ifkar wrapped a
scarf around his head against the sun and Naji reversed his
cap and tied one of his clean cloths around his neck. They
were hungry but decided to save what food they had for
the evening meal, hoping to get fresh supplies at a village
a little to the west the following day. They would buy
enough provisions for the next part of the journey, which

would take them to the north-east corner of Macedonia and its border with Serbia. Ifkar thought they had a three- or four-day walk to the border, but Naji believed this was a little optimistic.

Ifkar began to open up about his life, just as Naji had the night before. He explained he had very little schooling because of his brutal uncle, who made him work in his various businesses – a food store, a garage and an upholstery repair shop. And when there was nothing else to do he was set to sweeping the yard and cleaning a shack where a mistreated donkey was kept. Anything he knew he'd taught himself.

'Did you have a mother and father?' Naji asked.

'My mother died when I was seven and my father sent me to my uncle because he could not look after all his children. We were four. I was the eldest so I had to leave the home. I never saw my brothers and sister again.'

'Why?'

Ifkar bent down to pick up a stone then straightened up with his armed raised; his eyes were focused on something in the scree in front of them. 'My father took them to Germany four years ago,' he said, 'but he never arranged for me to join them, as he promised he would. My uncle hated me even more because of that and punished me and forced me to work even harder.' As he finished the sentence, he threw the stone at a lizard that was sunning itself several metres away. The stone shattered against the rock, causing the lizard to leap vertically into the air. They both laughed.

'You nearly hit it.'

'I wasn't aiming for it,' said Ifkar. 'I just wanted to make it jump.'

'So, are you going to Germany to find your family?'

Ifkar's sunny expression faded. 'Before I ran away, my uncle he told me that my father wrote him to tell him he'd won a green card and was going to America. That's where my family is now – in Chicago.'

'But you can join them! You can go to the States and you can become an American citizen.'

Ifkar was shaking his head. 'My father does not want me.'

'How do you know?'

'It is simple – when he got the news about America, he did not come to fetch me. He knew where I was. He knew that my mother's brother was a cruel man.' Ifkar hung his head. Naji touched him on the arm and looked up into his face. The dog moved towards him and nuzzled Ifkar's hand, which made him smile.

'But you can go to America and find them,' said Naji. 'The authorities will tell you where they live in Chicago. How long ago did you leave your uncle's place?'

'Not sure exactly.'

'How can you be not sure, Ifkar?' said Naji, who was exact about such things.

'Maybe two and half years ago, when I was about your age.'

'Do you know how old you are?'

'Not exactly – maybe seventeen soon.'

'You don't know your birth date?'

He shook his head.

'Right, so in those two years your father probably tried to find you. He knows what happened to your people.'

'He thinks I'm dead.'

Naji thought quickly. 'When you stole that money from your uncle and ran away, what did you think your uncle would do?'

'He would have asked my father for the money. He would treat it like my father's debt.'

'Right, so your father knows that you left the area where your uncle lived and he will know you're still alive.'

'Why?'

'Because you escaped before IS came to your town and all those Yazidis were killed.'

'Maybe.'

'Did your uncle have an address for him?'

'I think so. But I don't have it.'

'If they are in America, Ifkar, you will find them. Your brothers and sister will be on Facebook.'

'I don't know Facebook. And I am not good at reading,' he added quietly.

'That's not a problem,' said Naji. 'I can fix all that – I can teach you to read and then we'll set you up an account for you and Moon.'

'Are you on Facebook?'

'I was once,' Naji replied, 'but in my country Facebook can get you into a lot of trouble.'

They stumbled on through the rocks and Ifkar pointed out many small wonders: some tiny, star-shaped flowers that were covered in spiders; pink and bright green mosses that grew beside the springs they encountered lower down the mountain; a vulture that was perched on the rocks above them, holding its wings out as if drying them. Everything seemed new and fresh to Naji and he felt perfectly at ease with Ifkar.

Samson had slept little and he felt lousy from too much red wine, which he'd drunk in the hope that it would knock him out for a few hours. He gulped some orange juice from a carton and looked up and down the valley, thinking that his mother was right and he needed to find something else to do. Suddenly his attention was drawn to a plume of smoke rising from the trees on the other side of the valley, about half a kilometre downstream – not far from where the migrants had been seen with their catch. He started the car and drove down to a spot directly across from the smoke. There was much less of it now, but occasionally he saw a hint of an orange glow among the dark trees above him. It was very hard to be certain, but he thought he spotted at least one figure sitting by the fire. He decided to take a closer look, but there was no suitable place to cross the river beneath the road. He would have to go downstream if he wanted to avoid getting soaked.

An hour later he had climbed up to the campsite and found a fire that had been intentionally put out, as well as rather an ingeniously made windbreak in which boughs had been woven together. A closer search around the fire revealed fish bones and the rind from a salami sausage. In the carpet of pine needles and leaf mould that formed the forest floor there were impressions left by two people who had bedded down for the night. Maybe it was going too far to conclude that one was deeper than the other, but it did seem to Samson that Naji – if this was indeed him – had slept closest to the fire. The stones around the fire were still warm, but the fire had been well doused and all the heat had gone from the ashes. Further away he found signs of human defecation and dog shit.

It had to be them, and he was angry with himself for missing them, though he told himself that they would have scarpered the moment they heard him approaching through the undergrowth. There was no clue as to which way they had gone, although they would obviously still keep going north. If it had been his decision, he would have chosen the high ground to walk in the early morning sun, for he had noticed when he was by the car that the forested ridge led to the rolling slopes of the mountains, which would be as good a route north as any. If they had gone high, he could work out – more or less – where they would end up, and he could drive to that point without a lot of difficulty. Sooner or later, they would have to leave the wilderness for food and drinking water.

Back at the car, he smoked half a cigarette then raised the binoculars and planted his elbows on the roof to steady them.

A sweep of the valley produced nothing, so he trained them to where the bare rock of the mountain began and the woods ended. Carefully he quartered the upper slopes. The binoculars skidded past something – a movement just below the skyline. He went back. A white animal was crossing a dark patch of rock. It was a large white dog, just as the German hikers had reported. Now he saw two figures, some distance behind the bounding dog. The smaller of the two, so tiny in the vast landscape, was clad in exactly the same colours as Naji had been wearing in the service station CCTV – a black and red jacket, blue jeans and a red cap. The taller of the two was in green trousers and a yellowish shirt. A pale-coloured scarf around his head trailed in the breeze behind him.

'Hello, Naji Touma,' Samson murmured. 'Now where are you off to?'

He watched for twenty minutes, until they disappeared behind the summit. Cursing to himself and feeling much in need of coffee, he pulled the map from the side pocket of his cargo pants. It was going to take some time for them to round the summit, and then it would be a lot harder for him to keep track of them, even from a new vantage point further up the road. He reckoned there were two possible routes down to the only village in the area, and he was sure they would take one of them. One thing he took from his observations of the morning was that Naji's companion knew what he was doing – it was smart of him to walk in the shade of the mountain, for it would not be so exhausting and they would use less water. And judging by the way the campfire and windbreak were constructed, this young migrant knew how to look after himself in the wild. So, at least Naji wasn't going to die of exposure, starvation or dehydration.

He got into the car and phoned Vuk. 'I need that bloody number, Vuk,' he said. 'Where are you?'

'In traffic,' growled Vuk, before a hacking cough robbed him of speech.

'Are you in Skopje yet?' Samson asked. 'Have you arranged the handover of the money? I sent you all the numbers you needed.'

'I get money now then I see bastard policeman in bar at eleven.'

'Right, call me when you have the number and I'll test it. It's important that I do it and you don't try it – okay? Then you're going to pick up Anastasia at the airport.'

'No – she miss plane. She come tomorrow, maybe later. She call me.'

'That was efficient of her.' He glanced at his own phone to see that he had a text from her. 'Okay, so let me know when you have the number. I'll make sure I stay in a place with network coverage. Any news about the other stuff?'

Vuk would know he was talking about the combined operation in Serbia and Bosnia. 'They watch two houses,' he said.

'Have they got a positive ID using the CCTV images we retrieved from the service station? Do they know its them for sure?'

'Same men, but they say nothing to me now.'

'That's to be expected, I guess. We'll speak as soon as you have the number,' he said, and hung up.

In reply to Anastasia's text he said she mustn't come if it was at all difficult, but it would be great to see her whenever she could make it. He was just sending the text when the encrypted phone in his lap vibrated with an incoming call.

'Yes,' he said to Sonia Fell without much enthusiasm. 'How can I help?'

'Look, he wants you to stop looking for Firefly, Paul. He understands why you've stuck with the case, but now he needs you to leave Macedonia and forget the whole business. That's what he's asked me to tell you.'

The 'he' was of course Nyman. 'I don't understand what possible objection he has against me looking for the boy. It has absolutely nothing to do with him – he made it clear he wasn't interested in the boy.'

Fell picked up the edge in his voice. 'The Macedonian authorities are going to deal with him – he stabbed a police officer.'

'A police officer that was almost certainly going to assault him sexually.'

'You have evidence for that? Look, respecting the Macedonian's pursuit of criminals on their own soil is obviously the basis of our ability to operate here, as you must appreciate. He has told them that we will back off.'

'Because he thinks he's about to make the arrests?'

'You know I can't say anything.'

Samson held his temper. 'So he got what he wanted – the boy was simply the means of tempting them into Europe. Is that right?'

'You know that's wrong. He had already left the Middle East before we were fully aware of his significance. There's no question of this being some kind of clever plot or manipulation. We have just moved on and adapted to the threat that Europe faces from these men. We must deal with the realities of life in the Balkans,' she concluded.

'Okay,' he said, certain that he was not going to give up on the boy and also mildly annoyed that Fell had been deployed to deal with him.

'Glad you see it that way,' she said. 'I thought you'd be angry. You've done such a fine job on this and I know you have invested much in Firefly. And of course we've got to this point entirely because of you.'

'Just one other thing,' said Samson. 'When did he agree formally with the Macedonians to leave the boy with them? Why?'

'We only had a request from the Macedonian government in the last half an hour.'

'That explains it.' This time he didn't bother to hide his feelings. Without waiting for Sonia's reply, he hung up.

He guessed that London would not yet have heard of this new instruction about giving up on Naji, so he rang Okiri's number on the encrypted phone. 'Just wondering about the boy's phone and whether there's anything on it that I should know about. I still have it with me, since no one seemed to want to take it off me yesterday. Did Jamie O'Neill find much?'

'You've still got the phone?' said Okiri. 'That's weird. Sonia should have taken it from you. Did you hear from her yet? She said she was going to speak to you – don't know what about.'

'I'll look forward to that, Chris. About Firefly's phone, did Jamie O'Neill come up with anything? He told me there were some interesting things on it.'

'Not sure about that. I'll look for you.' Okiri was silent as his fingers worked a keyboard. 'Cheltenham say they need to look at the phone itself, so I guess you had better get it to us ASAP.'

'Okay, so no chance of finding out what's on it remotely?'

'I guess not,' said Okiri. 'Is that all you wanted? I've got a lot on.'

Samson ended the call, then started the car, descended the rutted track to rejoin the road and began to move slowly north, watching the slopes of the mountains as he went. At first, he felt confident that he'd intercept the boy and his companion, but as he went he realised that they would have to go around three summits to avoid a series of precipitous cliffs before descending to the village. There was therefore a much greater area for him to search.

Eight hours later, watching from the deserted car park of a panorama above the village, he swung his binoculars from the storm clouds in the west and saw the flash of the white dog on a slope about a kilometre away. It was unmistakably

the same dog as he had seen before, yet there was no sign of
the boys. Soon after he spotted the animal, the mountains
were swallowed up by mist and rain, but at least he knew
their position and it seemed unlikely that they would continue to travel in the rain and gathering dark.

All day he had been phoning Vuk without success. The
cell phone reception was patchy in the mountains so he'd
used the satellite phone, but still got no response. He suspected Vuk had switched his phone off, or wasn't answering
because he hadn't got the number from the policeman. He
left another curt message before taking the road down to the
village. He came across a store that doubled as a café and bar,
where he was surprised to find a party in full swing. There
must have been fifty people there. No table was available
so he drank a beer at the bar and watched the proceedings,
which included speeches and unaccompanied songs. The
bartender, a young man with a neat beard who introduced
himself as Andrej, explained in passable English that most of
the party had been up the mountain to pay their respects to
the head of the family, who had died a year before. He was
Andrej's uncle and it was tradition to visit the departed more
or less on the anniversary, but never, for some reason, on
the exact day of the death. The patch of ground where this
ritual was held had been in the family since their Serb ances-
tors had come south into Macedonia three or four centuries
before. Once respects had been paid, tradition also dictated
that the party repair to the store, which had also belonged
to the family for as long as anyone could remember, there

to toast his memory with as much beer and quince brandy as they could drink, accompanied by cake and a mountain of cold lamb chops. People had come from all over, including a large middle-aged man who ran a repair shop in Milwaukee and a fitness-obsessed couple who'd made the trip from Germany and had run up the mountain for the ceremony. This had earned the disapproval of the older members of the party.

Samson didn't bother to enquire if any of them had come across the two young migrants, because it was evident that the group had visited a different part of the mountains – and anyway, most of them were too far gone. But as the evening wore on, he mentioned to Andrej that he needed a place to stay for the night.

'But why are you want to stay here? The city is only two hours away.'

'I need to be in this area tomorrow morning.'

'For the autumn colours?' he asked, a bit sarcastically.

'No,' he said quietly, 'I am trying to track two migrants, who are somewhere in those mountains – one of them is in great danger.'

Andrej looked away and lit a pipe – he evidently assumed Samson was some kind of policeman.

'It's important that I find him before others do,' Samson added. 'That's why I need to be here at first light. I think they'll come down to get food and water.'

'There were two migrants here earlier. They bought food.'

'Is that so? The ones I'm looking for have a white dog.

One is about thirteen years old, the other one is older and much taller.'

'No, the ones we served were grown men, well into their late twenties, and they did not have a dog with them.' He added that he had no problem with migrants and these two were polite and had thanked him for the groceries they bought. One spoke Serbian well and had a very good vocabulary.

Samson was sure that none of the men from Syria were fluent in Serbian. 'Anything else you remember about them?'

Andrej shook his head. 'No, but I do have a place for you to sleep. It'll cost you twenty euros.'

Samson agreed, but it was a long time before he was allowed to leave the party. Glass after glass of booze came his way. He took to moving the glasses in front of the pudgy-faced man from Milwaukee and they were soon emptied. At eleven, Andrej showed him to the loft of an old barn, a little way up the hill behind the village. The place was dry, though far from draught-proof. It had running water, a basic camp bed of canvas and metal rods, one dim overhead light and a picture of Mihailović, the Second World War Chetnik leader, printed on cardboard which had curled up with damp at the bottom.

He checked his phones for messages and emails before putting both on charge and going to bed.

They set up camp in the late afternoon and Naji, eyeing the black clouds that had appeared in the west, stretched his plastic sheet between the trees. It began raining at seven, well after they had collected enough dry firewood for the night and heated water for tea and eaten what little food they had left. Ifkar quickly cut some boughs to shield them from the rain on the summit side of the shelter and Naji diverted a rivulet running into their camp by using several flat stones. The rain stopped two hours later and they stoked the fire and watched the sparks shooting into the night air.

They slept well but were disturbed at first light by Moon, who had got up and was standing between them with hackles raised, emitting a low growl. They peered into the dark forest but couldn't see what she was looking at. Ifkar reached up to stroke her, but Moon shifted a few paces forward, the better to concentrate on the thing that was bothering her. Ifkar left his sleeping bag and told Naji to pass him his stick, which he rapidly began to sharpen into a spear.

'What is it?' asked Naji.

'Maybe a wolf.'

With the stick sharpened, Ifkar crouched by Moon. Naji put on his trainers and also moved to Moon's side.

'Something's out there,' said Ifkar. 'I heard it just now.'

Naji strained to listen, but he heard nothing above the wind in the trees. They waited, saying nothing. Moon's growl was now punctuated by a whine and a nervous shake of the head, as if she could not quite decide whether to charge into the undergrowth or stay to protect them. Then she was silent and they both heard the noise: the tread of something taking its time to move across the slope below them. From behind

it – to their right – came another sound, of a lighter creature scampering across the forest floor. Trembling all over,
Moon began to ready herself and barked three times. Ifkar
rose, holding the stick over his shoulder like a javelin. In his
left hand he gripped the short kitchen knife that he used for
everything. Naji took his throwing knife from his pack and
readied himself for the attack. Nothing happened. Then in
the light of the fire, which had flared into life after being
poked vigorously by Ifkar, they saw a huge, pale brown
face, with two darkened eye sockets and round ears, peering
at them from between two low boughs. The bear regarded
them with a mild interest, neither aggressive nor fearful,
studying them until a smaller face appeared by its side, at
which point it growled and shoved the cub away with its
snout. It sniffed and pawed the ground, then looked up again
and raised its head to scent them better. Moon responded
with a charge that was quickly aborted when the bear moved
forward and took a swipe at her. Ifkar launched his spear at
the bear and struck it between the shoulder blades, without
the slightest effect. The spear slid harmlessly to the ground.
The bear moved forward a couple more paces, close enough
for them to see the snot coming from its nose and smell its
pungent, earthy odour.

'What are we going to do?' shouted Naji.

Ifkar reached behind him and seized one of the flaming
logs with one hand. Naji grabbed another and they threw
them together. The logs cartwheeled through the air in a
shower of sparks. Ifkar's hit the bear on the top of its head

while Naji's landed at its feet and sent up a burst of flame that caused the bear to leap backward and let out a wounded roar. But still it would not go. Then, with both hands, Ifkar picked up the largest log, which they hadn't been able to break into smaller pieces to feed into the fire. Holding the flaming end out in front of him, he began to march towards the bear, with Moon and Naji following. The bear was now beginning to show signs of doubt. It shook its head violently, perhaps wondering at the smell of burned hair. It jumped backwards, lifting both front paws, and finally turned tail when Ifkar charged at her screaming.

Suddenly the bear and her cub were gone, and they didn't even hear their retreat down the mountain. Ifkar stood with the flaming log for a few moments, then turned and gave Naji a sheepish smile, which Naji did not return because he was so utterly overwhelmed by the experience. He sank to the wet ground and shook his head, repeating, 'It was so big.'

Ifkar came over and pulled him up by the hand. 'Come on, you'll get wet down there, Naji. There's still a little sausage left and I have a cigarette.'

They sat by the fire. Ifkar lit his cigarette and Naji took a couple of drags, which made him feel heady but not as nauseous as at Idomeni. They talked excitedly about the bear's eyes, its huge teeth and claws and the foul odour it left behind. Moon wagged her tail and danced about the camp, as though to take credit for vanquishing the enormous creature that had come out of the forest. Ifkar and Naji both agreed that while she'd baulked at attacking the bear,

Moon was undeniably responsible for saving their lives and deserved the end of the sausage.

They struck camp and arrived in the village two hours after the confrontation in the woods with the bear and its cub. They did not stop talking about the incident in all that time, and the prospect of buying some food and seeing civilisation, however rudimentary, had put a spring in their step. Moon was also full of the joys of being a dog with two doting masters and ran ahead, occasionally chasing red squirrels.

Until they passed a woman carrying a large bundle of faggots on her back who waved a stick at them, they were unaware how dirty and dishevelled they looked. They noticed a disused washhouse that was covered in ivy and brambles standing by a little Orthodox church. Inside they found a bench, a stone slab for pummelling clothes and, more importantly, a trickle of mountain stream water coming from a spout that was covered in limescale. A frog sat on the slab, eying them, until Ifkar stripped off his clothes and flicked his T-shirt at it. Naji cleaned himself as vigorously as if he were about to attend prayers, while Ifkar took great care in washing his feet with the soap given to Naji at Gevgelija – he said his feet and trainers smelled worse than the bear. They hung around waiting for the store to open, which it did for two woodsmen who arrived on a narrow-wheelbase tractor with an exhaust funnel. One sat on the drawbar at the back with his legs dangling and a small chainsaw across his thighs. Naji and Ifkar followed the men in and heaped food and cans of beer and soft drinks into a wire basket, having first shown that they had money to a young woman with very large breasts who was in the process of clearing up the bar at the back of the shop. They went back to the washhouse, where they reckoned they could eat breakfast in peace, for the woman and the two woodsmen were giving them suspicious glances, which made Naji eager to leave the village.

While they ate, he took out the map and started to plot the next stage of their journey to the Serbian border, but Ifkar wanted only to talk about the storekeeper's breasts and did not seem especially interested. Naji argued that it would be safer and quicker by the mountains, and anyway, they would have the option to join the road in the next valley if the weather worsened. Ifkar nodded but kept looking out of the washhouse at the storekeeper, who was sweeping dust from the shop into the road.

They chose the mountain route, which led them out of the village and up a grassy lane, also taken by the woodsmen on their tractor. Whereas the first hills they had walked through were mostly covered with conifers, the trees on the lower slopes of this mountain were deciduous, with autumn leaves of gold and sometimes blood-red. Neither had seen anything like it before. Naji remembered the phone he had stolen, which still had a lot of power in it. He pulled it out and took a picture of himself with Ifkar and Moon against the foliage. When he found a place with reasonable reception, he emailed it to Munira with a short note telling her about his new friend and the dog. He added his new number and a request for hers.

THIRTEEN

Samson wasn't hungover, but he had slept fitfully and was not entirely awake when his satellite phone sprang into life at the bottom of the camp bed, where he'd left it on charge.

'Yes,' he said, noticing that there was no caller ID, a sure sign that it was London.

'Is that you?' demanded Sonia Fell.

'Yes.'

'It doesn't sound like you. Where are you?'

'It's hard to explain – how can I help?'

'I'm calling because I know you talked to Chris Okiri after I spoke to you yesterday and that he gave you certain help in regard to Firefly's phone that was counter to the Chief's express wishes. You didn't tell Chris that you'd spoken to me and that you had been stood down from this project.'

'That, surely, is not my fault,' he said sharply. 'I assumed he knew. Internal communications are not under my control.'

'Of course he couldn't have known. We had only just agreed the situation with the Macedonian government, who are actively searching for the boy.'

'Okay.'

'Okay what?'

'You've bollocked me, now you can get on with your day and I can get on with mine.'

'Do you understand what I'm saying? I'm telling you to go back to London and forget all about the boy. Forget Firefly.'

'Yes, I heard, but it can't have escaped your notice that I'm no longer working for the Office and that you're not in a position to order me anywhere.'

'But you can confirm for me that you're not searching for the boy.'

'I am not confirming anything of the sort. Let me remind you that what I'm doing is the subject of a private contract, which has nothing to do with you or your masters.' He had in mind an arrangement with Denis Hisami, which he could easily fix with one call, although it didn't exist at that moment.

'That makes no difference. We want you out of the country.'

Samson said nothing.

Fell cleared her throat and continued, 'I should perhaps tell you that intelligence now suggests that Firefly was witness to and may have taken part in atrocities carried out by Al-munajil's group. We believe he is a killer, Paul, and we now regard him as a serious security risk, which is why the

Macedonian police are pursuing him. That's their end of the operation – dealing with the boy.'

'Honestly, do you believe that?'

'I have to believe the intelligence, Paul.'

'You've got video?'

'I'm not aware of any, but these young boys all end up brainwashed and killing for their masters.'

'Does that make him any less the victim?'

'We're not child psychologists, Paul. We're involved in a massively important security operation. The boy has led us to the terrorist cell – that is what we needed.'

There was no point arguing. 'Well, I hope that's all working out,' he said.

'Thank you for that. Now I must ask you not to contact Jamie O'Neill or Chris Okiri or anyone else on this matter. As far as you are concerned, this is all closed – the boy no longer exists.'

'Fine,' he said, reaching for his trousers. Fell before breakfast was a fucking nightmare – thank God he'd never been to bed with her.

'And we will need the phone you have in your possession,' she said crisply. 'Can you be sure to drop it at the British embassy before you leave Skopje, preferably today?'

'I'll see what I can do, Sonia.'

'You're stalling, Paul. Please, just do what the Chief asks.'

'If that's all,' he said, now weary of Fell's manner as well as her bloody ambition. 'I'll say goodbye and go and find something to eat.'

He washed in ice-cold water, dressed and slung his bag in the car before heading to the store. He reckoned it would be an hour or so before Naji and his companion descended into the village from the spot where he had seen the dog, and it would be easy enough for him to watch their progress from his observation post at the panorama. He needed to be there soon, but knew absolutely that he was not going to repeat the experience of the previous day of starting the day without coffee. Fell's call had already put him in a poor mood. What she had told him did not make the slightest difference to his desire to find and help the boy, for he had always recognised the possibility that he was dealing with a child soldier. Naji's closeness to the monster who was named after a machete implied this.

He found Andrej drifting around the back of the bar with a pipe stuck in his mouth, distractedly picking up glasses and putting them down again. Samson bought some coffee and a couple of flaky pastry rolls filled with cheese and watched him while sipping his hot drink. He ordered a second cup and went to the door to light a cigarette and look at the mountains, heartrendingly beautiful that morning – golden foliage and bare, pale rock, glowing softly in the early morning light. The moment was disturbed by the woman who'd served him erupting with a scream of dismay, which brought Andrej hurrying to the front of the store to stare at the shelf in question.

He turned to Samson. 'Your two young migrants were here this morning. My sister says they stole some things.'

'Chocolate?' asked Samson.

Andrej looked surprised. 'Yes, how did you know? Chocolate bars and cans of beer. They had a dog.'

'That's them. What time was this?'

Andrej consulted his sister. 'An hour ago. She says they followed the Nikolov brothers, who work in the forest up the track.' He pointed north.

'I'll pay for the items they stole,' said Samson, thinking that Andrej might report the crime and it would give the police a precise location for Naji. He handed him twenty euros for the night in his barn and twenty-five to cover breakfast and what the boys had stolen. Then he asked Andrej to show him the route they had taken and was led to a paddock above the barn. The view was good, and using his binoculars he quickly found the two figures and the dog. They had left the forest and were on open ground, moving purposefully across the side of the mountain, their heads bent to the wind. Instead of bounding ahead, the dog walked a little behind.

'Must be cold up there,' murmured Samson. 'How far do they have to go until they can drop down into another valley?'

Andrej shrugged. 'Depends which route they go. Perhaps no more than a day's walk to Pudnik.'

Samson took out the map from his side pocket and folded it to a manageable size.

'The ground gets higher here,' said Andrej, his finger on the map. 'They can die there from cold if they do not have more clothes. Even now it is very low temperature, and at night . . .' He flipped his hand as if waving out a match.

'They must be making for Pudnik then. How far is that from here by car?'

Andrej nodded. 'An hour, maybe more.'

Samson found them again with the binoculars. The gap between the lead figure and Naji and the dog had grown larger. There was no sign of Naji flagging; it was probably that his stride was shorter than his companion's. Then something else attracted Samson's attention, way off to the right. He moved the binoculars and focused on two figures in dark clothing who appeared to be following the same route as Naji and his friend.

'Are these the brothers you mentioned?' Samson said, handing the binoculars to Andrej.

It took a while for Andrej to find them, and then he shook his head. 'No, that's not the Nikolov brothers – they go nowhere without a tractor.' He looked again. 'Could be the two men who came into the store yesterday. They both wore dark clothing.'

'Everyone wears dark clothing,' said Samson. He took the binoculars from Andrej and felt for the satellite phone with his free hand. He dialled Vuk. Eventually he answered.

'I need that number now,' said Samson roughly.

'Is problem.'

'Have you got the number?'

'No, he want more money.'

'How much?'

'Five thousand euros.'

Samson thought quickly. If the Macedonian authorities

were indeed searching for the boy, the policeman was taking
a risk in not reporting his phone stolen, because it could be
used to pinpoint the location of the boy. So perhaps he could
be justified in demanding such a large sum.

'Did the cop say anything about a big police operation to
find the boy?' he asked, still holding the binoculars with one
hand and tracking the men moving steadily up the slope.

'No, he say nothing.'

'How did he react when you mentioned that place he
took Naji?'

'He say nothing. He don't give two shits. He fucking
policeman.'

'Okay, call Denis Hisami's people in ten minutes, by
which time I will have spoken to him. I know he will help
with the money. It's vital I have that number as soon as you
get it, so text or call me when you can. Then I need you to
meet me at a village called Pudnik tonight. You can find it
on the map.' He repeated the name of the village a couple
of times, then hung up and turned to Andrej.

'So this is really important?' said Andrej.

'You could say that. There are a lot of people who want
that little guy dead because of what he knows. Any idea how
I can get up that mountain quickly?'

He removed the unlit pipe from his beard and looked up
the mountain. 'Grivo has dirt bike.'

'Who's Grivo?'

'Cousin. I will call for you.'

He went off, while Samson rang Denis Hisami and

explained in a roundabout way – because he was not sure who might be listening to Hisami's phone – why he needed the number so urgently.

'You can see him now?'

'Yes, on the hillside ahead of me, which is why I need to get going.'

'Sounds like you could use some help out there.'

'Maybe later. If we get to him, we're going to have to find somewhere safe for him. How's it going your end?'

'We're close,' said Hisami, 'very close to identifying the man who is responsible for Aysel's death.'

'He's talking?'

'Yes, when he's got his drugs. Slowly we are getting there. The authorities are being most accommodating.'

'I bet,' said Samson, thinking that Hisami's money had prompted all the cooperation he needed. 'Thanks for everything – I'm grateful.'

'My pleasure,' said Hisami. 'We will be in touch soon, no doubt.'

Samson reduced the contents of his rucksack to just his hat, gloves, the two phones and their chargers, bread, water and some energy bars, leaving the rest in the boot of the hire car. He exchanged phone numbers with Andrej and gave him the key to the car, saying that if he didn't return, a man called Vuk would collect it. Grivo – a near replica of Andrej but in a black beanie, khaki jacket and work boots – appeared on a black Yamaha dirt bike, which had a raised rear mudguard that doubled as the pillion seat. Samson took out twenty euros and gave it to him. Before they left, Andrej rushed out of the store with a walking stick that had a leather wrist cord at one end and big metal ferrule at the other and told Samson that he would be a fool not to take it.

The way was muddy from the previous night's rain and the bike kept sliding into deep puddles, which required Samson to dismount so that Grivo could gun his machine back onto firmer ground. Samson was twice sprayed with liquid mud. It all took a lot longer than he had expected and several times they both had to get off the bike and walk through the woods. At length, they remounted the bike, pushed through a plantation of small conifers and sped onto the open ground. Grivo pulled up and shouted over his shoulder for directions. There was no sign of any of the four figures, but Samson knew which way they had gone and pointed left, noticing at the same time that mist was spilling down the western flank of the mountain and onto the route that Naji and his friend had taken, pursued by the other two.

Grivo put the bike into gear and yelled for Samson to hang on. They climbed for a hundred metres then traversed a slope with a firm, gritty surface on which a few stunted shrubs grew. Samson noticed the village come into view below them and realised that they'd reached the point where the pair had been when he first spotted them forty-five minutes before. Suddenly, Grivo skidded the bike to a halt, sending up a spray of grit, and started calling to someone. A shepherd, wearing a big woollen coat and a round hat and carrying a long stick, emerged from the boulders fifty metres up the slope. He waved back, whistled to his dog and started coming down towards them. While they waited for him, Samson looked around, impressed by the stark, monochrome landscape and the mountain steaming like a cauldron above them. Way off in the valley, beyond the village, shafts of light picked out settlements, ploughed fields and brilliant stands of yellow poplar.

The old shepherd and Grivo greeted each other warmly – Samson assumed they were related. They lit cigarettes and the shepherd uncorked and proffered a flask of slivovitz, which he'd whisked out from a leather satchel. Grivo insisted that Samson went first with it. The alcohol burned his throat and warmed his stomach. A long exchange followed, in which Grivo appeared to be asking about everything other than the migrants, but presently the man, pointing with his stick, and adding detail with a curving motion of his hand, indicated that the pair with the dog had gone down and around the mountain to avoid the talus, the stretch of huge flat rocks that had fallen as if sliced from the crags above.

Samson asked Grivo to ask the shepherd about the other two men. They had gone through the talus, which told him they knew nothing about mountains and were probably just relying on a phone to navigate. It looked like a good shortcut on the map, but when the rocks were wet they were treacherous to cross, as the shepherd knew to his cost. He said they'd be clambering through those rocks for a long time.

They bade him goodbye and set off down the slope, avoiding the patches where springs had turned the grit to mud, and passed below the rocks. Then they climbed again, but saw nothing of Naji and his friend. They pressed on for about fifteen minutes, until they reached a perfectly flat plateau where there was lush grass and a bog with large pools of water. Grivo turned off the engine and told Samson that he couldn't go any further and didn't have the time to carry the bike across the bog, but that he would show Samson the best way through the soft ground. Samson got off and planted his stick in the ground before pulling on his gloves. He was extremely doubtful about the wisdom of continuing on foot, but then Grivo nudged him and pointed to two tiny figures and a dog on the next mountain. Without saying a word, he swung his arm to the right and Samson picked out the two men in pursuit, who must have traversed the talus with surprising speed, or climbed above them and crossed the boggy ground on the far side of the plateau.

They were about three hundred metres away. Samson took out his binoculars and focused on the men. He watched for a minute before establishing that neither was the long-faced man, Ibrahim, he had seen in the service station video. Maybe they were just a couple of innocent migrants. He switched to watch Naji and his friend, who were crossing a piece of ground lit by the sun. They seemed unaware of the men keeping pace behind them. Certainly they did not look back. They were now walking together and Samson thought they might be talking as they went.

He let the binoculars drop. Inside his backpack, one of his phones was ringing.

★

The going was hard and Naji was already tired and lagging behind Ifkar. His optimism was fading and he began to dwell upon his darkest fears: that he wouldn't make it to Germany; that his family, who were relying on him, would never see him again; and that they'd spend the rest of their days in the vast camp in Turkey, surrounded by sickness and despair, without hope of anything better to come. The more he had these thoughts, the heavier his backpack seemed and the harder it was to put one foot in front of the other. It didn't seem to have occurred to Ifkar that Naji might need a rest or the odd word of encouragement. He, too, was with his own thoughts, though Naji suspected that his handsome friend was not a person to stay on a subject for very long, or think very deeply about his life. Ifkar existed in the moment like no person Naji had ever met before. He and the dog were similar in that way. Maybe that's why Moon was so attached to him, though Naji did notice that even Moon preferred his company to Ifkar's that morning. Perhaps she didn't feel like racing ahead either.

For an hour Naji didn't say anything, but his temper snapped when he tripped and fell into a pool of water and his jeans got soaked and covered in mud. He shouted to Ifkar to slow down and swore at him, calling him everything under the sun including the son of a whore, which he immediately apologised for. Ifkar didn't seem to mind. That was Ifkar — stuff washed over him — but from then on they walked together with their heads bowed to the wind, and that made Naji feel much better. He took out one of the chocolate bars he'd stolen, and they saw how long they could keep a chunk in their mouths without it melting. As usual, chocolate stimulated Naji's conversation and he was soon describing ways he thought he would make money in Germany, which were chiefly centred round the phone repair business.

Earlier, they had decided to head for Pudnik, because the road from the town led to a major route and Naji wondered if it would be possible to sneak onto a truck to get over the Serbian border. Ifkar doubted it would be easy to hide Moon on a truck and he was sure he didn't want to cross without her, but he agreed to Naji's plan anyway because he didn't have another.

After they'd agreed that Naji was the winner of the chocolate competition and should be allowed the last piece, they left the plateau, trudged round a smaller mountain and skirted a spur, where they were hit by a cold blast of air, more mist and some drops of rain. Just as Naji was saying that it wasn't going to be more than a shower, Ifkar shouted that he had seen a stone explode a few metres ahead of them. They examined the shattered stone, then looked up and around, searching for the cause, for they had had heard no sound at all. They could see very little due to the mist.

Naji shrugged. 'Maybe you kicked another stone without noticing. Maybe a bird dropped something.' He looked around again. 'Maybe you imagined it.'

'Maybe not,' shouted Ifkar over the wind. They moved down to a patch of short, densely packed conifers, which gave them shelter. The pine needles tickled their faces as they pushed through, making them laugh.

Five minutes later, the policeman's phone began to sound with a heavy metal ringtone in Naji's backpack. Ifkar swung round with a look of surprise; Naji held his stick up and strummed an imaginary guitar.

'Aren't you going to answer it?'

Naji shook his head and kept strumming until the phone went silent.

'Why?'

'Because it's a call for the pervert cop. It could be him phoning to see if I'll answer.'

Ifkar agreed that it was better not to answer.

Later, they stopped to eat and rest at a point where they could see the town below them. It was larger than they'd expected after looking at the map, with warehouses and factories and three smokestacks that belched thick, grey smoke. The wind brought an acrid smell up the mountain. Naji dozed on the dry ground beneath a tree, using Moon as a pillow. Then the phone sprang to life again. There had been four or five calls in the last hour and each time he'd let them ring out, but this time the phone pinged with a message and he took it out of the backpack, thinking he would put it on silent. The screen was illuminated with the beginning of a text message in Arabic. To his astonishment, it began, *From your sister Munira.*

He opened the message. *I tried calling but no answer. You need to hide. Two men are following you on the mountain. A man who speaks Arabic is trying to help you. He is a friend. You must call him. Call me and I will explain.*

His hands shook as he immediately dialled the number, but the call wouldn't go through. He tried several times without success. He thought for a few seconds, then, with many reservations, he dialled the number she had added for the man she said was trying to help him. His mind swirled with questions. He had given Munira his number when he sent her the email with the photo earlier that day, so that explained how she had called him, but who had contacted her? How did that person know her number? How did he know where he was? How did they know men were following him?

That call didn't go through either, which was explained by just one bar at the top of the screen – enough for a text message maybe, but not a call. He wrote a text, but it refused to leave the phone. Then he told Ifkar that his sister had contacted him to say that someone was following them, and he needed to find a place with a much stronger signal. At first Ifkar didn't take him seriously – they hadn't seen a person on the mountains for days. 'No one knows where we are,' he said, although Naji noticed some doubt in his eyes.

'What about that splintered stone?' Naji demanded. 'You think that might have been a bullet?' He felt more fearful than at any moment since he was drowning in the ocean. Not only were Al-munajil and his men tracking him, but the darkness of Syria had followed him across the sea and into the heart of these mountains. Maybe he'd never shake it off.

Ifkar looked at him steadily but didn't answer the question about the splintered stone. 'We should go down to the village so you can make the calls – there will be a better signal down there.' He laid a hand on Naji's shoulder. 'It will be okay, you'll see.'

Naji nodded with a weak smile. In this new friendship of theirs, neither was dominant, despite the difference in age. There were times when Naji led with his ideas and bounce, but Ifkar's unflappable strength took over at other moments and Naji was content to follow.

Sensing they were about to leave, Moon got up and stretched her back legs, one after the other. They shouldered their packs and set off through the pines, moving as stealthily as they knew how and stopping every few minutes to listen to the forest.

Samson answered the phone to Vuk, who gave him the number of the policeman's cell phone, also texting it to him make sure Samson had it right.

'There is problem. Bastard want another five thousand tomorrow. If we don't give it, he cancel phone.'

Samson absorbed this. 'Did he say anything about the police searching for Naji?'

'Yes, Naji is big time terrorist. They say he killed plenty people.'

'He told you that?'

'Yes, this is why he wants five thousand tomorrow.'

Samson understood perfectly – the policeman would take another five thousand from Vuk, then either cancel the phone or, if the Macedonian authorities had the technology, suggest his colleagues track it. The thing that really interested him was that the Macedonians now believed Naji was a killer, and they could only have got that from Nyman or Sonia Fell. MI6 plainly had no further use for Naji, which to his mind was a mistake, but worse still was that they were shedding responsibility for the Syrian boy and were happy for him to vanish into some grim detention centre.

'You didn't say whether the police were actively searching for Naji,' said Samson.

'For me, I do not think they look for Naji. No big time operation. If they find Naji maybe they feel lucky.'

'That's my guess, too,' said Samson and hung up.

During the call he had watched the distant figures of Naji and his friend being swallowed by the mist, which had rolled down the slopes on the other side of the plateau. The two other men, it seemed to him, veered to the right just before disappearing in the mist. He thanked Grivo, who pointed out the sticks that marked the way through the bog before also starting the bike and departing with a wave.

There was no time to lose, but Samson was careful to think through the various courses of action. To call Naji out of the blue would be obviously the most direct way of alerting him to the possible danger of the two men, but there would be too much explaining to do and Naji would be bound to suspect his motives. Using Naji's own phone, which was in his pocket, wouldn't make any difference; in fact, it would probably make him even more alarmed. Instead, Samson dialled the number for Naji's sister, which he'd prised from the reluctant Sonia Fell two days before.

He got through on the second attempt and, speaking in Arabic, gave his name, said he was a colleague of Fell's and told her that he needed help to bring Naji to safety.

There was a lot of noise in the background and then a woman's voice repeatedly asking Munira who was on the phone. It was a friend of hers, she explained. He told her to find somewhere quieter.

He began again. 'We think some of the individuals Naji was associating with in your country – the men from Iraq – are here in Macedonia and are looking for him. I believe you know who these men are and why they are so dangerous.'

'Yes,' she said, but he could hear the doubt in her voice.

'If I meant Naji harm, I wouldn't be calling you, would I?' She said nothing to that either.

'Okay,' said Samson, 'I understand your caution, but I need your help right now. Naji has a new phone and I want you to call him on it.'

'I know, he sent me the number.'

'Can I check the number with you?' He read out the number Vuk had given him and she confirmed it was correct. 'Great, thanks,' he said. At last he was getting somewhere. 'Naji has a friend and they're with a dog, a lovely, big, white dog that is protecting them. They are walking across some hills. I hope to catch them up. But I do need your help.'

'How?'

'I want you to speak to Naji and tell him that I am a friend and I'm going to help him. Naji is not far from me, but the trouble is that I saw two other men on the mountain.

They could be innocent refugees, like Naji, but I just want to make sure he knows they are behind him and for him to take precautions.'

'Who are you?' the girl demanded.

'I work with Sonia, the lady you met two days ago. I live in London, though originally I am from a village in Lebanon. I was once a refugee, too. But for most of my life I have lived in the UK. I was hired by the people Sonia works for to find Naji because he may have valuable information that will save lives.' He paused before adding, 'Munira, I am not lying to you. I really need you to call Naji now.'

'We didn't like that woman who came to talk to us,' she said.

'She's just doing her job the best way she knows how. Maybe she was in a hurry. Look, this is really important, Munira. We haven't much time. Please will you talk to him? I could try, but I don't think he will take any notice of me.'

'I will call him,' she said, and hung up.

He crossed the boggy ground with ease and took Naji's course, rather than the higher line across the slope he thought the two men had followed. He walked quickly and was alert to everything that was going on around him, just as he had been in his crossings of the Turkish border into Syria. He noticed the slight changes in the ground, which on the whole was firmer than on the first mountain, and the capricious nature of the mist, which by turns obscured the mountain then the valleys below, smothering him so that he could barely make out his own boots then lifting so that he could suddenly see a hundred metres ahead of him.

He'd been going for about forty-five minutes and was confident that he would catch Naji in the next hour or so when he heard voices. He stopped in his tracks and bent his ear to the mountain above him. The voices came again, moving high on the slope above him. The rhythm of the speech suggested Arabic, although he couldn't hear what was being said. There were two voices and neither belonged to a thirteen-year old boy. He waited so he could work out exactly where they were coming from. The voices moved ahead of him, then stopped altogether.

He went for another hundred metres, pausing and listening. He was aware of a sudden drop in temperature and the mist being pushed along by a sharp new wind from his right. He had the impression of looking out of the cockpit of an aeroplane onto the clouds, seeing flashes of the mountains on either side – a long dark slope to his left, a dark spur to his right and some wild, shaggy goats peering over a parapet of rock, as still as if they'd been hewn from stone. The wind was getting stronger by the minute, making the ties on the outside of his pack hum and snap against the fabric. He continued with his head bent against the wind, thankful for the beanie he was wearing and the stick Andrej had pressed into his hand.

Five minutes later, he was moving down the slope to get out of the wind when he was brought up short by the sound of two shots being fired, as clear as if someone were cracking a whip beside him. He crouched down against a large rock, though certain that he was not the target. He waited. The mountain was silent again. He took out the satellite phone and dialled Munira.

'Did you get through?' he asked.

'No,' she said. 'I try many times.'

'Text him and email him. He may look to see if you replied to the one he sent this morning.'

'I've emailed him,' she said.

'Can you text him also? Then I will call him. We'll speak later.'

'Please tell me what's happening – we are very worried for Naji.'

'I will when I know,' he said.

Munira was silent.

'Are you there?' he went on. 'Is there something the matter?' He glanced up the mountain to make sure he still had the cover of the mist.

'Yes, I am here. It is a difficult time – we all are very worried. It's my little sister Yasmin. She is sick. My mother has gone with her to the camp medical facility. It is hard having a brother and a sister in danger at the same time.'

'I understand,' he said sympathetically. 'I will do everything I can to help Naji. Good luck with your sister. We will speak soon.' Although Samson was capable of an exceptionally cool objectivity in his work, he felt for the widow and children of Faris Touma, and understood all too well what they were going through. The added anxiety of knowing that Naji was on the road by himself must be almost unendurable. He said goodbye, pleased that he seemed to have gained her confidence.

He dialled the policeman's number three times, but got no response from Naji. He stood up from the rock and continued down the mountain, away from the source of the gunfire, as well as the wind that had made him suddenly feel so stiff. When he'd dropped to eleven hundred metres, he followed a contour on the satnav map that led to an area of green – the sprawling forests through which Naji would have to pass to reach Pudnik.

Naji and Ifkar ignored the paths and forestry tracks they encountered, crossing over them and moving through the dripping trees. The forest seemed to go on forever, but that suited them fine because they had no plan to enter Pudnik yet – they simply needed to find good reception so Naji could call Munira. So far, the service was worse in the trees than up the mountain – Naji didn't have even one bar. They walked without speaking, although Ifkar occasionally gave Naji reassuring glances and murmured endearments to Moon.

In the middle of the afternoon, as a watery sun broke through the cloud, they stumbled into a clearing full of tall grasses and found eight young migrants – six men and two women – sitting under a tree in the centre of the clearing. Ifkar glanced at Naji, who murmured that maybe it would be better if they didn't get involved. But as they turned to go back into the trees, one of the young men shouted out, '*As-salaam alaykum ya ikhwani*' – Peace be upon you, brothers.

They gave the traditional reply: '*Wa'alaykumu as-salaam*' – And upon you be peace.

One of the girls called out, 'Would you like some nuts? These are the best.' She held out her hand.

'Shall we get some nuts?' Ifkar asked, smiling at the girls. 'We can find out about the border.'

They walked towards the group and saw that they had a pile of walnuts, around which the fleshy green outer shells were littered. Everyone was seated on the ground.

'Where did you find the dog?' a man asked.

'She found me,' Ifkar replied, grinning.

'And where are you from?'

They didn't answer.

'Syria, Iraq, Afghanistan?' the man persisted.

'We came from hell and now we are in paradise,' said Ifkar, looking down at the two young women who were stripping the nuts. Naji was amazed by Ifkar's sudden confidence. The women looked up at him with interest; one pulled back the scarf on her cheek and smiled.

'Where are you going? Are you going to cross the border?' one of the young men asked. 'They are putting up a fence between Serbia and Macedonia – maybe they have already completed it.'

Ifkar shrugged. 'Maybe,' he said, taking one of the nuts and cracking it in his hand. He picked out the two halves and gave one to Naji. 'But there are always means of getting over.'

'With a dog?'

'Sure, with a dog.'

'Take some more nuts,' said one of the women. 'We have lots. Does your young friend talk?'

Ifkar turned to Naji and looked down at him with sympathy. 'He's not right in the head. He is simple.' Naji gave his most gormless smile. He was enjoying this.

'Where are you all from?' asked Ifkar, bending to scoop up a handful of nuts.

'We six are from Aleppo,' said the man who had done most of the talking, gesturing towards the two women and three men who were together. Naji had noticed how people on the road generally kept as clean and tidy as possible, but these people were dishevelled and looked exhausted. 'It's been hard,' he continued. 'We have no money because a people smuggler stole from us. Then three of us got sick with food poisoning and it knocked us back for weeks. The time limit on our papers ran out so we cannot cross the border to Serbia legally, and we cannot risk being sent back to Greece.' He gave his name as Rafiq, and introduced the others in his party. He told them that they were either related or were friends and had known each other all their lives.

'Your dog is beautiful,' said one of the women. 'I don't like dogs usually, but this one is really something – like a white lion.'

Ifkar smiled at her and she giggled.

Rafiq looked over to the other two men. 'And our brothers here joined us half an hour ago,' he said. 'They walked out of the forest, just like you. They are headed for the border, so we have just agreed to all go together.' Naji saw a flicker of unease in Rafiq's face, as though he did not know what to say next. He a bad feeling about the men who'd walked out of the forest. One had a couple of days' growth and a mass of curly black hair, but it was the hard, dead look in his eyes that struck Naji. He'd only just noticed it because both men had been smiling manically. And there was something familiar about the fidgety behaviour of the other man, who sat cross-legged, smoking, and whose gaze moved restlessly across the group under the tree. Al-munajil used to get the same look when he used that drug that kept him awake and made him unpredictable and extremely violent. Naji shot a glance at Ifkar, who knew exactly what he was thinking, though he did not allow his sunny demeanour to change. And Moon seemed to pick up something because she let out several squeaks, which always meant she was impatient to be on her way.

'Well, thank you for the nuts,' said Ifkar. He wished them good fortune and said '*Al-wadā*' – So long.

They would have left right then, but the phone in Naji's pocket started vibrating. He took it out and moved away to answer. One of the two men muttered, 'Not so retarded that he can't use a phone.'

At that moment, Naji heard his sister's voice and his heart leapt.

'Oh, Allah be praised – you're alive!' she said through tears of relief. 'I was so worried. Did you get my text?'

'It's so good to hear you, dear sister.' Naji was on the edge of tears also and he moved a little further away from the walnut tree.

'There's so much to say,' she sobbed. 'I don't have an idea where to start.'

'Then you must try not to cry. Tell me everything in the right order. Tell me how everyone is.'

'Oh Naji!' Munira sobbed again.

'Who is this man who contacted you?' said Naji. 'I do not understand why he wants me.'

She controlled herself. 'You spoke to someone – a woman in Greece. Was she a doctor? You told her things and you said what's on your phone. They sent a woman spy to speak to our mother – all the way from London.'

'They? Who's they?'

'British spies.'

'How do you know the woman was a spy?'

'Her questions were those of a spy.'

'How do you know what a spy says?'

'I just do! Listen!' He couldn't help but smile. 'Look, Naji – they even gave me this phone so I could make international calls. What do you know that is so important to them, Naji? Why have they sent a man to save you? He is with you in the mountains and he says two men are following you and they may hurt you.' She stopped for a second to get her breath. 'I can barely believe I am saying this to you – it's all so strange and frightening. His name is Paul – Paul Samson. He speaks Arabic and he's been hired to protect you by the lady spy. I talked to him twice. I trust him, Naji. He wants you to call him. Will you do that? Will you promise to do that immediately? You have his number. I sent a text with it.'

Naji's head was spinning. 'How do they . . . What do they . . . I mean . . .'

'Ask him to explain. Promise you'll call him, Naji. I know he will help you.'

'I will,' he said, still struggling with the idea that anyone could have found him in these mountains, and amazed that his phone was the subject of such interest, because he hadn't mentioned anything to the woman in Greece about his phone. There were things on it, but how could anyone know that? And anyway, the phone was long gone.

'How is everyone?' he asked again.

'Yasmin is not well.' Munira's voice faltered. 'I cannot lie – we are all very anxious about her, Naji. She is sick.'

'What with?'

She cleared her throat loudly – she was trying to control herself. 'She has a sickness called meningitis. It is dangerous. Our mother is with her now. She is having treatment.'

'Is she going to be all right?'

'We must pray for her, dear Naji.'

He turned away from the walnut tree, his eyes brimming with tears. 'I will,' he said, blinking furiously. 'I will pray.'

'And call that man now. Please do that for me, Naji, so I don't have to worry about you. And call me again. Tell me what's going on.'

'Yes,' he said. He nearly asked how his father was doing,

but something stopped him – the shadowy taboo in his mind that prevented him thinking about his dad now blocked the question. He said goodbye and allowed the hand holding the phone to fall to his side. He felt utterly exhausted, but he told himself he had been walking for nine hours. That made him think of the challenge ahead of him and very soon the image of Yasmin left his mind, for that was the only way he could survive on the road. He sneaked a look at the people beneath the walnut tree – they were eating nuts and laughing – and then he dialled the number.

Seconds seemed to pass before the call went through. When the voice answered, he was silent. 'Hello? Who is this?' said a man in Arabic.

'This is Naji Touma.'

'Great! I very much want to help you and your friend, Naji. I believe I am quite close to you.'

Naji was about to ask the man who he was and how he knew which number to call when there was a sudden rush of air to his left and one of the men took hold of him roughly, prising the phone out of his hand in one rapid movement that was impossible for Naji to resist. And then he was aware of a lot of shouting coming from beneath the tree. Somebody yelled, 'Don't shoot!' He heard a ferocious sound, halfway between a growl and a bark, and he was aware of a white blur to his right. The man who had got hold of him screamed at the first bite. The gun fired from somewhere behind them. Naji ducked but Moon kept on and forced his assailant to the ground. Naji saw her teeth bared and her ears flattened like a wolf's. She repeatedly lunged for his throat and face, and each time she pulled back there were more lacerations on the man's cheeks and jaw and also on the arm he was using to defend himself. Blood spatters appeared on her dazzling white coat. Naji knew it wouldn't be long before she ripped his throat out. This man with the curly black hair and the hard look in his eyes was the individual who was now going to pay for all the brutality she had suffered in her life.

She straddled him and took the front half of his head in her jaw, which opened wider than Naji could ever have imagined, and began to shake him. The man's eyes bulged with helpless terror and blood poured from somewhere on his scalp. Another shot rang out and Moon let go with a yelp and fell back. The man struggled to get to his feet but slumped back, his face a mess of blood and skin.

Naji turned to see the second man moving towards him with the gun pointing at Moon, and he realised he meant to finish her off, but for some reason – maybe the sight of his companion's face – he hesitated for a fraction of a second and that gave Ifkar the chance to rush him, which he did with incredible force, knocking the man sideways. As he toppled, he let off a couple more shots, the second of which seemed to cause Ifkar to jerk upwards. There were more screams from the party beneath the tree, but none of them came to help. Naji dived to wrest the gun from the man's hand as Ifkar stamped on his arm and chest. As soon as Naji had the gun, Ifkar stopped beating him and stood back to contemplate his victim. The man plainly thought he was going to be executed by Naji, who had the gun levelled at his forehead, and he let his head fall back onto the grass with a bitter smile, which seemed to acknowledge that after all his years of violence and fighting he was going to be killed by a kid. Naji moved back several feet so he could cover both men and assess the situation. They weren't going to cause any more trouble – that was plain – but he raised the gun anyway, aimed carefully at its owner and gave him a long, hard stare. Not long ago he'd seen a man executed by Al-munajil – or rather, he'd seen his body keel over just after the shot had been delivered to the side of his head. The terrible ease of this movement and of the extinction had stayed with him. He lowered the gun, ran a dozen metres, drew his arm back and flung it as far as he could into the trees.

The last few minutes had passed with such speed that Naji doubted he had taken more than a couple of breaths, but now things slowed down. As the gun sailed through the air, he noticed big black birds of prey flying in a spiral high above the clearing. In that moment, he remembered his father remarking once how odd it was that birds continued as normal whatever the chaos and brutality humans contrived in the world below them. They mated and hunted and migrated as though nothing was happening.

He turned back in this oddly detached state and saw his friend kneeling by Moon. He was telling her she wasn't hurt badly – just a long flesh wound on her flank and maybe a broken rib. It was as if she understood him perfectly, because she shook her head and then commenced a rhythmic licking of the gash on her side. He rose and threw a look towards the man she had savaged. He went over to him and sat on his haunches with his hands resting on his knees.

'He'll be okay. It looks worse than it is,' he said to the two women, who had moved forward. 'If you take him to the village they will look after him.' From his pack, he pulled a large pot of antiseptic ointment, which Naji knew he'd used to treat Moon when he rescued her all those months ago, and asked the women to smear it on the man's cuts to keep them from getting infected.

'What about you? You're bleeding!' said one of the young women after they had applied the cream. Ifkar looked nonchalantly at his right side. She motioned for him to remove his jacket. Naji saw his bloody shirt and T-shirt, which the women lifted from his torso. They knew what they were doing; they had come from Aleppo, and wounds like this were nothing new to them. The bullet had cut through his flesh twice – on the right side of his chest and then through the skin on the other side of his armpit, close to the lateral muscle. They dabbed the blood away from the wounds and spread the cream, though Ifkar insisted they go easy because he wanted to save some for when Moon had finished licking her injury. He grinned mischievously at their touch and told Naji it didn't hurt at all, but Naji knew this wouldn't last. He had once been in the back of Al-munajil's pickup with a young fighter who was hit in the leg. In fact, it wasn't long after they left the body of the executed man in the *wadi*. The fighter climbed in saying he was fine, but by the end of the journey he was screaming.

As they bandaged Ifkar's gunshot wounds as best they

could with spare headscarves, the women murmured their admiration of his impressive build. Naji remembered how the well-endowed store assistant had given Ifkar a double take and stared at his eyes, allowing Naji to lift a couple more chocolate bars from the display. Ifkar held something for women that he was only just beginning to appreciate, and these two seemed full of things they wanted to say to him. They mentioned, quite casually, that the pair with the gun had threatened them when Naji and Ifkar stumbled into the clearing. The men had only been there for ten minutes and they seemed friendly enough, but the moment they spotted Naji they became deadly serious, showed them the gun and told them to call Naji and Ifkar over and to act normally. They said Naji had stolen a phone that belonged to them.

Ifkar nodded his understanding, but Naji felt less forgiving. His friend and the dog, which he loved as though he'd known her all his life, were both pretty badly hurt and would need rest and treatment. Their wounds weren't going to heal themselves. As Ifkar was helped into his clothes, Naji paced up and down, hoping his mind would clear and he would have an idea what to do next.

His thoughts were suddenly interrupted when the man who'd been savaged by Moon jumped up as if he had been given a shot of adrenalin and, screaming his head off, ran to where his rucksack lay beneath the tree. He seemed to have completely lost his mind. He aimed a kick at the other man, who struggled to his feet. They hoisted their bags as best they could, shot crazed looks towards Naji and Ifkar, then staggered off towards the trees, one with blood oozing through the cream on his face, the other clutching his side and moaning with each step.

'Zombies!' said Rafiq. Everyone grinned except Naji, although that was exactly what the pair looked like. He knew they were on Captagon – the drug that allowed men to go on when others were dropping with fatigue. If it hadn't been for Moon's courage and Ifkar's physical strength, he'd most likely be dead by now, because the pair had obviously been sent to find and kill him. But for the high wind on the top of the mountain, they would have heard that shot; maybe there had been more. But what really bothered him was that he had never seen these two in his life before. How many more like them were out there?

They had secured Ifkar's pack around his left shoulder and were about to leave the walnut tree when Naji realised that the two men had taken the policeman's phone. He had assumed it was on the ground, but somehow the man had kept hold of it while fending off Moon. With the phone had also gone his only means of contact with his sister and the one person who might be able to help him, Paul Samson. He cursed himself for not making sure it was in his possession while he held the gun. He could have waved it in the man's face and made him hand the phone over. He felt like an idiot – as usual, he'd screwed everything up. As they took their leave of the group with muted goodbyes, his mind filled with guilt about Ifkar and Moon, who had been injured only because they were with him.

FOURTEEN

The moment Samson received the call from the boy he stopped in his tracks. He answered in a way that he hoped would give Naji confidence that he meant him no harm. But then he heard pandemonium break out on the other end, with yelling, a dog going wild and two cracks of a firearm. The gun echoed around the hills and Samson realised he was not too far away. He could see nothing, but he marked the position on the wooded slopes and set off in that direction.

To his astonishment, the phone call remained live. He heard two more shots quite close to the phone's microphone, which also rang out in the forest and allowed him to confirm the direction of the gunfire. He stopped again, listening intently and trying – with no little anguish – to work out what was going on and who had been hurt. He heard a man groaning close to the phone, and in the background, several other people were speaking excitedly in Arabic. He waited, barely breathing. Then he heard the boy's voice. Yes, he was pretty sure it was Naji. He had survived the attack and it seemed he and others were in control of the situation. Why the hell didn't he speak? 'Naji! Naji! Talk to me!' Samson said urgently into the phone. 'It's Paul. What's happening there? Naji, are you all right?'

No reply came.

He set off again, the phone pressed to his ear to make sure he wasn't missing anything. For a good ten minutes little changed – he heard the same groans and chatter in the background. Then there was a rustling as someone picked up the phone. This was followed by a lot of yelling from one individual, most of it in Arabic, but he also thought he heard a few words of the local language. That was impor-tant – the woman in the store had mentioned that the two migrants whom she had served spoke some Macedonian, or seemed to know some Serbian – he didn't remember which it was. He waited. There were now just two men talking; the agitation in their voices had subsided. He could hear them moving through the trees. One asked in Arabic, 'Have you got the phone?' When the other replied 'Yes,' he heard the first man say, 'That's all that matters,' before the call was ended. The individual must have glanced at the phone and seen that the screen was lit. It was significant that these men set such store in possessing what they must believe was Naji's phone.

It took him a further forty minutes to locate the empty clearing, where a perfectly symmetrical walnut tree stood like a child's drawing in the centre of an expanse of grass.

He saw that the grass was flattened under the tree where people had sat. Piles of green walnut husks were scattered about, along with cigarette butts, and there were spots of blood on the dead grass and a bloody rag discarded by the tree. He was no clearer about what had occurred, except that everyone who had been in this quiet, almost sacred place had apparently left alive. He listened to the forest for a few seconds but heard only the swaying of the trees and the call of a few birds. The temperature had dropped and the light was dimming. He needed to find a way down to Pudnik, but first he called Vuk.

'Where are you?'

'Am in Pudnik,' said Vuk. 'This shit town with shit people. Too many migrants here.' He stopped to take an audible drag on his cigarette.

Samson shook his head. 'The boy is probably headed to Pudnik. He's with a tall guy and they have a big white dog. It's late so they may look for somewhere to sleep.'

'Okay, I watch for them.'

'If I find the track I can see now on the satellite map, I'll be with you in about an hour. Just let me know the moment you see them. By the way, I'm pretty sure they don't have the phone any longer. I'll explain when I see you. The priority is obviously to watch for the boy and call me if you spot him.'

'I not fucking idiot – I know this,' Vuk protested, before the connection dropped in the middle of another sentence about Samson's car. Samson redialled but didn't get through.

He walked to the northern side of the clearing and plunged into the woods. After ten minutes of searching, he found a path. He took a couple of tumbles on the way down, cracking his knee, but by chance found a shortcut and, far away in the gloom of the forest, glimpsed two figures making their way down to the town. Despite the pain in his knee he forced himself on and saw them twice more. He noticed that they did not have a dog with them.

When he reached Pudnik, it was almost dark. Straddling a dirty, fast-flowing river, the town had an abandoned air, with several communist-era factories standing empty and unlit on the outskirts. As he hurried to the centre, Samson noted hints of winter in the activities of the townsfolk – hearths being fired up, wood being chopped and stacked, welders working on a snowplough under clamp lights.

Along the way he made multiple calls to Vuk to say that he had arrived, but they produced no response and he eventually found his way to a draughty market square, next to a bus station, where migrants stood in groups around makeshift braziers or sheltered behind the awnings of stalls set up for the following day's market.

At the bus station, a young couple were operating a hot drinks stand that was doing a brisk trade in soup and coffee. He bought a black coffee and listened to migrants' stories of being terrorised by police dogs and forced at gunpoint over Bulgaria's border with Macedonia. Now they had to find their way into Serbia, without the correct papers, and then head north to Croatia, but their number had been swollen by fresh arrivals from the south. These were people who had been blown off course on their trek north. They were sheltering in a large warehouse adjacent to the bus station. It was rumoured that buses would arrive to take some, or all, of them from Pudnik to the official border crossing with Serbia, north of Kumanovo. No one had any idea what to expect. Their faces were pinched with strain, their clothes filthy.

All the time he kept an eye on the road for the boys and the dog, but as the evening wore on he became certain that they'd camped somewhere in the forest, where they would be far better off than these people. They were doing it their own way and were probably even more determined now to avoid contact with other migrants. Yet he was certain of one thing: they couldn't make progress to the north without at some stage passing through the town. The terrain was just too challenging to choose any other route.

He was also sure that the two men he had seen on the mountain and in the forest must be in the crowds somewhere, so he focused his energies on finding them. He checked the huge warehouse and discovered another mass of people under a tin roof that groaned and shuddered in the wind. It was too dark to see properly, and people shrank from his gaze. Outside, he called Vuk again and left a testy message on his voicemail. He was tired and short-tempered and there was something about Vuk's boozy nonchalance that got under his skin. Where the hell was he? He cast about, dimly aware that he was slipping into autopilot. In Syria he had noticed that when he was caught up in the chase, his decisions often came without any conscious deliberation – and it worried him that he relied too much on his instincts. He was feeling a profound frustration from not catching up with Naji that day and now, as he saw three buses roll into the station, he feared he would lose the two men who had attacked the boy. Although they still represented a considerable threat, he thought that they were more likely to try to escape with what they believed was the prize they'd been sent by ISIS to retrieve – Naji's phone. But then, it wasn't Naji's phone, and they may already have discovered that, which meant they were still a danger to him.

He watched the buses pull up and the huddled crowds stir and begin to gather around them expectantly, but the doors remained firmly shut. It was a desperate scene made more stark and dramatic by the floodlights that cast long, grotesque shadows across the market.

He called Vuk again. This time he picked up.

'Where the fuck are you?'

'I have good surprise for Mr Samson.'

He sounded drunk. Samson ignored the remark about the surprise. 'Listen, there's an officer called Arron Simcek from the Macedonian Administration for Security and Counterintelligence. He was the man on the helicopter when we handed over Al Kufra, with the cropped hair and black leather jacket. Get hold of him and tell him that there are a couple of likely terrorists here in Pudnik. In the meantime, he has to make sure that this crowd don't board the buses going to the Serbian border, so he should talk to the local police. Then he needs to get here as soon as possible. How far is it from Skopje?'

'Maybe one hour and half hour.'

'Where are you? You're meant to be here, watching for the boy.'

'I get car and make surprise for Mr Samson.'

Samson held his temper. 'Just get hold of Simcek and tell him to meet me in the bus station at Pudnik.'

Fifteen minutes later a police squad car drifted into the station. Samson was pleased to see two police officers get out and talk to the bus drivers. A further hour and a half passed before three unmarked cars and two police Range Rovers tore into the station. Armed men rapidly cordoned off the area and Samson went over to talk to Simcek, who listened with scepticism, his gaze shifting from Samson's face to the crowd in front of them.

When Samson finished, he said, 'The reason we came was because of Al Kufra, who has proved useful to us. But if you don't know what these men look like, how are we to find them? There are two, maybe three hundred people here.'

'I have an idea,' said Samson. 'It worked for Al Kufra. First we need to get everyone together out here.'

People were flushed out of the warehouse and moved from the far corners of the marketplace. Speaking through an interpreter, Simcek asked for silence, as though he was going to make an announcement. He held up his hand, waiting for people to stop moving and the children to settle down. When eventually the only thing anyone could hear was the sound from an eddy of leaves by one of the stalls, he told his men to take up positions in the crowd. He nodded to Samson, who took out his phone and dialled the number. A muffled ringing came from deep within the crowd, way off to Samson's right. Two uniformed officers immediately descended on a man whose face was hidden by a hood, then grabbed the individual standing next to him. Samson watched as the men were pushed at gunpoint to the front of the crowd. Simcek pulled back the hood of one to reveal a swollen and badly lacerated face, then removed the second man's beanie. This one sported a bruise on his face and was clutching his right arm with his left.

Samson was surprised that such an unimpressive pair constituted the assassination team sent into the mountains to kill Naji. They were handcuffed and taken away in Simcek's vehicle.

After leaving the group at the walnut tree, Naji and Ifkar went deep into the forest and found a shallow dip in the land, at the end of which was a large flat rock that looked like a massive gravestone. Naji felt the ground by the rock – it was bone dry, thanks to the many dense pines above it. He told Ifkar to rest while he stretched his plastic sheet across a frame of sticks to make a roof. He cut pine boughs for the sides of the shelter and laid some under the plastic to create a springy bed. At the end he built a fire against the flat rock, so it would reflect the heat. Ifkar and Moon huddled close to one side of the fire and Naji began cooking the rice, beans and salted lamb they'd bought that morning. By juggling their odd collection of receptacles he managed to get the ingredients hot and edible more or less at the same time. Ifkar congratulated him, but the pain was showing in his face and every time he bumped his arm or moved it he suppressed a cry. When they'd finished, Naji boiled water to clean his and Moon's injuries, but by that time it was dark and very hard to see. After the one of the most exhausting and terrifying days of their lives, all three slept soundly in the snug shelter.

Samson woke to the sound of Vuk's Zippo lighter, which was followed by a mixed aroma of lighter fuel and cigarette smoke that reached him before he opened his eyes.

It was 6.30 a.m. and he had fallen asleep sitting on a couple of wooden pallets, a few metres from a police van that remained on the road between the bus station and the market square. The other vehicles had long since departed with the two suspects. He'd waited until he was sure that Naji was nowhere around and then, having had no word from Vuk, settled on the pallets out of the wind to smoke and wait for dawn. He had been asleep for no more than hour, but in that time the market had begun to come to life with stallholders unloading goods and produce.

'Surprise for you. I have surprise for you,' announced Vuk.

Samson clambered to his feet, stretched and took in Vuk's

grey stubble and bloodshot eyes. 'Where the hell were you? I was calling your bloody phone all night.'

Vuk shrugged, as though this had as much to do with him as the weather. 'I have surprise for you.'

Samson put up his hand to stop him. One of his two phones was vibrating in his pocket.

There was no caller ID. 'Yes,' he said into the phone.

'We understand you're still in Macedonia,' said Sonia Fell.

'And good morning to you, Sonia.'

'We've learned that you were involved in the arrest of two men in the north. The Chief wants to know what you're still doing in-country?'

'In-country! We're not in a fucking war zone, dear!'

'He wants to know why you're still there,' she said stiffly. He could tell this really got under her skin.

'I mean this in the politest possible way, Sonia, but it's none of his goddamn business. I thought we'd been through this. I'm a free agent.'

'Are you still in pursuit of Firefly? Have you got to him?'

'No.'

'No to which question?'

'Both.'

'Then what are you doing? Is Vuk with you?'

'No.'

'You're in Macedonia illegally. You can be arrested.'

'I doubt it. Simcek has just taken delivery of two suspects, as you know. They were in possession of a phone that belonged to the policeman who was stabbed, which may suggest to the authorities that they were responsible for that attack. The men may also have local links, which the Macedonians rightly believe is important for their own security. And, by the way, I make that three suspects I've brought in this week. What's your score, Sonia? Are you still watching that . . . ?'

'Refrain from discussing operational details,' she snapped. 'All we need to know from you is whether you're going to leave today of your own free will or whether we are going—'

'There's something I've never understood about this,' said Samson wearily. 'This investigation is all my work – I've got you so far! Why are you now so keen for me to leave? What the hell is the problem?'

'I cannot answer that question. I am simply telling you that unless you leave you will be—'

'Sorry, didn't hear that, Sonia. You're breaking up, Sonia. Can you repeat that?'

'Unless you agree to leave now you will be—'

'Hello? Hello! Can you hear me, Sonia? Oh damn! I've lost you.'

He ended the call and turned to Vuk. 'What do you know about Bosnia?'

Vuk pouted doubtfully. 'They are waiting. They are watching. They not tell Vuk Divjak nothing because Vuk not work for them. My people, they say your people watching houses and factory in Bosnia-Herzegovina. Big-time operation – many, many people. This everything I know.'

'So they're sure Al-munajil and the other two are there?'

'Maybe – I do not know this.'

'I thought the British were still paying you?'

He shook his head. 'I have new boss with plenty money now.'

'You're not thinking of me, I hope.'

Vuk snorted a laugh and began coughing. He felt for the flask in one of the hand-warmer pockets in the front of his jacket, took a mouthful and banged his chest violently with his fist.

'What happened last night, Vuk? Why didn't you answer? You could have called me back.'

'Was busy with new boss.'

'Who is your new boss?'

'In moment I tell you.'

Samson stamped his feet and rubbed his hands and looked around, now bored with Vuk's game. With the activity in the marketplace, migrants were stirring and beginning to look around for sustenance. 'I need coffee,' he said. His eyes travelled across the market stalls in search of a stand selling hot drinks. The stall that had been worked the night before by the young couple had gone. Then he saw two policemen making towards him, with a third man in plain clothes, who pointed straight at him. He bent down and slipped all three phones into the side pocket of his backpack.

'Vuk, can you pick up my pack?'

'Your pack?'

'Yeah, my backpack! Pick it up and walk away from me.

Do it now! It's got Naji's phone in it. Guard it with your life.'

Vuk hooked the bag over one shoulder and moved away into a group of men unloading crates of tools and electrical goods from a truck.

Samson patted his pockets and pulled out a pack of cigarettes. By the time he had lit up, Vuk had disappeared.

'You!' said the plain-clothes officer in English. 'You are coming with us.'

'Oh really,' said Samson. 'Why's that?'

'You are here illegally. You were instructed by border police to leave the country. You did not obey that instruction and you are now under arrest.'

'What if I tell you that I'm leaving today?'

The man nodded and the uniformed police officers each took one of his arms. 'It is too late for that, Mr Samson.'

'You were here last night, weren't you?' said Samson, now recognising the officer. 'You have two terrorist suspects under arrest because of my help.'

The man turned away and Samson was frogmarched to a waiting car.

Naji was first to wake. It had snowed a little during the night and pellets of ice had gathered in tiny drifts beyond the cover of the trees. He heaped pine logs onto the fire to make tea and nudged Ifkar awake. He was slow to come to, but eventually he took the tin cup, held it in both hands and blew on it. Moon raised her head and then let it flop back, ignoring the sliver of lamb that Naji held out to her. It was obvious to him that neither could travel that day.

Naji busied himself collecting more wood and repairing the shelter, then warmed the bread on the fire and placed a slice of hard cheese on it for Ifkar's breakfast. He was worried about his friend's pallor and glassy-eyed listlessness. He coaxed him to eat, saying he needed fuel to make new blood and defend himself against infection. Ifkar smiled weakly and did his best, eating a little, but then deflected Naji's attention to Moon. Together they made her drink and forced some meat into her mouth, which she consented to swallow.

All three dozed for a while. By mid-morning Ifkar was getting worse. His forehead was hot to the touch and he complained of a raging thirst. Naji had no idea what to do – he was too large to help down into the town and Naji was sure he wouldn't be able to get medical aid to him on the mountain, even if he found someone. There was only one thing for it – he would leave them and go to find drugs, water and food. He stoked the fire with a large, dry tree branch, and placed a pile of wood beside Ifkar so he could keep the fire going. He left his sharpened stick and a knife, and at Ikfar's suggestion put the remaining food in a plastic bag and hung it on a tree a little distance away, because the day before they'd wondered if the bear had been attracted by the smell of food. He set off, and after hurrying downhill for five minutes found a track that wound down the mountain to the town. He marked the spot where he had joined the

track by tying a rag to a sapling then raced on with only the
dread of losing Ifkar and Moon in his mind. He reached the
town in under an hour. At any other time he'd have taken
care to scout out the place and watch for Al-munajil's men,
but he went quickly to the centre and found a large general store that had a few basic medical supplies for sale. He
bought packets of bandages and plasters, although he knew
they wouldn't be enough to cover Ifkar's gunshot wounds,
and as much food and water as he could stuff into his pack.
Outside the store he stopped to listen. Familiar sounds were
coming down the street – the calls of market stallholders
are the same the world over – and he followed them to an
open-air market that was full of colour in the fleeting sunlight. A large number of migrants milled about and there
was almost a festive atmosphere. He learned from a group of
men gathered around a stall specialising in tools that several
buses had already departed to take people to the Serbian
border, and many more were promised that afternoon.

He knew a lot about markets, and at any other time he
would have lingered among the stalls to watch, but as soon
as he realised there was nothing he could buy to help Ifkar,
he decided to leave. At that moment he became aware of a
woman in a headscarf staring at him from the other side of
a fruit stall. For a moment their eyes met. She smiled, then
started waving excitedly and calling his name. He pulled his
cap down and started to push through the crowd. But she
moved quickly and in no time she had caught up with him
and grabbed hold of his arm – not roughly, but with enough

strength to prevent his escape. He turned to see the woman, who was not much taller than him, beaming and fanning her face after the exertion of her dash through the crowd. 'Oh Naji, it's wonderful to see you again.'

For some reason he noticed her huge breasts and thought how Ikfar would admire them. But who was she? There was something vaguely familiar about the stout figure and the chubby, friendly face. She laid her hand on his arm, shaking her head. 'Naji! Don't you remember us?' She turned to a stocky man who was carrying a baby on his chest. 'Fatimah and Hassan!' she continued, her eyes popping. 'The Antars! We were on your boat – you saved our little girl when we sank. You saved our little Marya! We have her because of you, Naji. Because of you, Naji!'

She lifted the baby from the sling and held her out in front of him. 'This is Marya, who you saved from the sea. Don't you recognise her?'

He nodded, though one baby looked like another to him. Even though he had spent so long looking at this baby's face, he could not remember her. Marya stuck her hand out and touched his nose and her parents roared with laughter. Naji groaned inwardly. At the camp, he'd been embarrassed when the couple had come with tears in their eyes to shower him with kisses, and now Fatimah was determined to go through the same mortifying performance, telling those who had gathered around them that Naji was a true hero. He protested that he wasn't a hero at all – all he'd done was reach for a life jacket when he was about to drown in the ocean.

He didn't know there was baby in it. But no one heard him. They touched him and patted his back and one man said that to hear of such selfless action restored his faith in humanity.

Marya was returned to the sling and a dummy was put into her mouth. Naji thought this was good moment to go and attempted to wriggle free from Fatimah's grasp. 'Where are you going?' she cried. 'Aren't you going with us on the bus? Please travel with us, Naji! We may be able to help you.'

He shook his head. 'I have a friend who is sick and I must return to him. He's very sick.'

'Helping everyone except yourself – as usual,' said Fatimah. She glanced at her husband, who nodded his admiration. 'There must be something we can do for you, dear Naji? We owe you everything.'

He shook his head resolutely. 'No, there's nothing you can do for me. It's kind of you, but . . .' He stopped. 'Have you got a phone I can use? I need to call my sister.'

'Yes, of course! We bought a replacement in Lesbos.' She held out her hand to her husband without looking at him. He placed the phone in her hand and she passed it to Naji.

He'd memorised his sister's new number, but unfortunately not the number of the Englishman named Samson. He moved away a little and dialled.

She answered immediately.

'Munira – it's me.'

'Oh, Naji! Naji – you're all right! Thank God!' She let out a sob of relief.

'Yes, I'm fine, but I don't have that phone any longer

– someone stole it before I could call that man. Tell him I'm in the same place. But I am looking after a friend who is hurt and—'

Munira told him to shut up. This shocked him – she never spoke like that, even in anger, and now he realised that there was something strange about her voice. 'Naji, listen to me. She died – our little sister Yasmin died. This morning she left us.' The news came in gasps that ended with a moan of grief.

At first, Naji had no idea what she was saying, for with the battle of the walnut tree and his total preoccupation with Ifkar and Moon, he'd forgotten completely about his sister's illness. It was a couple of seconds before the realisation dropped like a stone in his being. Yasmin was dead, and there was nothing he could do to bring her back – no act of courage or self-sacrifice. Nothing. She was gone and he was responsible, for he hadn't reached Germany and brought his family to safety. And in his mind stirred that other dark truth that he'd kept tethered and hidden for so long.

He staggered a little. The hand holding the phone dropped from his ear and he sank to the ground. Fatimah caught him and helped him to a low wall, where Naji sat with his head hanging and tears coursing down his cheeks. The woman took the phone from him and spoke to Munira and listened gravely. Then she handed the phone back to Naji. 'Speak to her, dear child. She needs to hear your voice.'

He couldn't manage anything except to mumble that he was desperately sorry and that it was all his fault: bringing Al-munajil into their home so that he spied on her and determined to marry her was his fault. That was the reason they had had to leave Syria and go to the camp and that was the reason Yasmin had caught the disease. Munira stopped him in mid-flow and told him to think straight – how could he, a young boy, be held responsible for the evil of a man like Al-munajil, or for the conditions in the camp that caused their sister to catch meningitis? Was he responsible for the war? Was it Naji Touma's fault that hundreds of thousands of people lay dead in ruined cities across their homeland?

He had to agree that it wasn't.

'This is the life that has been chosen for us – that's all there is to say about it,' said Munira. She stopped and Naji heard his beloved sister take several deep breaths to control herself before she stumbled through an account of the funeral they would hold for Yasmin the following day. 'We can survive this disaster as long you stay safe, dear brother. You must call the man who will help you. Promise me that you will do that.'

He told her about his phone, but not how he'd lost it, and she said she'd call Paul Samson, but Naji must stay in one place until he arrived. He replied that he couldn't do that because he was looking after a friend who was sick, but that he could meet Samson in Pudnik market, where he was at that moment, the following morning.

He made her repeat the arrangement several times to make sure she had got it right. After they had told each other how much they loved each other and Naji had sent his love to his mother and his middle sister, Jada, she hung up. He gave the phone back to Fatimah. His hand trembled and tears were still running down his cheeks. She opened her arms and he let himself fall into them and be held against her breasts, right there in the marketplace with everyone watching and wondering what was going on.

'I heard you blaming yourself just then,' Fatimah said in his ear. 'That is wrong, Naji. You saved our baby, and my life, too, because I could not have lived without her. Do you understand?' She took his head in her hands and held it so that he could see her face. 'We owe you everything, Naji. During these terrible times you must remember that three strangers will never ever forget until their dying day what you did for them.'

He nodded and wiped away his tears. But she held him for a little longer and that made him feel better, or at least able to go on.

The scene had attracted the attention of two medical volunteers, a young man and a middle-aged woman. They had rushed to Pudnik with a mobile treatment centre because large numbers of people had arrived from the south and east at the same time, many of them injured from their encounters with the Bulgarian police. The young man, a tall blond with blue spectacle frames, asked Fatimah if there was anything they could do, and she explained that Naji had just had some very bad news. 'Perhaps we can at least clean and dress the graze on his arm,' said the woman in good Arabic. 'It looks like it might be infected.' Naji turned his arm and saw the graze on his elbow for the first time. He shook his head and said it didn't bother him – he had to be going.

'It won't take long,' said the woman, putting an arm round his shoulder. 'Our vehicle is just over there.' Numb with grief, Naji allowed himself to be steered to a camper van parked at the side of the bus station, next to the marketplace. Fatimah and her husband followed with the baby.

Inside the van, Naji insisted on standing, which meant the woman had to sit to treat him. She applied iodine, which stained his arm golden brown, dressed the graze with lint and stuck it down with strips of plaster. As this was being done, Fatimah leaned through the door and started telling the pair how brave Naji was and how he had saved her child and was travelling to Germany on his own. Naji gave her an exasperated look and willed her to shut up, but she went on and on, and threw in the observation that many kids were vanishing on the migrant trail. The aid workers glanced at each other, then the woman started asking Naji searching questions about his journey. He looked her straight in the eye and told her that he was travelling with two cousins, who were both over eighteen years old. Fatimah did not hide her surprise at this news.

'Your cousins, why are they not here with you now?' asked the female aid worker.

'I will go and find them,' Naji said confidently.

'Why don't we come, too?' she said pleasantly. 'It will be nice to meet them, and we can make sure they know how to look after that arm of yours.' In English, she told her colleague to make a call and say they had come across another unaccompanied minor. Naji recognised the phrase from the camp in Lesbos, where he'd heard it too many times, but his expression gave nothing away. She turned to squirt antiseptic gel into her hands and then worked it between her fingers. The blond man smiled at him and bent to pick up a box of latex gloves that had fallen behind the little counter on which lay two trays of disinfected instruments. Naji saw his chance. In one fluid movement he scooped up a wad of large dressings, the roll of lint and bottle of iodine, ducked past the woman and jumped through the doorway of the van. He collided with Fatimah, causing her to spin round with a shriek of surprise. For a few vital seconds she blocked the exit for the blond medic, who'd reached out to grab Naji but missed him.

Naji ran from the bus station and plunged into the crowds in the market, where he began to weave through the stalls in an expert fashion – fleeing someone in a market was not a new experience for him. Soon, he was back in the dismal streets of Pudnik and heading for the far side of town. Somewhere in his being, the pain of his loss throbbed, but now he consciously focused on Ifkar and Moon, for in the immediate reality of the Balkan Mountains they were all he had.

He longed to see Ifkar and show him everything he had managed to get hold of in Pudnik, but as approached the spot he'd marked with the rag, he saw a small tractor and trailer parked a little way up the track. The engine was still going and a layer of blue exhaust had settled over the path. Voices came from the direction of the shelter where Ifkar and Moon lay. Naji crept through the trees with his heart beating so fast he thought it might be heard. But he hardly made a sound as he moved over the beds of leaves and pine needles, and he was able approach to within a few metres of the camp without making a noise. He lifted a branch and saw two figures moving around the shelter – an old couple. They had swept back the plastic sheet and moved some of the boughs that Naji had arranged. They were bent over Ifkar and Moon; neither appeared to be moving. He glimpsed Moon's coat but he couldn't see Ifkar. The fire was still alight. He shifted his weight from one foot to the other and a twig snapped. Both heads turned towards him, and two pairs of eyes searched the forest. The woman, whom Naji guessed was in her sixties, wore three coats of different lengths, a patterned cotton scarf over her head and a woollen one around her neck. She smiled tentatively in Naji's direction, although she couldn't see him, and murmured something to her companion. He straightened and started towards Naji. He was a large man of about the same age, wearing a black cap with earflaps and a faded green parka with a fur-trimmed hood. Naji shrank into the bushes, but the man came near to where he was hiding and said something softly, then he simply put his hand out. He spoke again. Although it meant nothing to Naji, he guessed the man was saying hello. He waited a few seconds, then edged forward and showed himself. The man nodded and grinned, then turned to go back to the shelter. Naji followed.

On the ground by the shelter were two baskets full of fat

mushrooms and a few small yellow ones. Naji understood immediately that they'd been collecting them for food and had come across the shelter by chance. He slipped past the couple and knelt down by Ifkar, who opened his eyes with a wild expression as Moon gave a lazy wag of her tail. Naji touched him on his good shoulder and said that he'd got all the bandages necessary, plus the iodine. Ifkar nodded drowsily. He was sweating and also shivering. 'I cannot walk today,' he told Naji apologetically.

'We don't have to go anywhere – we have plenty of food,' said Naji. 'How long have these two been here?'

'Not long – the woman came first, then her husband.'

The woman nodded approvingly and kept repeating, '*Dobro momče* – good boy, good boy.'

Naji began to take one of the larger bandages out of its packet, but the man tapped him on the shoulder, wagged his finger and gestured in the direction of the tractor. Naji kept on unwrapping the bandage. The man touched him again and began to mime carrying Ifkar to the tractor and going up the mountain with the dog to their place, which he described by drawing walls either side of him in the air and a pitched roof over his head. To this he added the actions of eating with a knife and fork and sleeping, which he did by putting both hands together and pressing them against one cheek. He seemed to enjoy the miming and he made the woman smile.

Naji looked up at him. He trusted no one except Ifkar, but this old couple seemed nice, and besides, the three of them had very few options. Ifkar needed much more attention than he could give him out in the open. He nodded without looking up at the man, who laid a hand briefly on Naji's shoulder then set about cutting and stripping two small trees to make straight poles. He went off to his tractor and returned with four drive belts for some kind of machinery, possibly a log saw, which he nailed with tacks at regular intervals along the poles. Next he seized Naji's treasured plastic sheet, folded it lengthways and fixed it to the poles with more tacks. In no time at all, he'd made a stretcher. Now he considered how to move Ifkar from beside the fire onto the stretcher, for they had already discovered that the slightest touch on the right-hand side of his torso caused him to screw up his face and suppress a cry. Naji and the woman took hold of his legs, while the man worked his hands under Ifkar's back, as though he was going to lift a heavy log, and on the count of three they moved him to the stretcher. The man took hold of two poles at one end, while Naji and the woman grasped a pole each. Before they set off, Naji called over to Moon, who staggered to her feet and prepared to follow them. Progress was slow, their path blocked by fallen trees and dense clumps of saplings, and after struggling for ten minutes or so the man told them to lower Ifkar while he went to fetch his tractor, which he drove straight into the undergrowth, flattening the young trees before him. They lifted Ifkar onto the trailer. Then the man, who never stopped grinning throughout, put his hand down to Moon's nose and spoke to her softly. She rubbed against his leg, which Naji knew was a good sign, and he stroked her some more before picking her up and placing her on the trailer alongside Ifkar.

He turned to Naji and pressed his hand to his chest. 'Darko,' he said with his largest grin, his eyes disappearing into his huge red face. With a theatrical flourish, he announced 'Irina,' and just to make certain that Naji understood these were their names, he repeated them several times. Naji did likewise for himself, Ifkar and Moon. Then the man suddenly slapped his forehead and did an elaborate mime to say he'd forgotten the basket of mushrooms. Naji went back with him to collect a few things from the camp, particularly his throwing knife, which was in the spot where he'd left it for Ifkar. When he started gathering cooking vessels and the rest of their paraphernalia, the man revolved his hand to indicate they would come back another time for their belongings. Naji began to protest, but the man tapped his watch and beckoned good-naturedly to him and they returned to the tractor.

Now overwhelmed by exhaustion and close to tears, he clambered onto the trailer to sit beside Moon and Ifkar, while the woman wedged herself in the tiny cab with her husband. They set off up the track and were soon trundling across rolling pastures with Pudnik below them. By the time they reached the couple's farm, Naji had keeled over and fallen asleep on Moon.

FIFTEEN

Samson was led from the car into a large complex some way out of town. He was searched and taken to an interview room with a table, four chairs and no window. He was there for two hours before the door opened and Simcek of the Macedonian Administration for Security and Counter-intelligence entered his life for the third time that week. On this occasion he was accompanied by an eager young thug in a tight suit, with a scar that sliced across his right eyebrow and continued on his cheek for a couple of centimetres.

Samson looked up and smiled as they walked in. 'I mind starting the day without coffee more than being arrested.'

Simcek sat down. He did not smile. 'Is that so? Perhaps we should give you some time to reconsider that remark in one of our prisons, where I am afraid the room service is not what it should be.'

Samson sniffed the musty basement air and looked around. 'It's a big facility for a relatively small town. Built by Tito in the communist years, no doubt. Even so, it seems very large.'

Simcek studied him. 'There are problems in this district. Eight policemen were killed here this year. There's a hard core of troublemakers – Albanians.' He stopped and sighed. 'But now you're the problem. I have orders from the highest level to make sure that you leave our country today.'

'Can I ask why? I have done nothing but help your government. Al Kufra is an important catch for you, and the two men from last night are bound to be useful.'

'And we are grateful, but you are no longer needed here. You entered the country illegally and you were told to leave within a specified period by the border police in Gevgelija.'

Samson lifted his hands in surrender. 'Okay, but if I'd left when I was told to, you wouldn't have arrested those men. By the way, have you got any idea who those two were working for?'

'You can make guesses as well as I can,' said Simcek.

'Who put them on that mountain? Are they local? Where do they come from?'

'The suspects both required medical treatment and we have not spoken to them for any length of time yet. One of the men had been badly mauled. It's remarkable that he got so far after he was attacked.'

Samson tried again. 'Are they linked to Al-munajil?'

Simcek didn't react.

'I thought maybe you could help me out – since I've helped you.'

'You are in the country illegally and you are helping a criminal, the boy who attempted to murder one of our police officers.'

'I am not helping him – I haven't found him – and anyway, he's not a criminal. He's too young, as you know. I looked up the Macedonian criminal code on my journey. Yes, really – I looked it up. There's a consolidated version in English online. The kid is a minor and cannot be found guilty of a crime. And even if you could charge him, he would be able to claim self-defence, because you and I both know that police officer is a predatory paedophile.'

'You have no evidence of that.'

'The man at the gas station said the officer often picked up young migrants there – always young boys. I wonder what happened to those boys, because near where the officer was found with a stab wound there is an abandoned house. I'm no expert but I'd place a large bet that the turned earth at the rear of that building indicates a fresh grave.'

The young thug began shaking his head. Simcek said, 'You cannot defame a member of the security forces like this.'

'Is that why you are so interested in the boy?' asked Samson. 'Is it that you don't want him to reveal what happened to him there?'

'You need to mind what you're saying,' said Simcek.

'That's it, isn't it? You've done a deal. Your government has had me taken off the case because you want to make sure he is silenced, or at the very least that he's never found and therefore cannot testify about the policeman. That makes me think that the policeman has more influence than I originally thought – maybe he's the son of someone high up.' At this, Simcek leaned forward and slapped Samson hard across the right side of his face with such force that Samson nearly fell from the chair. But apart from putting his hand up to feel where Simcek's ring had broken the skin, he did not react. He was shocked, because he was certain MI6 had not asked for this, but he knew that to protest would be to invite the intervention of the young ruffian.

'Now we will proceed,' said Simcek quietly. 'We are in possession of the phone that the two men took from the boy. This tells us that you made calls to him throughout yesterday and before. We also know that he made calls to a cell phone in Turkey.'

'Yes, to his sister.'

'How did you know the boy stole the police officer's phone and how did you then acquire that number?'

'I made a guess that Naji had taken the phone because, as you know, his own phone had been stolen and he needed a way of staying in touch with his family. We tracked down the policeman and gave him money – five thousand euros. We wanted to stop him cancelling the phone, so that I could talk to the boy. The policeman asked for a second payment of the same amount, but by that time the two men in your custody had taken the phone.'

This was clearly all news to Simcek, but he did his best not to seem surprised. He couldn't very well doubt that the police officer had accepted the money, because the man had made no attempt to cancel the phone service, the normal reaction of someone who has had their phone stolen.

'So you made an arrangement to meet Naji Touma?'

Samson shook his head. 'He was attacked as I was speaking to him, so we did not make a rendezvous. I don't know what happened to him – Naji could be dead, for all I know. I heard several shots. But the two men in your custody can tell you exactly what occurred.'

'When we searched them last night, they had no weapons. Are you suggesting they threw away their guns?'

Samson met his gaze. 'Who knows, but to answer your question, I have no rendezvous with the boy and I have no idea where he is. I hoped that he might turn up in the bus station; that's why I waited there all night.'

Simcek looked him over. 'Where is the backpack you had with you last night? Where is the phone you were using?'

'When your men arrested me I didn't have time to retrieve it from a friend. But I believe it is safe, if that is what's worrying you.' Samson wondered if Simcek was after the really important phone – the one that Naji had brought across the sea from Turkey. But maybe he didn't know about it; maybe in their haste to capture Al-munajil and his gang, SIS had completely forgotten about the phone, or at least not thought to mention it to Simcek. There was no reason MI6 would alert Simcek to its existence, particularly as they seemed to have lost interest in Naji and any information he might have. For all intents and purposes, they seemed not to care whether he lived or died.

There were a few more half-hearted plays by Simcek, during which Samson reminded him that he was close to Denis Hisami, who'd had access to the Al Kufra interrogation, and also to Macy Harp, who was well connected in the Balkans, but he sensed the interview was ending. For as long as Simcek could say to his superiors that Samson had no plans to meet the boy and there was no hope of locating him in the mountains, and, moreover, that Samson was on a plane out of the country, nothing more could be expected of him.

A few minutes later, Simcek and his sidekick rose together. 'You will wait here until we can escort you to the airport,' said Simcek.

'What about my backpack?'

'That's of no interest to us. I'm sure your friend will arrange for its return.'

'Any chance of some coffee?' said Samson.

Simcek got up. 'I'll see what we can do,' he said.

No coffee arrived and he was left in the interview room for a further five hours, which hung very heavily indeed because he knew that this day would be crucial for Naji. If he had survived whatever had occurred in that clearing, he would urgently need help, for he'd probably reached the end of his strength and resourcefulness, and was almost certainly as frightened as hell. Samson knew enough about Naji to assume that he would get hold of another phone and try to make contact with him again. It was agonising to think that the boy's calls were going unanswered, unless of course Vuk had the wit to answer them, but there was no guarantee of that. If he was put on a plane out of Macedonia, or pushed over the border, Vuk would be the boy's only hope.

He was good at keeping himself occupied when forced into inactivity – he'd had to be in Syria, where he'd spent days holed up until it was safe to move or his contact turned up. Now, as he sat in the Macedonian interview room, he found himself thinking about Anastasia quite a bit, which surprised him, and when he had exhausted the memory of their conversations, he reverted to his strategy for the forthcoming race and Dark Narcissus's chances.

At three o'clock he was transferred to a room at ground level and given a bottle of water. His cigarettes, wallet and passport were all returned to him. Ten minutes later, he was placed in the back of an unmarked SUV, blue lights flashing behind its radiator grill, and driven at speed to Skopje airport. When they arrived, the two officers, who had said nothing during the hour-long trip, handcuffed him and marched him to the Lufthansa desk. The ticket was waiting for him. The woman behind the desk smiled as if nothing was untoward and wished him a pleasant flight to Vienna. The officers removed the handcuffs and led him to the security check. Only when he'd passed through and was waiting in line for the immigration booth did they leave him and head for the exit.

Samson watched them all the way to the car park, then began to consider ways of passing back through security.

'How are you doing there?' said an American voice from

behind him. Samson turned to see a man of about his height and age. 'If you give me your passport, we can expedite your deportation,' he murmured with a grin. He handed Samson a fob. 'Mr Hisami has arranged a car for you. It's out front, right by the door. Tell them you've forgotten to turn the lights off – they'll let you go back.'

Samson took out his passport and slipped it to the man.

'Don't worry – you'll have it back by tomorrow morning.'

'Thanks,' said Samson.

'Don't thank me – I get to have dinner in Vienna. Oh, I need your boarding pass, too.'

'It's inside the passport,' said Samson.

'There's a friend in the vehicle. They'll tell you where to go. So, I guess you're all set.'

'Great,' said Samson. 'I'll see you tomorrow.'

'You got it.'

Samson began to simulate forgetfulness and returned to the uniformed security guards to explain about the car, which was just visible from their desk. They told him he would have to go through the check again and he had better hurry if he was hoping to make the Vienna flight. He said he'd have to risk it. He jogged across the terminal floor, went through the automatic doors, pressed the fob to make sure he'd got the right vehicle and climbed in.

'Hello, Mr Spy,' said a female voice over his shoulder.

Samson whipped round to see Anastasia's grinning face. 'What the! How long have you been here?'

She roared with laughter. 'Such a good joke! I thought

spies were meant to check the back seat before they got into a car.'

He smiled – it was good to see her. 'Are you going to join me, or are you enjoying yourself too much back there?'

She got out, hopped into the passenger seat and gave him a peck on the cheek.

'When did you get here?' he asked.

'Late last night. Your weird friend Vuk picked me up.'

'But he was in the square with me this morning.'

'Yes, we were going to surprise you but then you went and got arrested – most inconvenient of you. Still, I met Denis Hisami.'

'How?'

'He's at Pudnik – well, near there, in a hotel.'

The penny dropped. 'Vuk is working for him now. And who was that man in there?'

'Jim Tulliver. He works for Denis. He calls himself Denis's "man of affairs". He set the destination on the satnav.' She pressed the screen and the route guidance began.

He looked over the controls of the car and moved off. 'We're going back to Pudnik, right?' he said.

'Yes, to find Naji.'

'To find Naji,' he repeated. 'Did Denis explain why he was in Macedonia?'

She shook her head and looked out of the side window. 'It is an appalling story. He didn't say much, except to tell me what you went through to try to find his sister. She sounds a wonderful person.'

'She was – after all those months of looking for her I began to feel I knew her, almost like a friend.'

'Is that the same with Naji?'

'No, I find it hard to imagine knowing Naji – he's like a little sprite dodging from place to place. A firefly.'

'You think he's still alive?'

'Absolutely.' They stopped at a junction and he turned to her. 'I'm certain he got out of that clearing with his friend and the dog. Don't ask me how, I just know. I think the Macedonians know, too, because they interrogated the two men that were arrested last night. Simcek wouldn't tell me anything.'

As they joined the motorway, Samson began to describe all that had happened in the last few days in the hope that Anastasia could give him some kind of reading of Naji's psychological state and maybe an idea of what he would do next. But after he'd finished she was silent for several minutes and he had to prompt her. 'So, where do you think his head is? What sort mental state is he in?'

'It's hard to say. Naji is highly motivated – the most motivated child that I have ever met. I believe he has both intrinsic and extrinsic motivation. He is determined to get things done and achieve goals because it gives him satisfaction. Did you know that he had the highest grades in his class and he was studying with kids that were much older than him? When Syria broke apart and his father was arrested and school ended, he didn't stop reading and learning. He has a hunger for things that make him think. At the camp, I had

to keep finding him books because he read them so quickly –
even in English – and nothing was too hard or specialised for
him. And then, of course, he has a high degree of extrinsic
motivation, also.'

'What's the difference?'

'Extrinsic motivation is when we are motivated by external
rewards – money, praise, group acceptance et cetera, et cetera.'

'And Naji's reward will be to bring his family to safety
because he loves them very deeply.'

'Yes, plus his dead father's praise – that's very important
to him.'

'We had someone visit the family in Turkey. She said that
Naji doesn't accept his father's death.'

'Didn't I tell you that? Actually I spoke to the woman.
She called me.'

'Yes, Sonia Fell,' said Samson. 'What did you think?'

'Of her? I didn't like her at all – too pushy – so I didn't tell
her much. But let's rewind: I believe Naji is subconsciously
waiting to recognise the huge fact of his father's death until
he has achieved what he set out to do, which is to bring his
family to a safe country. Then maybe he will allow himself
to give in to the grief and come to terms with his loss.'

'That sounds like it will be a huge problem for him.'

'Yes, but for now he has made a kind of pact with himself to concentrate on surviving on his own out there. The
secret that he's keeping from himself won't stay hidden
forever.' She stopped and looked at the lights of Skopje disappearing to their left. 'I believe he may have taken on the

responsibility for everything that happened to his family, especially his father's death.'

'But how could he do that? He didn't cause his father's arrest and torture, or his father's blindness.'

'Yes, but he brought that IS man into their home, which eventually forced them to leave for Turkey and may have caused his father's stroke. I got all that from your friend Sonia, including the name of the man – Al-munajil.' She paused. He turned to her and saw her smile in the glow of the dashboard. 'I got more out of her than she did from me.'

'Naturally – you're a shrink.'

'I won't dignify that with a reaction,' she said, shaking her head with exasperation.

She switched on the interior light and put the back of her hand up to the wound on Samson's cheek where Simcek had hit him. 'By the way, you need a bandage on this – it's actually quite a nasty cut. Did you know you have a lump of dried blood on your cheek? How did you do that?'

'Not sure,' he said.

'Right,' she said sceptically. 'I'll take a look when we get there.'

It was remarkable how at ease they were. There was no tension, and neither felt the need to fill the silence that ensued for the next half hour. Anastasia checked her phone and listened to music.

At length she pulled out her earbuds and asked, 'How do you plan to find him?'

'His sister Munira is the only hope we have. I'm sure Naji

will try to call her. I hope he calls me. Maybe he already has. I wish Vuk had thought of sending the phone in the car with you.'

'He was asleep.'

'Yeah, he made a night of it.' He looked at her again. 'I will be relying on you, if we find him. He trusts you and I'm not sure I'll be good at talking to a boy of his age.'

'You said that before. It's nonsense: you were a war refugee when you were a boy; you lost your father when you were young; and you've been to Syria and you know the hell that boy has escaped from. There's no one better qualified. Relax, Naji is more grown up than most adults – at least he takes responsibility.'

The satnav led them up a winding road that seemed to go on forever. When eventually the illuminated monastery that now served as a hotel came into sight, high on a cliff above the road, she said, 'Denis has taken over the whole hotel, which I guess pleased the manager because there are no other guests. It's a magical place. He said he likes it so much he might even buy it.'

'When you're as rich as Denis, I guess the trick is to know when not to buy something.'

'That's a wise thing for a gambler to say.'

'How do you know about that?'

'That you gamble? Sonia told me. She implied you lost your job because of it.' Anastasia patted him on the leg. 'But I didn't believe her. I mean, I didn't believe that it was a problem.'

'It isn't – I have the occasional bet.'

'Sizeable, was the word she used, or vast.'

'Okay, I have the occasional sizeable bet, and I make money.'

'She doesn't like you, Paul. Did you try to get her into bed?'

'Did I try? No.'

'Maybe that's why.'

They crossed a narrow bridge and entered a dimly lit, cobbled courtyard. The beam from the headlights swung over a portico of four arches, each topped with a cupola. Samson pulled up by the other vehicles, noticing his hire car among them. Then he saw Vuk hurrying from the main door, a phone in his hand.

SIXTEEN

Naji woke up in an old armchair in front of a wood burner. Ifkar had been placed on a rickety chaise longue that was covered in worn red velvet. The old couple were bent over him. The woman held his arm while the man examined his wounds, spectacles perched on the end of his nose. Ifkar's eyes were closed but he let out the occasional moan, so Naji knew he was conscious. The couple consulted each other, then the old man went to a little table under a light and picked up the phone and dialled, checking each digit against a number written on a list on the wall. He started to speak rapidly, looking up at the ceiling and gesticulating. Occasionally he glanced at his wife for reassurance and she nodded eagerly, sometimes repeating the things he said. Naji prayed they weren't talking to the police or anyone in authority who would ask who they were and why Ifkar had a bullet wound, but he didn't know how to make his fears understood and so he just looked on as the old guy

ended the phone call and went back to feel Ifkar's brow
and pulse.

He searched the room for Moon. She turned out to be
lying beside his chair, staring between her paws at the fire,
though every so often she raised her head to check on Ifkar.
The woman noticed Naji was awake and came over and
smiled down at him. She ruffled his hair before leaving the
room and soon he heard noises from the kitchen, which
instantly took him back to his childhood home and the
sound of his mother preparing meals with his two older
sisters. Little Yasmin had been too young to help then and
had sat in the corner of the kitchen in a baby chair with
wheels, which the three other Touma children had all used
before her. He thought of her fleetingly and then pushed his
entire family from his mind, even poor, dead Yasmin, and
concentrated on Ifkar, who suddenly opened his eyes with
a startled look. 'Where are we?' he asked.

'With friends,' said Naji.

Naji got up and wandered around the room, looking at
old black and white photographs of men in national costume
and a picture of a warrior on a white horse, a sword carving
the air above his head. He peered at the many ornaments
and wondered why anyone would think such junk worth
keeping.

With the old couple's eyes following him, he reached a
shelf on which stood two photographs of a young man. In
one he was sitting astride a red motorbike, leaning over the
handlebars with a big grin; in the other he was in uniform,

standing to attention with a hat held under his arm. Propped against the wall between the two photographs were a religious icon and a silver Orthodox cross; in front of these were a wristwatch and an engraved vase containing a few of the dark red flowers Naji had seen still blooming on the mountainside. He turned to the couple. The woman placed her hands over her heart and said, 'Našiot sin, našiot sin – Dimitrij.' Naji realised that Dimitrij was their son and that he was dead. He nodded solemnly to show that he understood and studied the photographs again, not knowing what he should do next. Eventually they turned their attention back to Ifkar and Naji returned to the chair.

The old guy kept glancing at the clock that ticked loudly in the corner of the room; he seemed anxious and, maybe to distract himself, he went and fetched the two baskets of mushrooms from the kitchen and started cleaning each one with a brush and a damp cloth. When he caught Naji's look of amazement, he rubbed his thumb and forefinger together to indicate that the mushrooms would earn him plenty of money. Naji knew that Europeans ate many unclean things, but the idea that anyone would pay good money for fungus that grew in the forest was baffling to him.

When the old woman handed him a bowl of lamb and vegetable stew and rice, he poked around, looking for evidence of fungus, but found none and ended up enjoying the stew very much. From his chair he called over to Ifkar and told him he should eat as much as possible. But there was usually never a problem with Ifkar's appetite, even now when he was half delirious with pain. He consumed two bowls of stew, the man holding his head up while the woman spooned it into him.

The clock had just struck nine when they heard the noise of a vehicle outside. When the old guy opened the door and switched on a light in the yard, Naji got up and peered out from behind him. A hooded figure climbed off a quad bike, unstrapped a bag from the rear rack and waved, before trudging up a dozen or more steps into the light. Naji was surprised to see a woman's face under the hood. The old guy patted her on the back and she squeezed past him into the living room, where she removed her anorak and fleece. She was tall and had a wide face and dark hair, which she shook out as she removed the hat she'd worn under the hood. Her name was Jasna and she was a brisk and practical woman with little time for pleasantries. She dropped the bag beside Ifkar, examined the bandages that Naji had stolen from the medical centre, and asked over her shoulder if he spoke English. When he replied that he did, she said she wanted to know exactly what had happened to them. Naji opted for a highly edited version of the events under the walnut tree, which had them being mugged for the phone he was carrying.

She gave Ifkar a couple of shots in his bottom, having rolled him onto his side, and then began to clean the wounds with the hot water the old lady brought in a plastic bowl. There was no serious infection, she said, and that meant she could stitch him up, but first he'd need a local anaesthetic.

While she waited for it to take effect, she asked Naji how long they'd been travelling together, where they'd come from and how they had managed for so long out in the open, for she could see that they were both exhausted and needed a shower. Jasna did not mince her words, and when Naji gave a rather hazy account of the last few weeks, implying that Ifkar and he were related, she flung him a sceptical look just to make sure he didn't think she was a fool. But without making any comment she translated for the man and his wife, who nodded with interest and said they were pleased to help any young folk – wherever they came from – now that Dimitrij had been taken from them.

As she sewed up Ifkar, she said, 'Your friend has a chest infection – that's why he's feverish. I have given him antibiotics. The wound will heal but he must treat it with respect because the stitches could tear.' While the old man held him in a sitting position, she dressed his wounds and bandaged his arm to his chest so that he couldn't move it. They let him back gently onto a cushion and the farmer's wife threw a rug over him.

Jasna peeled off her gloves. 'You're lucky that you've been rescued by the kindest people in the valley. I treat all their animals.'

Naji thought he'd misunderstood her. 'Animals?'

'Yes, I am a veterinarian – trained in the United States. There's really no difference between treating a gunshot wound in a human and an animal. It's the same mess, the same shock and the same risk of infection. Your friend will

be okay in a day or two. Then you can dress the wound, as
I have done, and bandage him up again. Use plenty of that
iodine. Now, let me look at your beautiful friend here,'
she said, moving to Moon's side. 'My goodness, what a fine
specimen she is!'

'Sister of boy is calling,' Vuk said, thrusting the phone into
his hand.

Samson nodded and walked a few paces away from the
car, coming to a halt next to a parapet, beyond which there
was a black void. 'Munira, I am sorry I couldn't take your
call before now,' he said in Arabic. 'Have you spoken to
Naji?'

'Yes. But we must speak in English. I do not want my
mother to understand what I am saying.'

'Okay,' Samson said, switching to English. 'That's good
news. Where is he now?' He nodded to Anastasia, who indicated she was going inside.

'I do not know where he is. He will meet you in market.
The city of Pudnik in morning tomorrow. He promise he
will be there.'

'That's very good – well done. Does he have a phone?'

'No, he make call with another person's phone. A Syrian
woman. She was in market with Naji today.'

'He was in the market today!' Samson grimaced to Anastasia a few feet away. 'I'm sorry I wasn't there to see him.'

'Listen, please, sir. I told Naji some bad news – our sister
Yasmin died. He is very . . .' She struggled for the word.

'Upset,' said Samson.

'Yes. He cried. Naji never cries.'

'I am very sorry to hear about your sister.'

'Naji, he is with friend. He is looking after friend who is sick.'

'Did he say where he was?'

'No, I do not know. I am sorry to forget to ask. We are in shock but we have each other and I have my good friend Rihanna helping us.'

'That's good, but be careful what you say about Naji. This is very important, Munira. Very important you don't tell people anything.'

'I trust Rihanna with my life.'

'Good,' said Samson. 'The arrangement is that we meet in the marketplace in Pudnik tomorrow. I will have someone with me that Naji knows and trusts.'

'Will you tell me when you find him?'

'Of course, and you know to call this number if there is anything you need.'

'Thank you, sir,' she said, before hanging up.

Inside the monastery, there was no sign of anyone apart from the hotel staff. He was led to a room with white walls and traces of ancient religious murals. He showered and put on the clean clothes that Vuk had retrieved from the boot of the hire car. Before going in search of Denis Hisami he smoked a cigarette, drank a beer from the mini bar and thought about how he could watch the square without being spotted by Simcek's people – the answer was that he'd have to rely on Vuk and Anastasia. He wondered if GCHQ were still monitoring his communications. If they were, it would mean his former colleagues in London would know he was still in Macedonia. But maybe they had their minds on the operation in Bosnia. He powered down both his phones and removed their batteries. Naji's phone was already switched off, but he took the battery from that as well.

He found Hisami alone in a panelled sitting room that was hung with ancient-looking tapestries depicting hunting scenes. He was going through a stack of legal documents on the table in front of him. He marked his place, squared the stack, rose and shook Samson's hand. 'Paul, it's good to see you. Can I get you something?

Samson shook his head and sat down in the chair indicated by Hisami.

'Business waits for no man, I'm afraid. This all has to be read and signed and in New York in twenty-four hours' time. It's my biggest deal yet, and certainly the biggest risk yet. I am going into television.'

'Old media?' said Samson, noting that although Hisami smiled, he looked strained and seemed to have aged.

'Old but reliable media,' he said. 'Owning content is all these days. Content is my north star.' He slapped his hands on his thighs. 'Oh yes, talking of risks, I put five thousand pounds on the horse Snow Hat with your man Judah, as you asked me to do, and I noticed the price came in immediately. Snow Hat is at 5–2.'

'Thank you for that,' said Samson. 'I haven't had a chance

to look at the odds yet, but the race isn't until the day after tomorrow, so there's time enough.'

Hisami examined him. 'Do you mind my asking how much you are going to put on?'

Samson said he wasn't sure, which was true. He wondered how much sleep Hisami had had recently.

'And your horse? Have the odds moved out in the way you hoped?'

'I haven't looked yet,' Samson replied.

'I'll be interested to see what happens.'

'Well, you won't be out of pocket,' said Samson. 'It's between Snow Hat and the horse I favour.'

'And you're not going to say which horse that is?' said Hisami, knitting his fingers around one knee and rocking slightly.

Samson smiled and shook his head.

'Well, perhaps when you've placed your bet . . .'

'Possibly,' said Samson.

'You keep your cards close to your chest, Paul.'

Samson smiled again. He could easily tell Hisami what he was planning, but he was innately secretive about this side of his life, because it allowed him to keep his options open and he was superstitious about telling people about it.

Hisami moved his hands from his knees and folded them under his chin. 'Now to less pleasant matters. I had a long talk with your friend Anastasia this afternoon, once we knew we'd found a way out of your problems with Mr Simcek.'

'Thank you for that, by the way – it promised to be awkward for me.'

'Actually, it was all Jim Tulliver's idea. He knew the border police wouldn't examine the passport he carried too thoroughly, and when he landed in Austria twenty minutes ago he simply used his American passport – immigration checks never match a passport with the name on the ticket, of course. It worked out fine – I just received a text from him. It helped that I got on well with Simcek and suggested he put you on that flight.'

'It was a good plan,' said Samson, touching the cut on his cheek, which had suddenly began to throb.

'Maybe you should put a dressing on it.'

'I will.'

'But your absence today gave me the chance to talk to Anastasia and hear about the work she's doing. What a fine person she is!'

'Yes,' said Samson, aware of a tiny flicker of possessiveness. 'And she knows Naji, which is going to be important. I have made an arrangement with his eldest sister that we meet in Pudnik market in the morning. She told me that their youngest sibling – a girl – died in the refugee camp, so I do not know what sort of state he'll be in. He's certainly going to need Anastasia's help.'

'Poor boy – it's good that she's here. A wise initiative by you.' Hisami took one of his long pauses and looked Samson candidly in the eye. 'Actually, she helped me a great deal. I have found the last few days extraordinarily hard, as you warned I would. But I didn't appreciate it would be this tough. As I told you, I loved my sister dearly and . . .' His voice failed him and he stopped to compose himself. 'Let me just say Anastasia is good at allowing one to confront the results of pure evil. She's the best listener I've come across. She gives herself entirely to the person to whom she is listening and absorbs some of that person's grief. It's a remarkable ability.'

Samson waited a moment before saying, 'She's had a lot of experience in Lesbos. The pain she deals with on daily basis is unbearable – she is very strong.'

Hisami nodded and his expression moved rapidly from hurt to anger. 'It seems that Aysel was murdered – tortured then murdered for refusing to comply with the demands of the man who bought her from Al Kufra.'

'I am so sorry,' said Samson. 'I'm afraid I suspected that.'

'It was kind of you not to tell me your fears. But now we know all the details from Al Kufra. The story even shocked Simcek, who was conducting the interrogation. The evidence found on that phone is enough to mount a proper war crimes trial against these men. It really is the most important find of recent years and we have you to thank for it.'

'It was sheer accident,' said Samson.

'No, it was due to your determination, and I thank you for it – really!' He sighed, as though settling something in his mind. 'I have to tell you that the individual who violated and murdered my sister was Al-munajil, also known as Abu Wassim, or the Commander. There can be no doubt about this. Al Kufra showed us all the evidence, including film and messages from Al-munajil. Al Kufra was a witness. Although a person of unspeakable depravity, even he was appalled and, knowing what I do now, I can believe that.' He stopped. 'She was very badly tortured over a long period. The many women catalogued on his phone all suffered, but none quite like Aysel.'

Samson was silent. Everything they knew about this individual, nicknamed 'machete', complied with this new information. Naji must have had some inkling of what he was doing, possibly even of the treatment of Dr Hisami, which was why he did everything to protect Munira and get his family out of Syria.

Hisami was not the sort of person who invited physical contact, but Samson momentarily laid a hand on his arm and said he appreciated very well what he was going through. 'Thank you,' Hisami said. 'It helps to know that you under-stand; it helps that you tried so very hard to rescue her.'

Another long silence followed. 'I could really use a drink,' Hisami said eventually, looking up from the logs in the grate. 'Perhaps you will join me?'

'Of course,' said Samson.

Hisami shook the little hand bell and ordered cognac, which was exactly what Samson felt like.

'There is one thing that seems important,' Hisami said when the waitress had left. 'Al Kufra was on the run because he had been dealing in drugs and had abused his position. He got wind and fled before he was seized and executed. He says that Al-munajil's only purpose in Europe is to avoid a similar fate and that he can do this by tracking down and eliminating the person who copied all his files and fled to Europe with them on their phone. Al Kufra had no idea the boy in the group he travelled with was that very person. As you know, he only stole Naji's phone because Naji took a picture of the group with him in it.'

'Did Simcek understand the significance of this?' Samson asked quickly. 'Did he inform the British and the other European intelligence agencies?'

'I've no idea. I assume he did. Why do you ask?'

'Al-munajil has no reason to travel north if his only purpose is to track down Naji. We know his people are actively searching for Naji in Macedonia because of the two men that shot at him the day before yesterday – the two men Simcek has under arrest. They were employed to kill Naji and get his phone. They took a phone from him but it happened to be the wrong one. However, that was why they were out on the mountain yesterday.'

The waitress returned with the drinks. As she set them down, Hisami opened his hands to Samson, urging him to continue.

'The point is that Al-munajil knows Naji is in this area,' said Samson. 'There's no way he would go to another country if he knew Naji was here, which he does. If Simcek hasn't shared that with the other agencies it means that he is going to try to capture Al-munajil himself.'

'And that's why he didn't mind you being here – because he thinks you'll lead him to Naji and Al-munajil won't be far behind.'

'That's possible. Frankly, I don't mind who gets Al-munajil, just so long as he's caught.'

'But all those intelligence agencies cannot be mistaken, surely. Vuk told me that it was a huge operation.'

'Maybe,' said Samson. 'What we have to do is make sure we get to Naji in the market tomorrow, and I don't want bloody Simcek arresting him.'

'Well, you have Vuk and me and Anastasia,' said Hisami. 'Jim Tulliver will have to go back to New York on the plane with these papers.'

'What about the other people that were in Skopje with you?'

'They had to leave. I have a problem back in the States that needs their immediate attention. My plane is practically running a shuttle service between the States and the Balkans.'

'Nothing serious?'

'It is, but I want to see this through with you. And my relationship with Simcek may be useful.'

'Can you ask him about the two men he's got in custody? He told me they hadn't been properly interviewed because they were being treated for multiple lacerations and other injuries. They were in a dreadful state but I'm sure he's talked to them and I'd very much like to know what he got from them – where they came from, who hired them and how the hell they came to track Naji down.'

'I will try, but right now I need to complete these papers. I have a long evening in front of me, I'm afraid. Would you mind if I didn't join you for dinner?'

'I'm beat anyway,' replied Samson, getting up.

'You'll find the chef is pretty good.'

Samson looked around the hotel but couldn't find Anastasia or Vuk, so went to his room and slumped in a chair for five minutes before picking up the phone and asking for her room.

'Hi, you want dinner?' he asked. 'We could order in.'

'I've already ordered for us both – cabbage rolls and *turli tava*, which I think is like a stew. And a very good wine, because I'm on vacation. Give me ten to have a shower.'

He washed and shaved and thought not about Anastasia but Naji. Then he did some calculations on the bedside notepad and left his room with the paper in his back pocket. Anastasia greeted him with a glass of red wine. She was wearing black jeans and a fine beige cashmere cardigan over a white shirt and a silver necklace. She smiled but seemed sombre. Samson's eyes unromantically went straight to the coffee table. 'Would you mind if I used your laptop for a few minutes?'

'What for? Spy stuff?'

'No, horse stuff – I want to look up something.'

He went onto the BetRosso gambling site, keyed in his membership number and looked up the prices for the Lovatt Champions Long Distance Cup, which was to be run over one mile and seven furlongs. Snow Hat was at 5–2 but Dark Narcissus had only moved two points, out to 18–1. Samson scratched his chin and thought. It didn't seem likely to move out any further, and even though there was a big field of nineteen runners, there was always the possibility that someone would spot Dark Narcissus and suddenly get a feeling about it and cause the price to fall. He sat back and did some calculations in his head.

'What're you doing?' she asked, perching on the side of his armchair.

'Wondering if I should wait until tomorrow to make my play.'

'Is this a big bet?'

'By most standards, yes.' He sat back and looked up at her, having decided that he would wait and add a reverse forecast into the plan, which would allow him to pick Snow Hat and Dark Narcissus as first and second, in either order. He explained this to her but she soon closed her eyes then moved to the sofa. He cursed himself for being so obsessive. Anastasia had, after all, haunted his thoughts in the past few days, her significance growing every day he was on the road, although he had not actually acknowledged that until this moment. 'I am so sorry.' He paused, genuinely surprised by his insensitivity. 'There you are looking so fresh and beautiful and all I could do was look at the damned computer. My apologies – I am not usually as dull as this.'

She gave him that confidential smile of hers and let him off the hook. 'Well, you've had a long day and little sleep – you can be forgiven.'

'Not really,' he said. 'I am appalled by my behaviour.'

'Why do you gamble?' she asked.

'To make money – most gamblers bet because they like the risk. I don't get my kicks like that.'

She wrinkled her nose doubtfully. 'There must be an easier way to earn a living, and I don't mean going into Syria.'

'This will be my second bet this year,' he said, aware that he was protesting too much. 'I have been waiting for this race.'

'And you enjoy it?'

'To be honest, I feel sick during the race. And even if I win, I still feel sick.'

'It is nevertheless a risk, and even when you win you don't feel good. Seems like you have a bit of a problem there.' She picked up her glass and examined him over the rim as she drank.

Samson shrugged and smiled ruefully. 'Maybe, but I do make money and I am very cautious – I mean exceptionally so.'

'Was your father a gambler?'

'He played poker and chemin de fer in a club near the restaurant in Mayfair. It's a version of the card game baccarat. He made money – well, that's what he always told us, and most of the time I believed him.' He stopped and watched her for a second. 'Sorry, I was being an idiot.'

She reached across to him and put her hand to his cheek. 'Let me just do something about this – it's annoying me.' She disappeared into the bathroom and came back with an adhesive dressing. 'Come into the light,' she said. She divided the strip equally into two then placed the two halves over the cut. He smelled her scent and her breath at the same time and despite his exhausted state felt desire stir in him. She moved her head back to admire her work and squinted at him with a kind of professional interest.

'What?' he said, and kissed her briefly on the lips.

She smiled and then put her head to one side. 'Just thinking about the risks you take in your life. Denis said that the second time you went into Syria to find his sister you were nearly killed. A group kidnapped you – is that right?'

'Not quite,' said Samson, sitting down heavily, now feeling a lot less amorous. He reached for his glass. 'There was a disagreement about the money I was paying the people who were helping me talk to contacts in Iraq and Syria. They wanted more for the work, which had admittedly become much more dangerous. They held me until they'd collected funds in Gaziantep in Turkey.' He stopped and took a sip of wine. 'My goodness, this is really good.'

'What happened?'

'The building they were holding me in was hit by a bomb. Two men were killed. They were just atomised – simply vanished.'

'And you weren't hurt?'

'Knocked out for bit and I lost my hearing for a couple of weeks.'

'Did you escape then?'

'No, I needed them. I stayed and helped an injured man, but it was thirty-six hours before anyone arrived. They were grateful I'd been with him, although the truth was that I really had no option. It would have been crazy to try to reach the border on my own, and besides, they'd taken my boots, so I couldn't run. It's hard to move around a war zone in your socks.' He pointed to his feet. 'These are the very boots.'

She glanced at the scuffed, dusty leather of Samson's boots for a moment. 'Then what?'

'We continued as before, but I'd lost valuable time and they understood that those two men were dead because they had extorted a few thousand dollars from me; otherwise, none of us would have been in that building. So things were pretty tense, but they did continue to work with me after the money was released.'

'Why was it an issue? Denis is so wealthy.'

'At that stage, I was financing the trip, along with my associate in London, Macy Harp, because Denis was exploring other avenues. I thought we had a good lead and Denis had already paid us a lot. But you don't go into Syria flashing a lot of dollars, unless you want to be held for a very large ransom. I told them I had limited funds. I had to work within what I thought the market was for a woman like Aysel.' He threw her an apologetic look. 'But you don't want to hear all this.'

'I'm not shocked. We've helped many women and girls who have been raped. It's part of life in the camp.'

'The irony is that I found the one man in the world who could have helped me free Aysel – Al Kufra.'

'Why did Denis want to be involved with his interrogation?'

Samson was silent, staring into the light of the table lamp

for a few seconds. 'He was bearing witness to her death in some way,' he said eventually. 'Denis had to know exactly what happened to her. Maybe he was taking on some of her pain, if you see what I mean.'

'I think you are right – we spoke of these things today.'

'He said you helped him a lot.'

'I doubt it. Confronting evil like that is very hard, because you can't explain it in normal human terms. But my impression from one meeting is that Denis is very strong – he has been through a lot in his lifetime.'

They sat in silence, and then she reached out and placed her hand on his uninjured cheek. 'I like you, Paul. I like you very much. But this life of yours – this life of risk – seems, well, so very solitary.'

He shook his head, smiling. 'I have lots of friends, Anastasia. And there have been quite a few relationships, too.'

She smiled. 'I am sure there have. You're attractive. How did they cope with this secret life of risk?'

He didn't answer. Samson was used to this kind of questioning from girlfriends, but he was amused by her sweet and irrefutable candour. 'You got me,' he said, opening his hands in mock submission.

'And you got me,' she said, and she leaned in and kissed him.

'But that was a rapid analysis for such a short acquaintance,' he said. 'You always do that?'

'Only to people I really like. I hope you didn't think I was rude.' She pulled back.

He shook his head.

When the food arrived, they agreed to talk about other things and consumed the stew with relish. Afterwards, they went out onto the balcony to smoke and finish the wine in the chilly updraught from the canyon below the monastery.

'Was your father a ladies' man, too?' she asked with a mischievous grin.

'That expression is a bit archaic, isn't it? He wasn't, and no, I'm not either.'

'Well, mine was,' she said. 'Couldn't help it – had to get every woman he met into bed. Eventually my mother grew tired of being humiliated and divorced him. He never got over it and died at fifty-nine.'

'Were you close?'

She shook her head. 'I was far too boring for him – he liked jokes and merriment and he never took anything seriously, even his businesses. I was too serious, and when I was a teenager I called him out on his infidelities, which he didn't like at all. I was immediately sent to boarding school in the States to shut me up. Then I went to college in the UK, and then he died. And, no, I have no unresolved issues about that. My father made his choices. He was a scoundrel, and he didn't know how to love or be loved. End of story.'

'But he'd be proud of what you're doing now?'

She thought about that. 'No, I think he'd be mystified. Plus, he would hate all the migrants coming into his country. He was basically a racist – as so many of that generation were.' She sighed. 'My mother always missed him. Long after they were divorced she bought the aftershave he used – it was a particularly type you could only find in London – and she sprayed it around her apartment to remind herself of his presence. She still loved him. But, no, he would not have understood what I do, or the need for it.'

Samson stubbed out his cigarette on the underside of a stone table and flicked the butt into the void. 'Well, I think you do a wonderful job and, by the way, you did help Denis.'

As if it were the most natural thing in the world, they leaned in to one another and kissed again. 'It really is like we've known each other for years,' she said.

'You'd have groaned if I'd come out with that. But it's true. I thought about you a lot over the last few days – you just kept popping into my mind.'

'That's because you needed me to help you.'

'Yes,' he admitted. 'I do need you for Naji. But your beauty just kept growing in my mind. When I watched you with those children in Pinto's documentary, I realised how astoundingly beautiful you are – but it's a kind of secret beauty.'

'Not sure if that's a compliment or not.' She kissed him again, and stroked his chin and examined him. 'You look tired – maybe we should wait.' She moved her head back a little. Her brows knitted and she lifted her eyes to read his. 'When it does happen,' she said, 'you should know that I don't want anything from you. And the really, really important part is' – she stopped and looked at him hard – 'I don't expect you to want anything from me. Understand?'

'Right,' he said, 'but what if I want to settle down with a mortgage, pet insurance and two sets of school fees?'

'You are hardly the man for that. But if that's what you want, you'll have to find someone else, though I don't think there's a suitable candidate in this hotel.' And then she was in his arms and kissing him with the passion that he'd known lay beneath her efficient exterior; he'd known it since he'd first met her at the refugee camp. He told her this, and she smiled then frowned. 'You know those two men from England who came in asking questions about the religious education of migrant children while you were there? They returned one more time. My colleague realised they were only interested in the boy who was saved by the dolphin, because they kept on coming back to him. They were curious about you, too. I am really sorry – I should have told you. I kept forgetting.'

'Did you tell Sonia Fell?'

'Yes, but she wasn't interested.'

'Of course she wasn't. But it confirms what I suspected – that a big operation was put in place to find Naji. That's what they were there for.'

She broke free. 'We can't really go to bed and make love when Naji's out there, can we?'

He shook his head. 'That's an entirely academic consideration, given my state. I need sleep. I'm beat.'

They went inside and were very soon lying in Anastasia's bed, she on her side and he on his back. He fell asleep immediately, without noticing the hand resting on his chest, or her breath on his face.

★

He woke and went straight to the capsule coffee machine on the other side of the room and made two cups of black coffee. He placed one on Anastasia's bedside table, pausing momentarily to admire her face in the faint glow from the radio alarm clock. She stirred and stretched and looked up into his face. 'Aren't we good?' she said.

'Coffee,' he said, then bent down and kissed her on the forehead.

He moved to the window. It was still dark and the exterior lights wore halos in the dense fog. He sat down at the coffee table, opened up Anastasia' s laptop and looked at the prices for the Ascot race. Snow Hat had come into 2–1 and was now the clear favourite. His eyes ran down the runners, which had been reduced to seventeen overnight. He let out an expletive when he saw the price on Dark Narcissus had dropped by six points and was now at 12–1. He would have to move quickly before the price was reduced further.

He emailed Macy Harp and asked him to activate the network of punters who would be used to disguise the true size of his main bet by placing many small bets on Dark Narcissus around the country. Each member of the network would make money, however the horse performed, and they were free to place their own bets – but only after they had secured Samson's wager. The total outlay would be £25,000, plus a reverse forecast that he would text to Judah at ten that morning, just before the main bet went on. This was not quite his largest bet ever, but it would clean him out if it all went wrong. Nothing else made him this nervous, even waiting in a bombed-out building for help to arrive.

Macy Harp emailed back: *Ah, so that's the one you've been waiting for. I can cover it all with the funds you have with us. By the way, I hear things are developing north of you. Call if you need further details.*

'So you've made your bet,' she called from the bed.

He gave her a guilty look. 'It's in the process of being laid. Can I use your phone? I'm keeping radio silence, and anyway, mine's next door.'

She yawned and took it from her bag and chucked it across the bed.

He dialled Macy Harp. 'What's going on?' he asked.

'They moved in at three your time,' Harp replied. 'In their wisdom, the European governments decided that it would be better to get these men under lock and key than wait for any information they might provide by leading them to others in Northern Europe. Their collective nerve gave out, much to the annoyance of certain parties in the UK, I gather. The French, who've had more attacks than all of Europe put together, insisted. That came from the president.'

'How many arrests? Any familiar names?'

'None of that is clear. It was a joint operation. They raided five properties. I suppose it's good news that the characters that have been pursuing your target are most likely already being questioned.'

'Anything in the media?' asked Samson.

'They never release anything. They don't want to tip off other parties around Europe.'

'Okay. Look, I'd better get on.'

'How's it going?'

'We may have a result today. I'll let you know.'

'By the way, I had an email from Denis last night. He said he's going to cover your time since that other group stopped picking up the bills. Said it was the least he could do.'

'That's good of him.'

'Good luck this afternoon, Paul. The going looks perfect and the weather's not too cold. I wish you were here to watch the race.'

He said goodbye and handed the phone to Anastasia.

'What is it?' she asked, seeing something in his face.

'Not sure,' he said, moving to make another cup of coffee. 'Probably the usual dread before a race.'

She shook her head disapprovingly, leapt out of bed with an athletic grace that surprised him and went to the bathroom. She didn't bother to close the door as she stepped into the shower, and he watched her with candid admiration as they continued to chat. 'You seem in pretty good shape,' he said.

'Nonsense,' she said, turning off the water after a few minutes. 'I'm not at all in shape – not like I used to be. I've danced since I was ten – I wanted to make it my life once, but didn't have the dedication, and I should have started much earlier.'

'I think you're just fine,' he said, as she reached for the towel, her face filled with pleasure.

SEVENTEEN

They were in the square just before light, though it had taken some time for their convoy to creep down from the monastery in the fog, which didn't improve as they reached the valley. It smothered Pudnik and choked its townsfolk. Matters weren't helped by the arrival of scores of farm vehicles, towing trailers full of livestock and pumping exhaust into the town's inert air. The numbers of migrants had swollen due to God knows what new expulsion in the east or sudden change in the flow of suffering from the south, and groups hung about watching the market activity, as they had the day before, although the mood was more pessimistic. The buses that were to take them to the Serbian border had not materialised, and there were rumours of border closures and new obstacles all the way to Austria.

Vuk drove his own vehicle, Samson was in the rented car and Anastasia and Hisami were in the SUV that Samson had driven from the airport the night before. He didn't particularly want Hisami along with them, because Simcek's people might spot him and wonder what he was doing in Pudnik, but now that Samson was on Hisami's payroll he confined himself to asking him to stay in the vehicle. And of course he too would have to remain concealed because of Simcek. That meant Anastasia and Vuk would be the only ones in the market looking for Naji. If Vuk saw him first, it was agreed that he would wait until Anastasia could approach the boy. In the meantime, they would communicate by phone, although Samson was reluctant to switch on any of his phones, and instead was relying on a primitive set Vuk had given him, but without a charger that he could plug into the car.

He parked up between the bus station and the market-place, but the fog meant that he couldn't see to the other side of the market. And there were too many police and plain-clothes security agents moving among the stalls and around the bus station for him to risk leaving the car, even with his hood up and a scarf tied round most of his face. He could see Hisami's vehicle parked on the far side of the bus station, and a quick look through his binoculars told him that the billionaire was warming to the task of surveillance by sitting well down in his seat and reading a newspaper.

Nothing happened for an hour, and then Anastasia called. 'I have found the couple whose baby Naji saved. The woman, Fatimah, just rushed up to me.'

'Really?'

'Yes, it's astonishing. I thought they'd be in Germany

by now, but they haven't got the right papers. They were here yesterday and Naji borrowed their phone to call his family. That's when he got the news about his younger sister. Fatimah comforted him and helped him to a first aid station where he stole some dressings and fled. What happened next is interesting. The man at the first aid station ran after him and saw which way he left the town, but Naji was moving too fast and he gave up chasing him.'

'His companion must be quite seriously hurt, and that means he can't be far away. Are you with the couple now?

'Yes.'

'Do they know which way Naji went?'

'No, but the medical aid worker is here and he does. He's working a mobile facility. We're right by that.'

He held up his binoculars, swept the far side of the market and spotted a camper van adjacent to the bus station ticket office. 'I see where you are,' he said. 'It's important that you know which street Naji took and that you watch at the spot where it enters the market.'

'Got it – I'll call you.'

'And I'll let Denis and Vuk know what's happening.'

The vet, Jasna, stayed long into the evening, drinking plum brandy with the old couple, Darko and Irina. She told Naji that Moon had been in much more danger than Ifkar, for she had an infection in her wound. While examining the dog, she noticed the signs of mistreatment in her past: scars beneath her coat and one knotty lump on her leg, which might have been caused by a poorly set broken bone when she was a puppy. She made Naji feel the lump. It was then that he told her the story of her rescue from the cruel shepherd in Bulgaria, which Jasna relayed in detail to the old couple, who were evidently shocked. They clearly loved animals.

Naji had never encountered a woman like Jasna before. She was beautiful in a way, though she was forthright and sat with her legs apart, slapping her thigh when she laughed. Yet she was also tender with Moon and Ifkar. She complimented him on his English – a sure way to Naji's heart – and asked him about his life in Syria and how he and Ifkar came to be travelling together. He replied that they had met just a few days ago but after their experiences in the mountains – being charged by a bear and shot at – it seemed like a lifetime. He told her about both incidents, but did not go into a lot of detail on the second and certainly didn't say that he and the phone he was carrying were the reason they were attacked. Eventually, he asked if she knew a way he could get down to the market the next morning to meet a man who was going to help him. She translated to Darko, who exploded with laughter. Jasna turned to Naji and explained that he would be leaving on his tractor at dawn to meet the mushroom buyer in Pudnik market.

That was how Naji came to be in Darko's trailer next morning, holding on to two long flower boxes filled with polished fungi, each wrapped in tissue paper and lying in a bed of dried moss. Visibility was no more than a few metres, which meant the journey on the pot-holed track took over an hour. The eerie shapes of the trees fascinated Naji, but he was happy he didn't have to slog through the forest on foot, for he certainly would have got lost. Darko sang along to a radio playing folk music in his cab and sometimes turned round to beam at Naji and wave his cigarette hand at him.

Naji might have enjoyed the trip more if he hadn't been so on edge. Ifkar and Moon had both improved overnight and Ifkar was eating well, even for him – something that hugely pleased Irina, who had stood back with her hands clasped around her middle, watching him as her husband got ready to leave. His anxieties about Ifkar and Moon had been replaced by new worries about not knowing what Samson looked like, plus the fear that the market would be filled with Al-munajil's men. Naji had now had time to process the fact that two men he'd never seen before had followed them over the mountain and shot at them. Had those men just been lucky, or were there so many of them looking for him that one group or another was bound to find him? He knew that they wouldn't be long satisfied with the phone they'd taken. Once they realised it wasn't his, they would start looking for him again.

They chugged into town behind several other tractors with trailers and a vehicle with caterpillar tracks that sent black smoke into the air and held everyone up. Darko found a space near one of the market entrances, parked and swung down from his cab, indicating that Naji should pick up one of the boxes. Naji followed him into a smoky café where men were seated drinking coffee and clinking shot glasses, which they held with their little fingers pointing out. The mushroom buyer was at a table alone, leafing through invoices. He raised the corner of each box, peeped inside and nodded his approval. Then the haggling began. It was as if Naji wasn't there, although the other men in the café were interested to know what Darko was doing with a migrant boy. He tugged at Darko's parka and tapped his watch – how long did he have in the market square? Darko opened his hands and seemed to say that he should take as long as he needed.

Naji slipped out, pulling his cap down and wrapping the lower half of his face in the scarf Irina had insisted on tying round his neck as he left the farm. He walked towards the main market area, noticing that it was a very different event to the day before, with many more farmers and pens for animals. He paused at one with four puppies for sale, and another that contained a goat that was butting the sides of the pen. For the first time in many weeks he was without his backpack. This made him feel a little odd but also much freer, and he darted between the pens and the stalls, merging here and there with groups of men, picking up information and looking out for anyone who might be Samson. He learned that the additional buses that had been promised to take people to the Serbian border hadn't turned up, and that meant Fatimah and Hassan Antar must be in the crowds with their baby. He might be able persuade Fatimah to lend him her phone again, then he would call Munira and she could tell Samson to meet him by the church with the big tower, one minute's walk from the market. Otherwise he could try borrowing a phone, or stealing one. He had to do something, or he would never find the Englishman in this crowd with all this fog.

The crappy little phone that Vuk had loaned Samson sprang into life.

'Yes,' said Samson irritably. Three uniformed policemen were standing just a few metres away, blocking his view of most of the market and the bus station.

'Boss, they got no person.'

'Who's got no person?'

'Bosnia-Herzgovina! Your people make raid on houses and factory and get no person. No Al-munajil. No Ibrahim. No Usaim. No fat guy that drives fat fucking pickup. No one fucking person in houses – just lot of old women in beds.'

'They raided the properties they had under observation and no one was there – is that what you're saying?'

'That's what I say to you, boss,' said Vuk, with a tone that suggested Samson was an idiot.

'But Aco, Simeon and Lupcho followed them into Serbia and then Bosnia. I was led to believe they saw them in the pickup going north in Serbia? What the hell happened?'

'I don't know. Maybe switch few days ago.'

'You're saying they were never in Bosnia?'

'Yes.'

'Do you know what my people are doing? What are they planning to do?'

'No, this is all what Lupcho know.'

The phone started protesting. Samson looked at the screen. 'I need a charger, Vuk – the bloody battery's running out on your phone.'

'Okay, I bring it for you.'

'Wait!' Samson said. Something was going on thirty metres away from him. A Mercedes SUV with darkened glass had pulled up and the policemen that had been standing in front of Samson's car hurried over. One of them spoke into his radio, and several other uniformed cops who'd been patrolling the market approached the Mercedes. The driver's door opened and the thuggish young officer who had been with Simcek during Samson's interview got out. Then Simcek himself appeared from the other side of the car and gestured for the police to move into the open space in front of Samson. 'It's Simcek,' whispered Samson. 'He's right by me. I can't move.' He straightened in the seat so his face couldn't be seen and turned slightly away, though Simcek now had his back to him.

'He's showing them photographs. They are looking for someone.' He paused. 'Jesus, I wonder if he thinks Al-munajil is here. That would explain why Simcek has stayed in Pudnik.'

'Al-munajil here in Pudnik – that figures,' said Vuk, as if he had thought this all along.

'Maybe. Look, I'm right in front of the truck with the

green cover. As soon as you see the police move away, bring that bloody charger. Where are you, by the way?'

'With Mr Hisami.'

'Well, tell him to stay put – I don't want him leaving the car and running into Simcek.'

He hung up and waited a full ten minutes as Simcek continued to brief his men. Then the phone rang again. This time it was Anastasia. 'Naji's here,' she said breathlessly. 'We were talking then he saw someone and ran off.'

'Where are you?'

'In the streets beyond the marketplace – it's really hard to describe. It all looks the same. I'm looking for him now.'

'I can't move. Try to get hold of the boy and wait somewhere until I can come. Have you told Vuk?'

'No, you were both on the phone – I couldn't get through. I'll call him.'

'I'll tell him to come to you.'

Samson hung up and dialled Vuk, but before the call could connect the battery died. He swore and dropped the phone in his lap. Another two or three minutes passed before the briefing ended and Simcek returned to his car. Samson eased the driver's door open, rolled out of the seat and moved with his head down to behind the cattle truck, where he turned to see if the police had spotted him. They hadn't – in fact, they were now dispersing in every direction except his. He waited a couple of beats before choosing the best line between the stalls and jogging through the crowds to the other side of the market.

★

Naji's methodical search ended suddenly in the last line of market stalls when his eyes fell on Dr Anastasia, the woman who had been so good to him in the camp in Greece. She was wearing a white bobble hat and a dark olive puffer jacket and was facing away from him, talking to the woman from the mobile medical centre. He circled them to make sure it really was the doctor, wondering what she was doing talking to the aid worker. It looked like they knew each other, which he guessed wasn't impossible. For one crazy moment he thought that she might have come all the way from Greece to take him back to the camp. But then she happened to look in his direction and their eyes met and her face lit up, and he sort of knew that wasn't the reason she was there. She left the woman from the medical centre and hurried towards him. There was a part of him that still wanted to run, but her smile held him to the spot and he became aware of a sudden desire to tell her everything that had happened to him and about his little sister's death.

'Naji,' she said, as she reached him and took his hands in hers. 'Oh Naji, we've been searching for you everywhere. I'm so pleased to find you.' She held him at arms' length with a worried expression. 'You've lost so much weight!'

He looked down self-consciously. It wasn't what she'd said, it was the warmth in her face. And she was so very beautiful. All the kids in the camp thought so.

'What a journey you've been on,' she said, cupping his face with the palm of her hand. 'I'm truly amazed by you, dear Naji. You are so brave.' He might well have collapsed into her arms then and there, but he noticed that when she mentioned his name for a third time a head whipped round in a group of men to his left. The face was mostly hidden by a hood and was turned to Naji for only a fraction of a second, but that was enough for him to recognise Ibrahim. He froze. Anastasia gripped his arms and asked what was the matter. He looked down and muttered, 'They're here.'

'Who?' she demanded, looking around. 'Who's here?

He wrenched himself free, and flinging her a look of anguish, he sprinted away. But he did not go straight to the café. Instead, he ran in the opposite direction and then for about ten minutes darted back and forth through Pudnik's murky streets, occasionally pausing to see if he had been followed. Eventually, he went to the street where Darko's tractor was parked and slipped into the café. Darko was sitting alone, counting out notes on the table. He was smoking a sweet-smelling cheroot and in front of him were three empty shot glasses. A fourth was filled to the brim with a dark orange liquid, which he jokingly proffered to Naji as he approached. Naij couldn't believe he had drunk so much – he'd only been away for forty-five minutes.

He tugged at Darko's sleeve and frantically gestured that they must leave, trying to communicate his terror. But Darko was not to be hurried. He chucked back the contents of the last glass on the table, returned the cheroot to his lips, patted his pockets, stood, straightened his cap in the mirror, waved to the bartender then, wrapping an arm round Naji's shoulders, aimed himself at the door and set off unsteadily.

When they reached the tractor, Darko handed Naji the key and gestured that he should put it in the ignition then perch to the right of the driver's seat, which he had seen Irina do the day before. After a couple of attempts, Darko managed to haul himself through the door and plant his bottom on the seat, but this seemed to take it out of him and he had to rest his head on the wheel for a few seconds. Finally he started the engine, which he did by pulling out a choke button and pumping the accelerator, then with a great effort of concentration he reversed the tractor and trailer so he could clear the car in front of them.

Now they were moving slowly towards the outskirts of Pudnik, the tractor's two tiny headlights making a double prong ahead of them in the fog. As well as watching out for anyone who might be following, Naji kept his eyes on the road, and twice in the first few hundred metres of their journey he had to move the wheel to stop them scraping a line of parked cars on their right. Darko didn't seem to mind his intervention, and puffed away at the cheroot with a tipsy grin on his face. At a set of traffic lights, where they were turning left, they became stuck behind a truck that had broken down and Darko had to put his mind to reversing once more to steer round it. As they turned into the much smaller road and began to climb, Naji became aware of a voice screaming his name. He glanced down. Anastasia was running alongside the tractor and waving wildly at them. He tapped Darko's shoulder and pointed to her, but it seemed that now he had set course for home nothing was going to deter him, and he accelerated. Naji made a helpless gesture. At first Anastasia quickened her pace, then she dropped behind the trailer, grabbed hold of the tailgate, jumped up and scrambled over it. Naji was amazed. He couldn't believe that the beautiful doctor could vault into a moving trailer, and he waved excitedly to her. Then, as Darko accelerated more, he saw panic sweep her face. She clutched the pockets of her jacket, stood up and felt her jeans, then stared back down the road, aghast. Naji understood exactly what had happened – she had lost her phone when she was running or jumping into the trailer. He tried to get Darko to stop but the old man refused to take any notice. By then he had his hands full keeping the tractor on the road.

Samson circled back to Hisami's car, having searched the market and streets around it. He found Vuk lounging against the side of the car, smoking and talking to Hisami. He got in the back seat and opened the window so Vuk could hear him. 'That phone you gave me is dead,' he said. 'I've had to switch mine on, which I didn't bloody well need. Did you hear from Anastasia? I can't get her.'

'She called,' said Vuk, bridling at Samson's tone.

'And?'

'She say she found Naji. She talk to him. Then he run away because he saw man. Then she see boy again on tractor and she follow him.'

'What man?'

'She did not say what man.'

'Jesus wept. Didn't you ask her?'

'No. She go to follow tractor.'

'A tractor – she's following a bloody tractor? Where to?'

Vuk shrugged and stamped his cigarette into the tarmac.

'Why isn't she answering then? I've called her half a dozen times in the last five minutes – it's ringing out.'

'Can I help?' asked Hisami calmly.

'We need to find Anastasia and the boy. I'm certain that while every intelligence agency in Europe has apparently been conducting a surveillance operation on an old people's home in Bosnia, the Macedonian intelligence service had reason to believe that Al-munajil and his team never left their country. I just saw Simcek handing out mugshots to his officers. It suggests they've got hard information about their presence in Pudnik. Maybe Simcek knocked the information out of the two men I helped them arrest the day before yesterday.' He stopped to think. 'Simcek didn't want me here, because I was competition in the hunt for Al-munajil. He wants the kudos of arresting the lot by himself.'

Hisami turned to him and said, 'With your phone on, they'll know you're here.'

'Yes, but that's the least of our worries. If Naji fled because he recognised someone then there's every chance he and Anastasia have been followed. So let's think about where they might have gone. From the direction he ran yesterday, we know that Naji is somewhere to the south of Pudnik. So if we take the tractor story at face value and Vuk has got the right word, it means Naji has found help, probably at a farm in the mountains not very far from where his friend was shot. Does that make sense?'

Hisami nodded. Vuk looked annoyed and said, 'Tractor is tractor.'

'And we know from the number of bandages Naji stole that his friend is probably quite badly hurt and cannot travel,' continued Samson. 'I'd guess they are pretty close to where they were attacked.'

'That all seems logical,' said Hisami.

'So, here's what we're going to do. I'll take your car up the mountain, and Vuk, you will drive Mr Hisami back to the hotel in your car.'

'I am coming with you,' said Hisami.

'That's not possible,' said Samson, in an equally matter-of-fact tone.

'Well, this happens to be my vehicle and you are also working for me, Paul.'

'You have shareholders, investors – people that rely on you. And someone should be in Pudnik in case Anastasia returns.'

Hisami shook his head slowly. 'We all know that Anastasia will stay with that tractor if she's seen Naji on it,' he said. 'I'm coming with you and that's all there is to it. Vuk will stay here.'

'There's a lot of ground to cover. It's probably going to be a fruitless search.'

'All the more reason for you to have company. Shall we go?'

Samson's phone rang. He answered, noting that it wasn't Anastasia calling.

'Hi,' said the caller. 'It's Jamie O'Neill.' Samson grimaced. 'I was just hoping you might give us a bit of help.'

'How?' asked Samson, surprised that O'Neill had not immediately mentioned that he knew he was still in Macedonia and not Austria.

'Can you turn on your encrypted phone? Then we can talk.'

Samson hung up, switched on the satellite phone, waited it for to fire up then called O'Neill's number.

'The thing is, we've become very interested in Firefly's phone in the last few hours. Of course, we copied everything from it a few days ago when you took it from Al Kufra, but there are things we don't understand, in particular some screen grabs that he stored in his photos several months ago. Do you have the phone with you?'

'Yes,' said Samson, delving inside his leather jacket. He turned Naji's battered phone on and went to the camera roll. 'What am I looking for?'

'It's an album called "Sikinsabbi", which I think translates roughly from the Arabic as "knife boy", though you would know better than me.'

'Kind of,' said Samson.

'Right, go to the first photos at the top.'

Samson scrolled to the top and saw a series of geometric structures that resembled buildings and were made out of layers of vivid colours. 'Yes, I've seen them before. He did a drawing along the same lines in the camp. What are they?'

'We think they're a computer constructed by Firefly in an online game. It looks like a fully functioning computer to the people at Cheltenham. There are quite a few of them out there, mostly made by kids showing off to each other.'

'I don't quite . . .'

'They construct computers in the virtual world of online games, and they use them like any other computer to store information, but naturally only the person who builds the computer knows how to access and use it. If Naji has information, that's almost certainly where he's stored it. Cheltenham is trying to locate this structure on the web but have had no success so far. They think it likely that he hid the access codes somewhere on the phone, but they haven't found them either. So, all we need to know from the boy is where this computer is and how to get into it. This has become a very urgent matter, Paul.'

'What about the others in the north? The action there?' Samson asked, knowing that O'Neill would understand he was talking about the joint operation in Bosnia.

'Can't tell – things are still unclear. But this request I am making about the phone comes from the very top.'

'You do know that our arrangement was terminated this week,' said Samson. 'They said they didn't need my help.'

'I'll find out about that, but would you mind helping out?'

'As long as you keep that particular party off my back and get word to the locals to leave me alone.'

'Consider it done. Thanks a lot. Hear from you soon.'

Samson said goodbye and opened the rear door. 'If you're

coming,' he said to Hisami, 'you'd better get in the passenger seat, because I'm driving.' Hisami nodded and got out, while Samson took some cigarettes from Vuk. 'Don't do one of your vanishing acts,' he told him. 'Stay on the phone! If Anastasia calls, she's likely to try your number because she doesn't know I'm using my own phone.'

'I not vanish,' said Vuk solemnly.

Naji was doing most of the steering by the time they cleared the forest, following a track marked with posts that were topped with orange paint and small plywood double arrows that pointed up and down the hill. He had noticed them on the way down, although Darko hadn't used them to navigate because he knew the way so well. But they were helpful going back to the mountain farm in the fog. They also had their own tyre tracks to follow and those of the vet's quad bike. When he could, Naji waved to Anastasia, who was clinging to one side of the trailer to stop being thrown about. He didn't have a lot of time to think, but he certainly asked himself what she was doing in Pudnik and why she was so desperate to find him. But mostly his thoughts were haunted by the cruel gaze that had settled on him from beneath Ibrahim's hood. And that was the main reason he glanced behind the trailer so often as they crossed the slope to the hanging valley where Darko's farmhouse lay hidden behind a clump of pine trees.

At the sound of the tractor entering the yard below the house, Irina rushed down the steps and started scolding

Darko, who waved to her good-naturedly before swinging his legs out of the cab and half-falling into her arms. Naji attempted to introduce Dr Anastasia, but Irina took little notice, and anyway, Naji was at a loss to know how to explain her presence in sign language. Instead, he shrugged.

'So this is where you've been hiding,' said Anastasia, looking around then peering hard into his face. 'How are you, Naji, apart from losing all that weight?'

He had never told her his name, but he liked her using it. He shrugged again. 'I saw Ibrahim,' he said. 'He is Al-munajil's man. Ibrahim goes nowhere without Al-munajil, so that means Al-munajil is here, too, and he will kill me. In the camp I told you about these men who want to kill me and you did not believe me.'

'I did believe you, but you ran away before I could help, Naji. However, now I am here and Paul Samson is in Pudnik and you will be safe.' She stopped to admire the horse, cattle and pigs that had poked their heads out of various stalls and were watching them with interest. 'This is a wonderful place you've found.'

'Ifkar – that is my friend – wants to remain here with Moon, who is his dog. She was shot, too.'

'Who was shooting at you?'

'Two of Al-munajil's men, but we beat them and they ran off. I threw their gun away. I wish I'd kept it. I was dumb.'

She smiled at him. 'No, you weren't. It was good you threw it away: it was symbolic.'

'Symbolic? What does that mean?'

'Ah! For once I have found a word you don't understand! It means you weren't just throwing the gun away – you were saying that you've had enough of all the violence you have witnessed. That action was a symbol of all your disgust.'

'I understand – but violence to defend yourself is good, no?'

'It's never good, but it is excusable, yes.' She shivered. 'Let's go in and I can meet your friends properly and then we can decide what to do.'

Inside the farmhouse, Darko had already been pushed into another room to sleep it off. Ifkar lay on the couch with his good arm crooked over his head. Beside him was Moon, who gave them a single tail wag. Ifkar was now much better, and it pleased Naji that Anastasia's looks caused him to blush and become completely tongue-tied when she greeted him with her few words of Arabic.

Irina brought them a drink that Anastasia identified as mountain tea, made from the flowers of a particular herb and used to treat colds and chest infections, and a cake called *kozinjak*. She wondered about the best way of contacting Samson; she was without her phone and she didn't know any of his or Vuk's numbers by heart. They talked about using the landline to call Naji's sister, who would be able to give them Samson's number, but then Anastasia remembered Samson was using Vuk's old phone, and of course Munira didn't have that number.

Naji rang his sister on the landline several times and left messages, giving a good description of where the farm was in relation to Pudnik, which he doubted would be relayed to Samson with any accuracy should he call her.

Anastasia also spoke a little Macedonian, and as Irina knew some Greek, they were able to converse quite well as they watched Ifkar consume nearly all the cake. Anastasia explained she was a psychologist and told Irina some of what Naji had been through in the last few months, including his near drowning and Yasmin's death. As the story unfolded, Irina looked more and more appalled and kept touching Naji's head, which irritated him quite a bit, partly because he didn't know what was being said.

At the end Anastasia turned to him and said, 'We do have a lot to talk about, don't we? I wonder when we will ever manage to do that.'

'When I have my family with me in Germany,' he replied.

'I'm sure you'll get there soon, but why Germany? Why not America? You speak such good English. You told me you wanted to become an engineer when we were in the camp together. Wouldn't it be easier to learn engineering in a language you understand?'

'I am learning to speak German. And my father does not like America because he says Americans hate Muslims and . . .' For some reason, he was unable to go on. He tried again to complete the sentence, but stalled again and stood in the centre of the room feeling foolish and also rather hot and breathless.

Anastasia was sitting on the edge of the chair that Naji had occupied the night before, the boy standing a little way from her. She leaned forward and took both his hands then rose and pulled him gently towards her and hugged him. With Ifkar looking on, Naji was rather embarrassed, but part of him momentarily relished the hug and he didn't resist.

She drew back to look in his eyes, as she had done in the market, and Naji felt the same temptation to crumple, but something in him wasn't ready to give in, and now all he could think of was escaping her embrace. She held on to him for a few seconds longer, but then he twisted downwards and slipped free. He rushed to the door, and wrenched it open, letting it bang closed behind him as he ran out. On the narrow wooden veranda he was stopped dead in his tracks by the sight of four men silhouetted against the lights of a vehicle that had freewheeled silently into the yard. His first crazy thought was that the figures looked like aliens haloed in the fog, but then one of them laughed and he knew Al-munajil had found him.

They first drove up the track Samson had used when he'd descended the mountain two days before, but after finding nothing they reversed all the way down, because there was no place to turn the car. They took a trail that wasn't displayed on either Hisami's phone map or the vehicle's satnav. There were some promising tyre marks in the mud, but a little way down the track Samson lost control of the heavy SUV and it slid into the undergrowth. Hisami immediately got out and built a bank of stones and logs to give the wheels purchase and after nearly an hour they got the vehicle back onto the track.

'You don't mind getting your hands dirty then?' shouted Samson as they roared onwards.

'I've dug out more vehicles than you ever will.'

'How come?'

'I did two years of military service before I went to college in the States.'

'Who with?'

Hisami said nothing. He carefully took off his glasses, blew on the lenses and polished them on the end of his cashmere scarf. He replaced them and looked at Samson. 'I served in the Peshmerga – the Kurdish forces in Iraq, Paul. But that's not public knowledge and I'd be grateful if you kept it to yourself.'

Samson glanced at the slight, dapper figure beside him with a certain amount of surprise. 'How come no one found out?' he asked.

'My sister and I changed our names when we came to America. New life, new name and I suppose a new past, though we did nothing reprehensible – nothing to be ashamed of. My sister served in the army also.'

'And that's why she returned?'

'She was trained in treating battlefield trauma – gunshot wounds and injuries caused by explosions. It was how she came to medicine as a young woman, and yes, that's why she went back.' He stopped. Then, in what Samson knew was a rare unguarded moment for him, Hisami said, 'Life's adventure is nothing without her.'

It wasn't self-pity, just a simple statement of loss. Samson had always known how dreadfully Hisami missed his sister, but knowing now what they had been through together, he understood what it meant to him even more.

A little way on, he braked sharply. 'Can you reach that?'

Hisami wound down his window and tugged at a rag tied to a tree.

'Looks like someone left a marker,' said Samson. He moved on but stopped again after they had rounded a bend, because a vehicle – almost certainly a tractor – had flattened the vegetation on the right-hand side of the track. There were marks made by the same vehicle turning. Samson took only a few minutes to find the camp and note the same signs of occupation he had seen on the hillside a few days before – a fire similarly constructed, though this one had been built against a huge flat stone, and dog and human excrement. In the fire, the remains of a huge tree stump lay, still just smouldering. Beside it were the cans they'd used for cooking and some bloody rags.

'They were here not long ago – we're on the right track.' He looked up into the trees. 'The light's fading – we'd better go.'

In the big, draughty barn, fifty metres down from the farm-house, Anastasia and Ifkar were tied to posts that supported a beam that ran laterally across the ceiling. Moving like an automaton, Naji himself had tightened the ropes that held Ifkar and Anastasia; when Ifkar had cried out as Ibrahim pulled his damaged arm around the post for Naji to bind his hands together, he'd showed no concern. Even the looks of astonishment and horror on Anastasia and Ifkar's faces did not register with him. He just did what he was told by Al-munajil's crew. Whatever they needed him to do was fine. That was the way he survived.

The moment he saw Al-munajil appear from the mist in the yard he lost all will to escape, or to defend the people who had helped and befriended him. He did nothing when Irina was pistol-whipped by Usaim and fell unconscious to the floor of the farmhouse, or when Darko received the same treatment, or the couple were tied to their bed with their heads bleeding. He did nothing when Moon was stamped on and kicked and sent limping to a corner of the room where she collapsed; nothing when Ifkar and Anastasia were dragged from the house and down the steps towards the barn, there to be roughed up and, in Anastasia's case, groped and humiliated on a cold stone floor that was covered with dried animal dung. His mind went dead, as it always did when Al-munajil and his men were doing unspeakable things. He'd seen the same cruelty from the back of Al-munajil's pickup on countless occasions. They intended for him to witness the floggings and executions, and they might have succeeded in hardening him to their violence had it not been for his parents' quiet goodness and the appalling prospect of Al-munajil taking his beloved sister as his wife. He'd kept something of himself to resist the monster, but you didn't do that by crossing him or disobeying him. And so he bound the arms that twenty minutes before had held him and comforted him, ignoring the pain he was inflicting and the terror in Anastasia's eyes.

When it was done, he stepped back, his eyes to the floor, and waited for Al-munajil's next order. But in his rasping, cracked voice, Al-munajil was fussing about the barn being unclean. There was old straw and hay strewn everywhere, and dried shit on the ground and broken equipment and piles of old chains, anyone could see that, but Al-munajil insisted that pigs had likely been slaughtered in the barn and told them he knew pigs' blood when he smelled it, however old. Someone needed to do something fast – that was what he was saying.

Usaim was in the farmhouse, guarding Darko and Irina and keeping watch on the tracks that led to the house from the west. Ibrahim was minding the barn door. Rafi, the fourth member of the gang, who seemed familiar to Naji, though he could not place him, was sent off to get something from the truck for Al-munajil to sit on. At the same time, he was told to hide the truck and check again that there were no mobile phones anywhere in the house.

During this time, Naji never lifted his gaze from the floor of the barn, but he could feel Al-munajil's eyes boring into the top of his head. He knew he would be killed in the most painful way Al-munajil's sick mind could concoct, and that made him shake and want to throw up, but he didn't understand why he wasn't tied up and being questioned about the data he had stolen.

★

Samson answered his personal phone with one hand, but the call dropped. He slowed the car and glanced at the screen. Out on the open hillside the reception was better than it had been in the forest, but it still wasn't good.

'Anastasia?' said Hisami.

'No. Looks like it's Naji's sister.'

He slowed the vehicle to walking pace, and when he saw bars appear on the screen he stopped and dialled the number. A young woman answered. 'Is that Munira?' asked Samson.

'Who is this?' came the voice.

'Can I speak with Munira? I'm a friend.'

'Yes, she's right here.'

Munira came on the line. 'I have a message for you,' she said.

'Who's that with you?' asked Samson.

'My friend.'

'Would you mind moving somewhere you can talk privately?'

When the rustling of her walk ceased, she said, 'Naji phoned me an hour and a half ago to describe where he was and he left a message.'

'What did he say?'

'He says he is in a farm with your friend, but it is difficult to find. It is by some trees, south-east of the town, in the mountains. He says it is six kilometres in distance but the road is hard – not really a road at all.'

Then she used an Arabic word that he didn't understand. '*Munkhafid.* What's that mean?' he asked.

Hisami replied before she could. 'A hollow, or a depression in the land.'

'Okay, I've got it,' he said to Munira. 'Anything else?'

'He says there are orange markers on sticks. If you find those sticks you will find the farm. That's all he said.'

'Do you have his number?'

'He left a number but I think it's wrong – it's ringing out.'

'Okay, thanks. I'll call when we've found him.'

He hung up and explained that Anastasia was with Naji and they had to find some orange sticks. 'This doesn't seem right,' he said, looking out onto the blank, grey hillside.

Hisami said he might have seen a stick some distance back – lower down. Then he said, 'You like Anastasia?'

'Yes, very much,' said Samson, turning the car.

'So do I,' said Hisami. 'She reminds me of my sister. She has the same moral imperative in her life.' He left it a beat before saying, 'Will you see her after this?'

'I'm not sure. She's very independent, you know.'

'I had noticed,' said Hisami. 'But will you try?'

Samson cottoned on. 'Why? Are you interested?'

Hisami said nothing.

'That man,' Al-munajil said suddenly to Naji, making Anastasia jump, 'did you recognise him?'

Naji shook his head. 'Which one, sir?'

He gestured after the man who'd left the barn – Rafi.

'No, sir,' Naji replied.

'He was on your raft,' said Ibrahim with a sadistic smile from the door.

Al-munajil took a few paces towards Naji, seized his jaw and forced him to look up. He had always avoided looking straight into Al-munajil's face, not because of the sheer ugliness of his features – the thin-lipped, scowling mouth, the flared nostrils and crooked teeth, or the pitted skin and blotches of raised brown pigment around his eye sockets – but because Al-munajil's stare was simply the most unforgiving and terrifying he had ever seen. For scores of people it had been the last thing they saw on this earth.

'Brother Rafi is a hero,' said Al-munajil, 'for it was he who risked his own life in the sea to sink your raft with his knife. But you didn't drown as we intended, Naji. You lived, while all those good Muslims died.'

Naji couldn't help himself. 'He sank the boat?'

'At the point of maximum danger in the crossing,' said Al-munajil, 'he made sure your boat was doomed and he committed his life to the holy cause, but Allah the Mighty and Majestic decided to spare his life and he was saved at the point of death.' Al-munajil snorted, then let him go and went over to Anastasia. He snatched her face with a force that made her cry out. 'Then this meddling whore put you in a compound where we couldn't get to you, and you escaped and we were forced to follow you with the Western spies chasing us.' He looked back at Naji. 'We know what this bitch did – she told the authorities what you took from us. We have brothers in the camp that kept us informed about her actions. They had access to her office and her computer, and now she will pay for what she did.' Al-munajil's hand slipped from her jaw to her throat and, as he pushed upwards to choke her, his other hand felt her breast and kneaded it roughly. Then he rammed his fist between her legs. She let out a gasp of pain and kicked out and managed to connect with Al-munajil's knee. 'How dare you!' she screamed. 'Untie me now! Naji, untie me!'

Al-munajil rubbed his leg and contemplated Anastasia's defiant glare. Naji thought he was going to kill her there and then. 'What is the whore doctor saying?' he demanded.

'She says please not to hurt her,' said Naji, 'because it is I – Naji – who stole your data.'

He swivelled to face the boy. 'And that wasn't all you took, was it? You stole from the caliphate to pay for the escape of your family. Where else would you get that kind of money?' He grabbed him with both hands and shook him violently. Then, drawing a long, thin knife from his jacket, he spun Naji round and placed the blade across his throat. 'I should cut your blasphemous little head off now. That's what we did to the last man who was accused of skimming money from our group.' He forced Naji to a kneeling position and pulled his head back by the hair. Naji felt the blade on his skin again.

Anastasia screamed, but then Al-munajil hefted his boot against Naji's back and sent him sprawling. 'An execution like that is too good for the deceiving son of Satan. You will know what it is to administer pain to your friends before you yourself die by fire.' This last sentence came out in a broken, throaty whisper for, as Naji knew well, when Al-munajil's mind seethed with murderous hatred, his vocal cords went into spasm.

The barn door opened and Rafi returned with a striped blanket over his arm. He whispered to Al-munajil before wiping a wooden feed box down with his sleeve and laying the rug across it. Al-munajil gathered his coat and sat down with the manner of a noble Bedouin chieftain surveying his tribe. His gaze settled on Naji. 'They found nothing – not one mobile phone in the house. How is that, Naji? Where have you hidden the phone? And where is the whore's phone? A Western whore like her always carries a phone.'

'She lost hers and mine was stolen. A man took it when I was asleep.' Naji shook his head hopelessly. 'If I had it now, I would give it to you to stop all this.'

'That is a lie,' said Al-munajil. 'The two men that we sent to find you, they took a phone from you, but that was a dummy phone – the one you meant to be taken.'

'No, no,' cried Naji. 'That was the phone I stole because mine had already gone. I promise this is true.'

Sagging on the ropes that bound him and with his head lolling grotesquely, Ifkar murmured, 'It is true. Believe him.'

But Al-munajil did not hear. He spread his lips in the closest thing he had to a smile. 'You phoned your sister and sent messages to her – we know this, Naji. Indeed, we heard from sweet Munira very recently. You were kind enough to give her directions for the Western spy and that is how we found you so quickly.'

Naji's mind reeled. 'She . . . she hates and fears you – she would never help you.'

'Munira knows I have chosen her for my wife and she will soon learn that she has only one duty, and that is to me.' Again the lips splayed in their revolting manner.

'She would rather die,' he said. Suddenly he remembered Munira's friend, the girl who was always with her when they spoke. She must be Al-munajil's spy.

'We have wasted enough time,' said Al-munajil. 'Where's your phone?'

'I don't have it. I told you, sir, it was stolen. It's gone.' He was terrified, but there was also a part of Naji that had contempt for Al-munajil's technical incompetence. He was so dumb that he believed Naji would actually hide everything on a phone. Yes, he needed his own phone to get his bearings in his own maze, so to speak, but he remembered the reasoning behind most of his codes, so he could probably recreate them and, given time and concentration, he would be able to access everything.

'We shall begin,' said Al-munajil, taking out a gun from his pocket and holding the knife out to Naji. 'Take it! Go on – take it!' Naji took the knife, and Al-munajil levelled the gun at him. 'I trusted you. I privileged you with my attention. You had things that no boy could dream of and a chance to dedicate your life to the caliphate. You repaid me with treachery and now you will feel the consequences of that betrayal.' He paused, ran his tongue round his lips, opened his mouth and screamed, 'Stab her! Put the knife into the whore now! Do it.'

The force of the command, which cracked on the last few syllables, shook Naji. 'I cannot,' he said, aware that the hand holding the knife was shaking. 'She's done nothing. She helps Muslims. She cares for people.' The knife slipped from his grasp and clattered to the stone.

Al-munajil nodded to Ibrahim, who had approached Ifkar from behind the post. Naji glanced up as Ibrahim took hold of Ifkar's hand and plunged his own knife into his forearm – straight through, so that the blade appeared on the underside of the arm and went into the post. Ifkar's face froze in a rictus of agony before he let out a dreadful cry.

'Pick up my knife, little traitor,' said Al-munajil – very quiet, very calm. 'For now you must use it on the infidel Yazidi, or the whore doctor will get it in the belly, or wherever Ibrahim feels like stabbing her. You must kill the Yazidi to save her.'

Naji started shaking his head. 'No,' he said. He turned to Al-munajil, trembling violently, and raised his eyes. 'No,' he screamed, now confronting Al-munajil's limitless, dull savagery with all his being.

Al-munajil's mouth opened but no words came out.

'You want to know what I took and where I hid it,' continued Naji. 'If anything more happens to my friends, you will never learn.' Then he added, 'Do you know what a timed release function is?' Before Al-munajil could respond, he answered his own question. 'It means I have to log into the place where I've hidden all your information before a certain time. If I don't, the data I took from you and the phones and computers of your headquarters will be released onto the web.' He was aware of his own voice, high and thin in the echoing barn.

'You're lying to save your life,' said Al-munajil, his voice, by contrast, now a strangulated whisper. He cleared his throat violently and projected a gob of phlegm onto the ground.

'All that data will be released the moment I don't log in. You will have no more time – everything will be out there. They will know all about you.'

Al-munajil got up, took hold of Naji by the throat and squeezed his windpipe. Naji began to choke. Al-munajil watched and squeezed harder, then he seemed to think better of this, drew back and smashed the gun into the side of Naji's head several times. Naji did his best to duck and several of the blows missed, though the gun caught his ear and he felt blood trickle down his neck. 'You think you can save yourself with these lies?'

'No! I know you're going to kill me,' Naji shouted as the gun smashed into his head. 'I'm trying to save their lives, not mine.' He fell to the ground to escape the blows.

Al-munajil stopped, his arm still raised, and looked at Ibrahim.

'Maybe the data isn't valuable to you,' said Naji into the floor. 'Maybe your masters don't care about it.'

'Pick him up,' Al-munajil ordered Rafi, and returned to sit on the feed box. 'What did you steal that we don't know about?'

'Everything on your three phones, everything on your laptop, and I hacked the headquarters using your passwords. That was a big dump. I didn't look at it much, but there was data about sales of crude oil, money, bank accounts, foreign actions, military operations and social network communications – those kinds of things. Anything I could get. And I got all of it because your security is shit. I got so much I couldn't read it all.'

Al-munajil couldn't hide his reaction. 'You did this all the time you were with me?'

'Since the first time you gave me your phone to mend I have been copying all your communications data. But it's all on a site I've built to store it. It's like a hard drive, but I need time to access it, and that's the truth. You can choose to believe it or not but you won't have my help unless you release my friends.'

And now came the self-pity that Al-munajil always used to justify his worst actions. In his mind he and the fighters who butchered their way across Naji's homeland and beyond were always the victims. 'We were like brothers to you. We helped you. We gave you food and money for your family. I am to marry your sister, and you repay me like this!'

Ibrahim strode over to Naji and seized him by the neck. 'Let me finish him off now.'

'Don't be an idiot,' said Al-munajil. 'Let him go.'

Naji shook himself and reached up to inspect the cut high on the top of his head.

'Why?' said Al-munajil, still acting the aggrieved party.

'I saw what you and your people did. You made me watch and you even wanted me to kill for you. Ibrahim was going to force me to murder with his gun until I ran away. You were no better than the men who tortured my father. In fact, you were worse. I saw what you did to the women at that place.'

Al-munajil glowered at him for a moment, then asked where the data was hidden.

'I told you – it's on a website, but only I can access it and because I don't have my phone that will take a lot of time.'

'Why?'

'Because I have to work out the encryption I put in place and the key is on my phone.'

'Do it now on my phone,' said Al-munajil. 'Do it now.'

'I need the Internet. There is no coverage here. That's why the old people only have a landline. Look for yourself.'

Al-munajil got out his phone and beckoned the others to do the same.

'He's playing for time,' said Ibrahim.

'Yes, I am, because I want you to stop hurting my friends and let them go.' He looked down, aware that something was happening inside him that he'd never experienced before. He couldn't speak, and he waited a moment before saying, 'But you need this more than I do.' Suddenly Naji felt an overwhelming need to close his eyes, for everything to just stop. The tensions from the last three years, the violence he had seen – close at hand and the bombs from the air – all but drowning in the ocean, the trials of his journey, the constant fear, the loss of his little sister and on top of that the much, much greater loss that Anastasia had tried to make him confront now all swarmed in his mind. He began to sway. He was aware of Al-munajil telling Ibrahim to get water and Anastasia shouting in English that they should leave him alone because he was just a kid. Before collapsing he thought, 'Yes, I'm a kid, and I'm finished.'

EIGHTEEN

Samson and Hisami spotted a faint glow in the trees a few hundred metres ahead and drove to the top of a rubble track that curved sharply to their left, down to a farmhouse and several outbuildings that were all entirely hidden in a hollow.

'This is it,' said Samson, drifting to a stop and switching off the headlights. 'There's nothing else around. Best to leave the car here. We may not get it back up that slope.'

Hisami agreed. Samson turned off the engine and they got out. 'I'll go on ahead and see what's happening,' he said, moving off. He took a few paces but, having got no response, glanced back into the dark. 'You okay, Denis?'

'Yes.' The voice was muffled, as if Hisami was distracted, or perhaps bending down.

Samson assumed he was relieving himself and continued on down to the bottom. He noticed the tractor and trailer, and several stables with the top halves of their Dutch doors open. The lights were on in the house and cracks of light were coming from between the panels of a building further down the gradient. A caged lamp illuminated the yard. He got the impression of an orderly, well-maintained establishment where money was tight. Many running repairs had been made to the stables and the steps and the wooden rail that led up to the farmhouse. He paused and listened. Apart from the periodic lowing of a cow, he heard no sound. He started up the steps and was exactly halfway up when the farmhouse door banged. The shadow of a man hurried across the veranda and started moving down towards him. Too late, Samson saw that as well as the large water bottle under his arm, he was carrying a gun. Now he saw Samson. He stopped and raised the weapon. He already had a grin on his face as he said in Arabic, 'Welcome, British spy — we expected you.'

He knew this bastard: Al-munajil's right-hand man, Ibrahim Anzawi, thirty-five years of age, a native of the Sunni town of Latifya in Iraq and a man whose crimes were so extensive that he would certainly merit a drone strike on his own. And this bastard had him cold — there was absolutely nothing he could do.

Ibrahim whooped and yelled over his shoulder. Another man rushed from the house and joined him on the steps. Samson knew this one too — Usaim Abdel Zahra; twenty-eight, a petty criminal and black marketeer turned war criminal. He was brandishing a handgun. They kicked him down the steps and marched him to the barn with a gun at the nape of his neck. As they went, Samson noticed Usaim was limping.

He had an idea what to expect inside the barn, but nothing prepared him for the tableau of pain and despair that was illuminated by a single naked light. He took in Anastasia's appalled expression, though he didn't let his eyes meet hers, the young man on the post next to her, slumped and unconscious, with blood dripping from his arm, and Naji sitting on the floor with his arms clamped around his knees, rocking gently. Al-munajil rose from a box and moved towards him. As the draught from the door caught the bulb and made it swing, light and shadow swept across his face. He approached Samson and said, 'So we didn't lose them all. One of them stuck to us.'

'This one was in the market,' said Ibrahim. 'I saw him with my own eyes. He is the one who is speaking to Munira.'

'I know that, you fool,' Al-munajil said, spitting out the words. 'Did you check the vehicle?' Ibrahim shook his head and looked at Usaim, as though this had been his oversight.

When Usaim turned and took a few steps towards the door, Al-munajil looked as though he was going to have a seizure. 'Keys!' Usaim turned back. 'Didn't you search him before?'

'We thought it best to bring him in here first,' said Ibrahim. 'Do it now!'

Usaim moved to Samson's front and slapped him hard across the face. This is the one who is bullied by the others, Samson thought – he may be the cruellest of the four. Usaim wrenched the car fob from his jacket pocket and then pulled the three phones from two inside pockets, plus a money clip of euros, some change, a few loose cigarettes, a pocketknife and a flashlight key ring.

'Any ID?' said Al-munajil.

Usaim shook his head.

'Sometimes it adds to the pleasure to know who you're killing,' said Al-munajil.

'Paul Samson's the name,' said Samson coolly.

Al-munajil studied him. 'You are Arab.'

'British, and proud of it,' said Samson.

'No, you are Arab. You speak Arabic and you look Arab.'

'Lebanese-British. Proud of the first part, too. And you are Al-munajil, the butcher of men and tormentor of defenceless women and children – the man who has failed in just about everything in life except cutting people's heads off, which isn't so hard when you're called Machete.' This earned him a blow to the back of his head from Ibrahim, but Samson was expecting that. His purpose was to draw the fire from the others and to gain time, in the hope that Hisami had the sense to walk back to where there was a good signal and raise the alarm, but right now he wasn't holding out much hope for any of them.

'You will soon be dead,' said Al-munajil.

'That makes two of us,' replied Samson. 'Actually, your chances of leaving here alive are less than mine.' Another blow followed and this time Ibrahim drew blood. Al-munajil walked over and put his face so close to Samson's that he was aware of a bacterial stench, which told of the man's tooth decay and rotten gums. Everything that came from Al-munajil's mouth – the words, the voice and the breath – was nauseating.

'You will watch the others die and then you will die,' he said, and his voice cracked to a whisper. Samson just managed to turn away as Al-munajil cleared his throat and spat at him. 'We have business to complete,' he said, stepping back to cover Samson with his gun. 'Ibrahim, bring the boy to his senses. Usaim, check the car, dispose of the old people and come back. Then you will your have fun with the whore.'

Ibrahim marched over to Naji and emptied the water bottle over the boy, but it was Usaim banging the door as he left that shook Naji back to reality. He gave Anastasia a stricken, helpless look, which she acknowledged with a taut smile, though her eyes quickly fastened on his feet, or just a little above one of them. Naji rose slowly, dripping wet, and looked at Samson for the first time.

'You will show us how to find all the data you stole,' said Al-munajil.

'Let my friends go,' he said hopelessly. Al-munajil ignored him. Naji understood that everything had changed with the capture of the British spy. Samson somehow had made things worse. Then his eyes came to rest on the feed box where Samson's things had been piled. He couldn't believe what he was seeing. There were three phones, and one was the phone that had been stolen from his backpack a few days ago. The scratched red cover, the shattered corner of the screen, the tape holding everything together, the peeled-back corner of the Super Mario sticker – this was his phone. It was his phone! How had Al-munajil conjured it out of nowhere? If they had his phone, they could get everything they needed. It would take only a minute to find the encryption to operate the online computer he had built. He looked again. Yes, it was his.

The only person at that moment to realise the import of Naji's discovery was Samson, who also understood that Al-munajil didn't yet know what he had in his possession. Ibrahim's eyes had followed Naji's gaze and settled with mild interest on the three phones. Samson was sure he was on the point of working it out: once he had, they were all as good as dead. It would take no time to torture the boy into revealing what those screenshots in his camera roll meant and how they could be used to access his online computer. Or, worse still, they'd torture Anastasia in front of the boy. Al-munajil's men already knew she was theirs to do with what they wanted.

Samson stepped sideways and backwards, whirled round to Rafi behind him and dived for his weapon. It was a clumsy move and the distance between them meant that it was bound to end in failure – and pain. Before Al-munajil or Ibrahim had time to shout a warning, Rafi had clubbed Samson to the ground and straddled him, ready to set about his face with his gun.

'Wait!' shouted Ibrahim above Anastasia's screams. 'Wait! He's trying to distract us.' He shot forward and grabbed the phone. 'Look – this is the boy's phone!' He turned to Al-munajil, his face jutting and fanatical under the light. 'What spy goes around with a phone like this?' He pointed to the sticker. 'This is what we came for! This is the phone! Look at the boy's face – he knows this is his phone! And the British spy knows it's his phone, too.'

A silence fell in the barn. Al-munajil had been watching Naji. He put a hand on his shoulder in an almost avuncular manner and handed him the phone. There was no point in pretending any longer. He took the phone and turned it on. He was praying that the battery was down, but no, the phone was fully charged. He went to the phone's calculator, which he had rigged as a portal to a programme that generated his code. It would have taken several hours to recreate this on another phone, and that other device would have had to be the same model and age as his, but it would now be just a minute or two before the set was ready to access yondaworld.com, the virtual world where a good part of Naji's life had been spent building fantastic machines and chatting to obsessed engineering types during the months he was with Al-munajil's crew in Iraq and Syria. He worked hard, remembering 168 prime numbers between one and 1,000, tapping them into the screen in reverse order, except for the numbers that appeared halfway in the sequence, 431, 433 and 439, which he did not reverse.

Al-munajil looked over his shoulder, fascinated but uncomprehending. 'What are you doing? Show me.'

'I can't,' said Naji, 'you wouldn't understand.'

It was indeed complex: even if a person had known that the calculator was the place to gain access, there were several stages beyond typing in the prime numbers and not all of them were mathematical. The function buttons on the calculator – MR, memory recall; M+, add to memory; and M-, subtract from memory – all played a part, and they had to be pressed in the right order and the correct number of times for the next stage to begin. This generated a random code that Naji did not even know, but the way he had set things up in yondaworld.com meant that the virtual computer – the one that existed only on the web and in his mind – would recognise a code that flew from the calculator in the shape of a fluttering cartoon chicken. The trick was then to land the chicken by dragging it to the right positions, for which reason he had taken screen grabs of the four places the chicken had to land in the architecture of the online computer, otherwise it was very easy to get lost in the maze of strata and geometric shapes.

A string of digits appeared in the calculator's display: 1.1111111E20. This had no meaning other than to indicate the code was ready. Naji closed the calculator and saw the chicken on the display. He handed the phone to Al-munajil, even now prepared to take some pleasure in this numbskull's reaction to the chicken bobbing up and down at the bottom of the screen.

'What is this? Are you playing a joke?'

'No,' said Naji. 'That is the code. You have to place the bird at different locations in a computer I constructed in yondaworld.com, but you need the Internet and a reliable signal.'

This was all plainly beyond Al-munajil. He didn't even know what to ask about the code. 'How do I know you are not tricking me like you always do?'

Naji shrugged. 'You can try it up on the hill, where you'll get a signal. I have to be with you to put the bird in the right place, otherwise you won't be able to access the material.'

Al-munajil stood dumbly looking down at the phone. The wind had got up and was blowing through the cracks in the barn's timber walls, causing the light from the bulb to trace a perfect circle on the floor of the barn.

At that moment they heard the unmistakable sound of a gunshot.

Al-munajil looked up and said, 'Old man!' After the second shot he said, 'Old woman.' And when they heard a third, he grinned and said, 'Dog!'

It was at this point that Samson came to, though he had never been fully unconscious. His head and face hurt like hell, and his left eye socket was already so swollen he could not see out of it. His assailant had stopped beating him the moment Ibrahim made the discovery of the phone and, assuming Samson was unconscious, he'd got up and rushed over to watch Naji work the phone, over the shoulders of Al-munajil and Ibrahim. Samson had heard the gunfire and knew that now the end must be close. Although he'd missed most of Naji's explanation, he appreciated that Al-munajill had got what he wanted and had no further use for his three captives. And Naji would be disposed of, too, once Al-munajil had secured the database. Any help that Hisami might have managed to raise would certainly be too late for them.

Then Samson heard the car alarm and that made him wonder. Usaim had taken the key and fob from him. The car alarm would only have been set off if he had tried to unlock the car using the key instead of the fob. That didn't seem right, and besides, Usaim had been told to find and check the car before dealing with the people in the house. He shifted a little so he could see what was going on with his right eye. The men had taken no notice of the alarm whatsoever – they were too obsessed with what was on the phone.

Suddenly Anastasia addressed Naji quietly in English. 'You know the thing you stole from my desk in the camp? You remember, Naji? Be prepared to use it.' Ibrahim didn't know what she was saying but took a step towards her and slapped her hard. Yet even after the stinging blow, Anastasia kept on saying, 'Use it, Naji. You know you can.'

Naji did not appear to hear her. He knew what she was talking about, of course, but the truth was that he was pro-foundly shocked by the thought of Moon being shot. It didn't make sense that he was more upset about the dog's death than the killing of the kindly old couple who had given them food and shelter, but right now all he could do was think of that beautiful dog, the only dog he had ever loved in his life, and this made him angrier than he had ever been.

'We're done here,' snapped Al-munajil, grabbing Naji by the collar. 'Finish off the Yazidi scum and I will deal with this one.'

Naji thought Al-munajil was referring to him, but it was soon evident that he meant Samson, because he dragged him over to where the spy lay in a pool of blood and aimed the gun at his head. Samson moved his arm to shield his one good eye against the light, saw the gun and closed the eye. Al-munajil was enjoying the moment, and instead of firing straight away, he began a lecture about the inevitability of the caliphate's victory over the decadent West. Naji looked up at Anastasia. She held his gaze then nodded once.

Al-munajil had his arm wrapped around Naji's neck so that Naji was facing away from him, but he knew that his captor's heart was level with the top of his head. He lifted his right leg and bent the knee so that he could reach his ankle, as though he was scratching it. Just at that moment, the barn door opened and Usaim stood there. His hands were covered in blood. His face wore no expression whatsoever. 'Good work,' Al-munajil shouted to him. 'You will be rewarded with the flesh of this pretty Western whore.'

Usaim took a step forward, but it was now clear that he wasn't moving of his own accord. There was a man right behind him and he had Usaim by the scruff of the neck. He held a gun, which moved swiftly from behind Usaim's skull to fire first at Rafi, who was nearest and was hit with a bullet through the side of his head, then at Ibrahim, whose chest exploded before he had even had time to raise his own gun. Al-munajil backed away, gripped Naji even tighter and placed the gun at his temple

'Who are you?' said Al-munajil, his voice falling to a whisper.

'I am Denis Hisami, the brother of Aysel Hisami, whom you tortured and murdered. I've seen what you did to her and to countless other women and I'm here to make good her death and those of scores of nameless women.' He moved forward, pushing Usaim, who was hysterically pleading with them both not to shoot. Al-munajil let off a round, but he had didn't have a clear shot at Hisami, who was a little shorter than Usaim and was almost completely hidden. The bullet clipped the Arab's shoulder and he shrieked. Hisami held him up and swore in his ear and said he would shoot his balls off if he collapsed. Usaim staggered but managed to remain on his feet for the next few seconds, long enough for Hisami to move to his left, where there was less light, and heave Usaim to his right and shoot him. Usaim was dead before he hit the ground This did precisely what Hisami had intended which was momentarily to distract Al-munajil, who actually seemed to have lost track of him in the shadows.

'I'll kill the boy,' whispered Al-munajil, moving backwards and forcing Naji to lower his leg. 'I will finish him.'

Naji again raised his right leg, but this time grasped the throwing knife that had come in so handy since he'd taken it from Anastasia's desk. Moving it in a diagonal path in front of his torso he plunged it over his left shoulder and into Al-munajil's chest. At that very moment Hisami fired a bullet that entered Al-munajil's right temple.

Whether a knife to Al-munajil's heart or a bullet to his head ended his life would never be known, and it did not matter much. He sank to his knees and, like so many of his victims, keeled over to the ground without making a sound. Naji took a step forward, shook himself and placed his fingers in both ears to stop the ringing from the gunshots, then ran to Ifkar and began slashing and tearing at the ropes that held him to the post. Hisami was already at Anastasia's side and untying her bonds, but she was yelling, 'I'm okay. Leave me! Ifkar will bleed to death. Stop the bleeding!'

Samson, by now on his feet, lurched forward, stumbled over Ibrahim's body and made it to Naji just in time to help him lower Ifkar to the stone floor. He was conscious and murmuring gratitude to Naji. Samson saw that he was bleeding profusely, so clamped his hand over the knife wound and raised the young man's arm so it formed a right angle. Naji knew exactly what to do next and crab-crawled to Ibrahim's body, cut a strip from his shirt with the bloody knife and handed it to Samson, who made a tourniquet around Ifkar's bicep. As he did so, Ifkar began furiously to mutter Moon's name. 'Go, Naji,' he said. 'See if Moon is alive.'

Naji scrambled to his feet and was out of the barn before anyone could stop him. Anastasia rushed to join Samson on the stone floor and began to examine Ifkar. Her hands were shaking.

'He's going to be okay,' said Hisami, who was standing over them.

Anastasia wasn't so sure, and looked under his eyelids, felt the pulse at his neck and said his name a few times. Ifkar responded with a weak smile.

'I have to go,' Hisami said quietly. 'No one can know I

was here, do you understand? This must never get out. Help is on its way. I phoned Simcek.'

'Then we'd better think of a story,' said Samson above the noise of the rafters that were now shuddering in the wind.

'I will fix all that. Just go along with what Simcek tells you.' He placed a hand on Anastasia's shoulder. 'You going to be okay?'

She nodded. 'What about the old couple?'

'They're alive, but they will need treatment.'

He turned. Samson raised his hand and Hisami squeezed it. 'We'll speak,' he said, and left. Moments later they heard the sound of a car starting in the distance.

'I'd better go and find the boy,' said Samson, guiding Anastasia's hand to the wound so she'd keep the pressure on it. 'Can you hold on here?' She nodded. He touched her on the cheek and saw that the look of primeval dread had left her eyes. He got to his feet, went to collect the phones from the feed box and headed for the door.

Outside, the fog had been ripped from the mountainside by a wind that now tore through the deserted, dimly lit farmyard, rattling the stable doors and humming in the power cables overhead. He could hear the thump of helicopters to the north and he glimpsed several lights in the distance behind the trees. He started towards the farmhouse, only to find Naji standing stock-still in the dark at the bottom of the steps.

Samson called out, but Naji just shook his head and stared at the ground. 'What is it?' Samson said as he approached him.

Naji shrugged. 'Moon . . . I do not want to see her if she is dead.'

'We'll go in together,' Samson said, wrapping an arm around the boy. 'I know she's alive.'

Naji looked up into his eyes but said nothing.

'You made it,' said Samson. 'You made it all this way, Naji. You're safe and you will bring your family to Europe and they will be safe, too. You did all that!'

'And you found me,' said Naji.

'I was beginning to think I never would, but I guess I did. Now, let's go and find the dog.' He felt Naji's body tense as a helicopter suddenly appeared over the farmyard and a searchlight swept the ground and picked them out. Another circled round from the south to avoid the power cables and hovered over the flat ground where he and Hisami had parked. Before it touched down, armed men jumped to the ground. Naji, for so long reliant only on himself in the face of every possible danger, suddenly clutched at Samson's arm, and Samson responded by holding him close. 'They are here to help us,' he said, waving to the men.

The roar of the helicopters had brought a reaction in the farmhouse. A light came from the front door as it was flung open. The old man staggered out and, shielding his eyes from the searchlight with one hand, groped his way along the railings that separated the terrace from the drop into the yard. He shouted down to them but they could hear nothing. All they knew was that silhouetted in the light behind him was a large dog, also moving with some difficulty.

EPILOGUE

Naji slept in the Monastery Hotel, his arms raised above his head. Beside the bed were the backpack with the fraying strap he had brought all the way from Syria, two pairs of trainers, the goatskin-and-silver frame containing the photograph of his mother and his sisters, the shepherd's flute and his copy of *The Cosmic Detective: Exploring the Mysteries of our Universe,* twenty or so pages of which had been sacrificed to light fires. Even his filthy clothes had been laid out neatly.

Anastasia had taken charge of Naji immediately and insisted he would undergo no questioning until he was properly rested. Simcek went along with this on the condition that he and his people had full access to any intelligence the boy might have. He didn't appreciate the significance of the phone in Naji's pocket, of course; only Samson and Anastasia knew how it could be used to gain access to the particular part of the virtual world where the boy had stored all the data. So Simcek didn't demand Naji hand the phone over to him and it remained in the boy's pocket.

Anastasia had stayed with the boy through the night in case he woke, because his stillness and silence coming down the mountain in the police vehicle seemed to indicate shock. She also wanted to protect him from the numerous security people that had arrived in the hotel through the evening – particularly the British intelligence officers, who wanted to talk to him first and were preposterously claiming Naji as their rightful asset. This she managed without difficulty because Naji was a vulnerable minor, and as the psychologist who had helped him in Lesbos, she insisted that she was now the closest thing he had to a guardian.

Because of her own great shock at the violence and terror of the previous day, she slept little. She got up at dawn and peeped through the curtains onto a bright, still day that showed the autumn colours on the slopes around the hotel at their very best. She glanced at Naji tenderly then went barefoot through the connecting door to the next room to check on Samson, who had been stitched up at the hospital the night before. His face was grotesquely swollen on the left side and he'd lost a molar, but his sight was going to be all right. Once the nurse had cleared the blood away, Samson reported he could just see out of his left eye. The hospital had tried to keep him in overnight, along with the old couple and Ifkar, but he wasn't having it and Vuk had brought him back at ten and waited while he ate an omelette and fries in his room and then downed a beer and a brandy or two.

'How is he?' he murmured when he sensed Anastasia in the room with him.

'Okay, I think,' she whispered, moving to his side. She touched him on the shoulder. 'Poor Paul, does it hurt terribly?'

'Not so much now – the painkillers worked well.'

She sat down on the bed. 'Do we have to let them talk to him today?'

'Yes. They won't wait.'

'And Denis?'

'Hisami wasn't there! That's been agreed. Hisami went back to the States before all that happened.'

'Are we really going to be able to maintain that story?'

'Yes, it's now part of the record. I saw Simcek at the hospital last night and we went through it. He knew Al-munajil's gang were here – he never did buy the idea that they'd gone to Bosnia. So he deserves some praise for that and he's more than happy for his people to take credit for the killing of four dangerous terrorists. The story is that they busted in, there were some exchanges of fire and all four terrorists were killed. No one will expect you to go into any detail.'

'What about Naji?'

'I don't think that'll be a problem. You can stop them from asking intrusive questions on the basis that it might harm the boy psychologically. Besides, I'm not sure how much he'll remember.'

Samson let his hand flop to her knee. 'You going to be okay?'

'Just about.' She gave him a tense, slightly rueful smile.

'It's very shocking to encounter that kind of evil. I'd heard about such men from the refugees I treated in the camp, but to see it yourself . . .' He put his fingers to her lips, but she moved her head so she could continue. 'I spent most of the night wondering how Naji survived all those months with him. That's the other side of humanity, isn't it? The boy is a truly exceptional person.'

'Will he survive all he's seen?'

'I think he'll need a lot of help, but kids are more resilient than adults.'

She went round to the other side of the bed, crawled under the covers and lay with her hand across Samson's chest. 'Seeing you beaten like that was unbearable,' she said. 'I know why you went for that man – to buy us time. You helped save us, Paul.'

'Actually, I was trying to distract Al-munajil from seeing Naji's phone as well as buy us some time. Anyway, it was the least I could do – I got you into this mess.'

'No, it was surely I who got you into this mess,' she said, and kissed him with great care on the undamaged part of his cheek.

They dozed for a little while then ordered breakfast. When the trolley was wheeled into the room, Naji was woken by the smell of eggs and waffles. He wandered through the door and sat down and ate without saying anything. 'What do you want to do now?' asked Anastasia after he had finished.

'Talk to my family then see Ifkar and Moon,' he replied without looking at them.

'Oh, I have some news for you,' said Samson, smiling as best he could. 'A woman named Jasna came by the farm when she saw the lights of the helicopters. She's a veterinary surgeon and a friend of the family apparently, and she's up there now, looking after all the animals. The dog is in very good hands, I guess.'

Naji nodded, satisfied. 'Ifkar?'

'He's going to be fine. He'll be in the hospital for a few days. The old man, who was not as badly injured as his wife, said he wants your friend Ifkar and the dog to stay with them as long as they need. He's certain she will agree. Maybe that would be a good life for your friend and his dog.'

'For the old people also – their son is dead,' said Naji simply. Samson and Anastasia exchanged looks. There wasn't a lot that Naji missed.

Naji went over to the window, checked the reception on his phone and called his sister. In the event, Naji's mother, Nada, answered, which caught Naji off guard and for a few seconds he was unable to speak. Then he inhaled deeply, composed himself and told her that he was safe in a hotel with people who were looking after him. He said nothing about the events at the farmhouse and did not mention Al-munajil.

As Naji prepared to ring off, Samson thought he heard him promise his mother that he now had all that he needed to bring his family to Europe. He hung up and looked out of the window without saying anything, without moving. For a few seconds, all three of them gazed out on the wonder of the trees. Then Naji turned to them. His cheeks were streaked with tears but his eyes displayed all the resolution that had brought him from Syria to Europe.

'So how do you want to play this?' said Samson, in English so that Anastasia would understand. 'What do you want to do about the phone?'

Naji gave his usual shrug.

'It's your phone,' said Samson. 'You risked your life to bring it to Europe. I was hired to find you, not tell you what to do about that data. That's your decision.'

'Everything I do is for my family,' Naji replied in Arabic.

Anastasia grinned as Samson translated this. 'We're on your side,' she said. 'Whatever you want is fine with us.'

Five hours later they met Simcek, who made sure that Naji understood that no mention of Hisami's presence in the barn should be made – it would be difficult for the billionaire to explain to people in America how he had ended up with the skills of a Special Forces combatant. Simcek was completely frank with him and, speaking man to man, asked for Naji's confidence. Naji just nodded and said he couldn't remember what had happened.

They followed Simcek into the hotel's conference room, which held representatives of several European intelligence services, including all those who had attended the meeting at the British embassy in Skopje – Germany's BND, France's DGSE and DGSI, Belgium's VSSE and Britain's MI6 and MI5. Peter Nyman was wearing his usual expression of worldly dismay while Sonia Fell smiled brightly and tried to spread a sense of British success. Yet no one was deceived. MI6's claims to ownership of Naji and his material had been quickly abandoned when Naji said that he would share the information with anyone who might find it useful in the fight against men like Al-munajil.

Simcek showed Naji to a chair next to the projector, from which ran a lead that would allow him to plug in his phone.

Naji sat down and looked up to Samson. 'You can tell them now,' he said in Arabic, and pulled out his phone and placed it on the table.

'Firstly,' began Samson, 'I want to thank Arron Simcek of the Macedonian Administration for Security and Coun-terintelligence for all that he has done to neutralise four extremely dangerous individuals. We owe our lives to him and his colleagues and we are extremely grateful to him.' Simcek accepted the thanks with a nod.

Nyman coughed and looked at Samson hard. 'You were indeed lucky to be able to raise the alarm. We were won-dering how that was achieved?'

'Shall we do the operational debrief later?' said Samson, turning so that he could see Nyman with his good eye.

'We're so relieved that you are all here,' Nyman con-tinued. 'I just thought I'd say that. By the look of you, it was obviously a very near thing.'

'Shall we move on?' said Samson, not quite losing his patience – yet.

'But how was it done – how on earth did you raise the alarm?'

Naji suddenly pushed back his chair, got up and put his phone in his pocket. 'They do not want to hear me,' he said in Arabic. 'I go to see my friend Ifkar in the hospital.'

The man from DGSE, Louis Fremon, saved the situation in perfect Middle Arabic. 'Please, we are eager to hear what you have to tell us. We want very much to know how you can help us in the fight against men like Al-munajil. Don't go just yet.' The Frenchman looked pointedly down the table at his rumpled and fatigued British colleague.

Naji nodded to Fremon, then sat down again.

'My friend has one or two conditions that he needs agreement on,' Samson continued, 'before he shows you what he's brought out of Syria and Iraq at the greatest possible personal risk. I have some sense of what he will disclose and I can assure you all that it will be of great value. However, he wants an assurance that his family will be given sanctuary and citizenship anywhere of his choosing in the EU and that they will be given a home and money to begin a new life.'

There was silence. Then Nyman said, 'I'm sure this is all perfectly easy to arrange. Take it that we will see to a new home.'

Naji shook his head and whispered to Samson, who had to crane to hear him.

'He further wishes,' said Samson, 'that he and his two remaining sisters will be assured places in universities of their choosing, provided they meet the required academic standards. He hopes that the governments represented here will bear the costs jointly.'

Hans Spannagel of the BND began nodding vigorously. 'It will be our pleasure. I have had instructions from Berlin that Germany is content to take the lead in this,' he said. 'We are aware of the family's plight and are in a position to fly them to a reception centre close to Munich within the next three days. I am pleased to say Germany will welcome your family, young sir.'

Samson translated, but Naji was already smiling. 'I believe that is acceptable to my friend,' he said, and sat down next to Naji.

Naji switched on the phone and plugged it in so that the phone's screen was projected onto the wall at the darkened end of the conference room.

He moved quickly to the camera roll, paused on shots of the group of migrants in the orchard, which Al Kufra never did delete, and the swirl of firefly lights in the forest which had so appealed to the people in SIS headquarters, and eventually reached the screen grabs of computer architecture, which were remarkably similar to the blueprints of buildings. He enlarged each one before examining different parts of the structure intently then, seemingly satisfied, he closed the camera roll and opened the phone's calculator. At this point most of those around the table took out their own phones and began to film what was happening in front of them on the screen, though few probably appreciated he was entering the prime numbers between one and 1,000 in reverse order, except for the three numbers in the middle of the sequence, of course. He then turned to the calculator's function keys, which he touched in order with unerring speed, and a string of digits duly appeared in the calculator's display panel.

The code was ready. Naji sat back as the animated chicken bearing the newly generated code appeared on the screen. There were smiles around the room. He logged into his account on yondaworld.com and started navigating the towering maze of one of the virtual computers the site encourages its members to build. Dragging the chicken with his finger, he paused occasionally to consider his location before allowing it to land. Each time, a starburst indicated the chicken had hit the target correctly.

Then the screen went blank. Naji tapped it and suddenly it filled with a list of files. He opened one and murmured to Samson that he thought this was to do with petroleum sales. Another file contained hundreds pictures of young men and women, all unmistakably jihadists. There were files containing emails, texts, messages from social media, screen grabs of Internet bank accounts, invoices for weaponry, videos of explosions, contact lists taken from other phones, maps, endless sheets of figures and photographs of locations in Europe. He moved through them, talking animatedly in a mixture of Arabic and English, saying what he thought they were and how he had acquired particular files by hacking into systems at locations visited by Al-munajil. When prompted, he explained that he almost always gained access by using either the phones or a laptop that Al-munajil left lying around in the pickup. Without Al-munajil's lax attitude to security – which Naji had noticed the first time he repaired and adapted his phone – none of this would have been possible.

The room was duly impressed and arrangements were made for the hundreds of files to be copied and immediately shared among all the services present. Various encryption and computer experts appeared and went through the access procedure with Naji and murmured their appreciation of his unorthodox approach to encryption, which one German expert described as a combination of ingenuity, cunning and playfulness. Samson thought this was a fair description of the boy he had pursued around the Balkans.

At length, Naji began to tire, answering more of the experts' questions with an uncooperative shrug. Anastasia, who had kept her eye on him for all this time, began to look concerned. Suddenly he had had enough, and rose and unplugged the phone from the projector and put it into his pocket, which prompted a look of alarm from Sonia Fell. She leaned over to whisper to Peter Nyman.

'This is a rather good point my colleague makes,' he said to the room. 'Do we think it sensible that this young man is walking around with access to this information in his pocket?'

Samson, now also standing, shook his head. 'Instead of worrying about the phone, which, after all, is his property, I would suggest that someone around this table has the good grace to formally thank him for the great service he has rendered to the security of Europe. He has made your lives easier and those of European citizens much safer, at least for the time being.'

'You're right, and we *are* grateful,' said Fremon, 'but Monsieur Nyman is right – we cannot risk the other side knowing what we have in our possession. That is a basic tenet of our work.'

Samson looked down at Naji. 'Why don't you pay Naji the courtesy of asking him to delete the information, or at least his access to it?'

Naji eyed the Frenchmen and grinned. 'I just did that – didn't you see?'

Fremon returned the smile and said, 'I am sorry – you were too quick for us. I did not notice.'

'I have no use for the material,' Naji said. 'I kept it to hurt Al-munajil and stop him marrying Munira. That is all. Now he is dead and I do not need it.'

'I think we are all guilty of misjudging the clever young man we have in our midst,' said Fremon. He took a few paces and put out his hand. 'I thank you on behalf of the French people for the mission you have completed, Monsieur. You are an individual of rare gifts and courage, and we honour you.'

And then Fremon's colleague from the DGSI followed him, and eventually the whole room lined up to shake Naji's hand and offer their thanks, and even the eternally morose features of Nyman broke into something approaching good humour as he patted Naji on the back and expressed the gratitude of the British government.

Samson, Anastasia and Naji left the room together, with Naji leading the way, apparently unaffected by the praise heaped on him. He said he wanted to go outside and call his family and tell them the good news that they would soon be reunited in Germany. They walked with him to a high spot among the trees, where there was good reception, and waited a little way off while he made the call. When he'd finished, he sat down on a stump and looked up at the topmost branches, which were swaying in the wind and shedding a few of their leaves. He shivered and Anastasia went over to him and took him in her arms.

'You've done what you promised,' she told him. 'Your family will soon be in Europe and they'll be safe, all because of you.' She held him tightly against her down jacket and Naji smelled her scent and closed his eyes. 'You understand what I'm saying, don't you, Naji? You have fulfilled every part of your promise to your father, and he knows that. When you were on the road it was he who kept you going, but now it's time to start to think of life without him. Let him go. Let him be in peace.'

Naji struggled and but she held him and kissed the top of his head. 'You must come to terms with the loss; otherwise it will hurt you. Do it in your own time, but you should try to do it.' She let him go and bent down to pick up his cap, which had fallen to the ground, handing it to him with a smile. 'Okay?' she said.

Naji shrugged and then nodded. 'Yes,' he said, looking at the ground.

'Good.' She took his hand and they started back to the hotel, with Samson following some way behind.

When they reached the hotel's entrance, Samson remained outside to smoke his last cigarette, for he had decided while being treated in the hospital to quit. He noticed he had a text from a number he didn't recognise. *Glad our horse triumphed in the end*, it read.

He called the number, expecting to get Macy Harp, but when the phone was eventually answered he found he was speaking to Denis Hisami. 'Dark Narcissus was second,' said Samson. 'I checked this morning. Anyway, what do you mean by *our* horse?'

He heard a chuckle at the other end. 'Dark Narcissus won after Snow Hat was disqualified when traces of an illegal substance – the residue of medication used to treat ulcers, it turns out – showed up in the drug test. Surely you don't imagine that I wouldn't try to find out which horse you favoured. It was obvious what was happening when the price of Dark Narcissus came in on the morning of the race. So, having kept to our agreement, I placed a bet on Dark Narcissus. We were very, very lucky.'

Samson exhaled the smoke, stubbed out the cigarette and looked at the shafts of light from the setting sun play in the trees. 'Indeed we were,' he murmured.

ACKNOWLEDGEMENTS

My thanks are due firstly to Alexandra Tzanedaki, volunteer aid worker on the Greek island of Lesbos, without whom the first part of this series would not have been possible. I would also like to thank Anna Panou, a psychologist working in the Moria refugee camp, Lesbos, who was generous with her time during a very challenging period in 2016. That goes for members of Médecins du Monde, the United Nations High Commissioner for Refugees and some smaller aid agencies, all of whom gave me advice and help on my journey through the Balkans.

For this novel I have been reunited with my former editor Jane Wood. I thank her for her care and the huge improvements she has made. My thanks also go to Pamela Merritt who read the manuscript with her usual intelligent eye and to Roger Alton whose enthusiasm for the story gave me the confidence to launch into it. Finally, salutes to my literary agent Rebecca Carter of Janklow & Nesbit, who has given me unwavering support through the writing of *Firefly*, and Charles Collier of Tavistock Wood, who made valuable suggestions after reading the manuscript.

HP, London, 2017